# ON DARK HORIZONS

## ANTHONY LAKEN

For my Mother and Father.

# Contents

# CHAPTER ONE

Lord Elvgren Lovitz pulled at the hood around his face and prayed that no one had spotted him. It had been two weeks since he and his companions had fled the Burkeshi capital, Kurgobad. Two weeks since they had escaped the city he had helped to decimate.

He closed his eye, and the carnage began to replay in his mind. The dead lying at his feet, the pink gloop that had been their brains seeping out of their ears. The mad crush of people as they realised the extent of the tragedy that had befallen them. The ease with which he and his companions had used the madness to their advantage, slipping from the city like spectres.

'Wake up, One Eye, we gotta move,' a voice called from behind him.

He turned around to see the face of Dargo, a teenage cut-purse and miscreant who had become his closest friend. The boy took a step forwards, his wooden leg thumping on the ground. Elvgren's chest grew tight when he looked at the makeshift limb. *That's my fault as well,* he thought.

'What part of being a wanted man don't you understand, Gren? We ain't got the luxury of standing about,' Dargo said.

Elvgren shook his head and scratched at the scar running down and through where his left eye used to be.

'You're right, Dar. Let's get going.'

They set off down a wide road. Overhead, a crescent moon played peek-a-boo through the clouds, casting the town of Reltucca in fitful bursts of pale light. The town was situated in the country of Mandira. Elvgren and the rest of his companions had managed to sneak into it by paying fishermen to take them along the Eastern Continent's coast in stages, hopping from one town to the next, always on the move.

Around them, the cobbled-together hovels and shanties of the town's poorer populace began to creep in, the road turning into a tight funnel that eventually spat them out in front of a temple. The massive stone building knifed upwards, multi-limbed gods painted in every colour imaginable cavorting across its face, making the building throb with life.

'Where we s'posed to meet this bloke again?' Dargo asked.

'I think the note said by the statue of Gandra.'

'Which one is Gandra?'

Elvgren frowned, his one good eye glancing at the multitude of carvings in front of him. 'I don't know,' he said finally.

Dargo pinched the bridge of his nose and sighed. 'This whole fucking thing is madness, you know?' he said. 'How the hells do we even know these people are on the level?'

'They're priests, Dar, don't think you can get much more on the level than that,' Elvgren said, the beginnings of a headache forming like a gathering storm front. 'Plus, we need some help if we're going to make it to New Ledi and find a way home.'

'Whatever you say.'

'Look, let's just stand over by that one. At least, it'll give us a good view of anyone coming or going,' Elvgren said, pointing at the least fearsome statue he could spot.

Somewhere, a stray dog howled, the desperate sound making Elvgren shiver while he stood in the statue's shadow. He looked around the courtyard. The place was deserted. His gaze led up the steps of the temple to its door. Inside, he could just make out the flickering of a torch but nothing more.

'Good evening, young sirs,' a voice said in Elvgren's ear.

He spun around, hand moving to the ballistol stashed in the front of his trousers. Before him stood a man in his mid-forties, bald head gleaming in the moonlight. A swirling tattoo wormed its way from between the man's eyes, going over the top and down the back of his head. A robe of orange silk was wrapped around his middle.

'Peace,' the man said with a smile, 'I am a friend.'

'Prove it,' Dargo spat.

The man cocked his head to one side. 'If I had meant you harm, I would have slit your throats before announcing my presence. I assume by the way I startled you that you were unaware of the fact I have been observing you for the past fifteen minutes.'

Dargo's body remained rigid, his eyes fixed on the man.

'Easy, Dar,' Elvgren said, placing a hand on the boy's shoulder. 'Let's hear what he has to say.'

'A wise decision, my lord,' the man said. He clicked his fingers, and Elvgren saw two men who had been hidden in the shadows bow and head towards the temple.

'I see you weren't too sure about us either, old chap,' Elvgren said.

'I wanted to make sure of you myself. The description of you given by the Burkeshis is rather accurate, Lord Elvgren.'

'Pretty recognisable these days,' he replied, lifting his eyepatch and scratching his scar.

'Quite. I am Rihar Holki, High Priest at the temple.'

'You already seem to know me,' Elvgren said. 'And this here is Dargo.'

'A pleasure,' the priest said with a small bow.

Dargo narrowed his eyes and spat on the ground. 'How you gonna get us into New Ledi then?' he said.

'Dargo!' Elvgren cried.

'It's quite alright, my lord. The young man's bluntness is excusable, given your plight. But here is not the place to discuss such things. Please allow me to host you in my chambers.'

'Lead on,' Elvgren replied.

***

Bellina Ressa stared up at the ceiling above her head. A crack ran down its middle while an intrepid spider was busy constructing a web in the corner. She looked down at her hands, her breath shallow, then turned onto her side. A bowl of thin soup and a hunk of bread sat untouched on the bedside table. The smell of it made her stomach whirl, and she turned the other way.

'You can't carry on like this, Bellina,' a woman's voice said.

'Go away,' Bellina replied.

Instead, she heard the heavy footsteps of Major Cirona Bouchard enter the room.

'It's been three weeks, and you've hardly taken a bite to eat. If this keeps going you'll die.'

'I deserve to die after what I did.'

She felt the large, rough hands of the major grab her shoulders and spin her around. Bellina looked up into the face of Cirona. The woman's nostrils were flared, her jaw set tight.

'Don't you ever say that to me again.'

Bellina felt like a rock had wedged itself in her throat. Her bottom lip quivered before the tears fell. 'I-I'm s-sorry,' she said.

Cirona pulled her into a tight embrace. 'You don't need to be sorry either; none of this was your fault.'

'But my powers are what killed all those people. It was my fault the Burkeshis declared war.'

'Did you know what would happen once your cognopathic restraints were removed?' Cirona asked.

Bellina shook her head.

'Exactly. None of us did. And as for starting a war, you know what Marmossa and Kurkeshi were planning. The yaksit, the kaffars. They were getting ready to go to war with us and would have used any excuse to light the fuse.' Cirona paused and wet her lips. 'I suppose we won't get the full picture till we return to Estria and speak with your father.'

The blood began to pound in Bellina's veins. 'No, I suppose we won't,' she said.

Her mouth twisted into a sneer. *He'd better have some bloody answers,* Bellina thought. It was him who had pushed her into this situation. It was him who had pretended to love her, to care for her, to be her father. She felt her jaw ache. In the end, she had been just another pawn in one of his games. All along, he had only been interested in her cognopathic powers, in using her as a weapon.

'Anyway,' Cirona said, gently lying Bellina back down, 'if you and Torkwill don't get your health back, we'll never make it home.'

'How's he doing?' Bellina gave a small shudder, imagining just what would have happened to her and her companions if her fellow cognopath hadn't shielded them from her psychic blast.

'Torkwill? Well, he asked for some wine yesterday, so we think he's on the mend,' Cirona said with a laugh. Bellina gave a small smile.

There was a knock at the door, and she turned her head to see who it was. In the entrance, she could see the form of Holger, his broad shoulders almost the width of the frame.

'Am I interrupting,' he said, rubbing the back of his head. 'It's just that I heard talking and came to see if Belle was up.'

'Come in,' Bellina said.

Holger came into the room and stood at the foot of the bed.

'Would you leave us, Major?' Bellina asked.

Cirona bit her lip, eyes shooting between the pair. Eventually, she nodded and stood up. 'Alright,' she said, 'but make sure she gets some of that soup down her.' With that, the major clomped out of the room.

Holger's eyes locked with Bellina's, and he beamed from ear to ear. Bellina felt her stomach flutter slightly in response to his gaze.

He cleared his throat and said, 'Feeling any better?'

'After killing a thousand people? I suppose I'm as well as is to be expected.'

Holger flinched, holding up his hands. 'Alright, alright. I was just asking.'

Bellina felt a knot form in her stomach. 'I'm sorry,' she said. 'It's just that, every time I close my eyes, I see them. All those people. It's like there's something inside of me, something I don't understand any more, and it scares me.'

'I understand,' Holger said, perching himself on the end of her bed.

'What do you mean? How can you?' she asked.

'Look, Belle ... there's something I've been meaning to tell you—'

Outside, the sound of angry chanting and catcalls filled the air, cutting off Holger's sentence. They looked at each other, eyebrows raised. A few seconds later, Cirona came charging back into the room.

'What's going on?' Bellina asked her.

'There's a mob coming. They've got Gilroy, tied a noose around his neck … I think he's leading them here. We've got to move. Now!'

***

Elvgren and Dargo sat on the bare floor of the priest's quarters. The room contained a single low bed made of ropes strung between wooden posts and a torch for light. Other than that, it was empty. Elvgren watched the priest close his door, bar the window, then lower himself down opposite them.

'I hear you are looking for passage into New Ledi,' he said.

'That is true,' Elvgren replied.

'With how things are in Reltucca at the moment, that may not be as easy as it sounds. Burkeshi agitators are stirring up anti-Estrian sentiment as we speak. And there are many, not just here but in the whole of Mandira, who would love to see you dead.'

Wetting his lips, Elvgren said, 'I take it you're not one of them. Considering that you're meeting us?'

'Quite so, my lord.'

Dargo let out a snort. 'I don't like this, Gren. What does he want out of this?'

'For goodness sake, Dar!' Elvgren said with a sigh.

The priest held up his hand and smiled. 'The only thing I seek is peace. That is my job here. Estrian rule may not be perfect, but I distrust the words and promises of these Burkeshis. And they have shown scant regard for the religions in the countries they have invaded.'

'Better the Terror you know then?' Dargo said, tilting his head to one side.

'That is one way of putting it, yes,' the priest said.

'I hate to press the matter, but do you have a way of getting us out or not?' Elvgren said, tugging at his shirt front.

'I believe I have. One of the acolytes from the temple is taking a shipment of grain to New Ledi for the festival of Ilvetta. The wagon should be big enough to hide you and your companions in. You would have to leave tonight though.'

Outside, a massive roar went up. Elvgren, Dargo and the priest looked at each other then hurried to the window. Throwing open the shutters, they saw a mob descending on the temple. The light from their torches flickered fitfully, throwing the faces of those holding them into stuttering illumination. Elvgren felt as if his insides had just been plunged into ice.

'I think leaving tonight would be our best option,' he said.

***

Cirona opened the back door of the house and checked the alley was clear. The chants and hollers from the mob echoed around her, reverberating, distorting, till the sounds became the cries of animals. She turned around and nodded to the rest of the group. Holger was helping to support Bellina and Torkwill was leaning heavily against a wall. *They're not up to this*, she thought, closing her eyes and drawing in a deep breath.

'Let's go,' she said to them.

'What about Everett?' Holger asked.

'If he wasn't such a useless spy, he would never have been caught. None us made him go on those reconnaissance missions of his. He knew the risks. Now move,' Cirona said.

'One Eye ... and ... the street rat — what about them?' Torkwill said, wincing with each word.

'They know the drill,' Cirona replied. 'We meet at the East Gate.'

A look of unease passed over the rest of the group's faces, but they began to shuffle out of the door. Cirona waited till they were all out then ushered them up the alley. Ahead of her, she saw Torkwill sway on his feet then collapse into a pile of rubbish. A bottle rolled away down the alley, clinking and tinkling as it bounced along the cobbles. Rushing forwards, Cirona pulled Torkwill back to his feet. Then, from behind her, she heard the sound she had been dreading, the call of inquisitive voices at the other end of the alley.

She grimaced and turned her head towards the sounds. There stood two Mandirans, flaming torches in their hands. One of them was pointing up the alley towards the group, the other was gesturing to the rest of the mob.

'Shit!' she said.

'Whoops. S'pose this one's on me, eh?' Torkwill said.

'Forget it. Let's go.'

Torkwill pushed her away and slumped against the wall. 'Leave me. I ain't strong enough to run; I'll only slow you down,' he said.

'Stop being ridiculous, Torkwill,' Bellina said.

A shout echoed from the mob at the other end of the alley. Cirona saw at least ten Mandirans had gathered and were approaching their position.

'I'm sorry, Torkwill,' she said.

'Major, you can't be serious?' Bellina said.

'Don't worry, lass; I'll hold them off as long as I can,' Torkwill replied.

'But—'

'Hey! I won't take nay for an answer,' Torkwill said, offering Bellina a weak smile. 'I know I said I'd tell ye about yer mother, but there ain't time now. She was a great woman, lass. Go to the School of Cognometry; you'll find the truth there.'

Cirona watched as Bellina rushed forwards and wrapped her arms around Torkwill. Holger stared at the ground, a look of jealous anger flickering over his face. Placing a hand on the girl's shoulder, Cirona said, 'We have to go.'

Bellina nodded her head and wiped at her eyes.

'Thank you, Torkwill,' Cirona said.

'Don't mention it,' he said with a weak smile. 'Now go.'

With that, he set off towards the group of men, screaming, sword drawn. Bellina stood watching him, her hands clasped to her chest. Cirona grabbed hold of her and pulled her along.

'Major, wait!' Bellina cried.

Ignoring her pleas, Cirona set off. She ducked down a series of alleys and came towards one of the main roads. The street was choked with Mandirans, chanting and whooping, flaming Estrian flags in their hands. Cirona cursed under her breath and peered out over the crowd. Up ahead she could just make out the form of a Burkeshi on a raised platform. He seemed to be leading the maelstrom of hate.

'What do we do now?' Holger asked.

'We'll have to take the long way round,' Cirona replied and retraced her steps.

She turned left into a new alley and came to a stop. Dead ahead of her was a small group of Mandirans. Excited chatter escaped them as they saw the major and the others. Cirona gritted her teeth, let out a hissing sound and ran in the other direction.

All around them, more and more Mandirans poured out of the narrow backstreets, Cirona and Holger just managing to stay ahead of the pursuers. With the alleys blocked off, Cirona's options were limited, and she soon ran into what seemed like a dead end. A group of Mandirans crept towards them. Frantically, she looked about for an escape route.

'Over there!' Bellina called.

Cirona's gaze followed Bellina's fingers and fell upon a door set into a mud-brick wall. In a handful of strides, she covered the distance to the door and charged into it. The brittle wood gave way, and she found herself in a kitchen. A startled old lady looked up from where she was chopping vegetables.

'Sorry,' Cirona said, bustling through the house while the old woman spat a string of fast-paced obscenities at their backs.

They burst through the front door, and Cirona's heart sank. Another large crowd stood in front of them, this mob blocking the way to the East Gate.

Just then, she heard the sound of horses' hooves behind her, accompanied by shouts and screams. She turned around to see a carriage bearing down on them at breakneck speed. Three people sat atop the driver's seat. She just had time to register the faces of Elvgren, Dargo and what looked like a terrified priest.

'Hop on, Major!' Elvgren called as he sped past.

'Slow down first, you moron!' she called.

'I can't — the horses seem to be a tad upset,'

With a shake of her head, Cirona sprinted after the runaway carriage. The crowd parted before the vehicle's approach, leaving a wide swathe for the major and Holger to run through. Up ahead, she could see the massive doors of the East Gate. A pair of men on either side were trying to close it.

Cirona pulled a ballistol from her waistband and fired at the man on the left side. The bullet caught him in the shoulder, and he went twirling to the ground. His companion stopped what he was doing and rushed to his friend's aid, leaving the gate three quarters open.

Elvgren somehow managed to slow the horses as he tried to align the carriage with the gap. Holger grabbed onto the back of the wagon and swung himself inside. He leaned out towards Cirona, offering his hand. The major stretched out her fingers and just missed Holger's grasp.

She slipped forwards and caught hold of the carriage's back footboard. Her body bounced and scraped along the ground. The air was driven out of her and grit filled her eyes, mouth and nose. Her fingers began to lose their grip, and one final collision broke her hold.

At that moment, Cirona felt a thrumming coming from her back. The next thing she knew, she was levitating from the ground.

'I can't keep this up for long, Major,' Bellina cried. 'I still haven't regained full control of my powers.'

Cirona looked up into the disbelieving eyes of Holger and said, 'Your hand, you fool!'

Holger shook his head then leaned out towards them. This time, Cirona caught hold, and with the help of Bellina's cognokinetic powers, Holger managed to haul them in.

Once they were on board, Bellina gave a cry. Cirona helped her in a seated position. A thin trickle of blood escaped Bellina's nose.

'Bellina, are you alright?' she asked.

The cognopath looked wan, a sheen of sweat covering her forehead, but she managed a nod.

Cirona turned to look at the town they had just left. The mob stood in the partially opened gateway howling and throwing anything they could get their hands on. The projectiles fell short as the carriage made its escape.

# CHAPTER TWO

Sunlight caught the edges of the spinning coin, sending tiny shards of illumination into the air around it. Castros Del Var stole the coin from the air with a flick of his wrist and placed it on top of his right hand, covering it with his left.

'Call it, Whist!' Castros said, green eyes glinting, a wolfish smile playing at the corners of his mouth.

'Cass, this is stupid. I'm not gonna decide to risk my life on the spin of a fucking coin!' Whist said with a sigh of exasperation.

Del Var studied the man. He'd known Whist the majority of his life — from his fifteenth year to the present day, from Whist's first scraggly attempts at beard growth to the first signs of grey forging a path across his temples.

Whist was cautious, Castros was reckless. They knew each other inside out. That was why they made such a good team. Whist provided a good counterpoint to all his wilder ideas, but ultimately, the man would bow to Castros' orders. It was why he knew Whist would call it, the man worshipped Del Var, and Castros knew it.

He watched the tug of emotions play out across Whist's face. A twitching in the nose, a narrowing of the eyes, a pursing to the mouth.

'Fine! Heads,' Whist finally said, throwing up his hands in defeat.

Castros smiled broadly at him. 'Tails!' he said, after checking the coin. 'You lose, my man. We do this one my way.' He rolled the Estrian penny across his knuckles then made it disappear, palming it in his hand.

'Bet it was a bloody trick coin,' Whist said, muttering darkly.

'Oh, come on! Don't be a sore loser. Here, take the coin, get yourself something pretty.'

'Very funny, Cass! Look, if we're gonna do this, we'd better get going. The executions are set for midday.'

'Fine, fine. Let me just finish this.'

He clasped the small, cylindrical, clay mug in his hand and downed its contents. Castros felt the warmth and tang of the strong coffee flood through him. He sighed and smacked his lips theatrically; Whist rolled his eyes.

Del Var stood, slapping down the money for their drinks on the table, making sure to leave a generous tip.

He turned to look out at the sea. The cafe they were in had a fantastic view of the Tremoran coast. Seagulls careered over the turquoise waves, diving here and there at some prey. Clear and deep, Castros would have liked more time to admire the water some. He imagined the life he could have led if things had been different. If he had had less auspicious heritage.

*Bah!* he thought, banishing the reverie from his mind. This was the life he had chosen, and he wouldn't have it any other way.

The two men snaked their way through the maze of tables and out onto the wide boulevard. It had been a long time since Castros had been in Saprez, the capital of Tremore, but it was still the same as ever. The clean paved streets, the tall buildings with their elaborate facades, everything well kept and ordered. Del Var hated it. A city should have life, energy, grime and dirt. It should be lived in, and its history should be written on its face — new buildings jostling with the old in beautiful tension. But this idea of a city, built to a plan, the old destroyed to make way for the new, made his skin itch. Historical places, slums and hovels, all cleared away so that the Duke of Tremore and the rest of the nobility could walk around without having to hold scented handkerchiefs to their faces.

'Whereabouts will they be holding Dane?' Castros asked.

'In the Childran gaol. If our intel is right, he's been split off from the rest of the ringleaders, held in isolation at the very top. Don't want him starting another rebellion, I suppose,' Whist said, scratching at the dark stubble on his chin.

'Ha ha! See, it's what I've always said — they fear the truth of words more than swords and balliskets. He made a good fist of it, Dane did. Heard him and his rebels gave the duke merry hell down in the south of Tremore. But organisation was never one of his strong points.'

'Neither is his temperament! Look, Cass, I know you've been away awhile and you want to get a proper cell of insurgents set up, but is Dane really the best choice?'

'I hope you're not questioning my decision making, Whist?' Castros said, shooting a dark look at his companion before suddenly breaking into laughter. 'Of course, I'm sure! He's one of us — another survivor of the operation. Got to get him back.'

Del Var gritted his teeth as he turned away. Bloody right he had to get him back. Even though Whist and Dane had been minor accomplices on the attempt to assassinate the Emperor, so many years ago now, they'd had a rough time. Always running, always hiding, and without Castros to protect them — vulnerable. He had hated to leave them after the failure, but it had been his only choice … well, the only choice made available to him.

Despite not having his leadership, the two men had tried their hardest to carry on the cause. Forming workers' rights groups, printing the people's manifesto and distributing it, despite it being a capital offence, trying to organise rebellions like the failed one Dane had attempted to lead. Del Var was proud of them, and he'd be damned if he left them a second time, especially now he had his new weapons.

They walked down a street where a young boy was selling copies of the *Chronicler*. A large group had hemmed him in, and he was exchanging the newsprint for cash as fast as his little hands could manage.

'Wonder what's up? Think I'll nab one — best to keep abreast of current affairs, after all!' Del Var said, striding towards the boy.

'Cass we really don't—' Whist began

'Oh hush! We have plenty of time, you'll see.'

Castros barged his way into the crowd and purchased a copy from the boy, giving the lad a large tip and ruffling his hair. He looked down at the paper, and his eyes lit up.

'Burkesh blames Kurgobad deaths on Estria,' Del Var said. 'War imminent.'

'Twelve hells! Think there's any truth to it?' Whist asked.

'If you buy the *Estrian Chronicler* looking for truth, my friend, you will be sorely disappointed,' Del Var replied, handing the paper to Whist as they continued on towards the gaol.

After thirty minutes brisk walking, they arrived at the prison. Massive stone walls capped with spikes rose above them. Two guards stood alert beneath an arched doorway. Behind this entry point, the Childran gaol hovered like a ghoul. The ominous black stone was punctured with slit windows, open wounds, like sores on a pox victim. Whist turned towards him, raising his eyebrows.

'Well, boss, you wanted to infiltrate the prison. What do we do now?' he said.

A smile broke across Castros Del Var's face, and he began to walk a coin across the knuckles of his left hand.

'We're going to do something magical!'

Castros flipped back the fabric of his coat dramatically and pulled out a miniature bellows, which he sat in the palm of his hand. Next, he took a small, round, leather ball from his belt. It contained his own breath fused with sortilenergy. Carefully, he unstopped the top of the thin tube that extended from the top of the ball and screwed it into place behind the bellows. Overall, it had the look of a pipette.

'Fuck me, Cass! Is that a screamer?' Whist said.

'If you are referring to my means of distributing sortilaero then yes. Yes, it is.'

Though Whist was one of the few people in the world who knew that Castros was a demi-mage, the man had never seen Del Var use his powers. *Well, I couldn't use them before my exile*, thought Castros.

'Twelve hells, Castros! Where have you been?' Whist spluttered.

'You wouldn't believe me, if I told you,' Del Var replied with a smile. 'Come on, let's move out of the view of the guards. You know I love a spectacle, but I wouldn't like to be caught only two months after returning.'

***

Heels thumping dully on the pavement, the pair made their way to the back wall of the prison. After a quick check for patrolling guards, Castros nodded to Whist.

'Right, my good man, hold on tight and try not to get too aroused by my manliness,' Del Var said.

'Very fucking funny. You gonna tell me about all this?'

'Not now. One day, maybe.'

It wasn't that he didn't trust Whist — hells he was one of the only people he had told about his abilities — but he really did *not* want to get into the things he had experienced during his exile just yet.

Pulling Whist close, Castros wrapped his arm around the man's middle. He pointed the screamer at the ground and gave a hard squeeze on the bellows.

Assisted by the magically enhanced air, the pair shot into the sky like a firework. Bricks, mortar and the spikes of the wall flew past in a dizzying blur as they sped upwards. The pair arced over the wall and began to descend with a stomach-turning rapidity. Castros held his nerve and gave another short blast of the screamer. The force of the sortilaero blast slowed their fall, and they dropped to the ground with a gentle bump.

Scanning to his left and right, Castros saw no one in the wide courtyard they had landed in. Still, he knew their time was short. The guards in the watchtowers would discover them before too long, if they didn't move.

Del Var jerked his head towards the back of the main prison building, and they sprinted across the cobbles towards it. They pressed themselves close to the stone, out of the watchtowers' view, and Castros prayed they didn't run into any random patrols. He was counting on the Tremoran's arrogance at the impregnability of the gaol, hoping it would lead to lax security.

'For the love of the gods, Castros, this isn't infiltration. This is full-frontal assault! I hope you have some kind of plan?' Whist hissed in his ear.

'Of course, I do,' he lied. 'Have a little faith in your illustrious leader, eh?'

Del Var checked the rest of his arsenal. He had his water dispensers and the other air containers. He had about fifteen minutes of sortilenergy stored in his weapons, fifteen minutes of magic in exchange for a day storing and converting the power. *Still*, he thought, *fifteen minutes should be more than enough.*

'Which way to the cell?' Castros asked.

'That way. Dane's being held at the top of that tower. Only way through is to make your way up from the bottom. Gonna be hard to manage that, even *with* your new-found powers.'

That was one of the things Del Var loved about Whist — he took everything in his stride. *Whist sees a man he's known for years turn up with magical powers and just thinks, what the hells!* He knew that Whist would already be formulating strategies in his mind that incorporated Castros' new abilities. He gave his friend a slap on the back.

'We'll make our way up alright, but since my transformation, I must say I'm not too fond of stairs,' Castros said.

They sped towards the tower as alarm bells began to sound all over the prison grounds. *Shit*, Castros thought, *I was hoping for more time.*

Five guards came running at them from the base of the tower, balliskets primed for firing. The men set themselves up in front of Del Var and Whist.

'Shit it all! What do we do?' Whist cried.

'Just keep running for that tower. I'll do the rest.'

Castros pointed the screamer and gave a vicious squeeze when the men opened fire, the blast of air diverting the paths of the bullets. Looks of confusion followed by fear passed across the guards' faces as they realised what they were up against. Castros drank it in. *That's it lads*, he thought, *a mage is amongst you; what do you do now?* He cast a quick glance at Whist, he seemed dazed but was still running.

'Whist, draw your sword and hold this lot off. I'll be back in a few minutes,' Del Var said.

'A few … where the hells do you think you're going?'

'Up there,' Castros said, pointing at the top of the tower.

Giving Whist no more time to respond, he spurred his legs straight towards the guards with a mad fury. A few paces from them, Del Var blasted himself over their heads with a burst of sortilaero. Landing softly on the ground behind them, he continued his run, not breaking step once.

He reached the bottom of the tower and again gave a long squeeze on the screamer. He shot into the air and grabbed hold of the bars of the window to one of the cells high up in the tower. He looked up; he had a long way to go and hoped he hadn't underestimated how much sortilaero he would need.

Pushing with his feet against the black stone, Del Var threw himself backwards and propelled himself upwards with his screamer. He continued like this all the way to the top.

When he reached the uppermost window, Castros pulled out his waterskin and squirted the contents out. He willed the droplets into a ball and then made the sphere expand. It exploded with a sloshing sound against the wall and window of the tower. Still using the screamer to keep himself in the air, Castros willed the droplets of water into the bricks and mortar. He flared the sortilaqua outward, eroding the stones' bonding material, and the portion of tower wall covered in the water collapsed. Dust and debris showered downwards, making Del Var cough. He angled his screamer behind him and blasted himself into the cell.

He landed on the floor with a bone-crunching bump and skidded forwards. Dazed from his entry, Castros pulled himself unsteadily to his feet. He shook the fragments of wall from his person, creating a small dust cloud around him.

'That was quite the entrance, Cass, how about getting me out of these chains?' the voice of Dane called out to him.

Del Var stared across the cell and caught sight of his friend chained to the far wall. He made his way over to him, laughing.

'No, "How are you, boss? Where'd you get the powers?"' Del Var said.

'Nope. Don't care. Get me free,' the large Narvglander said, blue eyes peering out from beneath a tangled mass of blonde hair.

*Same old Dane*, Castros thought, *straight to the point.*

He examined the chains that were holding Dane to the wall. Not anything he should have a problem with, but he had to be careful to save enough power to escape.

Water formed into a whirling puddle in his hand and then shot towards the links in the chain just below Dane's wrists. It covered the metal, and he drew on his quickly depleting reserves of power to force the water to mesh with the atoms of the steel. Once Del Var could feel his energy inside the chains, he froze the sortilaqua, turning the metal to ice.

Without needing to be told, Dane pulled his arms sharply forwards, breaking his bonds. He stood up to his full, impressive height and stretched, joints cracking in response.

'Wahoo! Fuck me, that's better. Cheers boss. How we getting out of here?' Dane said.

*If Whist takes things in his stride*, Castros thought, *Dane, plain doesn't care*. Freedom, captivity, whichever way the pendulum of fate swung was all the same to the big man.

'Back the way I came—' Castros began.

He was cut off as the door to the cell flew open and three guards poured in. They stood huddled together in the doorway, their balliskets pointed at Dane and Castros' hearts.

'You, big man, get over there by the other one,' a guard ordered Dane, moving tentatively towards them.

'Can I kill 'em boss?' Dane said, rolling his shoulders.

'No. You know my rules,' Del Var said. 'Just get yourself over by me.'

Dane shrugged and walked over to Castros.

'Now, start backing towards the gap in the wall,' he whispered to the Narvglander.

Hands raised in surrender, Castros and Dane began to walk backwards towards the hole Del Var had blown in the cell. Looks of confusion passed over the guards' faces.

'Stop that! Stand still this instant. That man has to answer for his crimes! He must face the duke's justice!' one of the guards called out.

'Sorry, old chap, not today,' Castros said, throwing himself out of the hole, taking Dane with him.

The big man hullooed in free fall like a child on a merry-go-round, and Del Var wished he shared his companion's joy of madness. Forcing his heart back down from his throat, he pulled out the screamer. Ten paces from the ground he spewed out the last of the sortilaero from the container, creating an air cushion to catch them.

They sank the small distance to the ground like feathers caught in a breeze. Castros caught sight of Whist fighting off a handful of guards, spinning about the men with his expert grace and swordsmanship. Dane let out a deep howl and ran headfirst into the fray. Castros thought about stopping him, but he knew he needed to change the sortilaero container on his screamer if they were to have any chance of escape.

He hastily screwed the new container into place and sprinted towards his comrades. Barrelling past the guards, he placed the screamer in his teeth and grabbed Dane in one hand and Whist in the other, then he bit down as hard as he could, and they shot into the air, Dane cursing him the whole time for ruining his fun. Using the screamer in such an unusual way meant that they ascended on a diagonal instead of flying true. One of the spikes atop the wall caught against Del Var's leg, and he let out a startled cry, the screamer falling from his mouth.

*Fuck it*, he thought, *this will hurt later but there's nothing for it.* He took in a deep breath and fused the air hastily with his own life force, converting the sortilenergy quickly but painfully. As they plummeted back towards the ground he expelled the air he had turned into sortilaero.

It wasn't his most graceful landing from a spot of air walking ever, but it saved their lives, slowing them just enough to stop the crash being fatal.

Castros lay on the pavement, panting furiously. Whist and Dane were already up and pulling him to his feet.

'How ... was ... that ... for a homecoming?' Del Var said between desperate gasps.

'Fucking outstanding! What do you reckon, Whist?' Dane said.

'It was moronic, dangerous and far too conspicuous,' Whist said, frowning. 'I loved every second of it!'

Smiles broke across the faces of the three men. After all this time, it's like we haven't missed a beat, Castros thought.

'Well, that's me all magicked out for the day, probably tomorrow as well. Dane, give me a lift,' Del Var said.

'Aye, aye boss!' the big man replied, hoisting him effortlessly onto his shoulders.

Bells and cries reverberated all around them. What must have been the entire force of guards started to pour out of the gaol.

'Wouldn't be right if we weren't running away from someone, I suppose,' Whist said with a sigh before tearing away down the street, Dane and Castros following in his wake.

***

The fibres of the fake imperial moustache tickled Castros' nose, and he brought his hand up to cover a sneeze. He peeked his head around the corner of a building and checked that the route to the Saprez locomotron station was clear. The building stood in front of him, a wonder of glass and steel. Turning back towards Dane and Whist, he gave a brief nod and the disguised men made their way towards the station.

They had managed to lose their pursuers by heading into the sewers. The ever-resourceful Whist having already stashed their disguises in the subterranean waste system beforehand.

The trio had returned above ground dressed as successful businessmen.

They wore lavish greatcoats, silk shirts and bowler hats. The outfits should help them blend in for a short while, but given Dane's size, the threesome wouldn't withstand close scrutiny.

Leading the way, Castros strode into the station and weaved his way through the crowd. Dane *did* draw a lot of attention from stationmasters and porters, but he hoped they would assume the big man was his bodyguard.

They made their way towards the train departing for Victory, the Capital of the Estrian Empire. Gleaming in the sunlight that poured through the glass ceiling, sleek and black, the locomotron stretched like a panther reclining in the sun. At the front of the train, a silver eagle perched menacingly.

Del Var purchased their tickets from the booth and quickly looked back towards the entrance. His stomach gave a small twirl when he saw four watchmen talking to a porter. The porter pointed in Dane, Whist and Castros' general direction.

'Get a wriggle on lads, the Watch is on its way!' Del Var whispered to his companions.

They walked along the platform, looking for an unoccupied compartment. They found one in the middle of the locomotron. Clambering through the carriage door, Del Var, followed by Whist and Dane, settled himself into a plush velvet seat. Castros angled himself so he had a clear view back down the platform. He saw the stationmaster check his pocket watch and then give a blast on his whistle.

The locomotron chugged into life and began to pull away. Castros saw the watchmen burst through the crowd and confront the stationmaster. They were gesturing wildly, trying to get the man to stop the train. He merely shrugged in response. *In Estria, the locomotrons run on time, regardless of whether they're harbouring fugitives*, Del Var thought.

The sensual fabric of the seat enveloped Castros as he reclined. He felt the knot in his stomach uncoil, and he gave his companions a broad smile.

'There we go, men! Let's hope this is the start of many successful escapades!' Del Var said.

'There won't be too many more if we go barrelling into each one like you did at the gaol, Cass,' Whist replied.

'Oh, lighten up, you miserable bugger. We're here now, ain't we? No harm done,' Dane said.

'That's the spirit, my large friend. I've always found a positive attitude brings positive results,' Castros said, leaning forwards to slap Dane's shoulder affectionately. 'Good work on the disguises as well, Whist.'

'Thanks, boss. Once we get ourselves set up properly, I'll make sure we've got this kind of stuff stashed in all our bases. Got all sorts of things in the Workers' Party bases in the capital, but we could do with some in the other major cities. Shame we ain't got a cognopath, though; a shedder or a shrouder would come in handy.'

Del Var felt his insides sting. The pain must have registered on his face as Whist slapped his hand against his forehead.

'Sorry, Cass. I didn't mean to open old wounds.'

'It's alright. I miss Nairne every day, but you don't need to tiptoe around things with me. Plus, you have a point. When we get to Victory, we should see if we can bring a new cognopath into the fold.'

Silence fell across the group for a while, the only sound the steady clack of the wheels as the country flew by. Castros shuffled uneasily in his chair; he hated silences.

'I think I need a calling card,' he said.

'A what?' Dane asked.

'A calling card. A little token left behind to let our enemies know who has paid them a visit. I was thinking of leaving behind a white rose whenever we finish a job. What d'ya reckon?'

Dane and Whist looked at each other and burst into laughter.

'A fucking rose! Oh, Cass, I have missed your sense of humour,' Whist said, wiping at his eyes.

Castros pouted and sank back in his chair, staring out of the window sulkily. He hadn't been joking. His reaction fuelled the others' laughter, stoking them into full-blooded roars.

'Look out, Whist, we've upset the White Rose of Estria! Don't rub him the wrong way, or he'll throw petals at you!' Dane said.

'Alright, alright, leave it out, you two. Your discipline has gone to the dogs,' Castros said, unable to stop a small smile passing his lips. He knew the pair didn't mean any harm, and he enjoyed the banter with his friends. It was a stark contrast to the terrors of his exile.

Whist produced a deck of cards, and the trio sat playing Dead Man Down. The hours passed without incident, and any soul who thought of entering their compartment quickly changed their mind when they caught sight of Dane.

Castros threw down his cards and gestured that he was out. Dane and Whist continued as he stared out of the window. Victory, the Imperial capital, the Unfallen City, dominated his view. The dark stone of the vast Castrian Wall, the steep Olphant Hill rising sharply in the distance, and the brightness of thousands upon thousands of galvanic lights shining like a web of captured stars. They would soon be at their destination.

Stretching and flexing his muscles, Castros stood. His body responded with a deep ache. He didn't want to let on to his friends but using his own life force to quickly gather and use sortilenergy would have him in pain for days.

'I'm gonna go and grab a drink from the dining car,' he said to the pair, hoping alcohol would help lessen the pain.

Dane and Whist nodded without looking up from their cards. He opened the compartment door into the narrow gangway and made his way to down the locomotron.

In the dining car he ordered himself a shot of Gortrix thunderwater. He downed it in one and felt the liquor explode in his body. Two men walked into the carriage. He instantly didn't like the look of them. They had the self-satisfied air of vultures, watchmen promoted to the Lord Chancellor's intelligence department. The men looked towards him and then began to mutter amongst themselves. Castros turned back towards the way he had come and left the buffet car.

He hoped he was wrong about the pair, but his fears were proved right when he heard additional footsteps sound dully on the thick carpet behind him. He quickened his pace.

'You, man, stop in the name of the Emperor!' A voice called from behind him.

Castros broke into a run, his depleted body screaming in protest. As he passed his own compartment, he banged on the door. It shot open and the chasing vultures smashed into it.

'What's the big id—oh, I see,' said Whist, sticking his head out of the door and spotting the two prone men.

'Run!' Castros called behind him.

He raced down the corridor, the sound of Dane and Whist's running feet following behind him. Carriage after carriage flew past until Castros burst through a door and was confronted with the locomotron tracks receding into the distance.

'Shit! The end of the train. What now, boss?' Dane said as he and Whist caught up to him.

'Only one thing for it. We go up,' Del Var said, pointing to the roof of the locomotron.

'You've got to be kidding me, Cass!' Whist said, eyes bulging in disbelief.

'No time to argue,' Castros said, pointing towards the rapidly approaching vultures.

They pulled their way onto the roof and began to run back towards the front of the train. Castros couldn't say what he hoped to achieve with the tactic, but he had no intention of being caught.

Halfway along the locomotron a shot rang out from behind them. The trio stopped in their tracks and turned around, swaying side to side with the movement of the vehicle. Castros looked back and saw the two vultures. One held a smoking ballistol in the air, and the other pointed one towards them.

'Don't move, or we'll shoot. We have reason to believe one of you is the ringleader of the Tremore uprising and is sentenced to death. Come quietly now and make this easier on yourselves,' the man with the smoking ballistol shouted.

'Go fuck yerself!' Dane called back.

Though Castros wouldn't have put it in such blunt terms, he agreed with the sentiment. *What the hells should we do now*, he thought? It would be hard to fight on the roof of the locomotron and using any more sortilenergy was well out of the question — if he pushed himself further he would risk permanent injury, or worse. The locomotron sped over the bridge across the Tollfaith river, and an idea entered his mind.

'Follow my lead,' he whispered to his friends. 'Alright gents, you've got us we'll—Jump!' Del Var shouted.

Sprinting towards the edge of the locomotron, Castros heard the shot of the second ballistol and felt the sharp sting as it clipped his arm. He blocked out the pain and launched himself off the roof of the cabin.

The air ripped past his ears in a high-pitched squeal. From behind, he heard the curses and oaths of the vultures and the cries of his companions. Dark water rushed towards him and then swallowed him in an icy grip. His momentum took him deep beneath the surface. The world turned black around him.

Fighting with all his strength, Del Var broke the surface of the river. The current was bearing him along quickly. Frantically, he looked around him for his companions. Whist was just behind him, already making his way towards the steep walled banks of the river, but there was no sign of Dane. Where was he?

'Dane? Dane!' Castros called out.

Even further back than Whist, he saw a large, dark shape floundering in the water. *Shit! I forgot he's not a strong swimmer.* Battling against the current, he watched the big man sink beneath the water.

'Hang on Dane!' he cried.

Straining every muscle in his body, he fought towards his friend. He watched in horror as the man sank and rose three times. As hard as he tried, he couldn't make any headway. Castros stared in cold disbelief as Dane sank once more. Bubbles burst on the surface of the water and then all was still.

# CHAPTER THREE

Elvgren sighed and swatted at the flies that were landing and taking off from his body in intermittent bursts. The wide stretch of road that led to New Ledi was choked with other refugees seeking safe haven in the city. People, oxen, carts, all added to the mad crush and the smell was overwhelming.

As the sun beat down on his head, he longed to be back home in Estria, back where things made sense, and he wasn't hot all the time. He was sure his role in the defeat of Marmossa and Kurkeshi would have to be acknowledged by the Lord Chancellor and his family. He could already see the looks on his parents' faces as he arrived home, seemingly risen from the dead.

The only dark spot on his horizon was Holger. After the great buffoon had declared his feelings for Bellina, Elvgren had been dreaming of the day they could be shot of him. *Once we're back, I'll get the Lord Chancellor to pack him off somewhere*, he thought. After all, it was the Lord Chancellor, her father, who had set up his and Bellina's engagement.

Taking a deep breath, he pushed the thoughts aside. Everything was going to be fine. The respect and command he'd longed for would be his; all they had to do was get home.

In the distance, Elvgren could see the massive walls of New Ledi. They were monumental constructions of stone that reared up like a watchful snake. Cannons glinted in their embrasures, and tiny Estrian soldiers paraded the ramparts. The whole city had been designed by Estrian engineers — but built with local labour, of course — to be the seat of the Empire's control in Mandira. It was the closest thing to home they could hope for. Now, all they had to do was get in.

'This is bollocks, Gren,' Dargo said. He had reared up in the driver's seat like a startled cat and was peering ahead at the throng. The priest, who was on the driver's seat with them, furrowed his brow. 'I mean,' continued Dargo, 'you'd think they'd be rolling out the red carpet for us. We're heroes, ain't we? Got rid of Marmossa and Kurkeshi, didn't we?'

'I'm not sure how much of that news has got through,' Elvgren replied, wiping at the sweat pouring down his face.

'Bloody travesty is all I'm saying. I mean, Belle's half dead back there from taking down those mad bastards.'

'For the love of the gods, Dargo! It's too hot for your bloody moaning, unless you've got a plan that will move all this,' Elvgren said, gesturing in front of them at what seemed like the entire population of the world.

Elvgren watched Dargo recline in his seat, a pout on his lips. Then the boy's eyes lit up.

'Maybe, I have got a plan,' he said.

***

Cirona stared across the wagon at the sleeping form of Bellina, Holger by her side as he usually was, eyeing her avidly. *But is it passion in those eyes,* she thought, *or obsession?* The covered space provided some respite from the blistering heat, but the girl still seemed to be right on the edge of the land of the living. *It's because she used her powers to get us on board,* she thought for the thousandth time.

Inside her head, the doubts and the guilt that had plagued her since their flight from Kurgobad began to spill out. Reveeker's face as he was tortured to death in a Burkeshi dungeon, Torkwill's sacrifice, Bellina's face when Cirona had told her that the man she thought was her father had actually sent her to die.

A wave of sickness coursed through her body. She tried to swallow but her mouth felt like it was stuffed with cotton. How could she carry on after all she had done? Bellina didn't seem to blame her for the whole incident in Burkesh, the girl had placed the blame squarely on the Lord Chancellor, but that didn't stop the guilt.

Cirona tried to tell herself she had done it for her daughter. That she would have done anything to see her again, that she still would, but the words rang hollow in the barren waste of her heart. She had spent her life in service to Estria, had killed, sacrificed, and the stains on her soul had always washed off. This time, though, she wasn't so sure …

'Alright, Rona, which one of these sacks has got the oats in it again?' Dargo said, clambering into the back of the wagon and dragging her from her thoughts.

'What are you up to, Dar?' she said, her eyes narrowing.

'I'm getting us into that city before the Old Terrors come back, that's what,' he replied.

She shook her head and watched Dargo take a handful of oats and place them in a bowl. Then he took his waterskin and made a lumpy mixture on the wagon's floor. As he began to smear the concoction over his face and arms she couldn't help but laugh.

'Dargo, you look like you've got skin rot,' she said.

'Exactly!' Dargo replied with a wiggle of his eyebrows.

He climbed out of the wagon and Cirona followed him. She watched as he plopped to the ground in front of the horses and began to stagger about and moan. He soon got the attention of the people in front of him who took one look at his face and began to pull aside in disgust. Suppressing a laugh, Cirona moved to the front of the wagon and climbed up next to Elvgren and the priest.

'Alms!' Dargo was crying now, his hands clawing at the heavens. 'Alms for the sick. We've all got skin rot, whole wagon full of us! Please give us alms.'

'Bet he doesn't even know what alms are,' Elvgren said with a smile.

'I do not think this charade is respectable. It is bad luck to feign sickness,' the priest said.

'He's getting this lot moving,' Cirona said. 'If you disagree that much then hop off and form an orderly queue behind us.'

The priest's gaze flipped between the progress they were making and the pack of people and carts reforming the line behind them. In the end, he made a small disapproving noise and rested his head back.

Soon, they reached the gates, and Cirona saw two bored-looking guards. At the sight of the men, Dargo dropped his act and began to wipe the gloop off his face.

'Stay where you are,' one of the guards said, scratching at a rash on his chin.

'It's alright, it's only oats,' Dargo said, holding out his hand so the man could inspect it.

'What brings yer to New Ledi?' the guard said.

'What do you think brings us here?' Elvgren said. 'The rest of the country is revolting.'

'It's not that bad,' the other guard said.

'He means rebelling against … oh, forget it,' the first guard said to his colleague. 'You all Estrians?

'Except the priest, yes,' Cirona said.

'Won't mind us having a look in the back then?' the guard asked.

'Be my guest,' Cirona replied.

She hopped down from the driver's seat and followed the man round to the back of the wagon. Holger gave a start as the man climbed in, but Cirona held her hand up for peace. The guard cast a quick glance over Holger then turned his eyes to Bellina. His gaze fell on her eagle shaped power constraint, and he took in a sharp breath.

'You're … by the gods … why didn't you say who you were?' the guard jumped out of the wagon. 'Oi, Bert! Open the gate … and get the bloody Viceroy!'

***

Bellina felt as if she had been drained of her life force, as if some vital part of her had been ripped out. She sat up straight in the plush, gilded chair and tried to look as if she was paying attention.

The Viceroy of New Ledi had personally escorted them from the front gate. Bellina had been roused for the occasion and had just about been able to make a polite introduction to the man. From the back of the wagon, she had watched the jealous eyes of the Mandirans, who were seeking entrance to the city, glow with anger as Bellina and her companions crept inside the massive walls.

All around them, the impressive sights of New Ledi had swum into view: the massive Lumanist cathedral, the barracks, the Jaffle Hotel, and finally, the columned facade of the Viceroy's palace.

As she gazed around the office of the Viceroy, Bellina thought the interior matched the imposing exterior. She and her companions were seated in a large square room. Veined marble covered the floors, rising up into columns that climbed towards the ceiling, each one sculpted to look like trees native to Estria. A large mahogany table sat in front of their chairs, inlaid with intricate floral patterns and picked out with gold leaf.

Unfortunately, the Viceroy himself didn't match up to the splendour. He was a short, squat man, whose face was obscured by thick, white mutton chops that merged with his flyaway hair. His eyes and mouth were pinched into a small space on a large skull and a pair of gold-rimmed spectacles were perched on top of a prominent nose.

He reclined in his seat, peering over the tops of his glasses to look at them. His little legs dangled freely above the floor, thanks to the fact that he was sitting on top of at least five pillows.

'It seems,' the Viceroy began in a slow drawl, 'that I will have the honour of hosting some most auspicious guests. Heroes even.'

'I don't know if I would go that far,' Cirona said, shifting her gaze to Bellina.

The young cognopath certainly didn't feel like a hero. Even now, the faces of the innocent dead haunted her. She gave her head a small shake, but the thoughts would not relinquish their hold on her.

'After the incident in Burkesh, the Lord Chancellor put out a description of you all, more in hope than expectation, I fear. But here you are, safe and relatively sound by the looks of things.'

'Have you spoken to him? The Lord Chancellor, I mean,' Elvgren asked.

'I have. He is most pleased at your survival,' the Viceroy began.

Bellina narrowed her eyes and felt her jaw clench. *I bet he is*, she thought.

'Not to be rude, old chap, but what is he arranging in terms of transportation? I, for one, have rather had my fill of the Eastern Continent,' Elvgren said.

'He is sending a ship of the air. I could scarcely believe him when he told me, but apparently, you are already acquainted with it.'

'The *Sighing Wind*?' Dargo said, his face lighting up. 'We're gonna get to fly again?'

Elvgren turned a shade paler. 'Wonderful,' he said.

There was a sharp knock at the door.

'Enter,' the Viceroy said.

Everyone turned to see who had interrupted the meeting. Bellina's eyes grew into wheels, and she felt a shiver pass through her. In the doorway, stood a tall man with a face like a cracked boulder. He was covered from head to toe in burgundy robes marking him out as a purgista. If Bellina felt unease at the sight of the purgista, it was nothing compared to the look on Holger's face. His eyes were bulging, and a small whimper escaped his lips.

'Ah, Brother Dalcet, how nice of you to join us,' the Viceroy said.

'It is an honour to be before such esteemed guests,' the purgista replied.

'Is our little present for the Lord Chancellor ready?' the Viceroy asked.

'The gift is suitably restrained,' Dalcet said.

'Excellent, excellent,' the Viceroy replied, tugging at his facial hair. 'Is there anything else, Brother?'

'Yes. I need a word with you in private, my lord.'

The Viceroy stared long and hard into the purgista's face, the small man's brow crinkling. 'Very well,' he said.

He pressed a button located on top of his desk, and a train of Mandiran servants came into the room.

'These people will show you to your rooms and give you the tour,' The Viceroy said. 'I beg your pardon for not taking you myself.'

'Not at all, Viceroy,' Bellina managed to say. 'I am sure we are all most grateful for your hospitality.'

'Then I hope you pass on your good opinion of me to your father.'

*Oh, I'll pass it on*, Bellina thought, *that and a whole lot else besides.*

# CHAPTER FOUR

Castros Del Var was lost. *Lost in my own secret base*, he thought with a tired smile. In front of him stretched the tunnels of what the rest of his men had named the Warren. No one knew who had built the vast network of passageways that ran underneath Victory and out into its suburbs. Some claimed they were created by smugglers, others that it was made during the Mage Wars to get supplies, and people, in and out of the besieged city. Whoever it was, Castros was glad. The Warren had proved an excellent hideout over the years and allowed him and the rest of the Workers' Liberal Party unhindered access to the city above. And of course, he and Whist had added more tunnels to it in their turn.

Standing at an intersection of tunnels, Castros scratched his chin. Then he slapped his thigh and gave a small chuckle — right, he needed to go right. He set off, the sound of the printing machines churning out Workers' Party propaganda fading to a dull drone. By one exit, he passed a crate of pamphlets waiting to be taken to the surface and distributed in the poor districts of the capital. He stopped and picked one up, marvelling at the fact it was filled with ideas he and his fellows had come up with over twenty years ago. He replaced it with a sigh and carried on.

His walk soon took him past the deserted mess hall, sleeping quarters and the infirmary. This was one of Whist's additions. They did not have their own medificer but relied on the tender care of Butcher, an old army man, who knew how to tend a wound.

Butcher shared Castros' innate distrust of the medics. He too thought they were money-grubbing fraudsters. A bad hangover from a time when people thought rubbing chickens on your groin cured syphilis.

They both also shared an interest in the studies and progress being made by men like Dietmar Faralger and the Guild of Surgeons and Doctors. These were men of science, men who studied the human body to find out how it worked. Their achievements though were hindered and ridiculed by the Lumanists, who denounced them for meddling in the works of the Father. Seeing as the Lumanists, like the medificers, kept their position and status by controlling the population, keeping them ignorant, he understood why they didn't want people to find out that their bodies weren't made up of humours, bile, fairy dust or whatever else those in power decreed.

Finally, he arrived at Whist's room. He gave a jolly tattoo on the wood and waited. No answer came. Frowning, Castros turned the handle. The room beyond the door was sparse, only a bed and a work desk inside. Giving the room a quick scan, Del Var turned to leave then realised what he had mistaken for a balled-up sheet was his friend.

'So, you *are* in here, eh?' Castros said. Whist gave an undecipherable grunt. Grabbing the chair, Del Var moved it over to the bedside and sat down. 'How long are you going to keep this up, Whist?'

'Until it stops hurting,' Whist replied.

'Is this what Dane would have wanted? You curled up in a ball?'

'What would you know about what he wanted?' Whist said, wrenching himself into a sitting position. 'You were gone for ten *years*. Then you turn up with magical bloody powers and think you can just pick up right where you left off? It's my own fault, I suppose.' He gave a bitter laugh. 'I never should have let you talk me into any of this. Maybe then Dane would be alive.'

'Look, I know this is hard, but we have to keep going.'

'Well, excuse me if I don't possess your callous streak,' Whist said with a snort.

Castros ground his teeth and felt his body tense. 'Callous? Callous! Is that what you think I am? Dane's death hit me just as hard as you, Whist. You don't have the monopoly on sorrow,' Del Var said, running a hand through his hair. 'It's not callousness that keeps me going. All I know is that, if I stop for a second, just one, then I will be betraying the memory of everyone who has died for our cause.'

Whist let out a heavy sigh and scrubbed his hand over his face. 'I'm … I'm sorry, Cass. It's just, you know, Dane was one of the last originals. Now, it's just me and you.'

'All the more reason we keep fighting the good fight and recruit more to our numbers. You've done an excellent job here in my absence. All the members are well drilled and motivated. They love you, Whist; they need you.'

'They love *you*,' Whist replied.

'No. They look at me like some semi-mythical figure. But you … you're their general — the man who gets things done,' Castros said, reaching out his hand and squeezing Whist's shoulder. A chiming came from inside Del Var's coat pocket, and he plucked out his watch. 'By the gods! Is that the time already?'

'Going to see Constance, eh?' Whist asked.

'Yes. I think it's about time things were set in motion. Going to come and see me off?'

"Course,' Whist replied.

They walked back into the maze of tunnels.

'Right,' said Del Var. 'Which one of these leads towards the Olphant Hill?'

***

Appearing in the cool night air at the base of the Olphant Hill, Castros looked up. Rising above him, almost touching the night sky, was the collective home of Estrian nobility. The mansions and stately homes were up there. Galvanic lights shone out of them, lighting up the night like a false dawn.

Castros thought of the millions of men, women and children sitting, that moment, in the cold and the dark. Many of them not knowing when their next meal would be. This had to change.

He made his way up and around the hill. The cable cars going up and down went past him, taking some lord or lady back to their luxurious homes. He knew no one would pay him any mind, though. He was dressed as a manservant and anyone who saw him would assume he was just out on an errand for his masters. He also wasn't concerned that anyone would recognise him.

Even after the attempt on the Emperor's life, there were not many who knew what he looked like. Castros had become a faceless horror, a nightmare fairy tale the nobility whispered to each other on dark nights. And for some of them, he was going to make the nightmare a reality.

Soon he could see the high walls of his destination. The home of Aberoth Constance, champion of workers' rights. Castros had decided to put Lord Constance's devotion to the cause to the test.

Thanks to Whist's intel, he knew the house was lightly guarded despite the imposing walls. He also knew where to find the lord of the manor.

Using another screamer, he shot over the wall at the back of the house. Landing softly in the branches of a tall tree, Del Var did a quick scan of the grounds. He could see no guards.

A light was shining from a second-floor window. This was apparently Aberoth's study and was where the man spent most of his nights.

Running along the branch, Castros reached its tip and jumped. He gave another blast of sortilaero that carried him over to the windowsill. Castros clung on by his fingertips and pulled his head up to observe the room.

It was typical of any Estrian noble's study. Burgundy carpets, a booze cabinet, bookcases, a roaring fire fuelled with burning sortilenergy and a stout witch-oak table. At the table, Aberoth sat, head bowed over some papers, scribbling furiously. Most importantly, he sat facing away from the window.

Seeing it was safe, Castros pulled himself up onto the broad sill. Taking his waterskin out from his belt, he squirted a small amount into the lock. He froze it, took out a small hammer and gently broke the lock.

He opened the window and crept into the room. Standing behind Aberoth, Castros cleared his throat. Lord Constance jumped from his seat and turned around clutching his heart.

'Please, my lord, do be seated. Oh, and don't even dream of calling for your guards,' Castros said.

Aberoth took a deep breath and composed himself. He took his gold-rimmed spectacles from his rather prominent nose and began to polish them. His bald head was surrounded on the sides by a ring of white hair. A wrinkled brow sat above piercing blue eyes that shone with life. He seemed a strong and capable man. Castros was pleased.

'And who, pray tell, are you, young man?'

'I'm Castros Del Var,' he replied.

Castros had expected a strong reaction to his name and was surprised, and slightly disappointed, when he didn't get one.

'Really? Well, well that is a turn up for the books. The Lord Chancellor has long claimed you were dead. Though you could be any common burglar climbing through my window and claiming to be the scourge of the nobility to give me a fright. Do you have proof of what you claim?'

Castros took off his coat and rolled up his sleeve exposing his prison tattoo and number.

'Feel free to take the number down and check it out for yourself,' he said.

'I will, but I don't need to jot it down — I have an exceptional memory. Now, if it's not too much bother, could you please tell me why you are here?'

'You have done a lot of good things, Lord Constance. I think you could do more. Although I despise the nobility, I no longer believe that force will achieve my goals. Goals which I think you and I both share.'

'Believe me, my boy, I would love to do more, but I do not possess the power.'

'What if I could make you the most powerful man in the Empire?'

'I don't see the Lord Chancellor relinquishing control any time soon,' Aberoth said with an eyebrow raised quizzically.

'What if you had the power to override the Lord Chancellor?'

'What are you saying? For that I would have to be—'

'You would have to be the Emperor.'

# CHAPTER FIVE

Cirona gazed down from the battlements of New Ledi and frowned. They had been in the Mandiran capital for a week now and each day the mass of people outside the city walls had grown. Sickness was running high amongst the refugees while food was running low.

She watched a scuffle break out on the plain below. Two men were wrestling over a loaf of bread. Blows were exchanged then Cirona saw the unmistakable glint of a sword being drawn. She held her breath and gripped the wall in front of her. Then more people joined in and pulled the men apart. Letting out a sigh, Cirona wondered to herself how long it would be before all that simmering anger was directed at the walls of New Ledi.

Turning her eyes upwards, she scanned the heavens for sign of the airship. The *Sighing Wind* was nowhere to be seen. She prayed it wouldn't be much longer and not just because the mood towards Estrians on the Eastern Continent was turning poisonous.

Home. That was what she wanted. That and to see her daughter. Cirona wondered what that first meeting with her child would be like. Would they cry? Laugh? Would they notice they both had dimples or find out they both hated oranges? She stroked at her throat as her pulse quickened ever so slightly. Gods, she hoped it went well.

*It will be alright,* she told herself, tapping her fist against the wall. It was all going to be fine.

Spinning on her heel, Cirona now faced the city. She stared out over the low mud-brick buildings of the locals, her eyes being drawn towards the monumental constructions of the Estrians. *It's a magnificent place,* she thought, *it's just a shame about the incessant heat.*

She nodded to one of the patrolling guards and prepared to descend the wall when a series of howls and cries rose from the east. Squinting, she stared in that direction. A thin plume of smoke was rising up from the market quarter. *Didn't Elvgren and Dargo go there to do some shopping?*

'What the fuck have you done now, Lord Lovitz,' she muttered, sprinting down the stairs.

***

Elvgren stood looking at the vast array of silk garments and trinkets in front of him. There were shirts, billowing trousers and flyaway scarves. In his mind's eye he could see himself decked out in the gear, sauntering through a pleasure garden like a white Multan.

'How much for this?' Dargo said, pulling Elvgren from his daydream. The boy was holding up a thick gold bangle. The stallholder shrugged in return.

'No, no, no. You're doing it all wrong, Dar. These brown chaps can't understand if you talk to them like that,' Elvgren said.

'Alright, you have a go then.'

'HOW MUCH FOR THE SHINY, SHINY THING?' Elvgren bellowed at the man.

The stallholder narrowed his eyes then held up five fingers.

Elvgren smiled and counted out five rencats from his coin purse. 'You see, Dargo, the natives are not that bright. You have to talk to them as you would a child, if you want to get anywhere.'

'If you say so, Gren,' Dargo replied with a roll of his eyes.

The stallholder took the coins and passed Dargo the bangle. He slipped it on, admiring the way it glinted in the sunlight.

Elvgren smiled and patted the boy on his back. 'Let's see what else we can find, eh?'

The market was packed. The smell of countless spices and perfumes mingled with that of the people, grounded and heavenly all at once. Chickens clucked and scampered around underfoot. Sickly cows with exposed ribs mooed forlornly. And monkeys screeched from rooftops, coming down every so often to steal a piece of fruit. It was a lively place and Elvgren found it intoxicating.

'Gren? Gren!'

'What is it, Dargo?'

'I don't like the looks some of these locals are giving us,' he said, pointing at a group of hungry-looking men half hidden in the shadow of an alley.

Elvgren glanced at them and laughed. 'Don't be ridiculous, Dar. They wouldn't dare touch an Estrian. They'd be swinging from the palace gates if they so much as muttered a threat at us.'

'Didn't stop that mob in Reltucca attacking, did it?'

'New Ledi is different. This is our main hub in the east. There are tens of thousands of men stationed at the barracks.'

'Yeah, but how many of them are Estrian? From what I've seen, most of 'em are locals.'

'Oh, stop worrying. Look, one of them is coming over to us now.'

One of the men had indeed peeled himself away from his fellows and was making his way towards Elvgren and Dargo.

'HELLO!' Elvgren cried at the man.

The man flinched, holding both his hands out in front of him, and said, 'Please, my lord, I speak the common tongue most clearly. There is no need to make so much noise.'

'Excellent! How can we help you?' Elvgren said.

The man licked his lips and smiled. 'It is I who may be able to help you, my lord. A fine looking young man such as yourself must get very lonely so far from home. Perhaps you have heard of the samurs? Girls trained their whole lives in the mysterious ways of physical pleasure,' he said.

'I *have* heard tale of them,' Elvgren replied, eyebrows raised, body straight.

'Good, good. You are most well-educated, my lord. Myself and my friends know the cleanest and best pleasure house in the city—'

'I don't like this, Gren,' Dargo said, cutting in.

'Of course, minors are not allowed entry,' the man said, smiling at Dargo.

Elvgren flicked his gaze from Dargo to the man. He hadn't had a woman since before they left Estria. Tales of the samurs were legendary in the taverns of his homeland. Elvgren pulled at his ear. Why shouldn't he have some fun? Because he was betrothed? Being betrothed to Bellina Ressa was like being sworn to a dead cod.

'Dargo, you head back to the palace,' he said.

'But, Gren!'

'I'm a big boy; I can look after myself. Now, off you go,' Elvgren said, turning Dargo around by his shoulders and giving him a gentle push.

Before the boy could argue any more, Elvgren nodded at the man who set off towards his companions. Elvgren followed in his wake. *What in the world is Dargo so worried about?* He checked his sword was in his belt. Even if they did try anything, he would be prepared.

Soon, they came to a two-storey building. There was a veranda on the first floor where some women were sunning themselves. The front door was a carved arch with pillars picked out in swirling gold and a silk curtain separating the interior from the street.

'We are here, my lord,' the man said.

'Yes, we are,' Elvgren replied, licking his lips and making for the door. The man coughed. Turning back around Elvgren saw that his guide had his hand held out expectantly. He sighed then pressed a rencat into the man's palm.

'And what about my friends, my lord?' the man said. Elvgren dug in his purse and took out three more coins. 'Thank you, my lord. I shall announce your arrival, get you the best girl.'

With that the man slipped inside the curtain. Elvgren was left with the man's companions who stared at him through narrowed eyes. Elvgren smiled at them and nodded his head.

'They are ready for you, my lord,' the man said, reappearing from the pleasure house. 'Your woman is waiting in the second room of the first floor.'

'Excellent. Many thanks, old boy,' Elvgren replied and slipped inside.

The smell of incense inside the house was overpowering and Elvgren had to press a handkerchief to his mouth. The ground floor was an open rectangular space covered in thick Varashi rugs and opulent couches upon which women lounged. They were feeding each other grapes and barely looked up to see the young lord enter.

Maybe it was the headiness of the incense or the sight of the women, but Elvgren felt his body shiver with desire. He crossed the space in a few large strides then mounted the stairs two at a time. He quickly located the first room and knocked on the door.

'Come in,' a silken voice beckoned.

Elvgren smoothed down his hair, straightened out his clothes, then went in. The room beyond was like a reproduction of the ground floor in miniature, though this room had a bed and a brazier in the corner to burn the incense. A woman was lounging across the bed but stood when he entered. A loose, transparent garment of silk just covered the woman's chest and crotch.

'Welcome, my lord,' the woman said.

She pressed a clasp on her shoulder, and the silk fell away, leaving her naked. Elvgren swallowed hard, his gaze taking in the glistening copper skin, the large firm breasts, the long, elegant legs.

'Here, lie on the bed,' the samur said.

Elvgren did as he was told, collapsing onto the bed. The samur smiled and pushed him gently backwards, so he was lying down. She straddled him and produced a blindfold as if from nowhere.

'Er, hang on a minute,' Elvgren said.

The woman shushed him and wrapped the blindfold around his eyes. His heartbeat thundered in his chest, every slight touch from the samur magnified. She began to undress him. He felt the woman lift off his shirt then slip off his weapons and pull down his trousers.

'One moment, my lord,' she said.

Elvgren felt the absence of touch keenly. He waited, body quivering with anticipation. Then he felt the kiss of cold steel at his throat.

'W-what is the meaning of this?' he said.

'This is for my country — the one you and your kind have raped for the last fifty years!'

The samur was on top of him, her weight pinning him down. A freezing sweat began to pour from his body. He went to move his hands and felt the knife bite into his neck, a thin trickle of blood tracing a path down it.

'I am going to carve you into pieces, you swine. Your body shall be a message to your Empire,'

'N-now hang on a second! I can give you money, power,' Elvgren mumbled. The samur let out a laugh.

A massive commotion broke out downstairs. Elvgren felt the blade's pressure relent. Not needing an invitation, he swung his arms down in a clubbing motion and felt a satisfyingly meaty collision. He sat himself up and pushed, sending the woman sprawling to the ground.

He ripped the blindfold from around his head and made a grab for his weapons. Elvgren was quick but the samur was his match. Their hands locked on top of the sword's hilt. Naked, they both tussled on the floor for it. With a knee to his balls, the woman won the battle. In one swift motion, she sprung to her feet. She levelled the blade at his chest, eyes glinting.

There was another crash and screams from somewhere else in the brothel. The woman's eyes flicked away from Elvgren for a split second. He pounced, his shoulder crashing into the woman's stomach, sending her tumbling into the brazier.

It hit the floor with a bang, hot coals spilling onto the floor and table. The lush carpets and silks that covered the room caught alight and the fire spread with an astonishing speed. Elvgren screamed and made a break for the door. The samur caught him. He hit the floor hard, the tang of blood filling his mouth.

'This is the end for you,' the woman hissed in his ear.

At that moment, the door burst open.

'I know I'm only a minor and all that, but I think you're doing it wrong, Gren,' Dargo said.

Elvgren looked up to see the boy looming over him, a ballistol in his grasp.

'Alright, love, off you get,' he said.

The woman's eyes narrowed to slits, but she stood up, spitting into Elvgren's good eye as she did. The lord hauled himself to his feet and stood by Dargo's side.

'What now?' he said.

'Run,' Dargo replied.

The pair sprinted down the stairs, Dargo hollering and waving the ballistol as he went. The other samurs were already in a blind panic and flooding out of the building, coughing and spluttering from the smoke. Realising he was still stark naked, Elvgren grabbed a delicate piece of silk and wrapped it around his waist.

Outside the building, a massive crowd had gathered. Upon seeing the Estrians, they began to shout and curse. Elvgren and Dargo began to back away, the threat of the weapon managing to just hold the Mandirans at bay. Elvgren felt his chest grow tight and his mind whirl. How the hells were they going to get out of this?

Shots rang out from behind the mob of locals, then a large white horse split the gathering and Elvgren could make out the form of Major Bouchard in the saddle. Behind her was a line of soldiers. The mob turned to face the soldiers and Cirona took the opportunity to pull up the horse.

'Get on!' she bellowed.

Dargo and Elvgren both clambered up behind her and the major turned the horse to leave. Elvgren watched in horror as the mob charged the soldiers who let loose a volley of ballisket fire.

'Gods, damn it all!' Cirona cried. 'I told them not to fire. The Burkeshis will have a field day with this. And where the hells are your clothes, Lovitz?'

'Ah, well—'

'Never mind. We need to get back to the Viceroy's palace.'

Cirona dug her heels into the horse's flank, and they set off. A large portion of the mob set off after them. As the major led the horse through the streets of New Ledi, Elvgren saw that more and more people were joining the throng chasing them.

'I can see the palace,' Cirona said.

Elvgren turned his gaze forwards. Up ahead, the palace was coming into view.

'What are they doing?' Dargo said, pointing at the gates.

Elvgren squinted his eye and could just make out the forms of uniformed men pushing the iron gates closed.

***

Bellina lowered the four-poster bed to the floor with her mind and scanned for a headache or a nosebleed. There was nothing. It was the first time, for over a month, that the usage of her powers hadn't caused her significant pain. She held her chin high and allowed herself a smile.

With a stretch, she left her room, enjoying the lack of ache in her body. The stay at the Viceroy's palace had done her a world of good. She wandered down the corridor, the wooden floor beneath her feet gleaming. She passed the faces of the previous Viceroys, frowning from the walls, their eyes looking down at her with disapproval. She stuck her tongue out at them and carried on.

Before long, she found herself at the door to Holger's room. The door was ajar. She peered in. Holger was lying on his bed, hands behind his head, gaze fixed on the ceiling. She gave a light knock on the door, and he sat up with a start.

'Hello, Belle, how long have you been there?' he said

'All of five seconds,' she replied. 'Can I ...?'

'Yeah, course. Come in.'

Slipping past the door, Bellina entered the room. She looked at Holger who was perched on the edge of his bed, wringing his hands. His eyes had sunk back into his skull and were framed by dark purple rings. *Gods*, she thought, *has he slept at all the whole time we've been here?*

'A rencat for your thoughts, Master Holger?'

'Don't think they're worth it,' he replied with a limp smile.

'What's the matter? You've been down the whole week, and whenever you see the purgista ...'

At the mere mention of the name, Holger shivered. 'It's him ... the purgista. They just put the shits up me is all. Never been this close to one before, but if you're born in Narvale, you know all about them,' he said.

'Of course,' Bellina said, bringing her hand to her mouth. 'The purges after Narvale joined the Empire were particularly harsh, weren't they?'

'You can say that again,' Holger said, running a hand over his face. 'They ... they took my nan. I've only heard the story from my mum, but it must've been terrifying. They just appeared in the middle of the night. Looking for heretics and people of magical capabilities. My nan was a soothsayer, must've been almost seventy-five, but they dragged her from the house by her hair, denounced her in front of the whole village then ... then they burned her.'

'Holger ... I'm so sorry,' Bellina said, clasping a hand to her chest.

'It's not your fault, is it?' Holger said. 'My mother had to flee, though. Leave her village and set up somewhere else. Once purgistas get the bit between their teeth they like to check up on the rest of a family, make sure they don't start showing any powers. We lived in constant fear they would find us when we were growing up.'

'But that's ridiculous. I bet you grandmother didn't even have any magical powers,' Bellina said with a snort.

Holger looked up at her, his brows knit tight, eyes shining with a strange light. 'Well …' he began.

Just then a tremendous roar came from outside.

'What the hells was that?' Bellina said.

Holger's window looked out over the front courtyard of the palace. Bellina strode over to it and looked out. She could see a gaggle of soldiers trying to close the gate. Outside, a vast group of Mandirans was bearing down on the palace grounds. They seemed to be chasing a horse.

'Bloody hell! Isn't that the major riding that thing?' Holger said coming to join her.

'It is. I think Dargo and Elvgren are with her as well,' Bellina replied.

'They're not gonna make it,' Holger said, gripping the windowsill so tight his knuckles whitened.

*Please let them make it*, Bellina thought, her hands gripped in prayer. She watched as the space between the gates shrank and shrank. Bellina bit her lip. She could see that Cirona was leaning forwards, willing the horse on. Still the gap grew smaller. Then the horse stuck its head into the gap. Unable to push with the animal in the way the soldiers stopped for a second and the beast squeezed through. Straight away, Cirona leapt from the saddle and helped the men to close the gate.

'We better get down there and see if they need any help,' Holger said.

Bellina nodded and they set off for the courtyard. On the way, they ran into a bedraggled Viceroy. He barely noticed them as they all made their way to the gate. He burst into the courtyard in front of them and began issuing orders. Bellina rushed to the major's side. The woman was leaning against the gate, panting, a small cut on her forehead bleeding profusely.

'By the gods, Major, are you alright?' Bellina said.

'I'll live.'

'I'm fine by the way, my beloved!' Elvgren spat.

Bellina turned towards her betrothed, who stood before her, naked except for a flimsy piece of silk round his waist. 'Where are your clothes?' she said.

'Lost 'em in a brothel,' Dargo said, stuffing a smoking ballistol into the waist of his trousers.

'A what?' Bellina said.

'There's no time for bickering,' the Viceroy said. 'We have to get inside. Barricade the doors.'

Overhead, improvised missiles flew over the walls. An erratic drumming echoed off the steel gates. The handful of guards on the walls fired their balliskets into the crowd.

'We're doomed,' the Viceroy wailed, pulling great tufts out of his beard.

'No, we're not,' Cirona said with a smile, pointing at the sky.

Turning her head, Bellina looked up and saw the *Sighing Wind* — the world's first airship — hovering into view. 'Thank the gods,' she said.

'Blessed is the Father,' the purgista said, appearing as if from nowhere. On his back, he was carrying a body. The unconscious man was brown as a nut, black paint covering his eyes in a horizontal band.

'In the name of … is that a kaffar?' Elvgren said.

'It is. A gift for the Lord Chancellor. We thought a thorough interrogation might yield valuable information,' the purgista said.

'How in the world did you subdue him?' Bellina asked, thinking to her own battle with a kaffar.

'Purgistas have their ways,' the priest replied.

The gates to the palace shuddered horribly. The trapped congregation in the courtyard watched the airship's agonisingly slow progress. After what seemed an eternity, it came to a stop and a rope was lowered. Elvgren ran forwards and grabbed it.

'I think Belle should go first,' Holger said, pulling the rope from the lord's hands.

'Ah yes, of course,' Elvgren said. 'I was just testing to see if the rope could take her weight.'

'What's that supposed to mean?' Bellina said.

'Oh, be quiet and get on,' Elvgren said.

The gate groaned under the weight of the mob's attack. Needing no further prompting, Bellina ran forwards and grabbed the rope. She gave a tug on its end and went shooting into the air. A soldier was waiting for her inside. He helped her from the rope then pushed a lever, sending it back to the ground.

'Where is Melek?' Bellina asked, enquiring after the airship's creator.

'Supervising the construction of the air fleet, my lady,' the soldier said.

Bellina rushed outside to the *Sighing Wind's* viewing platform. Below her, she could see the whole sorry scene. Outside the gates of the palace, what seemed like the whole of New Ledi was bearing down on the palace. She could see that a large number of local troops had turned their weapons on their Estrian comrades and were shooting them down.

Cirona was the last on the rope. As the major ascended, Bellina saw the gates finally give way. The Mandirans swept forwards, a throbbing sea of flesh. Their guttural cries carried up to her as they stormed the palace.

'Bloody hells,' Holger whispered when he came to stand beside her. Bellina nodded her head, her mind spinning.

From behind her, she heard the soldier bark an order and the *Sighing Wind* set off. The airship picked up speed. Bellina watched, mouth slack, eyes wide, as New Ledi, centre of Estrian power on the Eastern Continent, burned.

# CHAPTER SIX

Castros stood on the Merchant's Arch and watched the sun setting behind a bank of grey clouds. The dying rays burst through the gaps like golden spears standing guard against the oncoming night. From his position on the bridge, he could see the docks and warehouses bunched together along the banks of the Tollfaith river.

Somewhere in the distance, a news-crier barked out the latest newsprint stories for the illiterate workers. Del Var could just hear the man bellowing about New Ledi being overrun by the locals. *Good for them*, Castros thought.

He sighed and closed his eyes, thinking of all the sunsets he had watched with Nairne. How she would laugh, her green eyes sparkling, jet-black hair rippling in the breeze. Sometimes, when he concentrated hard enough, it was like he could hear her, smell her.

All at once, the whistles went off, signalling the end of the working day. The dockhands and other workers began to swarm out of the buildings, grey men with grim faces, marching to their homes or more likely the pub. Castros' nostrils flared and he ground his teeth. This was no way for people to live.

The first of the workers to leave were now crossing the Merchant's Arch. They spoke in gruff tones, a multitude of accents competing with each other to be heard. They had been drawn from all corners of the Empire, starving dogs enticed to Victory with the promise of meat.

Castros gave a bitter laugh. There was no better life in Victory. The masses who came swapped one set of hardships for another. He knew the tricks factory owners used. They would send gangs of men out to befriend the new arrivals, offer them a place to stay, a job. All they had to do was sign a little piece of paper. Most were covered in Xs instead of names. The factory owners banked on this, for *if* the workers could read what was on those slips of paper they might reconsider.

The person signing would get a place to stay alright; it was just in the purpose-built tenements of Bottom Barrow — filthy, crowded hovels where most lived dozens to a house. Before long, the worker would find out that this charming piece of real estate came with a price. The contracts they signed were loan agreements stating that whatever factory owner had caught them would lend them the money for the home but would expect the debt, and its astronomical interest, to be paid off through hard labour. Thus, they were trapped. Many had no chance of paying off the debt in their lifetime and so it would pass to their children, ensnaring another generation to be exploited.

This was what Castros wanted to change, to destroy — the cycle of exploitation the Estrian Empire was founded upon, from the workers to the enslaved mages. Aberoth Constance was a man of conscience and had campaigned to have the working day reduced and sick pay for the workers. He was a good man; which was why Castros had chosen him. That, and the fact that he was third in line to the throne.

Castros had long since given up thinking that violence would achieve his ends — the gang's abortive attempt on the Emperor's life had taught him that. During his long exile, he'd had the time to think long and hard about how to reach his goals. It was then that he had realised change had to come from the top, and the highest seat in Estria was the Imperial Throne, despite what the Lord Chancellor liked to think.

A stronger, more idealistic man could sit on that throne and shake off the Lord Chancellor's scaled talons, a man like Aberoth. And Castros would be right beside him. First, all he had to do was discredit those closer in the line of succession or, if needs be, force them to stand aside. For that, though, he would need money, and he had a good idea where he was going to get it.

***

A sliver of moon shone out from a clear sky, the sickly light stroking the leaves on the tree above Castros' head. It was situated in one of the leafy suburbs that had sprung up around Victory. As only the aristocracy were allowed to live on the Olphant Hill, the rich merchants, traders and other captains of industry had decided to set up their homes in the countryside.

'We nearly there, boss?' a voice called from behind Castros.

Del Var turned to see the massive frame of Blunt, a blacksmith with an automaton arm, who had been with Whist since Castros was forced into exile. He had half expected to see Dane when he looked around and had to force the disappointment from his face.

'Not much further,' he replied.

Beckoning for Blunt to follow, Castros set off, stealing his way along the hedgerows and trees. They soon drew near to their destination. In front of them sat a large stately home. It was built in the mock-Dunstan style, the columned finery mimicking the home of a noble. Castros looked at the building's three storeys and plethora of windows and tried to calculate the cost of the property. Even at a conservative guess, he reckoned the price would keep a thousand workers fed, clothed and homed for a year or more. Castros felt a large vein in his temple begin to throb. He massaged his head, trying to regain his composure.

The house itself belonged to a Mr Findus Peyton, a shipping magnate who had a fondness for sacking large swathes of his workforce at random intervals throughout the year. Whist hadn't chosen Peyton for crimes against his workforce — there was little to distinguish between the majority of exploitative bosses on that front — but because the man had a deep mistrust of banks. This meant that dear old Findus kept his considerable wealth in a vault beneath his house. The vault, though, according to Whist's intel, had a peculiar safety feature. Each of the five doors that separated the vault from the basement grew heavier with each passing one. Peyton had a specifically trained force of guards who could lift the immense weights. Castros hoped that between Blunt's mechanically enhanced strength and his powers they would be able to get the job done.

Taking out a spyglass, Castros fixed his gaze on the building. It was surrounded by a massive wrought iron fence, with two guards standing by its gate. He waited and spotted a further two guards patrolling the grounds.

'Two on the front gate, Blunty. You think you can take them out without causing too much fuss?' Castros asked.

'You got it, boss,' the big man replied.

'Oh, and make sure you don't kill anyone. These men may work for an arsehole, but it doesn't mean they deserve to die for it.'

Blunt nodded.

Keeping an eye on Blunt with the spyglass, Del Var watched the man slink up to the house. With an explosion of movement Blunt dealt a blow with his real fist to the first guard's face before dispatching the second. Blunt gave Castros the all clear and he sprinted to the gate.

'Good work, my man,' Castros said.

'What do we do now?' Blunt asked.

'Now? Now it's time for a bit of magic.'

Taking his screamer from his pocket, Castros grabbed Blunt around the middle and gave the device a squeeze. The blast of magically infused air took them clean over the huge gate. They landed on the other side with a bump.

'You alright?' Castros asked.

'Yeah,' said a wide-eyed Blunt. 'I'd heard you had powers, like, but I never imagined they were that strong.'

'I'm a man of many mysteries, Blunty,' Del Var said with a wolfish grin then ran to the side of the house.

Crouched in the shadows, the two men made their way forwards. Soon, they came upon the patrolling guards. Del Var signalled to Blunt who sprang forwards, covering the distance between him and the men in a heartbeat. Blunt grabbed the guards' heads and brought them together with a loud crunch which made Castros wince.

'They're not dead, are they?' Del Var asked, coming to the big man's side.

'Nah, they'll sleep like babes then wake up with a fucker of a headache. Probably wish we *had* finished 'em off when they come to.'

Castros bent down and checked their breathing. Blunt was right — they were still amongst the living. He gave the blacksmith a brief nod then set off towards the servants' entrance. Given the late hour, there was no sign of life now the guards had been dispatched.

Taking the waterskin from his pocket, Del Var squirted some liquid into his hand. Having already infused it with his lifeforce, the water responded to his thoughts, swirling into a ball then shooting into the lock. The liquid seeped between the very atoms of the metal then, with a further prompt from Castros, it froze solid. He hit the now frozen lock with the back of his hand and smiled as it went tinkling to the floor.

'Fuck me!' Blunt said. 'No wonder mages were so feared.'

'Stop it, you flatterer,' Del Var said, covering his face up like a schoolgirl in mock coyness.

Pushing the door open, the pair sneaked into the mansion. They were in a large kitchen. Pots and pans lined the walls, all polished to a brilliant sheen. Crouching down low, Castros took the lead and beckoned for Blunt to follow.

As they approached the kitchen door they heard voices. It was a woman talking to a man. Castros held his breath while their footsteps came closer. He watched their shadows pass under the crack in the door and carry on past.

Castros puffed out his cheeks as he let loose a silent sigh then pushed the door open. Walking on the balls of their feet, the pair stole along a plush carpet. At the end of the corridor was a door. Del Var made his way towards it. While he busied himself with its lock, the sound of more voices carried to them.

'All of 'em out cold they were, Mr. Peyton, sir. I went out to take the lads the leftover pie like yer said, and I found them!' A woman was babbling hysterically.

'Yes, yes, Mrs Hubble. You run along now; I will get to the bottom of this. They're probably going for the vault. But there are twenty armed men down there; they won't get away. Hopefully, I'll get my hands on them first!' Castros heard Peyton reply.

'Bloody hell, Castros, they're coming!'

'I know, Blunty, but the door seems to be jammed.'

'Here, let me help.'

'No, no, that's quite alright; I've got this,' Del Var said, frowning as he gave the door another shove.

'Just let me—'

'No, leave it alone—'

In a blind panic, Blunt slammed into the door. The wood gave way suddenly under his considerable bulk, taking the big man by surprise. Not thinking, he reached out to steady himself and managed to grab Castros' cloak. The pair tumbled down a short set of stone steps that had been hidden behind the door and came to a stop on cool flagstones.

Del Var shook the stars from his eyes … and then he saw them. Five guards who had been playing cards around a small wooden table had leapt to their feet. Some went for balliskets, others for swords. Quickly, and with concealed movements, Castros squirted some more water into his hand. Blunt made a dash for the guards, but before he could even make it halfway towards them, five blobs of water shot past his head at ridiculous speed, connecting in the space between the guards' eyeballs.

'Can't let you have all the fun,' Castros said with a grin.

Blunt offered Castros his hand and helped to haul him to his feet. Del Var scanned the room, lips pressed together, face tight. Whist's intel had said this was the entrance to the vault, so where was the bloody door?

'Damn it to the Void!' Castros hissed. 'Where's the bloody entrance?'

'Maybe it's hidden?' Blunt said.

'You don't say?'

'Alright, shirty, keep yer hair on.'

Castros bit the inside of his cheek then said, 'Look, let's just start searching.'

The pair began a sweep of the room, fingers prying into any crevice they could find. Castros was just pulling on one of the light fixings when Blunt let out a cry.

'It's down here,' he said, 'a trapdoor hidden under the table. They made it look like stone, but it's actually wood.'

'Good work, Blunty. I knew you were the right man for the job,' Del Var said, placing a hand on the former blacksmith's shoulder.

'Now who's the flatterer?' the big man said, a huge grin splitting his face just the same.

Blunt stuck his fingers into the gap between the trapdoor and the floor and heaved it upwards, exposing the stairs to the underground vault. They made their way down the stairs and found themselves in a vast storeroom — barrels, boxes and crates all stacked up on shelves in neat little aisles. A man was in front of them, his back turned. Castros sent another ball of water at the man and he crumpled in a heap.

'Thought you said we weren't gonna kill anyone?' Blunt said. 'Those things look pretty lethal to me.'

'Appearances are deceptive, my good man. My water bullets may look deadly, but I've worked out the power needed to incapacitate a normal man without him dying. Now, if I've been informed correctly, we go left.'

They weaved their way through the aisles, taking out the guards as they went. Blunt dispatched the last of them with a chop to the back of the neck. With surprising deftness, he caught the man and positioned him against a wall. Castros looked up at it with a grin.

'We're here,' he said.

'Eh?' Blunt replied, scratching his chin. 'Don't see no vaults round here.'

'You have just, ever so tenderly, laid this sleeping darling next to it.'

'What? The wall?'

'Yes, the wall. If you look closely, you can see the handholds,' Castros said, crouching down and pointing them out.

'Better get to it then,' Blunt said.

He bent down and grabbed hold. With one effortless motion, he threw the fake wall upwards. This carried on two more times. Castros watched as the increasing weight of the walls took its toll on Blunt. By the time they reached the final one Blunt was pouring with sweat and had gone an alarming shade of purple.

'You sure about this?' Castros said as Blunt took hold of the final wall.

'Won't … know … if … we … don't … try,' Blunt replied.

Del Var watched as the man heaved with all his might. Veins bulged all over the big man's body, and the strain on the cogs and pistons of his automaton arm was audible. Despite the monumental effort he was making, the final wall had only risen by a foot.

'Can't … hold on,' Blunt wheezed.

In a heartbeat, Castros took out his screamer, positioned it under the gap Blunt had made, then squeezed. With the added power of the magically enhanced air, the wall flew upwards. Behind it was a regular iron gate clamped shut with a huge padlock. Behind *that* was the vault door itself. Castros disposed of the padlock then stood there.

'Right then, here we go,' Del Var said.

He poured out enough water from his skin to form a large puddle. As he hovered his hands over it, the water began to form into a ball that grew in size. When it was about the size of a beer keg, he sent it spinning forwards, coating the whole of the vault door in water. A second later, it froze.

'Well, that's the last of my sortilaqua gone, used up all of my sortilaero too. Up to you now, matey.'

'What do you want me to do?' the still wheezing Blunt replied.

'Smash it.'

'With what?'

'With what? Your fist of course — the metal one preferably.'

Blunt shook his head but balled his automaton fingers into a fist. He pulled back his arm ready to strike and adjusted a dial on the side of it. Inside the contraption, Del Var could see the vial of sortilenergy that fuelled the mechanical limb begin to bubble. Then, with one almighty blast, Blunt hit the frozen vault door. Chips of ice showered down over Castros, and the force of the blow reverberated around the room. Four punches of the same magnitude later, and Blunt had created an opening big enough for them to walk through. They peered inside and Castros noticed Blunt's jaw go slack. The whole room beyond seemed to throb with the dull gleam of gold.

'How the hells are we going to move this, Castros?' Blunt asked.

'Well, we're not going to go lugging around the bullion. We'll take the notes and gems — anything lightweight.'

'Sounds like you've done this before,' Blunt said with a crooked grin.

'A man has to eat,' Del Var replied with a shrug. 'Let's—'

Castros was cut off by the sound of someone clearing their throat behind them. The pair spun round and found themselves face-to-face with a small man with a pencil moustache and five more guards.

'Mr Peyton, I presume,' Castros said to the moustachioed man.

'Indeed,' Peyton replied, upper lip curling. 'I must commend you — no one else has ever made it all the way to the vault before. But now your little game ends.'

Peyton clicked his fingers and the guards advanced. Blunt made a move forwards, but Castros held him back.

'Well I didn't want it to come to this. I'm going to ache like the twelve hells tomorrow,' Del Var said.

With that he took in a huge breath and held it. For an instant, it seemed as if his chest was glowing. Then he let out a blast of air that sent Peyton and his men crashing into the wall behind them. Satisfied, Castros turned back towards the vault.

'You'll … you'll never get … away with this,' Peyton wheezed. 'That money is mine. I made it through my own sweat and endeavour.'

'No,' Del Var said, closing the distance between them and crouching down. 'You used the sweat and endeavour of honest men to steal this fortune. Isn't it fair that I steal it back?'

Before Peyton could reply, Castros sent a smart punch into his temple. He stood up, gave a crisp nod, then went to help Blunt gather their haul.

# CHAPTER SEVEN

Bellina stood on the observation deck of the *Sighing Wind* and watched as the early morning light caught the rooftops of Victory. The flight home had taken a little over five days, everyone cramped and arguing, but now they were home. She took in a deep breath, feeling a strange heaviness overcome her body. Soon, she would have to see *him*.

Calvin Ressa, Lord Chancellor, the man she had once thought was her father. But what did she think now? So many questions, so many emotions, everything bubbling up inside her. It was too much. She gripped the handrail and swallowed hard. One step at a time, she told herself, one step at a time.

'Home,' a voice said behind her.

Bellina turned and saw Major Bouchard come and stand beside her. 'Indeed,' she replied.

'What's it been? Four, five months? Feels like forever,' Cirona said.

'Mm,' Bellina murmured, feeling as if the conversation was coming to her from a million miles away.

Cirona stared into Bellina's eyes then cast her gaze to the floor. She bit her lip then said, 'I-I don't think I've had time to say it, what with all the running for our lives, but I'm sorry.'

Bellina turned to her, brow furrowed. 'What? Why?' she said.

Cirona grimaced. 'Because … because I was part of your father's deception too. I knew what he had planned, and I should have stopped things sooner and—'

'Major, stop,' Bellina said. 'Everything you did, you did out of love for your child, to see her. Everything my fa—the Lord Chancellor did was out of his own desires.'

'What are you going to say to him?'

'I … I don't know.'

At that moment, one of the soldiers tasked with flying the *Sighing Wind* appeared on the deck. His gaze bounced from the major to Bellina, unsure of who to address first.

'Out with it, man,' Cirona said eventually.

The soldier snapped to attention and said, 'Preparing to disembark, sir.

Your carriage is waiting for you at the North Gate.'

'Noted,' Cirona said. The soldier gave her a crisp salute then returned inside the airship.

****

The air fizzed around Bellina as the rope from the airship descended. It stopped a foot above the ground, and she hopped off as gracefully as she could manage. She watched the rope shoot back up, ready to take its next passenger, then turned on her heel. The North Gate rose in front of her, a missing tooth in the Castrian Wall.

Some ten feet away, she saw the carriage that had come to collect them. It was a large, open-topped affair, the sides white and gold, smothered with ostentatious mouldings, two massive ivory horses pawing at the ground at its front. Bellina narrowed her eyes and shook her head. *Unbelievable*, she thought, *he's going to use this as some kind of publicity stunt.*

'Now this is more like it!' Elvgren said, strutting towards her. Thankfully, the soldiers had come with a spare uniform, and he hadn't had to wear the towel the whole flight home.

'You enjoy being made to dance like a bear?'

'We're not being made to do anything, my love. We've earned this; *we are heroes*,' Elvgren said. He cocked his head to one side. 'Sounds like there's quite a crowd waiting for us too.'

Shaking her head and rolling her eyes, she watched as her betrothed sauntered to the carriage where the driver promptly opened the door for him.

Soon, everyone had descended from the airship. Cirona followed Dargo who set off at pace towards the carriage while Holger came and stood by Bellina's side.

'Where are the Viceroy and the purgista?' she asked.

'Apparently, they're being dropped off somewhere else,' Holger said. 'You sure you're up to this Belle?'

Bellina turned towards him and looked into his eyes. The concern in them — stunning in their ferocious intensity — made her heart jump. 'It's now or never, I suppose,' she said.

'We could always run away,' Holger replied, pawing at the ground with his foot.

'No. I will see this through,' she said. 'At least I won't be on my own.'

Holger's face broke into a grin and they both walked towards the carriage.

****

The carriage proceeded through the North Gate, along the Way of Laurels towards the Olphant Hill. The route was packed with cheering people. Bellina watched Elvgren wave majestically to the crowds, Dargo at his side pumping his fists like a winning gladiator. Cirona sat bolt upright, rigid as a corpse, looking at some point in the middle-distance. Holger had squirmed as far down as the seat would allow him.

As for herself, Bellina kept her eyes fixed on the slowly growing platform. The Estrian flag was draped along its bottom, and she could just make out a cluster of tiny figures at its top. *One of them is him*, she thought.

The carriage made it torturous progress forwards, slow enough that everyone could get a glimpse of the group who had toppled the Burkeshi hierarchy. *If only they knew the cost of their victory*, Bellina thought, her mind's eye filling with the corpses they had left in their wake. She brushed a tear from her eye and took a deep breath. *One thing at a time*, she told herself.

After what felt like an eternity, they came to a stop at the bottom of the platform. The driver came and opened the door, and Elvgren jumped to the floor to rapturous applause. He bowed to the crowd then pushed Dargo — who seemed equally eager to bask in the adulation — back inside the carriage and offered his hand to Bellina.

'My lady,' he said.

Bellina met his gaze and raised an eyebrow.

He leaned forwards and hissed, 'We are back home now, my love, certain things are expected of us.'

Forcing a smile, Bellina took his hand and exited the carriage, not daring to see if her "father" was there. Once they had all disembarked, a soldier came down from the platform, saluted, then beckoned them to follow. As she climbed the stairs, Bellina could feel every fibre of her being quiver. She thought she had been ready for this but—

'Bellina, my love,' she heard that familiar voice say.

A knot formed in her throat, stopping the air reaching her lungs. Her head felt like a ball of solid lead, but somehow, she managed to look up.

And there he was. The man who had raised her, the man she had thought loved her more than anything in the world. For a brief moment, a tiny flicker of her heart was relieved, glad to see him. Then her skin flushed, and a pounding began in her ears. Nostrils flared, she took a step towards him. She raised her arm ready to strike … her body froze.

At first, she thought her body had betrayed her. Then she realised she was unable to move at all. Without her willing it, her other arm rose and opened out to embrace the Lord Chancellor.

'What have you done to me?' she managed to hiss through teeth that felt as if they were glued together by mortar.

'We have much to discuss, daughter, and I knew you would be angry. Forgive me, but I have a cognopath hidden nearby who was tasked with stopping you from making a scene,' the Lord Chancellor whispered in her ear.

A silent tear rolled down her cheek. 'If you think I was going to make a scene here, just wait until we're alone,' she said.

The Lord Chancellor sighed and said, 'I shall take my chances.'

With that he moved off to greet the rest of the party. She watched in paralysed fury as Elvgren bowed elaborately, as Dargo tried to mimic him, as Holger botched his attempt at deference — which raised a small chuckle from the crowd and made the young man go red as the sunset — and finally, as Cirona gave her sharp salute.

The greetings dispensed with, her father strode to the front of the stage, Bellina and her companions sandwiched between him and the smiling diplomats and government officials. The crowd's noise rose to a swollen roar, the voices melding into one. The Lord Chancellor raised his arms for silence.

'Good people of Estria,' he boomed, his voice projected by some unseen piece of technology. 'I thank you for joining us to celebrate the return of these brave souls, souls we have mourned as having passed through the Weeping Veil and into Father Light's embrace. Instead, he has blessed us by sending them back. These men and women ... no, these *heroes* who plunged into the dark heart of our enemy and cut off its head!'

Again, the crowd unleashed a volley of noise. Bellina's body trembled as she tried to fight off whoever was controlling her movements. But the noise and surging emotions coursing through her body had weakened her.

'I'm sure I speak for all who have survived this perilous mission in thanking you for your heartfelt support, but now we must retire,' the Lord Chancellor continued. There was a groan from the crowd, but he raised his hand and smiled. 'Please, I am sure, in the days to come, you will be able to read and hear all about their exploits, but until then, I think they have earned a rest.'

Turning from the crowd, the Lord Chancellor gestured for the others to follow him and made towards the back of the stage. They descended a flight of wooden steps at the bottom of which various carriages waited.

'My lord,' Elvgren said, hurrying forwards. 'I hope you have not forgotten my reward for this mission, and that I have been able to make up for my error of judgement concerning the Lord Exchequer's Ball.'

'You have more than acquitted yourself, Lord Lovitz. In fact, I had rather fancied you would swoon at the first sight of trouble. But you have proved you're nothing if not … resilient.'

'Does that mean—' Elvgren began.

'I shall expect you at the Palace of Administration promptly at nine. But for now, the left carriage shall take you home to your family; I'm sure they are dying to see you.'

'Thank you, Lord Chancellor, you won't—'

'Just go, Lovitz, before I change my mind.'

Elvgren gave a smart nod and set off towards the vehicle, Dargo trailing behind him.

'Lord Chancellor—' Cirona called.

'Do not concern yourself, Major; your reward is being arranged as we speak. Please expect a carriage to collect you tomorrow morning. You shall travel by the middle coach.'

Cirona gave a sharp salute and stalked away, eyes firmly on the ground.

'Now then, I think we should be off too my—' the Lord Chancellor began.

'Belle, wait. What's wrong with you?' Holger cried.

Bellina watched as the man she had called Father turned, eyes glinting with malice. 'I'm sure you have been an invaluable asset young man, but you are addressing one of your betters. You are a pirate no more,' he said.

'How did you—'

'Mr Barbossa and Mr Crenshaw have filled me in on the details. I have granted you the same pardon for your crimes as I did them, in lieu of payment. They are awaiting you at the barracks along the with the young boy, Midge, and the inventor, Melek. The right carriage is yours.'

Holger stood before them, gaze ricocheting between the Lord Chancellor and Bellina. He looked deep into her eyes, his hand clenched.

'Go,' she managed to whisper.

His shoulders slumped, but he nodded his head and walked towards his ride.

Bellina felt her throat close up as she watched the carriages depart in different directions.

'Come along, my love,' the Lord Chancellor said, moving towards the vehicle that awaited them. 'We have much to sort out.'

Although her whole body tried to refuse to move, Bellina was dragged forwards like a marionette. *He will pay for this*, she thought, *he will pay.*

# CHAPTER EIGHT

'Well, that was something, eh, Gren?' Dargo said.

Elvgren lifted his spinning head and looked across the carriage at the boy. 'What's that?'

'Belle. Thought she was getting ready to smack that old, bald bloke right round his chops then she gives him a hug.'

'I suppose it was a bit odd …' Elvgren said, his gaze drifting out of the window, looking at nothing in particular.

'What's the matter with you?'

'Hmm? Me? I'm fine, just a bit overwhelmed by …' Again, Elvgren's gaze and concentration wandered.

Letting out a snort, Dargo crossed his arms and said, 'Fine, be that way,' and turned his own attention to the scenery passing them by.

Elvgren barely heard him. In fact, he was barely registering anything at all. He could feel the bump and rattle of the carriage around him, could see the sights of Victory he knew so well, but deep inside, a small voice was whispering the same word over and over — Wrong.

As they climbed the Olphant Hill, up the steep, winding road, he began to pull and fuss at his clothes, a tightness spreading across his chest. Soon, they would be there — his family home. Soon, he would see his parents. A dizziness stole over him, and he bent forwards, focusing his gaze on the floor.

'Bloody hells, Gren, is that your house?' Dargo cried.

Elvgren shot a glance out of the window and said, 'Yes. Yes, it is.'

They came to a stop, and the world around Elvgren became too bright, too loud. He heard every squeak and clunk of the driver jumping down from his seat, the crunch of the gravel as the man approached his door, the screech of the hinges as it opened. The light from outside poured in, swallowing him. Elvgren's throat felt scratchy and dry, the dizziness still churning his brain. The driver extended his hand, and he took it, his own trembling more than a fraction.

Next thing he knew, he was outside. He could see the steps leading up to his home stretch before him, skewed and distorted till they looked like an ancient pyramid. *Get a grip on yourself,* he thought. *After everything we've been through this is nothing.*

Still, the world around him seemed bizarre. Somewhere far away, he could hear Dargo chattering, but the auditory world that had engulfed him only moments before had now shrunk to his own heartbeat. As if pulled by invisible threads, he began to climb the steps. With each one, he heard the slamming of his heart and that word — Wrong — growing louder and louder.

Each step began to feel like a monumental effort, a miniature battle to be fought. Dargo was a touch ahead of him, looking back, concern writ large on his face. Elvgren tried to give the boy a smile, to pretend he was fine, but it came out as a grimace.

Somehow, he reached the top and there, before him, were his parents. He wiped the sweat from his brow and stared at their faces. For people who had thought they had lost their last surviving child, they seemed remarkably fresh, no haggard lines or loose flesh from weight loss. His mind flashed back to when his older brother Jeremias had died. Oh, they'd gnashed their teeth and pulled their hair then.

For a moment, Elvgren stood there, his mouth flapping. Where had all the witty things he'd planned to say gone? Where was the triumphant stance and conqueror's demeanour he had meant to return with? All that was left to him was one word — Wrong — blasting in his ears, rattling his skull.

His mother's taut face turned upwards in haughty disapproval, as ever, took in the scar and eyepatch her son now wore, then scanned the rest of him.

'Well, I suppose you've managed to not make a complete mess of this endeavour,' she said.

Elvgren blinked like a fish caught in a net. Wrong.

His mother turned her gaze towards Dargo, who was trying to flatten down his hair before wiping his hand on his trousers and extending it to her.

'And who,' she said, recoiling, 'is this?'

Wrong.

'Well? Are you going to answer me?'

Wrong.

'Do not ignore your mother, boy,' his father said.

Wrong, wrong, wrong, wrong, wrong...

'WRONG!' Elvgren said.

'What?' his mother asked, her voice dripping ice crystals.

'Wrong. This is wrong,' Elvgren replied, waving his arms around.

'You are wrong. How dare you speak to my friend like that.'

'If this is the quality of the friends you are keeping these days—' his father began.

'Shut up, shut up, shut up! You condescending old shit. This boy means more to me than my own brother did.'

Elvgren's mother clasped at her chest and gasped. 'How dare you speak of—'

'Oh heaven forfend, I dare besmirch the name of the golden Jeremiah. The boy who shat diamonds and pissed out rubies!' Elvgren said, jabbing a finger at his parents. 'He is dead, dead as they come, mother. Why not weep, smile, show some kind of fucking emotion for the son who stands before you?'

'I feel faint,' his mother cried, before swooning into his father's arms.

'Do you know what? Fuck it. I refuse to spend one more moment of my life inside that mausoleum you call a home. Come on, Dargo, we're leaving.'

Elvgren turned on his heel, shoulders back, chin held high. He had done it, he had finally told them what he thought. On legs that now felt as light as a baby's sigh, he bounded down the steps to where the carriage and the driver still waited.

'To the Merchant District,' Elvgren cried to the bemused man, who gave a stunned nod.

Clambering into the carriage, Elvgren waited for Dargo to get in before slamming the door and making an obscene gesture towards his parents.

'Ha! Well you certainly told them,' Dargo said.

'Yes. Yes, I did,' Elvgren replied, his face stretched into a grin.

'Where we gonna go now then?'

'To the finest lodgings in the capital!'

'Hate to burst your bubble there, matey, but how are we exactly gonna pay for that?'

'What?' Elvgren asked.

'We ain't got no money,' Dargo replied, holding out his hands.

Elvgren winced as the carriage began its descent of the Olphant Hill. 'Shit.'

# CHAPTER NINE

'You slept through the homecoming of Estria's newest heroes,' Whist said, tossing the morning's newsprint onto Castros' bed.

Del Var groaned and pulled the covers over his head.

'Now is that anyway for a fearless freedom fighter to behave?' Whist asked, pulling the covers back.

Castros hauled himself up and rubbed at his eyes. 'What time is it?' he said.

'About three in the afternoon,' Whist replied, leaning against the door frame and crossing his arms.

Picking up the paper, Castros scanned the front page. 'Ah, yes,' he said, 'the surviving adventurers of the Lord Chancellor's scheme to put the brown man in his place.' He shook his head. 'Thousands dead, uprisings all over the Empire's foreign territories, and still, the man has managed to turn a shitstorm into a summer's day with that homecoming parade.'

'Gotta admire his front, if nothing else — not many who can bluff as well as the LC,' Whist said.

'The day I admire anything that man does I would ask you to kindly put a bullet in my head.'

'Done,' Whist said with a nod.

Castros stood up and stretched, the after effects of yesterday's raid on the Peyton mansion catching up with him. He was using too much sortilenergy, especially the roughly generated magic he could create in a pinch. During his training, he had been told to use it as a last resort, that the fusion of mana and his own powers, when done on the fly, would begin to break his body down.

Creeping over to the washstand and mirror like an old man, he took a good look at himself. Flecks of grey were stealing in at his temples, frown lines etched across his brow as if chiselled in stone. Where was the young man he used to know? Castros gazed into his own eyes and found him lurking behind the sparkle that no amount of time seemed able to dim.

'So,' Del Var said, pouring water into the washbowl then splashing it over his face, 'have you finished counting up what me and Blunty managed to liberate last night?'

'Liberate?' Whist said with a snort. 'You can dress it up anyway you want, Cass, but it's still stealing.'

'Allow me some theatrics, Master Whist, otherwise you'll shatter my delusions of being a dashing rogue,' Castros said, drying his face and returning to sit on the edge of the bed.

'Fine, fine,' Whist said, throwing his hands in the air and sighing. 'After deductions for the Workers' Party, there's more than enough left over for your schemes.'

'Schemes?' Putting a hand to his chest in mock affront. 'You wound me, sir. I think the words you're looking for are: master plan!'

Whist rolled his eyes.

Castros tilted his head to the side and regarded his friend through furrowed brows. 'Is there something you want to say to me, Whist?'

'I don't know,' Whist replied, taking a deep breath. 'It's just … the Party has been making steady progress for so long now. The workers are finally starting to see us as an alternative, a force for change. Then you come blasting your way back into my life and the life of the Party, and … I'm just worried this is all going to turn out like the assassination attempt.'

Del Var rubbed at his face and then stood up. He walked over to Whist and grabbed his shoulders lightly. 'I will never let that happen again, Whist. I was young, reckless. The attempt on the Emperor's life taught me a lesson. I realised I had to find another way. Killing and destruction were not going to be the answer. But this plan will be different — it will succeed. You know I have the utmost respect for what you have achieved here in my absence, but that progress you speak of has been slow.'

'Talk about damning with faint praise,' Whist said.

Castros winced. 'That came out wrong. You know what I mean!'

'Do I, Cass?' Whist replied, shaking his head. He turned to walk from the room.

'Whist, wait.'

'The information *me* and *my* men have gathered for you is on the table. See you later.'

The whole room seemed to shudder when Whist slammed the door, leaving Castros staring at the floor.

***

Night was falling over Victory as Castros Del Var walked past the workers on their way home. Here, in the more affluent merchant and banking district, this meant that a sea of black-clad men with serious faces flowed around him. Many were wearing white armbands, a sign of joy for the return of the Lord Chancellor's heroes.

It was a perfect distraction to hide his own actions behind. With the money they had lifted from Peyton, the Workers' Liberal Party would now have the funds necessary to keep its members fed. He had banked on Peyton being too proud to report the crime. For a man like him there was nothing worse than having to show weakness, to let the world know he had been victimised. Still, he thought the man would probably have hired thugs to get revenge on him and Blunt. That was why he had told the big man to lie low. With his size and build, he was almost impossible to disguise, unlike Del Var who had been taking on other personas since he was young.

It was now time for Castros to use the surplus wealth to put the next phase of his plan into motion. He had promised Aberoth that he would make him Emperor. In exchange, he had asked the man to recognise the Workers' Liberal Party as a legitimate body and, as such, be represented in all political decisions. Aberoth had agreed. Now all Del Var needed to do was accomplish the small feat of gifting the man the Imperial Throne.

Castros knew it would be a hard task. One of the reasons Aberoth had been his choice, though, was his position in the line of succession. His family was third in line to the throne and, although the man had never jockeyed for the title like the other noble houses, he would still be more likely to be given the title if certain *accidents* should befall the two families higher up the list.

This was Castros' task for the evening. He had given Whist's intel gatherers the task of trailing the Falton heir and the Winston heir. And the other night, one of their spies had come up with something intriguing about the second in line, Terence Falton.

A moaning dirge broke out bringing Castros back to the present. He cocked his head to the side and listened. It was the sunset lament. *Unusual,* he thought, then he remembered that the newsprint had said there was to be a service for the lives lost in the mission to Burkesh.

The citizens of Estria were not quite as devout as those in the countries of Slyvantain, Escambria or Tremore, but still, many of them attended the Lumanist temples, unlike Gortrix and Narvale who were the biggest opponents of the religion. The Narvglanders, being the most recent country to come under the protectorate of the Empire, were reluctant to abandon their old ways. Gortrix, a country of scholars and learning, opposed Lumanism on the grounds that it was backwards and counterproductive.

Shaking his head, Castros broke free of his meandering thoughts and carried on his way. He needed to get to the Gilded Apple before it opened. Spurring his legs on, he made his way towards the Hovel Crossing and into Skelm's Den.

Almost instantly, the dark closed around him. Tall, narrow buildings pierced the sky, windowed daggers that promised menace. The stench of piss and shit emanating from the gutters smashed into his nose, and he had to fight back a wave of nausea.

Stepping over a man passed out in a pool of his own vomit, Del Var continued on his way. Ghost-like faces peered out, hollow-eyed, from doorways. They watched his progress hungrily. He hoped there wouldn't be trouble. He didn't have time to deal with it.

An old lady called out to him from a window. She was topless, jiggling her sagging tits. When he shook his head, she scowled and brought out a girl of about twelve. The girl's face was heavily made-up, but her tears had smudged what had been applied round her eyes. Castros turned his head away and spat, feeling sick to his stomach.

In Skelm's Den, everything was for sale. Though he found it disgusting, tonight Castros hoped to use this to his advantage.

Thirty soul-destroying minutes passed before, finally, Del Var stood outside the Gilded Apple. A red lantern hung from the door, illuminated by burning garwhale oil — nobody had thought it worth hooking the Den up with sortilenergy.

The sign hanging above the door showed a man's bare arse. It was blunt, but you got the message. He rapped his knuckles on the lopsided door three times and waited.

'Look, I don't care how randy you are, we ain't open!' a voice said as an eyehole opened.

'Hello, Frit,' Castros said with a smile.

The eye at the hole grew wide in surprise and the door flew open. Frit strode out of it. Earrings and bracelets jangled merrily on his person and a waft of perfume followed him. Standing with his hands on his hips provocatively, Frit suddenly leapt forwards and planted a kiss on Del Var's lips.

'Well?' Frit said, pulling himself away and raising an eyebrow.

'Sorry, Frit, still not doing anything for me. If I ever feel curious, you'll be my first port of call, though.'

'Hmm. Well, you can't blame a boy for trying. What brings you here, Cass? I thought you were dead.'

'Not dead, clearly. I'm here on business.'

'You'd better come in then,' Frit said, turning round and pulling a shawl around himself.

Castros ducked down and followed the pimp into his brothel. The room beyond was lit by a drooping, ornate chandelier that had seen better days. Dark red curtains blocked the windows and several couches sat atop a moth-eaten Varashi rug.

'Drink?' Frit asked, walking towards a large cabinet.

'No, thanks. I'll need to keep a clear head this evening, and I know how strong that swill you drink is.'

'Swill? How dare you! This is the finest Tremoran brandy.'

'Your customers might believe that but you can't get me to,' Del Var said with a grin.

'It's a good job you're handsome, love, or I'd smack you in the mouth.'

'Thought you charged extra for that,' Castros replied, and they both laughed.

Pouring himself a drink, Frit motioned to one of the couches. Castros lowered himself into one, an alarming twanging accompanying the motion. Frit sat down across from him and crossed his legs.

'It's good to see you, Cass, but you said you were here on business. What can I help you with?'

'I need information on one of your clients.'

'Now, Castros, how long do you think I'd keep in business if I gave out my patron's secrets to any bloke who walked in off the street?'

'I understand that, and I'm willing to pay.'

'Don't think you've got the—'

'I want to hire your entire staff for the evening,' Del Var said, producing a massive emerald.

Frit coughed and brandy shot from his mouth. 'Fuck me, Del Var! How'd you get that much coin?' Frit said, breaking out of the careful sing-song tones he usually tried to speak with.

'That doesn't matter. Can you help or not?' Castros said.

Frit looked thoughtful for a moment. 'I suppose. What do you need to know?'

'There's a man who comes in here most nights. Burly fella, scar down his left cheek.'

'I know him.'

'He doesn't stay, does he?'

'No, he picks a bloke and then leaves. Pays a ton for the privilege as well.'

'Right. Well, that man works for Terence Falton,' Castros said.

Frit let out a low whistle. 'I'll have to charge him more.'

'No. Don't. I want you to keep everything exactly as it always is. Falton's man can't think anything is wrong. When he comes in tonight, whoever he picks, I want them to leave me a trail. No matter how hard we've tried, he *always* manages to shake our tail.'

'This won't put my boys in danger, will it, Cass? I'm still not happy about the chicken dinner incident.'

'No, no, it'll be nothing like that. Just tell them to leave drops of this on the ground,' Castros said, handing Frit a waterskin.

'Alright. I want my payment now, though, Del Var; I know you.'

'Fine!' Castros said, sliding the emerald over the table. Frit's eyes grew wide. 'I assume by your look that that will cover it. I'll be watching outside.'

***

Stamping his feet to keep warm, Castros kept his eyes on the front door of the Gilded Apple. Checking his pocket watch, he saw that it was now one in the morning. The hours he had been on the roof opposite the brothel had not been spent in comfort.

Just when Del Var was thinking of packing it in for the night, bemoaning the loss of the emerald, he saw Falton's man. From the way the man walked, Castros could tell that he was on guard. He would not be easy prey.

The man ducked inside the Apple and returned fifteen minutes later with an effete young man in tow. He gave them a few minutes head start and then jumped off the roof, cushioning the landing with his screamer.

Following the faint traces of life force he could feel in the droplets of sortilaqua the whore was leaving, he soon caught sight of the pair. Falton's man was quick but careful, stopping to check for a tail every few minutes.

After a while, the man stopped suddenly before an alleyway. It was so unexpected Castros had to use the screamer again to shoot himself onto another roof. He ducked behind a chimney and cursed his carelessness. A heart-stopping minute passed before he gathered the courage to check on the street below. There was no one there.

Returning to the ground, Castros picked up the sortilaqua trail going into the alley. The trail came to an abrupt end in the middle of it. Del Var spun around on the spot, wondering where they could have gone. He reached out with his mind and could just detect a faint trace of life force from behind the alley wall.

Running his hand over it Castros felt that one of the bricks was loose. He pushed it inward hearing a dull click. A portion of the wall swung back. Checking to his left and right, he went in, closing the hidden door behind him.

A long, narrow corridor stretched ahead of Del Var, lit by galvanic lights. Mould and damp covered the wall and even his breathing seemed to create an echo in the space. Tiptoeing along, Castros walked round a bend in the corridor and came face-to-face with Falton's man who was standing in front of a door.

The bodyguard gave a start and went to draw a ballisket. Castros reached out to one of the droplets of sortilaqua that was still leaving a trail on the floor and sent it at the man's head. It hit him between the eyes and he collapsed to the floor.

Pressing his ear to the door, Del Var listened.

'Am I a filthy boy?' a timorous voice was asking

'Oh, the filthiest I've ever met.'

'D-do I … n-need a lesson?' the first voice asked.

'Oh, yes,' the second replied. Then Castros heard the sound of a whip cracking accompanied by moans.

Castros had seen some things in his life, but he didn't think he was prepared for what he might see behind that door. Swallowing hard, he turned the handle.

A sparse, cold room stood before him. A few lights flickered from the bare stone walls, illuminating the room's only piece of furniture — a bed. With his hands and legs tied to its posts, Castros could see, who had to be, Falton. He was face down, pale arse in the air while Frit's whore snapped a whip across it viciously. Del Var cleared his throat and the pair turned to look at him.

'I thought you'd never get here,' the whore said.

'Well, I'm here now. Untie this idiot, I need to talk to him. Oh, and here,' Castros said, tossing a bag of coins to him. 'That's for your time.'

'Thanks,' the whore replied and sashayed from the room.

Falton sat on the bed, his erect member shrivelling to nothing. He rubbed at his wrists where he had been tied.

'W-who are you? What did you do with Egor?'

'Egor's fine, just having a little nap. You should be more worried about yourself. What would the *Estrian Chronicler* do if it found out the second in line to the throne was into buggery?'

'Look, if you want money, you can have it. I'm rich. Just … please,

please don't tell anyone,' Falton said, beginning to cry.

'Don't worry, your secret is safe with me. As long as you do what I say. I want you to relinquish your claim to the throne *and* give your support to Aberoth Constance.'

'What? That's ridiculous. I would never—'

'Oh, yes, you will. You will make an announcement tomorrow regarding what I have said to you. If I don't read of your shock decision in the evening paper, the next story they run will be about your night-time indulgences. Do I make myself clear?'

'Y-yes,' Falton replied, his body shuddering with sobs.

'Oh, and it goes without saying, but speak word of me to no one.'

With that, Castros made his way towards the exit, stifling a laugh. *One down, one to go*, he told himself.

# CHAPTER TEN

Outside the window, dawn's piercing light stroked its fingers across the rooftops of Victory. Cirona paused, drinking in the scene. She let the fresh promise of a new day fill her for the briefest of moments before resuming her pacing of the floor.

She had been put up for the night in one of the finest hotels in the capital. She assumed she hadn't been taken to her room at the Lord Chancellor's mansion so he and his daughter could spend some time together. Her mind flicked to thoughts of Bellina. She hoped the girl was doing alright. Any other day, her concern for Bellina Ressa would have lingered, but today … today was different.

Finally, after all the trials and heartache, she was going to see her daughter. Just the idea of it made her body tingle and her heart pound. What if the carriage was late? What if her daughter's adopted family refused her entry? What if the sky fell down …?

*I'm being ridiculous*, she thought, *everything is going to work out fine*. This was her reward. Hadn't she earned it?

Once more, she began her frantic pacing, a caged animal just waiting for the door to spring loose. Every time her walking took her by the window, she paused, biting at her lip. The minutes slunk past like a scolded dog, the pounding in her heart building to chest-smashing proportions. Just when she thought she couldn't stand it any longer, there was a knock at the door.

'Major Bouchard?' a voice called.

'Y-yes?' Cirona replied, her voice rambling over different octaves.

'Your carriage has arrived.'

'Th-thank you. I … I will be out shortly.'

Pausing before the full-length, gilt-edged mirror, Cirona checked her appearance. For the first time in her life, she had allowed her hair to grow out. The unruly tangles now sat just below her ears. She fussed at the ceremonial uniform that had been waiting for her in the room, then let out an annoyed squawk. 'It's now or never,' she said to herself and promptly stalked from the room.

*** 

Cirona watched from the carriage window as they passed though the Castrian Wall, out into the leafy suburbs of Victory. The driver had given her no information about where they were headed, and she found it hard to sit still. *This is it, Trafford*, she thought, *I'll finally get to see our baby*.

After an hour's travel, the coach turned onto a side road and came before a pair of wrought iron gates. Two men stood either side of it. They nodded at the driver then pulled the gates open, allowing the visitors to pass. As they proceeded down the gravel drive, a magnificent mansion came into view. *My little girl lives here*, Cirona thought, a strange mix of joy and sadness playing a tug-of-war on her emotions. They trundled up to the house, but instead of stopping at the front door, the carriage took a right and slipped round the back of the house.

'Driver?' Cirona said, sticking her head out of the window. 'Why aren't we stopping at the front?'

'Beats me, love. They told me to drop you round back, so drop you round back I will.'

They came to a stop. Cirona leapt from the carriage before the driver could open the door for her. She stood before the servants' entrance, frowning. Why wasn't there anybody waiting to meet her?

'What now?' she called to the driver.

'Well, most times a person wants to get the owner of a home's attention they ring the bell, like,' the driver said, lighting up a pipe.

'Cheeky git,' she muttered.

Heat rising to her cheeks, Cirona turned back to the door and located the handle for the bell. She gave it a pull and heard the tinkling of it somewhere inside. The sound of feet clipping along a hard floor grew louder and then the door opened. A young maid with downcast eyes stood before her.

'Good morning, Major Bouchard,' the girl said.

'G-good morning to you. I-I am expected … I think, um, yes, it's about my d—'

The maid shot Cirona a warning look and placed a finger to her lips. Shocked by the girl's sudden fierceness, Cirona took a half step back. Then the servant returned her gaze to the floor, mumbled an apology and stood aside so the major could pass. Cirona swallowed, then stepped inside.

Beckoning with her hand, the maid led Bouchard up the thin, winding, servants' stairs. They stopped on the first-floor landing in front of a white door inlaid with gold. The maid gestured towards the door then scurried off. Cirona took a deep breath. Her hands were sweating as they reached out to knock on the wood. *Get a grip woman*, she told herself. *Weren't you the first through the breach at Narvale? Haven't you battled your way from Varash to Burkesh then back again? Just knock on the damn door!* What Cirona had intended to be a purposeful tattoo, turned into a timid tap on the wood.

'Enter,' a woman's voice called from inside.

Taking the brass door knob in her hand, the cool of the metal shocking against the warm dampness of her palms, Cirona opened the door. She froze mid-step, a surge of dizziness washing over her. The room beyond was occupied by a woman sat next to a table, she was working at a piece of embroidery and hadn't so much as looked up at Cirona's entry.

'Come inside please, Major; you're creating a draft,' the woman said.

'W-where is my—'

The woman cut her off by getting to her feet and striding over. Cirona was shocked to see that the woman was of a height with her. Their eyes met, the other woman's flashing.

'Young Anna does not know of her … parentage. As far as she is concerned, she is the child of Mr and Mrs Wilbourne. And it shall remain that way.'

'She, I mean, Anna, knows nothing about me? Her father?'

'No, she does not.'

'Then what am I supposed to say to her? I've been through the twelve hells just for this chance!'

'Anna believes you are a prospective employee. I have arranged for her to assist me in judging your suitability.'

'This … this isn't what I thought would … this can't be—'

'This is the most I am willing to offer. If it wasn't for the fact that my husband is in the Lord Chancellor's debt, I would never have allowed you to so much as set a foot inside this household.'

Cirona jerked back as if she has been struck. 'But … but …' she stammered.

'I would have thought a woman of military bearing would be more … emotionally stable than you, Major,' Mrs Wilbourne said.

There was a knock from a door on the other side of the room.

'That will be Anna. Come in, my love,' Mrs Wilbourne cried.

Time seemed to grind to a halt. Cirona turned, her body feeling like it was wading through a sea of syrup. The door crept open, then there she was. Anna. Her baby. She was already tall, the same dull, brown hair as Cirona's hanging from her head in well-maintained ringlets. She looked into her daughter's eyes. *They're just the same as Trafford's*, she thought,

*Surely, she'll recognise me, surely on some instinctive level she'll know her real mother.* Then the girl's brow furrowed, and her nose wrinkled.

'No good,' Anna said with a sniff and turned to walk from the room.

'But, Anna, you haven't even—' Mrs Wilbourne began.

'Her uniform is dusty, her hair is a positive rats' nest, and I can see the dirt underneath her fingernails from here. She simply won't do, Mother. Make sure Father screens them a bit more thoroughly next time,' Anna said, before continuing out of the room, her silk dress rustling behind her.

'There you have it, Major. I tried,' Mrs Wilbourne said, jingling a small bell.

'Wait … th-that's not how I—' Cirona stammered as two burly servants appeared at her side.

'I'm quite sure that isn't how you imagined this going, Major, but my time is pressing. Max and Eric will see you back to your carriage.'

Upon legs that felt like they belonged to another body, Cirona allowed herself to be guided back downstairs. Her head felt light, a petal caught in the breeze, as she was led outside.

'We done 'ere?' the driver called to Max and Eric.

'Yep,' one of them replied.

The next thing she knew she was inside the carriage, the driver gently geeing up the horses. Cirona felt her stomach clench.

'No,' she said, as the house shrank into the distance. 'No, no, no, no.'

Pressing her forehead against the window, Cirona let the tears take her.

**CHAPTER ELEVEN**

Bellina's eyes pulled themselves open, the lids gummy and hot. As her mind crawled itself into consciousness, the events of the previous day came back to her. The last thing she could recall was her arm, controlled by unseen hands, picking up what had obviously been a sleeping draught.

'Bastard,' she hissed at the ceiling.

With great effort, she swung her legs onto the floor and took in her surroundings. She was in her own room. A flutter of happiness tickled her insides, and she cursed herself for being weak. How could she feel happy about being here, in the house of the man who had lied to her for a lifetime?

There was a knock on the door, and without waiting for a response, it swept open. In front of her stood the Lord Chancellor.

'Good morning,' he said, closing the door behind him.

Mustering all the strength she could, Bellina crossed the distance between them and slapped him round the face. It was a lot less forceful then she had hoped.

'Have you got that out of your system?' he asked.

'Oh, not nearly,' Bellina replied, nostrils flaring.

'Please, take a seat, my love; you look unsteady.'

'Why don't you have one of your pet cognopaths make me?'

The Lord Chancellor ran a hand over his bald head. 'I'm sorry about yesterday. But it was important you didn't make one of your scenes,' he said.

'Of course! The Father only knows we wouldn't want a scene now, would we?'

Sighing the Lord Chancellor said, 'Yesterday, was a chance for the people to cheer, to feel proud. They needed it, Bellina — there has been scarce cause for it of late.'

'Unbelievable,' Bellina said, shaking her head. 'What about me? What about how I felt?'

'You know my feelings for you are paramount—' the Lord Chancellor began.

'Do I?' Bellina cut in. 'I don't know what to believe any more. The lies spill from your mouth like quicksilver. Tell me — have you ever really loved me? Or was it all part of your plan? Keep the human time bomb happy until I need to deploy her in the heart of my enemies.'

The Lord Chancellor fixed his gaze on hers. It was like staring into a frozen stream. For the first time in her life, Bellina caught a glimpse of the man so many feared and respected.

'They were, and still are, *our* enemies, Bellina. Our enemies. Not just mine and yours alone but every soul that calls the Estrian Empire home,' he said, pinching the bridge of his nose. 'Every day, I send men and women, some of them barely old enough to drink, off to fight those same enemies. Men and women with families, parents — people who love and care about them. How can I ask them to make that sacrifice, if I won't?'

Cheeks burning, Bellina stumbled back. The back of her legs came into contact with the bed and she crumpled onto it. The Lord Chancellor's words had stung her. She had never thought about it like that before. There was truth in what he said. How many people had gone off to fight, to protect their home and the people they cared about? How many had died in her lifetime to keep her safe?

'Y-you still lied to me. Why didn't you tell me the true nature of the mission, of the real danger?' she said, her throat thick.

'I took a calculated risk, Bellina. I never hoped you would die. What parent would? But did I know it was a possibility? Yes. And, by the grace of the Father, you came back to me alive,' the Lord Chancellor said, sitting down next to her on the bed.

The anger that had sustained her since the incident in Kurgobad gushed from her body. A dull ache crept into Bellina's stomach, a vast, cold emptiness. No, she needed the anger, the fury. She needed it to keep away the guilt, the self-loathing. She tried to tell herself it was another one of his lies. But when she looked into his eyes now, all she could see was love. Love and relief.

'Why? Why didn't you tell me you weren't my father?'

'Ah,' he replied, a frown creasing his brow. 'It was unfortunate you found out in such a way. It was never my intention to mislead you, my love. I always meant to tell you but … I found so much joy in you. So much love and pride. Is it wrong that I wished I *had* been your father?'

There was a pause. Then Bellina said, 'W-who were they? My … my real parents.'

'That is a story I am not ready to tell yet … perhaps not ever.'

Bellina looked up and found the Lord Chancellor's gaze. 'Then at least tell me — are we related at all?'

'Yes,' he replied. 'I am your grandfather.'

There was silence as Bellina digested this new piece of information. Finally, she said, 'So … you had another child? One that no one knows about …'

She watched as the man she now knew to be her grandfather tensed, his face twisting. 'Enough questions,' he said, 'especially ones that have answers I fear neither of us have the strength to bear at the moment.'

Even though her mind was reeling with questions, Bellina nodded. 'Very well … grandfather,' she said.

The Lord Chancellor let out a laugh and said, 'Good grief, that certainly makes me feel my age.' He took her hand and gave it a gentle kiss. 'Now sleep; you need to get your strength back.'

Bellina nodded again, then much to her own surprise, she wrapped her arms around her grandfather and said, 'I love you.'

'I love you too,' he replied.

# CHAPTER TWELVE

Elvgren stood in front of the Palace of Administration and took in a deep breath. The vast building rose in front of him. It's Gothic spires and intricate stonework, which used to seem so forbidding, now made him feel ten feet tall; even the statues of the Lumanist Martyrs looked as if they had a new-found respect for him.

Striding forwards like a king claiming a new territory, Elvgren made his way to the guards waiting at the door.

'Deputy Lord Chancellor,' they both said in unison, snapping him a salute.

Elvgren gave them a lofty nod, and they swung the massive doors open for him. Chin high, he entered. All the way along the walk from the entrance to the Lord Chancellor's office, Elvgren was greeted with respect bordering on reverence from the clerks he passed.

Soon, he stood before the office, shoulders swept back, chest puffed out like a jutting rock. He thought back to the cringing youth who had stood in the same spot after the debacle at the Lord Exchequer's Ball, it felt like that person had existed in another era. He gave three swift raps on the door and waited.

'Enter,' the voice of the Lord Chancellor said.

Turning the brass handle, Elvgren went in. The first thing that struck him about the office was its sparseness. The wood-panelled walls were unadorned with pictures of any kind. Above the fire, the mantle stood bare. The only furniture in the room was a large table, a pristine scribograph perched at its far end, and a collection of rather uncomfortable-looking mahogany chairs. Behind the table, sat the Lord Chancellor, a huge mullioned window bathing him in light.

'I trust you received the funds you requested?' he said, without looking up from a pile of papers.

'Yes, thank you, my lord,' Elvgren said.

'Good,' the Chancellor replied, scratching at his chin. 'Where is the boy you picked up? Dingo, was it?'

'Dargo, my lord.'

'Ah, yes, Dargo.'

'He is currently being fitted for an automaton leg,' Elvgren said.

'I see,' the Lord Chancellor said, eyes scanning a piece of parchment.

There was a knock on the door behind him and Elvgren gave a small jump.

'That will be the ministers now,' the Chancellor said. 'Come stand by my right hand, the symbolism of that should escape no one.'

Lungs full of the most satisfied breaths he had drawn in a mostly self-satisfied life, Elvgren took up the position indicated. The Lord Chancellor barked out permission to enter and two men sidled into the room.

'Lord Lovitz, may I introduce Scholar Hidengraft, head of our sortilenergy department, and Lord Reisen, the new Minister for Foreign Affairs.'

The two men bowed to Elvgren, who gave a short incline of his body in return. Gesturing at the seats, the Lord Chancellor encouraged them to sit; the minister and the scholar dutifully obliged.

'Lord Reisen, would you care to start?' the Lord Chancellor said.

'Certainly, my lord,' Reisen replied. The small man fussed at his clothes. Elvgren noticed his nails were bitten down to the quick. 'The situation on the Eastern Continent continues to er ... deteriorate. After the fall of New Ledi, our forces have been driven deep into the south of Mandira.

'The Burkeshis are still sending kaffars and naffirs to stoke up resentment. They now place the death toll in Kurgobad at ten thousand men, women and children.'

*Gods*, Elvgren thought, *that was us*.

'An exaggeration, I'm sure, but I trust your office is still suppressing any hint of this?' the Lord Chancellor asked.

'Yes, my lord. We have kept the story of it out of the newsprints. But ... um ... i-it may only be a matter of time before rumours start to circulate amongst the populace. I'm sure the Duke of Tremore would happily use such information against us; seeing as er ... his um ... opposition to the Burkeshi expedition was most vocal.'

'Let him. I will spin it as Tremoran cowardice. The louder the fly buzzes the sooner it gets swatted,' the Lord Chancellor said with a dismissive wave. 'How do things stand in Escambria?'

Reisen tugged at his collar, the bobble of his throat pounding up and down like a piston. 'Fractured, my lord. The head of the purgistas, Brother Garand, is still seeking your support for the position of Prima Lurista. In fact I received word from him only this morning with regards to the kaffar one of his men managed to bring back for us. He … er … seems to see it as some sort of gift.

'On top of that, he is stoking the flames of religious fervour by blaming the Empire's er … current troubles on a lack of faith and a reliance on technology. He intends to hold an "Inferno of Idolatry", a mass book burning in three days' time.'

The Lord Chancellor's face blanched. 'Are you sure?' he said. Reisen nodded his head like an enthusiastic puppy. 'This is deeply concerning,' the Chancellor continued, staring at his hands. 'What of the head lurista?'

'Brother Drucardo still has the support of a quarter of the Church's members behind him and also seeks to be Prima Lurista. Unfortunately, he loses ground to Garand's um … extremists every day.'

The Lord Chancellor rubbed at his eyes and said, 'What a fucking mess.'

Elvgren cleared his throat and asked, 'Why do we not simply appoint this Garand?'

Eyebrow raised, the Lord Chancellor fixed Elvgren with his granite stare. 'Firstly, the current Prima Lurista is not dead. Secondly, a purgista has not held that role in the past five hundred years. Finally, Garand is a hardliner. Making him head of the Lumanist Church would alienate the Narvglanders—'

'And the Gortrixians!' the scholar added, nostrils flaring.

'Yes, and the Gortrixians,' said the Lord Chancellor.

Elvgren chewed at his bottom lip. They depended on the rich mineral deposits of Narvgland, especially as it was the only place in the Empire where tharg's bane could be found. On top of that, Gortrix had always been a staunch ally to Estria and a check on the advances of its neighbour, Tremore.

On the other hand, the more fervent countries of Escambria, Tremore and Sylvantain would welcome a man like Garand with open arms.

'So, we're buggered every which way,' Elvgren muttered.

The Lord Chancellor shot him a grim smile and said, 'Welcome to politics.' He turned back to the Reisen and said, 'Enough. Scholar Hidengraft, what happy news do you bring me?'

Elvgren watched the minister take a handkerchief from his pocket and wipe his brow before turning his attention to the scholar.

'Regrettably, I am also the bearer of woeful tidings,' Hidengraft said with a sniff. 'The sortilenergy output continues to drop; we are deep into our reserves. At this rate, power outages are a distinct possibility.'

'Damn it to the Void,' the Lord Chancellor hissed. 'Have any of you morons managed to work out the reason yet?'

Hidengraft's cheek twitched at the rebuke. 'There are still a number of possibilities, my lord — weakening of the bloodlines due to our mage breeding programme, a wilful desire on the part of the mages to not pass on their powers, some have even suggested that the source of sortilenergy has weakened.'

'And which of these *theories* do you subscribe to?' the Lord Chancellor asked.

'Personally, I feel an injection of new blood into the breeding program would work wonders. If we could just capture a mass of these kaffars … who knows?'

'The fact that the gestation period for a mage is twenty-four months doesn't seem to factor into that,' the Lord Chancellor said.

'Yes, well …' Hidengraft bristled.

'Two years before the fruit of any such experiment would ripen. Even then, you cannot offer me concrete proof that it will work. No, I shall take the dragon by the snout on this one, introduce power rationing, say we need it for the war effort; at least it won't be a lie,' the Lord Chancellor said, sweeping a hand over his bald pate. 'Very well. Thank you, gentlemen, for your candour; you are dismissed.'

The two men shuffled out, the minister's head bowed, the scholar muttering under his breath. Elvgren sauntered around the table and plonked himself into one of the vacated chairs.

'Don't seem the most reliable of chaps,' he said.

'And you are, Lovitz?' the Lord Chancellor said. 'Did I give you leave to sit down?'

'Er … no, my lord,' Elvgren replied, jumping to his feet.

The Lord Chancellor gazed at Elvgren, his fingers drumming on the table top. 'I am impressed at your resilience, Lovitz. I quite expected you to die on that mission, but here you are. As I am a man of my word, I intend to groom you as best I can. But do not think for one second you have made up for the death of the Lord Exchequer,' he said, picking up another piece of paper. 'I am sending you to the Escambrian capital.'

'To Prinargo Luminaro? W-why, my lord?'

'One: so, I won't have to look at you. Two: I want you to meet with Garand and Drucardo. They have been clamouring for a meeting with myself, but as you can see, I have a few things to take care of here,' the Lord Chancellor said, massaging his temples. 'There is also another matter that needs addressing, one for which I had hoped we would have more time.'

'What is it, my lord?' Elvgren asked.

'The libraries of the Lumanist churches are full of ancient knowledge, particularly the one located at the Palace of Radiance. There is a particular tome I have been trying to get my hands on for years, but the bastards have thwarted my every attempt. This inferno they have planned is forcing my hand sooner than I would like.

'Bellina shall accompany you on this trip. We shall say you are going to have your betrothal blessed by the Prima Lurista. Bellina shall then use her powers to infiltrate the library and take the book.'

'Is she up to the task?' Elvgren said. 'The last I saw her she looked a bit peaky.'

'Do not doubt my daughter's capabilities, Lovitz,' the Chancellor said. 'But you shall have some support. Major Bouchard's presence at your side will raise few eyebrows, and I have some more capable hands who may prove useful.'

'V-very well, Lord Chancellor; I won't let you down.'

The Lord Chancellor gave a snort and began to scribble on the paper he held. Elvgren remained where he stood, cheeks burning.

'Erm …' he said.

'For the love of … Go, Lovitz, you insufferable cretin!' the Lord Chancellor cried, waving his hand at the door.

Elvgren turned and made for the door as fast as he could. He shot into the hallway and collided with a clerk carrying a stack of notes.

'You clod!' Elvgren bellowed at the man as he bent to pick up the scattered paper.

'I … I am sorry, my lord,' the man said.

'Damn right, you are!' Elvgren said, before giving the man a kick in the rear and storming towards the entrance.

# CHAPTER THIRTEEN

Bellina stood in the early morning chill, a shawl pulled tightly around her shoulders. Her feet sank into the soft ground, dew clinging to the grass like glistening gemstones. It seemed she was the first to arrive at the embarkation point. Her carriage waited off to the side, the driver yawning and the breath from the horses rising in little clouds. The only other thing in the field around her was the world's second ever airship.

She had left the relative comfort of her vehicle to inspect the airship. It seemed bigger than the *Sighing Wind*, more intimidating, and she was sure she could see the snouts of cannons protruding from its bow.

From behind her she heard the creak of wheels and turned to face the noise. Three carriages were making their way along the road her own had followed. They came to a stop and the first one opened its doors. Bellina watched Elvgren tumble out, creased and crumpled, with Dargo close behind.

'You've had your automaton leg fitted, Dar,' Bellina said, walking towards them.

'I'm fine, my beloved, don't worry about me,' Elvgren said sniffily.

'I make it my prerogative not to,' Bellina replied.

'Don't listen to him, Belle. His highness here has been moaning about the early start the whole ride over,' Dargo said. He pulled up his trouser leg and continued, 'What do yer think, eh? Amazing innit?'

'Automaton limbs are rather impressive,' Bellina said, admiring the pistons and gears, before her eyes caught sight of the small vorotorium cell that powered the leg, sortilenergy swirling and spiking inside it. She shivered.

'Wanna see how high I can jump?' Dargo asked, eyes glinting.

'No, Dargo,' Elvgren cut in. 'We already have to pay the innkeeper for that hole you made.'

'Ah, come on, Gren, that was before I knew how to adjust the power properly!'

'Perhaps later, Dar,' Bellina said.

'Fine,' Dargo replied, a pout twisting his mouth.

'Who are in the other carriages?' Bellina asked.

'I imagine one is the major. Buggered if I know who's in the other one,' Elvgren answered.

They didn't have to wait long to find out. As if on cue, the door to the middle carriage flew open and a young woman jumped out. She was tall and athletically built, long legs stretching up from the ground. A narrow face topped with raven-coloured hair looked nervously about her. Catching sight of Bellina and the others she made her faltering way over to them before kneeling in front of Bellina.

'Master Bellina,' she said.

Looking at her closer, Bellina noticed that she was in her early twenties, just a few years older than herself. 'I beg your pardon?' Bellina replied.

'Y-you are Master Bellina, are you not?' the young woman asked.

'I am Lady Bellina Ressa,' Bellina said, her eyes narrowing. 'Who are you and *why* are you calling me Master?'

'I ... I am Dahlia Terracruz,' the woman said, before clearing her throat, 'and I'm calling you Master because you are ... ahem ... a Master of Cognometry. Y-you defeated Alcastus *and* have control of your power conduit.'

Bellina cocked her head to the side and pursed her lips. 'So, you're a cognopath?' she asked.

'O-of course, Master; it is all part of the plan.'

'Plan?'

'Y-your father's plan. The one to get the book?' Dahlia said, biting her lip. 'S-surely you were informed?'

'I have not seen my father these past few days. As you can imagine he is rather busy,' Bellina replied, feeling her neck and jaw stiffen.

'N-not from the Lord Chancellor but from Major Bouchard, your guard. She was ... um ... supposed to fill you all in.'

Truth be told, Bellina hadn't seen Cirona since they returned, but she was damned if she was going to let some upstart cast aspersions on the major.

'I'm sure Major Bouchard has a valid reason for this oversight,' Bellina said, her voice pure frost.

'Actually, where *is* the major?' Elvgren said.

'Must be in there,' Dargo said, pointing to the last carriage.

Together, they set off towards it. Bellina paused before the door and extended her hand to knock. She froze. From inside she could hear the sound of snoring. Bellina frowned; it wasn't like the major to oversleep. She gave a series of raps and waited for a reply. None came.

'Major? Major!' Elvgren yelled banging on the side of the carriage.

There was a snort and then the door flew open, Cirona hanging on to the handle, seemingly for support.

'Alright, One Eye,' she said, 'I'm coming ain't I?'

'Major, are you feeling well?' Bellina asked.

'I'm fine, m'lady. Nuffin a bit o fresh air won't sort out,' Cirona said climbing out of the carriage on unsteady feet.

'She's fucking sloshed,' Dargo said.

'Who tol' you that, eh? I'm fine.'

'Let's just get you onto the ship for now,' Bellina said, moving to Cirona's side and supporting her. 'Elvgren, come and help.'

Elvgren moved round to the major's other side and propped her up. He wrinkled his nose and said, 'Gods, Major, when was the last time you bathed?'

'Elvgren!' Bellina hissed.

'S'alright, I *have* missed a bath or two,' Cirona said, pulling them in tight against her. 'We've been through it, eh? Us lot? I love yer, I do.'

'Th-thank you, Major, we … er … love you too,' Bellina said.

As they began to make their way towards the airship, Elvgren said, 'Erm … Major, do you have the details of this plan. As … well … we have an extra cognopath and don't really know what to do with her.'

'Oh, that. She's s'posed to pretend to be Bellina or some such bollocks. Got it written down somewhere. Hang on a minute, we ain't getting on another one o them, are we?' Cirona said, pointing at the airship.

'I'm afraid so,' Bellina said.

'Ah, for fuck's sake!' the major groaned.

With great difficulty Bellina and Elvgren managed to get Cirona to the airship. Bellina waved up at it, and a few seconds later, five ropes with round platforms on the bottom shot down.

'For the love of the Father — please hold on tight, Major,' Bellina said.

'Yeah, yeah, stop fussing,' Bouchard replied.

Bellina, Elvgren, Dahlia and Dargo grabbed their own ropes. Once they were all on, they began to race into the air, Dargo whooping and yelling all the way up. They came to a stop in a square room lined with weapons. *It really is different from the* Sighing Wind, Bellina thought. The whole group poured through a door and found themselves in a mess room. Bellina scanned her eyes around it and saw …

'Barboza!' Bellina cried, rushing forwards and throwing her arms around the giant Timbokan.

'My lady,' he replied, returning her embrace. 'Welcome to the *Flying Vagabond*.'

'Don't tell me—'

'That's right. I am once more a captain and, as such, was given the honour of naming this fine vessel,' Barboza said, puffing out his chest. 'I'm sure you'll enjoy the improvements. Melek has extended the size of the gondola considerably. There are cabins, a galley kitchen, even a flushing toilet. Plus, the engine and vorotorium cell are now onboard, meaning we can land if needs be.'

'That's wonderful, Captain, but er … you do know how to fly this thing, eh?' Elvgren asked.

'Crenshaw knows what all those levers and gauges do,' Barboza said, waving his hands.

'Good job one of us does, eh, Bar?'

'Crenshaw,' Bellina said, giving the man a hug.

'M'lady,' Crenshaw replied with a smile and a wink.

'Don't forget me, Belle,' a small voice piped up.

'As if I could, Midge,' Bellina said, kneeling down to give the small boy a squeeze.

'I'll take one of those if you're dishing 'em out,' another voice said.

Bellina looked up and saw Holger standing in the doorway of the control room. She took a step forwards, a strange fluttering in her stomach. A smile built on her lips. She reached out a hand and Elvgren cleared his throat loudly. For a second, she drew her fingers back, then punched Holger lightly on the arm.

'You'll take that and like it,' Bellina said.

'It's good to see you, Belle.'

'And why pray tell are you even here?' Elvgren asked, his voice sharp as the edge of a cleaver.

'Belle's er … dad sorted me out. Didn't have no money and didn't fancy going out to sea again, so he suggested joining the Imperial Air Fleet.'

'I suppose being based in Victory and near enough to meddle in mine and Bellina's relationship had nothing to do with it?'

'How many times you seen Belle since we been back? How many letters you sent her?'

'Well, I don't see as that's any—'

'Whatever,' Holger said.

'Who the fuck do you think you're talking to, you jumped up little shitstain? I am the Deputy Lord Chancellor!'

'Thought that was just for show, like you and Belle?'

'Why you …!' Elvgren said, lunging forwards.

'Easy, Gren, easy,' Dargo said, jumping in front of Elvgren.

'Let him go if he wants to try it,' Holger said.

'Twelve hells, stop it, both of you,' Bellina said.

'He started it.'

'No, he did!'

'All of you, shut the fuck up!' Cirona bellowed, before puking all over the floor.

***

Cirona looked down at the world below, trees and buildings shrunk to doll's house proportions, and felt her head spin. The puke had done her some good, but it was going to take more than one upchuck to cleanse her system. *And why would I want to do that anyway?* she thought, drawing a hip flask and taking a swig.

'Is that really wise, Major?'

Turning her head, Cirona saw Bellina come onto the observation platform.

'Can't think of anything more so at the moment,' Bouchard replied.

Joining her at the platform's rail, Bellina said, 'I take it things didn't go to plan with your daughter?'

Cirona snorted. 'You can say that again.'

'What happened?'

Bouchard took a hard swallow and said, 'She … she doesn't know anything about me or … Trafford. Being raised by some wealthy merchant. Turned her into a right little madam.'

'I'm sorry, Major,' Bellina said, placing a hand on Cirona's arm.

'Don't be. I should have known. I just … I don't know … thought there would be this link between us, that she would recognise me. Instead she called me filthy and told me to piss off,' Cirona said, feeling the prick of tears in the corner of her eyes.

'I'm here for you, Major, you know that, don't you?' Bellina said.

'I do,' Cirona replied. She looked at the young woman beside her and felt a warmth rush from her stomach. 'Enough about me and my problems. How did things go with the Lord Chancellor?'

'We … we managed to reach some kind of truce. The love between us is still there; as for trust, I'm not so sure that will ever completely recover,' Bellina said, taking a deep breath.

The pair fell into silence as the *Flying Vagabond* raced towards its destination. In the distance, Cirona saw the sun gleaming, its rays splintered into shards as it hit the glass roofs of the hundreds of churches below; it was like the ground beneath them was strewn with gigantic diamonds.

'By the Father, that's quite the sight,' Bellina said.

'And I thought Prinargo Luminaro was incredible at ground level.'

'There must be hundreds of churches down there to produce that,' Bellina whispered. 'And to think we are the first people to see it like this.'

Just then the airship gave a violent lurch. Already unsteady, Cirona's feet slipped, and she went crashing into Bellina. The pair hit the wooden deck with a bump.

'What the hells is going on?' Cirona exclaimed.

A shudder passed through the *Flying Vagabond*, and the vessel began to plummet. Cirona felt herself slide down the viewing platform and connect with the rail, the air driven from her lungs.

'Major, we need to get inside!' Bellina said. She was hanging on to the door frame, holding out her hand to Cirona.

Fighting against the pull of the descending airship, Cirona managed to get to her feet. She fought her way towards Bellina and groped for her hand. Their fingers connected … the ship plunged again, and she slid back down the platform.

'Get yourself inside, my lady,' Cirona cried.

'Major, no!' Bellina replied, her hand still thrust towards her.

Cirona watched, horror-struck, as the *Vagabond's* nose dropped again, the angle of the platform now almost vertical. *Not good*, Cirona thought as her desperate fingers tried to gain some purchase, the ridiculous level of understatement pulling a panic-stricken snicker from her mouth. Bellina let out a cry, and Bouchard saw that her grip on the door frame was loosening.

Lying flat on her stomach, Cirona braced her feet against the railing and stretched out to her full height. Bellina's legs were dangling in front of her. She grabbed them in her hands.

'Major, what are you doing?' Bellina said.

'On the count of three, push off from my hands and get inside.'

'Major … I can't.'

'Yes, you can. One … two … three.'

Cirona felt Bellina launch upwards. The force of the push, though, sent her flying backwards. The middle of her spine connected with the guardrail. The world inversed for a moment as her body flipped over it. Through sheer instinct, she shot out a hand and managed to grab one of the iron posts.

'Hang on, Major,' Bellina cried. 'Somebody, help!'

Body swaying Cirona tried to get her other hand onto a post but it was just out of reach. The muscles in her arm quivered like a newborn calf. *Gods save me*, she thought, *of all the ways to go*. The airship levelled out, but her strength was failing her. Her vision shrank to just the view of her hand clinging on. She watched as her little finger slipped loose, then the next one. The pressure on the remaining two was immense. With a gasp she felt her middle finger snap and her grip fail. A scream ripped from her mouth as she began to free fall.

'Oh no you don't!' a deep voice bellowed.

Her fall came to a sudden stop. Cirona looked up to see the massive form of Barboza, blonde wig askew, leaning over the rail, his gigantic hand wrapped around her arm. With an almighty heave he lifted her up and back onto the platform.

Cirona lay on the deck, heart ricocheting off her ribs. She drew in a deep, shuddering breath and hauled her body into a sitting position. She could still feel the airship descending.

'What the fuck have you done to this thing, Barboza!?' she said.

'You're welcome, Major,' Barboza huffed.

'Why in the twelve hells are we falling?'

'It is not my fault, woman; I did not build this contraption.'

'Well nothing like this ever happened on the *Sighing Wind*.'

'If you want to blame someone then—' Barboza began.

'Stop it, the pair of you,' Bellina called. 'Get inside. Crenshaw says he has to perform an emergency landing.'

With a final sideways glance at Barboza, Cirona climbed to her feet and walked inside.

'Brace yourselves!' Crenshaw hollered from the flight deck.

Her stomach did a flip as the *Flying Vagabond* plummeted once more. Then, with a bone-jarring crash, the airship hit the ground, sending everyone on board sprawling. Cirona's skull crashed into a table and stars jumped in her eyes. She shook her head and looked around her. Elvgren was on his feet, face white as a phantom, helping Dargo up. The other cognopath and Holger were steadying Bellina.

'Well,' said Crenshaw appearing from the flight deck, 'let's go and see the damage.'

Barboza offered the major his hand but she waved it away. Gripping the edge of a table, she got to her feet and joined the others following Crenshaw to the engine room.

'Bloody hells,' Crenshaw said, letting out a low whistle. 'Blooming aspirators shot. It's a miracle we made it this far.'

'How did that happen?' Dargo asked.

'Faulty piece maybe,' Crenshaw replied.

'Or sabotage,' Barboza said, a wild look in his eye. 'You know I thought I saw *him* back in—'

'Not this again, Bar. He ain't here. You're jumping at shadows again.'

'I told you, we tarried too long in Victory — this proves it!'

'What are you talking about?' Bellina said.

'It's nothing m'lady, just Barboza being paranoid,' Crenshaw said.

'Can you fix … this?' Elvgren asked, waving his hand at the tharg engine.

'Should be able to pick up a spare part in Prinargo,' Crenshaw replied, scratching his chin. 'Looks like we'll be walking the rest of the way, mind.'

# CHAPTER FOURTEEN

Elvgren wiped the sweat from his brow and tried to get his breath under control. They had set a relentless pace, trekking across the field the *Vagabond* had landed in and through a wood of spindly trees that surrounded Prinargo Luminaro. Now they were in sight of their destination.

'Fucking hells, look at the size of those bastards,' Dargo said.

Following Dargo's pointed finger, Elvgren saw two massive kneeling statues flanking a gate in the city wall. Their hands were gripped together in prayer, a knotted cord for self-flagellation by their knees. The faces on the statues held a look of utmost ecstasy, while their backs and arms were cut to pieces.

'It would seem this is known as the Penitence Gate for good reason,' Barbossa said.

'Now there's an understatement,' a much sobered Cirona added.

'I don't like them,' Midge said, grabbing Bellina's hand.

'It's alright, Midge, they're just statues; they can't hurt you,' she replied.

'Well, there's no point standing out here, eh? Let's go and see what they've got planned for us,' Elvgren said, the thought of another parade through the streets filling him with glee.

Striding ahead, Elvgren swept between the statues without another glance and through the open gates into Prinargo Luminaro. In front of him, he saw a narrow street lined with shops and houses, the facades painted in delicate pastel shades. Men and women were going about their business, while a group of children chased a ball in the shade of a lemon tree. To the side, a group of men sat at a shopfront being served coffee; the scent of it was so strong, Elvgren could taste its bitter tang at the back of his throat.

What he couldn't see was anything resembling the pomp that had greeted their return to Victory. No crowds, no carriages, no bunting, just the everyday scenes you would find in most busy cities.

His heart shrivelled within him, and he kicked at the ground. 'Is this some kind of joke?' Elvgren said, his one good eye glancing around him. 'We came in the right gate, didn't we?'

'Yes,' Bellina said. 'We were to arrive at the Penitence Gate before midday. Does anyone have the time?'

'I make it just past ten,' Crenshaw said, looking at the face of a battered pocket watch.

'This is unacceptable!' Elvgren said.

'I'm afraid, in this city, nothing comes before the gods,' Barbossa said, 'not even the swashbuckling Deputy Lord Chancellor and his lady love.'

'Been here before, eh, Captain?' Dargo asked with a grin.

'Yes, just the once. Many moons ago,' Barbossa replied.

Just then a cry rose up from the street beyond. Elvgren and the others turned to look. They saw a scrawny youth in the brown robes of a novice clarista pick himself up from the floor and apologise profusely to the unfortunate gentleman he had collided with. Far from being annoyed, the man bowed to the clarista and offered him what looked like a shank of meat. The young man declined, his face reddening, and hurried towards Elvgren.

'Deputy Lord Chancellor, please forgive my lateness,' the clarista said.

Elvgren looked him up and down. 'So, not only am I kept waiting, but they send me a boy with hair like a nest built by a frenetic bird and what I can only hope are food stains down his robes.'

'Elvgren!' Bellina hissed.

'No, no, his lordship is quite right. I am a mess,' the clarista said, shuffling his feet. 'I beg your forgiveness for this also. It has been quite the morning. I'm just glad I made it here before Garand's men.'

'And why, pray tell, is that?' Bellina said.

'There is no time, my lady; they could arrive at any minute and you must speak to Brother Drucardo before then.'

'Very well, lead on,' Elvgren said.

'Thank you. I have two carriages waiting at the end of the street,' the clarista said.

'I'm afraid we need to do some shopping first, otherwise we'll be the proud crew of a broken airship,' Crenshaw said, scratching his chin.

'Very well,' the clarista said, biting his lip. 'Use the carriage for your errands but be at the Palace of Radiance no later than twelve.'

'You have me word,' Crenshaw replied.

'I'll come with you,' Cirona said, her voice thick with alcohol once more. She held her hip flask over her open mouth and smacked the last drops from its bottom. 'Gotta do some shopping of me own.'

'Sh-should we not accompany the lord and lady?' Dahlia said to Cirona. It was the first thing Elvgren had heard her say since their introduction.

'Screw it. They'll be alright. What are these nutjobs going to do? Preach 'em to death?' Cirona replied.

'I have no need for another shadow,' Bellina said to Dahlia, her eyebrow arched dangerously. 'You will accompany the others.'

'Yes, fine, all of you just do whatever you please. Let's just get on, shall we?' Elvgren said. 'And there had bloody well better be some bunting somewhere in this city!'

***

Cirona took a swig from the bottle of Gortrix thunderwater she had procured and sighed. The booze was killing the pain in her back and ribs but was doing nothing for the dull, aching void that had taken up residence in her chest. She had lost a lot of things in her life but always, at the back of her mind, had been the idea of reconciliation with her daughter.

What had she thought would happen? Some miraculous coming together? She had known her daughter had been adopted, and shouldn't she be happy that it was in a well-to-do family who could provide a good life for her? A witch's brew of emotion ran through her — hurt, jealousy, anger, loneliness. Her mind was spinning with it, though that could have been the booze.

'Argh,' Cirona said and took another swig.

'Wh-what did you say, Major?' Dahlia said.

'Nothing,' Cirona replied.

She wasn't sure what to make of this new addition to the party. There was a timidity to her that ground against Cirona's patience, a virtue already worn paper thin by the pain — mental and physical — that she was in. That pain grew inside of her, a poisonous bloom. She wanted it gone, to force it out.

'Tell me,' Cirona said, standing up and planting her feet wide. 'What do you expect to get out of this little escapade?'

'I ... um ... it is my duty to protect—' Dahlia began.

'Bollocks. You're a cognopath — locked up, reviled. Why would you give two shits about protecting the Empire?'

'Please M-Major, you know my abilities are supposed to be a secret on this mission. A-and of course I care about the Empire; I am still a citizen of Estria,' Dahlia said, puffing out her chest.

'Maybe a third-class one, just above the mages, just below the poor,' Cirona said. She stepped forwards and grabbed a hold of Dahlia's shirt. Leaning in, she hissed in the cognopath's ear, 'You're nothing, just a tool to be used. Serving the Empire, civic duty, it's all a pile of shit. All our Empire does is benefit the minority at the expense of the rest of us, sucking you in and spitting you out again. And after you've served, given everything you have, there's no reward, no happy ending.'

'M-Major, people are looking. Please unhand me,' Dahlia said, her reddened face looking around her.

'You're nothing, less than nothing. I have your power restraint right here. And look what some other servants of Estria, doing nothing but their duty, of course, have built into it … the suppression button, just in case you step out of line. Are you stepping out of line, girl?'

'P-please,' Dahlia said, her eyes wide, chin trembling, 'P-please n-not th-that.'

Cirona bared her teeth, finger wavering over the button. *Make her hurt*, a cold hissing voice called from the back of her brain, *make her realise what true pain is.*

'Major? What are you doing?' a small voice said.

Looking down, Cirona saw Midge's round face looking up at her, his eyes scared and confused. What the hells *was* she doing? Her hands let go of Dahlia and fell to her side.

'Everything alright, Major?' Barbossa asked.

As Cirona looked towards him to answer, her gaze was caught by a peculiar site. High up on the roof of a building to her left, she could see the figure of a man. He had the ebony skin of a Timbokan, a top hat resting on his head, and what looked like a necklace of chicken-bones hanging down his chest. Whoever he was, he was staring intently at the captain.

'You see that?' she said, turning to Barbossa.

'What?' Barbossa replied.

Cirona pointed her finger towards the rooftop but the man had gone. 'Huh, that's weird. Never mind,' she said, thinking that the thunderwater must've been stronger than she was used to.

'Got the aspirator,' Crenshaw said, joining the group.

'Then let us make haste to the palace,' Barbossa said, turning in the opposite direction to his destination.

'Good job we're taking a carriage, innit?' Crenshaw said, turning the captain to face the right way.

They crossed the crowded street to where their vehicle was waiting, and Cirona watched as everyone climbed inside. She wanted to run, to hide, to be anywhere but here. But she still had her duty to perform. She took another massive swig of the thunderwater and wiped her lips. The alcohol rippled through her body, a tide of fire. *Duty*, she thought. *Fuck duty! Where has it ever got me?*

'I'll catch you up,' she said and slammed the carriage door before setting off to find the nearest bar.

***

As their carriage made its path up the Way of Light, Elvgren saw the Palace of Radiance come into view. The main body of the building was flanked by two protruding wings, reaching out as if in embrace. Along the walls, columns rose, cutting the building into neat sections. The pediment above the main entrance writhed with gleaming gold figures. Topping off the whole palace was a tremendous roof of domed glass, the sun's light bouncing off it, dazzling the eye.

'Bloody hells! That's something you wouldn't see in Tavarar,' Dargo said, his face lighting up.

Elvgren gave a weak smile and nodded his head. The clarista had said nothing about why their presence was so urgent, merely repeating that Brother Drucardo needed to see them, brow furrowed while he pinched his bottom lip. Bellina too had sat in silence, but Elvgren had got used to that.

The carriage finished its ascent and came to a stop in the courtyard before the palace. Two more claristas were waiting to open the doors. Once out, the group was bustled inside the building, along floors decorated with stunning mosaics depicting scenes from the Book of Luminescence, past arched recesses filled with statues of saints and martyrs, until they stood before a set of double doors covered in gold decoration. One of the claristas knocked.

'Come in,' a voice called.

The claristas opened the door, bowed and left. The room beyond was large, oak panelling lining the walls, while thick rugs covered the floor. A collection of comfortable-looking couches and seats were studded here and there. Facing one of the windows was an ornate writing desk strewn with papers. To the side of this stood Brother Drucardo.

The lurista had the look of a slender man grown thinner under extreme duress. His face was gaunt, cheekbones standing out in sharp relief. Two pools of black engulfed his eyes, wrinkles like maps of rivers and their tributaries tracing out from them.

'My lord and lady,' Drucardo said, bowing low, 'I am glad you made it to me first.'

'Whatever is the matter, Brother?' Bellina asked, her eyes narrowed.

'It is about the blessing ceremony,' Drucardo replied, gesturing for them to take a seat. 'As I am sure you're aware, myself and Brother Garand are in the midst of a schism.'

'Yes, he's a hard-line blood-and-thunder sort, while you are more soft,' Elvgren said.

Drucardo held his hands out towards them and said, 'I'm not sure I would put it like that exactly, but for the sake of argument, let's say yes.'

'Garand has been using the current turmoil the Empire finds itself in to accuse us all of a lack of piety — particularly the northern countries — claiming that our recent woes are the judgement of the Father. I'm afraid, in troubled times, people are often drawn to the extremes, the middle ground lost in the dust of those abandoning it.'

'Yes, yes, extremes, fire and brimstone from the pulpit. But what has that got to do with us?' Elvgren said, tapping his foot.

'Garand has decided to use today's blessing as a test, so to speak,' the lurista said, his gaze falling to the floor.

Bellina cocked her head to the side and said, 'What kind of *test?*'

Drucardo cleared his throat and replied, 'Well … he … er … wants to bring back the *traditional* blessing ceremony.'

'What's that entail then?' Elvgren said, waving his hand. 'Some sort of special mumbo jumbo he wants to say?'

'No. It … it requires the … um … betrothed to walk the distance from their homes to the church. Seeing as you will be staying at the palace and blessed in our adjacent cathedral, it would be a walk of a few hundred yards to be completed … well … naked,' Drucardo said, a flush spreading across his cheeks. 'I was hoping, if I found you first, we could find a way around it.'

Dargo let out a snort of laughter, and Elvgren shot him a warning stare. Bellina had somehow turned whiter than her usual pallor, her nostrils quivering.

'If he expects me to parade myself through the streets of this city naked than he has another thing coming. How dare he seek to insult the dignity of a lady in that fashion,' she said. 'Lord Elvgren, tell me you are of the same mind.'

Elvgren looked at her for a moment. A bolt of lightning scorched through him while his mind considered a naked Bellina, then he came to his senses.

'There is no—' Elvgren began before the doors to the room flew open.

In the doorway stood a tall, wiry figure. A shaggy thicket of dark hair hung around a narrow face, a pair of wolfish eyes staring greedily outward. Two flustered-looking claristas stood to his side.

'We told him you were occupied, Brother,' one of the claristas said, 'but he insisted.'

'That's quite alright,' Drucardo said to the claristas before addressing the man. 'Welcome, Brother Garand.'

'Why, thank you, *Brother* Drucardo,' Garand said, closing the doors on the harassed claristas. 'It would seem you have had the honour of receiving our esteemed guests before me.'

Garand's mouth twisted into a mutated smile. Drucardo met his gaze, the air between them searing with tension.

'Have you told these young lovebirds of the changes to the ceremony?' Garand asked.

'I have,' Drucardo replied.

'I trust such eminent symbols of the Empire have no qualms about the requirements?'

Elvgren could feel his pulse rocketing upwards. He took a hard swallow, his gaze darting from Garand to Bellina. *Think*, he told himself, *think; what does this man want to get out of this?* Then it came to him. Garand wanted a spectacle, a show to parade the north's lack of due reverence. And if there was one thing Lord Elvgren Lovitz knew how to do, it was put on a show.

'Brother Garand,' Elvgren said, forcing his most ingratiating smile to his lips. 'Of course, we agree.'

Bellina stamped on his foot but Elvgren ignored it. 'In fact, as devout Lumanists we believe it does not go far enough.'

'Really?' Garand said, his wide, unblinking stare boring into Elvgren.

'In fact, Brother Drucardo suggested to us that we should complete our little stroll wearing hair clothes to rid ourselves of impurity before we declare our undying love before the Father.'

'Is that so, Brother Drucardo?' Garand said with a hint of amusement.

'It is,' Drucardo replied. To Elvgren's great surprise, the lurista didn't miss a beat.

'As such, I would like Brother Drucardo to lead us to the cathedral,' Elvgren said.

'Who could possibly deny such a request,' Garand said. 'But allow me to add one thing. To be truly rid of impurity requires scourging; there's nothing like a scourging to cleanse the soul. I think six lashes each should suffice.'

Taking a step back, Elvgren felt his mind begin to whir. How could he get them out of this one? He looked at Bellina, her eyes wide, hand clasped to her chest and felt a twang of guilt.

'Brother Garand,' Elvgren said, 'does it not say in the Lumens 3:21 that a husband should bear the weight of a wife's woes.'

'Indeed, it does, my lord.'

'Then I suppose that could be interpreted to allow me to receive the blows in my love's stead?'

Garand stroked his chin. 'I suppose it could. Very well then, we have an agreement. I shall make arrangements for the clothes,' he said, then stalked from the room

As one, Elvgren and the others let out their breath.

'Talk about making a rod for your own back,' Dargo said, rocking back and forth on his heels.

'An inspired piece of politics, Lord Lovitz,' Drucardo said. 'Giving me credit for the hair clothes should win me back some of the brothers who have thrown their lot in with Garand and the purgistas.'

'Fantastic,' Elvgren said, his head spinning.

'Why?' Bellina said, staring deep into his eyes. 'Why would you do this for me?'

'I don't really know,' Elvgren replied, dropping back, stunned, onto a couch.

***

Bellina gazed down the processional way that led from the palace to the cathedral. The sun now blazed from its zenith, its light catching and refracting in the building's glass dome until it seemed like the roof was on fire. In front of her and Elvgren, the path was lined with luristas, their white robes making them look like marble pillars. On the other side, stood the purgistas, their burgundy robes the colour of drying blood. Behind them, filling the cathedral courtyard was a mass of Escambrians, heads bowed as if in prayer.

The heat was intense, a sinuous curling beast that strangled and crushed, making Bellina's chest ache. Sweat snaked its way down her brow as she wondered to herself just what the hells they had let themselves in for.

From behind them came the sound of footsteps. Bellina turned her head and saw Brother Drucardo pass through Dargo, Barbossa and the rest. There was a muted muttering from the crowd as he took position in front of her and Elvgren. Moments later, Garand appeared. He strutted forwards to a great roar of approval. Giving the crowd a brief wave, he joined Drucardo. The lurista opened his mouth to say something, but Garand got in first.

'It is my honour to lead these two souls to their joining,' he said, his wide eyes staring up towards the heavens. 'Let this walk of contrition gain them the blessing of the Father.'

Garand began to move ahead. Bellina's fingers began to tingle and a wave of nausea oozed in her stomach. She looked back at their group; Dargo seemed to be suppressing a torrent of laughter, Barbossa smiled and nodded while Holger gazed at the ground, his fists clenching and unclenching at his sides. *Where is Cirona?* she thought, realising just how much she had come to rely on the major's presence for comfort.

'We must advance,' the voice of Drucardo hissed at her.

Head heavy, Bellina began to walk forwards. The simple hair dress they had given her to wear chafed at her skin with every step. *At least I'm not naked.* Looking across at Elvgren, she could see he was also struggling with the clothing, sneaking little scratches that would make no difference to his discomfort. His face had gone so white he could have passed for a phantom. *The lashes*, she thought, *by the gods how will he take the lashes.*

She returned her gaze to the backs of Drucardo and Garand. It felt like they had been walking for an eternity, but the cathedral seemed no closer. She tried to look up at the sky, to focus on something else, but it was too blue — a dome painted by an artist who had only heard tell of what colour it should be.

Looking at the ground instead, she forced herself onwards. Her mind was a blank, overridden by the constant rubbing of her dress and the heat, so when Drucardo and Garand stopped, she almost walked straight into them.

'We are here,' Drucardo said, turning towards her, offering a smile Bellina could only assume he thought was comforting.

She stared past him, taking in the massive gabled doorway, the arches, windows and saints in their recessed niches, tons of marble and stone pressing down towards her. It made her feel tiny, a minute fleck of lint in the pocket of eternity. *That's what it's designed to do, you idiot,* a voice in her head piped up. *Don't let it intimidate you.*

'Are you ready?' Garand asked her, white teeth flashing in a sneer.

Bellina took a deep breath and thrust out her chin. 'Yes,' she said.

'And you, my *lord*?' the purgista said to Elvgren.

'What? Yes, yes; let's just get this over with,' he replied, scratching at his neck and arms.

Garand gave an exaggerated bow then stalked into the building. Drucardo, Elvgren and Bellina followed him in. As she got her first glance of the cathedral's interior, Bellina felt her breath catch. The space around them was massive, with room enough to fit thousands, columns and arches rearing up, stretching almost impossibly to the glass roof overhead. Everywhere she looked was the glint of gold, the light from above making it shimmer like a field of wheat ready for harvest.

Her eyes were led along to the main altar, to a monumental carving of the creation story that took up the whole back wall. At the top was Mother Darkness, her weeping form created from onyx, arms clutched to her chest in despair as her robes fluttered down, enveloping a circular window. The window was made of stained glass — oranges, reds and yellows merging together to mesmerising effect. In front of the window, bathed in fire, was Father Light. He was carved from ivory, depicted in his benevolent form, youthful, fresh face wide with innocence. His left hand was outstretched, a world made of jade swirling into existence beneath his fingers. Below the world, helping to support it, were the Holy Four: Firuter, Gaindor, Cantrive and Aquinas. Beneath *them* spewed a swarm of fleeing figures, looks of sheer terror etched into their faces. *The old gods*, she thought to herself.

'It is quite something, is it not?' Drucardo said to her.

'Yes,' she managed to whisper back.

Around her, she heard the sounds of a large amount of people trying to be quiet. Bellina turned and watched the space fill up. Her gaze ricocheted left to right until she spotted the rest of their group settling in at the back.

A sudden unnatural silence fell across the assembly. Returning her gaze to the altar, she saw what looked like a walking corpse making its way to the middle, a lurista and purgista helping him; it took her a few seconds to recognise the withered body that stood before her as the Prima Lurista. Bellina raised her eyebrows. *How the hells is he going to lead the blessing?* she thought. The head of the Lumanist faith took a silver staff from an aid and rested himself heavily upon it.

'Righteous siblings,' the Prima Lurista intoned. Bellina was staggered by the rich resonance of his voice. 'We are gathered today to bless the proposed joining of Lord Elvgren Lovitz and the Lady Bellina Ressa.

'These esteemed nobles stand before us humble, full of contrition, asking that we raise our voices in prayer to bring forth the blessing of the Father. Please join me now.

'Father of Light show us the way. Lead us with your brightness from the grip of the dark. Look down on this gathering and hear our plea.

These two young souls, filled with love only for each other and yourself, grant them the grace of your favour. Peace be.'

'Peace be,' Bellina said along with the rest.

The Prima Lurista took two stuttering steps forwards and placed a kiss on her brow before doing the same to Elvgren.

'Now,' the old priest said, 'as a sign of penance, the Lord Lovitz has agreed to sacrifice his body in the name of love — love not only for his intended bride but also the Father.'

A spasm of chatter struck the crowd. Bellina turned her head and saw a massive purgista appear as if from nowhere, a multi-thonged flail in his hand. Bellina bit her lip as she surveyed the knotted lumps that dotted each lethal looking strap. She turned her gaze to Elvgren and saw the bobble of his throat plunge up and down. *This isn't right*, she thought, *I have to stop this.*

The bracelet that controlled her powers sat snugly on her wrist. Just a couple of clicks and she could put a stop to this madness, but what would be the cost?

'Kneel,' the purgista said, coming up to stand beside Elvgren, his deep voice bouncing around the cavernous space.

She watched as Elvgren licked his lips. On his face, she could see the beads of sweat mingling, twisting together into a sheen of perspiration. Body trembling, Elvgren collapsed to his knees. She had to stop this. Putting her arms behind her back, Bellina began to edge her fingers towards the buttons of her power controls.

There was a tearing sound that made her jump. The purgista had ripped the shirt from Elvgren's back in one swipe. Breath hitching and catching in her throat, she reached out with her index finger, its pad stroking the gem. At that moment, she caught Elvgren's gaze. He shook his head. A moment of shared understanding passed between them that had nothing to do with her cognopathic skills. If she did something now, all they were supposed to accomplish would be lost.

She watched the purgista draw back the flail, the straps making the sound of rain as they pattered against each other. *I won't look away*, she told herself, *I won't look away.* But when the purgista went to deliver the blow, she winced. A sound like massive bellows sucking in air met her ears as the crowd drew its breath. What she didn't hear was the sound of the flail striking home. Opening her eyes, she saw Garand standing in front of his fellow purgista, staying his hand.

'Let it not be said that we are unmoved by such devotion,' he cried, a look of utmost ecstasy on his face. 'Let it not be said that we know nothing of mercy. This day, Lord Lovitz has proved his commitment not just to his betrothed but to the Father. I shall take his penance for him.'

Bellina stood shaking her head as the assembled crowd went wild at Garand's proclamation. In one swift motion, he drew off his robes to reveal a back covered with scars, deep grooved lines in his flesh like drought-struck rivers.

'Brother Garand, I—' the flail wielding purgista began.

Garand held up his hand and said to the Prima Lurista, 'Your Magnificence, I humbly beg you — allow me to do this penance.'

The Prima Lurista nodded gravely. *They're all mad*, Bellina thought. Then she remembered Elvgren and went to help him from the floor. She knelt beside him, noticing how tense he was, his jaw clenched firm.

'It's alright,' she said to him, taking hold of his arm.

Elvgren stood. He punched his own leg and muttered, 'That deranged bastard. He's stolen the show. No one will remember Drucardo now.'

As the first blow landed, Bellina gazed around and saw the looks of morbid admiration on the crowd's faces and knew he was right.

# CHAPTER FIFTEEN

Cirona's head rested on the table in front of her. She had drifted into sleep at some point and her eyelids felt gummy. Her unfocused gaze lolled around the room she found herself in. It was a tavern of some sort. With a sudden jerk, she snapped her body into a sitting position, her brain trying its best to keep up. For a few moments it rocked like a storm-tossed ship then settled into a gentle see-sawing.

Fuck, she was drunk.

With a rub of her eyes, more of the room came into focus. There was a straggly tail of customers seated here and there on the other side of the room, all eyeing her as if she had the plague. *Fuck 'em*, she thought, and reached out for a mug on the table — the gods only knew what its contents were. She brought it to her lips and, to her immense disappointment, found it empty. This just would not do.

'Barkeep,' she bellowed, 'fill 'er up!'

A nervous-looking man at the bar came over to her, his hands worrying a rag that looked as if it had had all the worry it could take. His eyes were a watery blue, small and furtive. Beneath them sat a nose trying its best to reach a shade of red usually seen on boiled lobsters.

'I am sorry … madam,' he said, licking his lips, his r's rolling in that peculiar Escambrian way. 'But the money you … er … gave me earlier has run out.'

Cirona's addled brain considered this for a moment. 'The fuck it has,' she said, 'there was enough in there to keep me drinking in a shithole like this for a month.'

The bartender took a step back, his hands rising in front of him in defence, the rag flopping uselessly from them. 'I-If you recall madam, you … um … bought the room a round … several rounds.'

'Bollocks!' she roared, lurching to her feet, her seat flying away from her with a clatter. She grabbed the barkeep by his sweat-stained shirt and heaved him into the air. 'You trying to cheat me, eh? Trying to mug off the big Estrian, you little shitstain?'

'P-please, madam, i-i-it's true. All of it!' he said, eyes large and round as cartwheels. Behind him, the tavern's ragged huddle of patrons murmured.

'The rest o you lot got a fucking problem now then?' she said, tossing the bartender aside. 'Come on then, you bunch of faggots, give it a try.' She looked into their eyes and saw a dark loathing in them that brought her to her senses.

What was she doing? What the *fuck* was she doing? She looked down at the terrified barkeep, his back pressed against the wall, looking for all the world like an overgrown mouse. Cirona opened her mouth to say sorry, but it seemed too small and pathetic a word. Instead, she stalked outside without a backwards glance.

The sun was low in the sky now, its daily circuit almost complete. A few puffs of cloud shone a weak pink. *Pretty*, she thought and stumbled on, legs weighing somewhere in the region of fifteen tons. The streets around her were almost deserted and the thought suddenly occurred to her that there was somewhere she was supposed to be. The idea danced on the edge of her mind, stepping deftly out of her grasp. A plan? Yes, that was it … something to do with a plan.

Then her stomach began to revolve like a carousel, and she had to dart into the nearest alley, where she unloaded her guts. She stood, arms supporting her, against the wall. Her mouth was flooded with the sour taste of puke and the beginnings of a catastrophic headache began to bud at her temples.

The act of vomiting had cleared her head partially. It was then that she got the feeling that she was being watched. Years of battle and training had honed this sense to a razor's edge, and she cursed herself for not noticing sooner. Her hand reached out for the short sword attached to her hip. Her tongue licked her lips.

Drawing the weapon, she backed up against the wall, covering her back, and looked around her. The alley was deserted, save for a cat who paused from washing itself long enough to shoot her that look of contempt that felines save specially for humans.

There was nothing else.

With a sigh, Cirona went to put her weapon back. For a split second, her ears caught the sound of flapping, like a thousand crows taking flight as one. Something collided with her back, and she went sprawling forwards. The air whooshed from her lungs in one whooping blast. Her short sword spun from her hand and came to rest just out of her grasp. She groped towards it, even though, in her heart of hearts, she knew it was futile.

A pair of armodile-skin shoes came into view, the toes shrinking into a thin point topped with silver. She watched the shoes stroll leisurely to her sword and boot it categorically out of reach. The scaled leather of the shoes grew in her vision. For a chilling second, she was sure, whoever her assailant was, they were about to drive that silver point into her face. Cirona tried to roll away but didn't get far.

A massive hand clamped against her throat, hauling her into the air. She had never been manhandled like this in her life. Cirona found herself looking into the hooded eyes of the Timbokan she had seen earlier. The ebony skin of his face was covered in scars, a spider's web of ruined flesh.

'Where is he?' the man hissed.

'What? Who?'

'Barbossa.'

***

'Where the bloody hells is she?' Elvgren said, stopping his pacing for a moment to look out of the window. The sun was setting across the Palace of Radiance, the fiery globe nothing more than half a coin on the horizon. In the absence of the major, Dahlia had filled them in on the nature of the plan. He knew, if it had any chance of succeeding, their window of opportunity was as narrow as an arrow slit.

'I … I am afraid she isn't coming,' Dahlia said, chewing at the inside of her cheek. 'Perhaps, it would be best if we called the whole thing off?'

For a moment, Elvgren's mind flirted with the idea, his sense of self-preservation was certainly attracted to it. After all, it was a lot of trouble to go to just to steal a poxy book.

'Have some spine, woman.' Bellina shot her words at Dahlia, snapping Elvgren out of his reverie. 'We came for the book, and we will not leave until it is safely in our possession.'

Elvgren sighed and looked back at the room. 'Captain Barbossa, are you and Crenshaw capable of shouldering the major's task?' he said.

The giant Timbokan gave a start, his pompadour wig slipping a touch. Elvgren noted how wide and staring the man's eyes were. Barbossa's need for blinking had deserted him at some point during the day and his eyes had become criss-crossed with shots of blood,

'Hmm? What did you say, boy?' the captain replied.

'Don't worry, we'll be able to help you out. We've all spent time up in the crow's nest, and Midge has the eyes of a hawk,' Crenshaw said. He turned and muttered at Barbossa. Elvgren was sure he heard the words, 'Pull yourself together!'

Elvgren was having reservations about Barbossa. The man had become twitchy and ragged around the edges. His stomach dropped, plunging to his boots and settling there. Gods, but he could use the major right now. Not the drunken mess that had been their recent companion but the surefooted, hugely decorated soldier he had first encountered. *Well*, he thought, *needs must.*

'Bellina, will this change affect your performance?' Elvgren asked.

Bellina let out a snort. 'Of course not,' she said.

Well, wasn't this lovely — their muscle was probably face down in a puddle of her own vomit, the captain of their transport was a nervous wreck and Bellina, linchpin of it all, was acting like a cat who'd had its tail stepped on.

'Good,' Elvgren replied. 'See if you can send word to Bouchard with your powers, then we'll be off.'

***

Cirona's fingers clawed at the hands clamped round her throat, she may as well have been scratching at a steel post. The Timbokan's eyes, so white against the darkness of his face, drilled into her, pushing, searching to the very core of her.

'I will ask you once more,' the man said. 'Where is Barbossa?'

His hands loosened just enough for her to reply. 'Fuck you,' she spat.

'Unwise,' the man replied.

He grabbed a hunk of her hair and threw her to the other side of the alley. Cirona collided with the wall, pain lancing up her back like a parade of horses had just crossed it. Lungs gasping for air, she cursed herself. If only she hadn't been drinking, this idiot would have been short work for her.

Panting, she watched as the man took a small cloth doll from an inner pocket of his jacket. She saw him stuff something into the back of it then take a necklace from round his neck. Cirona realised with dull horror that it was made of bones, bones that looked human. The man was muttering under his breath incessantly, lips working overtime while words poured out. Teeth as white as bleached bone jutted over his lip, and he bit into the soft flesh. Blood cascaded down his chin, dribbling over the bone necklace and onto the doll. *That's it*, Cirona thought, *you keep up this nonsense; I've almost got my breath back.*

Behind her back, Cirona's fingers began to search for anything that she could use as a weapon. Her heart leapt as they wrapped around the neck of a bottle. It was a miracle that she hadn't crushed it in her fall, but it was the kind of luck she was going to need to get out of this one.

Breath now coming in something resembling normal fashion, she began to climb to her feet, making sure to keep the bottle obscured from the man's view. She took a step forwards, then another. Still he continued his chanting. Well, she wasn't going to let such an opportunity pass her by. With a lunge she closed the distance, lips drawn back in a feral snarl, the bottle's jagged edge aimed straight at the man's throat.

She froze.

The Timbokan was still in front of her, the doll held before him, the world's most bizarre shield. He smiled. It was a smile Cirona had seen before, the smile a card player has when laying down a winning hand, the smile a jilted lover gets when they see their former love fall on hard times. It was the smile of vicious, self-satisfied triumph.

'Woman, I am Kana Vooshu. With my name spoken you are now under my control,' he said.

'The fuck I am,' Cirona replied, willing her arm to move. It trembled like a baby bird but did not move.

'The pact is made,' he said with a bow. 'You will now follow my every instruction. You will not speak, less commanded. You will not move, less I will it. Understand me?'

Cirona's nostrils flared, her chest rising and falling to the steady beat of rage coursing through her body.

'Answer me,' Vooshu said.

Her mind began to throb. *Won't do it, won't do it,* she thought. But her jaw moved treacherously, traitorous lips spilling out the words. 'I understand.'

'Now, take me to Barbossa.'

She nodded then set off. Things didn't seem so bad now. It was all fine. Vooshu was an old friend, and it just so happened they shared a mutual acquaintance in Barbossa. She was sure the captain would be thrilled to see his old friend, Kana.

At the back of her brain, she thought she heard a voice. It was familiar but the words were barely audible, as if they were being spoken through a snowstorm. *Major?* the voice said. *Major ... hear me ... alright?* Then it was gone.

She smiled, thinking how surprised and delighted Barbossa was going to be. Her pace quickened. Yes, she just couldn't wait to see the look on his face.

***

Elvgren looked to the woman at his side and smiled. Bellina was resplendent, a fine gown of gold silk embroidered with swirling platinum thread covered her, hugging all the right places, and through some miracle of tailoring, even manufacturing some cleavage. His betrothed was linked to his arm, leaning upon him for support. He took a long look down her dress and, desire stirring within him, sighed. Everything would be perfect, if this were actually Bellina.

He allowed himself the luxury of the fantasy for a few more moments then whispered, 'Bellina would never take my arm in such a fashion.'

Dahlia, who was using the cognopathic shrouding ability to maintain the ruse, gave a start. 'R-really, my lord? Please forgive me,' she said and withdrew her arm.

'Try to stand a bit straighter too. That's it. Now all you've got to do is pretend you're looking at a walking, talking piece of dog shit when you speak to me, and no one will know the difference,' Elvgren said with a smile.

Dahlia did not return it. Instead, she shifted from foot to foot and fiddled with her dress. A tremor passed through her. Elvgren studied her face and could just make out a thin sheen of sweat. He wanted to tell her not to worry, that it would all be alright ... but the words wouldn't come.

Gods, but he'd had enough of Lumanist mumbo jumbo for the day. He looked to his left expecting to see Dargo, but he wasn't there, having decided instead to stay at the palace. *Probably trying to steal the silverware*, Elvgren thought with a sigh.

Around them, the sounds of the congregation settling in rose — the hushed conversations, the shuffling of feet and the creak of the wooden benches as seats were taken. Then, from behind him, he heard the clank of incense burners being shaken — the cloying, sickly sweet smell invading his nostrils, filling his mouth and throat, until he wanted to gag.

He turned his head, along with the rest of the assembly, and saw a procession of purgistas and luristas making their way towards the main altar. The luristas were wearing their finest vestments, geometric representations of the sun's rays picked out on them in fluid gold. The purgistas, meanwhile, had followed the example set by Garand and wore the same simple robes he had seen them in all day.

Leading the procession, leaning like a storm-bent tree on his staff, was the Prima Lurista. *Gods, how much longer has he got?* Elvgren thought to himself as he gazed at the pained expression caused by each step taken by the head of the Lumanist faith.

After what seemed like an age, the procession came to a stop at the altar. The purgistas and luristas fanned out and formed a line behind the Prima, who stepped forwards. The old man turned his attention to a shaft of light that ran from the main altar to just above the front entrance of the cathedral. The light struck a line above the main doors. At the top was a blazing, golden sun. At the bottom was a silver moon; the ray hovered just above it. Ten minutes passed in silence before the light dipped below the moon. Then it began.

A deep, mournful moan rose from those gathered. Without warning, it rose to something just below a scream, then fell again. The sunset lament had begun. Elvgren felt the hairs on the back of his neck leap to attention. He licked his lips and tried to hold his head high, but the noise was overwhelming, mingling and joining with the sound coming from all the other churches in Prinargo Luminaro, merging into a portent of darkness, a crow sitting atop a tombstone.

Just when Elvgren thought he could take no more, the dirge ceased. The Prima Lurista stepped forwards and said, 'Righteous siblings, we are gathered to observe and mourn the passing of this day's light. As we do every night, let us take pause to give thanks for the Father's gift.'

Elvgren bowed his head along with the rest.

'Now,' the Prima Lurista continued, 'Brother Garand has been given the honour of leading today's sermon, given the unfortunate illness that Brother Drucardo has come down with. Brother Garand, if you would.'

Garand bowed reverently to the Prima Lurista and made his way to the altar. For the first time in his life, Elvgren prayed it would be a long sermon; gods knew they would need as much time as they could get.

'Righteous siblings. Given the nature of today's ceremonies, I would like to devote my sermon to the subject of love,' Garand said, his wild eyes fixing upon Elvgren and Dahlia. *He knows something's up*, Elvgren's mind screamed, *he knows*. Blind panic flooded through him and it was all he could do not to lunge from his seat and make a run for it.

'We have celebrated here today the love between man and woman. Pure, devoted; one more link in the chain of fate that binds us all, one more cog turning in the machine of infinity. The strength of feeling shared between these two is undeniable. May the Father bless and favour them.'

He paused here as the congregation murmured a 'Peace Be'.

'But now I would like to take a moment to offer a word of warning. A warning to those who would betray the purity of love to deceive for their own ends. A warning we should all heed.

'In the words of the Father's Third Avatar, "Hark and listen to my voice. Beware the mouth that kisses for it contains the teeth that tear. Beware the lips that smile for they conceal the tongue that lies. Let no worldly love come between the love for the Father, as no purer truth exists." Peace Be.'

And with that, Garand walked away. There were confused mutterings from the congregation, and even the Prima Lurista looked bemused at the brevity of the sermon. But Elvgren wasn't confused. Garand's words had struck his chest with the force of a runaway locomotron. *Everything*, his mind hissed, *he knows everything*.

'My lord,' Dahlia said, pulling Elvgren's mind back to reality. 'My lord, they are leaving.'

Elvgren jumped to his feet as if a flame had been held under his arse. His good eye swivelled over the crowd. He could see the procession of purgistas and luristas towards the front, but now all their cowls were up, he couldn't spot Garand.

'Shit,' he said, thumping a fist into his seat. 'We've lost him.'

***

Bellina felt a small breeze gust around her, tickling the edges of her clothes and making her shiver; well, it was mostly the breeze. Despite the fact that she had been through much trickier situations *and* that the purgistas who usually guarded the library would be occupied in the cathedral, Bellina just couldn't shake the feeling that she wasn't so much putting her foot into the lion's den as dancing in front of it with slabs of meat dangling from her neck.

Brother Drucardo was ever so slightly in front of her, leading the way. He was moving forwards in short, twitchy steps, as if an invisible hand was tugging him at random intervals. They were walking through the Palace of Radiance, her shedding technique making them nigh on undetectable, though so far, they had not encountered a soul. Somehow, this made Bellina more nervous.

'This is it,' Drucardo said, coming to a stop in front of a pair of large wooden doors.

She gave a small nod, and Drucardo opened them. They stepped inside, and Bellina surveyed the room. The ceiling was vaulted, each arch and curve covered in paintings and gold leaf. Bookcases stood to attention in orderly lines that stretched back as far as the eye could see. The left-hand wall was pitted with windows, the day's last rays of light spilling into the room, catching dust motes mid-dance.

From outside came a low wailing. At first, Bellina could not place it, then it hit her. 'The sunset lament,' she said.

'Yes,' Drucardo replied, 'we must hurry.'

Like spectres, they flitted between the cases, the heady aroma of old books filling Bellina's nostrils and reminding her of her father's … no, *grandfather's* library. Just as she thought that the room would go on forever, Drucardo came to a stop, though why he had she could not tell. Before them was a wall, a painting of some ancient lurista frowning down at them.

'Why are we—' Bellina began. Drucardo held up his hand then moved the picture aside. Behind it was a time-worn keyhole, the metal around its cavity scratched and notched. The lurista took an equally abused key from around his neck and fitted it into the slot. With surprisingly little noise the portion of the wall containing the picture swung inward. Bellina followed Drucardo through and watched him press a button sending the hidden door back into place.

'Well, that was all very dramatic,' she said, 'but how much further is it?'

Drucardo cleared his throat. 'N-not far now,' he said.

He led the way through a room that could have been grandfather to the one they had just left. The ceilings were still vaulted, bookcases still lined the way, but there was no ornamentation here, no gold, just bare stone and a heavy sense of quiet, as if the men who had used the place had etched their piety into the walls.

'This way,' Drucardo said.

Bellina trailed in his wake, her eyes growing accustomed to the darkness around her. Once or twice, she tripped and had to bite down on the cry that wanted to escape her throat. In front of her, Drucardo came to a sudden stop, and she barrelled into him.

'Are you alright, my lady?' he asked, lending her his arm for support.

'Yes, I'm fine, but why in the world have we—'

She didn't need to finish her question. In front of her, she saw a mountain of books. What looked like a quarter of the room had been given over to it, different colour patches on the floor giving away where the bookcases had stood until recently. Her head jerked up and a gasp escaped her lips. *So many*, she thought, *there are so many of them*. Stepping forwards, she ran her hand over the nearest book, its leather binding cool in her hand, like the skin of some frightened animal.

'This … this is obscene,' she said.

'I know,' Drucardo replied. 'There are a thousand years of knowledge bound up in these books, and tomorrow, Garand puts a torch to them.'

'How are we going to find the right one?' she said.

Drucardo gave a humourless smile and said, 'Garand and the purgistas are nothing if not thorough. I have the inventory of all the books in this pile. If you tell me the name, I can see if it's in there. Then we'll just have to pray that we can find it before the men stationed to guard them come back.'

'It's called *Radiana Magnifica*,' Bellina replied.

Drucardo produced a list from his pocket and ran his eyes down it. 'Should be in the pile, somewhere,' he said. 'There's even a description here: Red binding, title embossed in gold.'

'I suppose any clue is better than none,' Bellina said, looking hopelessly at the mound of books.

Drucardo nodded and they began to search. The minutes flew by. Once or twice, Bellina's heart skipped as she caught sight of a red book, but none of them were right. She pulled another from in front of her and started an avalanche of parchment and leather. Drucardo gave a startled cry.

'I'm alright,' she called to him, 'just a minor book-fall.'

'I am glad, my lady, but that was not the reason for my cry,' he said hurrying over to her. 'Look here, where the book is listed. You see there? That red dot means it has been deemed particularly inflammatory.'

Without waiting for an answer, he scuttled off towards an arched doorway in the far wall, his feet slipping on tumbled books.

'My lady,' Drucardo exclaimed. 'Come here quickly I—'

Bellina felt her stomach tighten, as if a giant pair of hands were squeezing her innards. She licked her lips as a cold sweat broke out over her skin.

'Brother Drucardo?' she said. There was no reply.

She edged towards the door and peered in. The darkness in the room beyond was thick, a groping soup that seemed to coil from the door and snatch at her clothes.

'Brother!' she called as loud as she dared. Still nothing.

She stood on the threshold of the room, scalp prickling, telling herself that nothing was the matter, that Drucardo had perhaps fallen and banged his head, fighting the feeling in her legs that was saying 'Run!' she went in. Her foot caught on something and she almost fell. Looking down, Bellina saw it was the lurista.

'Brother!' she said, crouching down and flipping him over.

As she turned Drucardo onto his back, his eyes flew open. With a speed she would not have credited him, Drucardo pounced, taking her legs from under her. Bellina flailed her arms madly in the dark, trying to connect with any part of the lurista. Then something was covering her mouth and nose, a noxious smell penetrating.

'I'm sorry,' Drucardo whispered as Bellina scratched and clawed at his arms. 'I'm so, so, sorry.'

***

Cirona reached the top of the Way of Light and paused. Her eyes floated down the winding path they had ascended, taking in the view. The sun was slipping beneath the horizon, coating the buildings in a blanket of fire. The glass domes of the churches burned especially bright, torches scattered over the landscape by some careless god.

'Beautiful,' she whispered.

Kana Vooshu let out a grunt. 'Move,' he said. Cirona was more than happy to oblige.

In fact, she was happy to follow all of her old friend's suggestions. Each time she did, a wave of euphoria coursed through her body, and it felt like she was gliding instead of walking …

*Stop.*

'What was that?' she asked Vooshu amiably.

'I have not spoken, woman. It was just the wind.'

The wind. That was it. Just the wind.

*Fight him! This man is a liar!*

*It's in my head*, Cirona thought. Pain lanced across her brain, an electric bolt of agony ripping from the back of her skull to just above her eyes. She paused mid-stride, feeling like she was made of glass, that one missed step would send her into a million sparkling pieces.

'We are wasting time,' Vooshu said, rounding on her. 'Just think how happy our friend will be when he sees us both together.'

*Happy. Of course, Barbossa would be happy. What had they stopped for?* Cirona shook her head as if she was trying to get a rattle out of it and began walking again; in fact, she was nigh on running. If only there wasn't that dull pulse at the back of her mind. If that wasn't there, everything would be perfect.

They reached the top of the hill and came to a stop in front of a gate. A pair of guards were leaning heavily on their spears, passing a wineskin between them. At the sight of Cirona and Vooshu they snapped to attention a little too quickly, the skin dropping to the ground, its contents spilling on the ground like blood while they pointed their wobbling spears.

'Halt,' one of the guards said, an almighty belch escaping his lips. 'Who goes there?'

'I am Major Bouchard, and this is my friend, Kana Vooshu,' Cirona said.

The guards looked at each other then back at Bouchard and Kana. 'We were told to expect you, Major,' the second guard said, 'but we have had no word about this … er … gentleman.'

'Excuse me, good man, but I am a delegate of Timboko, come to offer our humble wishes of good will to Lady Ressa and Lord Lovitz,' Vooshu said.

Of course, Kana was a Timbokan delegate! How in the hells had she managed to forget that?

'Is this true, Major?' one of the guards asked.

'Yes, of course it is. Do you think I would bring someone who wishes to do harm with me?' Cirona said, fixing the guards with a glare that had been known to make hardened soldiers wilt, and to her satisfaction, the two mildly pissed guards in front of her crumbled.

'Forgive us, Major, Delegate Vooshu. Please, go through. You'll have to hurry, though, or you'll miss the sunset lament.'

'Then it seems I will have to offer my apologies as well,' Vooshu said, striding past the men.

Cirona followed him, giving the guards one final glare. They were now in the vast expanse if the palace's courtyard, the building cradling them on three sides. Vooshu stopped and took out a small, wooden figure, laying it gently in the open palm of his right hand. He whispered something to it and the figure began to twitch, moving itself to point north-west.

'He is close,' Kana said. 'Now to draw him out. Take out your sword, Major.'

Cirona smiled and took out her sword.

'Now, point the tip at your stomach. That's it, not too hard … yet.'

The major continued to smile, the cold kiss of the sword a distant feeling, a sensation filtering through a quilt of contentment.

'Barbossa!' Vooshu roared. 'I know you are here, come out!'

Nothing but silence greeted his cry. *Strange the captain doesn't want to see his friend*, Cirona thought.

*He is no friend. Take the sword and stick him right between his fucking shoulders!* the small voice at the back of her mind screamed.

Cirona's hand trembled.

'I will kill this woman if you do not show yourself, Barbossa. Can you hear me? Do you want another death on your conscience, coward?' Still only silence greeted Vooshu's cries. 'You have until the count of three. One … two … thr—'

'I am here,' Barbossa said, striding across the courtyard, Crenshaw, Midge and Holger in his wake. 'Leave the woman out of this.'

'Wh-what's going on, captain,' Midge said, his eyes wide.

'Who the hells is this man?' Holger asked, looking at Vooshu, his brow furrowed.

'He is a vooshu, a holy man from my country. He has come to take me away,' Barbossa said.

'Don't do this, Bar. We'll find a way out of this; we always have before,' Crenshaw said.

'No,' Barbossa replied. 'The time for running is over. I will not let him harm the major.' He turned to the vooshu. 'I submit. Let Rona go.'

Kana laughed. It was a high, wild sound. 'Submit? Submit! No. Any chance you had of submitting passed decades ago. The elders have decreed that you die. Woman. Kill this man … kill all of them.'

***

'Come on!' Elvgren called over his shoulder to Dahlia, pushing his way through the swamp of people in front of him. His eye darted about like a hyperactive bird, scanning, searching for a glimpse of Garand. From up ahead, outside of the cathedral, he heard startled cries and shouts of anger.

Finally succeeding in escaping the clutches of the crowd, Elvgren came to a halt. From every angle, he could see guards converging on the courtyard. Some were surrounding the Prima Lurista and his entourage, helping to guide them towards the palace.

'What the hells is going on here?' Elvgren said to a man on his left.

It took a moment for the man's slack jaw to form words. 'A woman, big, going crazy,' he managed to get out.

*Major*, Elvgren thought, *what the fuck are you up to now.*

From the corner of his eye, Elvgren saw movement. The purgistas had split off from the huddle, forming a tight circle around the Prima Lurista. Then Elvgren saw him. Garand was talking with one of the guards. *No*, Elvgren thought, *he's giving him orders*. He made a move to follow after them when a scream erupted from the centre of the courtyard.

There was the major, howling and brandishing her sword. He could see Barbossa and another Timbokan as well as Midge, Crenshaw and Holger. Elvgren's eye darted between the retreating back of Garand and the wild swinging of the major. Praying that Bellina and Drucardo had already found the blasted book, he set off for Cirona.

'Da—I mean, Bellina, get in the palace and look for you know who,' Elvgren said. Dahlia nodded and headed towards the building.

Grabbing a sword from the hand of a stunned guard, Elvgren entered the fray. The major was fenced in, a caged animal making mad lunges at her captors. The Timbokan stood at her back, a smile on his lips. Barbossa, Holger and Crenshaw were stood in front of Midge.

'You are the coward, Kana Vooshu!' Barbossa bellowed at his countryman. 'Your quarrel is with me. Let the woman and the others be.'

Kana merely smiled and stroked the head of a doll he held in his hand. He held the doll up and whispered something to it. The major let out a scream of pure rage, the tendons in her neck looking like knotted cord, before aiming another wild swing in the direction of Barbossa, missing the man by inches.

*Bouchard is a better swordsman than this, even drunk*, Elvgren thought. *If she wanted to kill she would have by now.* But something seemed to be holding her back, checking her blows at the last second.

'Major!' Elvgren called. 'Stop this instant. I don't know what piss-water you've been drinking, but this madness ends now.'

'This one is also expendable,' the vooshu said.

Cirona howled and came at Elvgren. His grip on the sword tightened, his knuckles turning the colour of milk. As the major bore down on him, he realised just how big she was. He watched her advance, frozen to the spot, as if a winter's frost had stolen over his body. He watched Cirona's sword swing upwards, its edge gleaming like ice-fire, then saw it swing back down with the inevitability of a pendulum. It took his brain a few seconds to realise he was cut.

***

Bellina's eyelids flickered open, a foul stench under her nose. She coughed, drawing in a great lungful of air, her hand moving instinctively to her chest, but she found her hand would not move; she was tied to something. Looking down, she saw that her hands and legs were chained to the wall behind her.

'Ah, Lady Bellina … I am addressing the real you, am I not? Only I saw your exact double in the cathedral not five minutes ago,' a familiar voice said.

Looking up, Bellina saw the wild form of Garand standing before her, a vial of smelling salts in his hand. Her eyes narrowed, nose wrinkling, lips curling into a sneer.

'Untie me this instant,' she hissed.

'Oho!' Garand said, walking the length of the small but opulent room they were in, towards a chair. 'I'm sure that tone has got you exactly what you have wanted over the years. But I am not your servant. You do not command me.'

'I have no idea what you think you're doing, but my father will not stand for this … the *Empire* will not stand for this,' she said, not really knowing what was coming out of her mouth. The only thing she did know was that a raging torrent of anger now coursed through every atom of her body.

'Unfortunately for you, I know exactly what I am doing. I was fairly sure your little sojourn to Prinargo Luminaro was not simply for the blessing ceremony. It was my belief that you and your *beloved* would try to stir the pot here against me. Imagine my surprise when I found out you were after this,' Garand said.

From a table to his side, he picked up a massive tome. The book was at least five inches thick, its red binding pocked and scarred like a plague victim.

'The *Radiana Magnifica*,' Garand said. 'What does your father know of it, and why does he want it?'

'As if I would tell you,' Bellina said.

'You will, in time,' Garand said with a smile. 'Purgistas are good at getting the information we seek. But before I torture you, perhaps I can show you something that will make this whole thing move along at a quicker speed.'

Garand walked across the room and pulled a sheet from over the ugliest statue Bellina had ever seen. It was of an old man, face contorted in a silent scream, hands stretched in front of him in a futile gesture of protection. Bellina looked at the statue in disgust, not quite knowing why Garand was showing her this; then it dawned on her.

'The Prima Lurista,' she said. 'What have you done to him?'

'Are you trying to tell me you were sent all this way, and your father didn't tell you about a purgista's true power?' Garand said, raising an eyebrow.

'O-of course he did. We know everything about you,' Bellina replied, as worms of confusion squirmed in her stomach.

Garand stood stock still, his head tilted to one side as he regarded her. Then he burst into a deep laugh that shook him from head to toe.

'You don't know. You don't know any of it, do you?' he said, wiping at his eyes. 'Kept in the dark, once again. I was sure you would have learnt after the debacle in Burkesh not to take the man purely on face value, but here you are. It must be nice for him to have such a well-trained pet at his side.'

'I'll show you who's the pet!' Bellina cried, reaching out with her mind, determined to steal into Garand's brain and leave him a gibbering wreck. Instead, it was like she had just headbutted the wall, and she reeled back in shock and pain.

'That won't work on me and not just because I have these,' Garand said, twirling Bellina and Dahlia's control conduits around his fingers.

Bellina felt her whole body break out in a cold sweat. She was helpless. *No*, she told herself. *No, you're not. Look closely. He hasn't turned all your powers off completely. He obviously doesn't know how to work the controls.* She found that her cognokinetic skills were still vaguely working. More in hope than expectation she focused on her restraints. Forcing back a yelp of surprise, Bellina realised they were yielding. Time. That was what she needed now, and she was going to play for it.

'What are you?' she asked.

Garand's smile deepened, his eyes flashing like cold steel. 'Now, that is the question,' he said. 'I and my brothers are one of the dirtiest secrets of this Empire, one that would prevent the sleep of many a citizen. We are mages.'

'No,' Bellina said, thoughts crashing into each other, trying to make sense of what she had just heard. 'It's not true.'

'I assure you, it is,' Garand replied in the deliberate tones of one trying to explain something to a child. 'Once upon a time, purgistas had a different name — the Ruzmagi. We have the power to change the status of the world around us and to inflict ailments. Still you look as if you don't believe me. Perhaps a demonstration is in order.'

With that, Garand took a small, round pebble from his pocket. For a moment he held it in his hand, running his fingers over it. Then he threw it at a chair. Bellina sucked in a quick breath, her mouth hanging open. The part of the chair the pebble had struck had turned to stone.

*Pull yourself together*, a voice inside her head called. *Keep playing for time. The chains are almost loose. Be ready.*

'Why?' she managed to say. 'Why are you doing all of this?'

'Because I am the creator's avatar,' Garand said, his face tilted towards the heavens, his arms outstretched.

'You think someone like you has been chosen by the Father?'

'I do not speak of the Father. I speak of the real creator — Mother Darkness,' he said triumphantly. 'She came to me, came when I was at my lowest point, came when I no longer knew where to turn. She told me what I had to do.'

Before she even knew it, the words were out of her mouth. 'What did she tell you to do?'

'Help destroy this rotting Empire. To pull it like a decaying tooth and drain the pus. She told me to cherish this book, that a devil would send his minions to claim it, that was when it would be time. Ten years I have waited for this moment, and now her, *our*, time is at hand.'

'I would say you're mad but that's obvious from a hundred feet away,' Bellina spat.

'Perhaps, I am. Perhaps, being touched by a god can only send the human mind insane. But then again, perhaps not,' Garand said. He walked towards Bellina and crouched down in front of her. 'Last chance. Tell me what you know.'

'I know this is going to hurt,' Bellina said.

She lunged forwards, her chains finally breaking, and drove her forehead into the bridge of Garand's nose. The purgista's arms windmilled as he tried to keep his balance, the control conduits flying from his grasp. Bellina gave him a shove with her mind that sent him sprawling onto his back and lunged after the controls.

Even though her chains were free of the wall they still impeded her movement. She reached for the conduit, the iron restraints making it feel as if boulders were weighting down her thin arms. Her fingertips brushed its side.

Without warning, she was pulled back and flipped onto her back. Garand straddled her chest, blood pouring from his shattered nose, a large splinter of wood in his hand. Bellina's mouth was dry, her heart smashing in her chest as if it was trying to break free. She flailed and clawed, hammering her fists against Garand, but it was as useful as trying to melt an iceberg by breathing on it.

'I shall enjoy burning you in my fire tonight,' Garand hissed.

***

Elvgren touched a hand to his stomach. It came away tacky and red. His eyes bulged and a small whimper escaped his trembling lips.

'I'm dying,' he whispered, looking up dumbly as the major prepared to swing her sword once more. The blade paused above her head and then stopped.

'No, you're not, you bloody idiot,' Holger cried, dangling around Cirona's neck. 'The cut's shallow. Now move!'

Elvgren rolled out of the way and watched the major whip her body forwards, sending Holger crashing to the ground. She righted herself as Holger groaned on the ground, then took a swing at him.

'I'm not the idiot, you are!' Elvgren said, as his sword blocked Cirona's, wishing he could have thought of something more witty to say.

'You're both a pair of idiots,' Dargo said, appearing from nowhere and kicking Bouchard's legs from under her with his automaton one.

'Dargo,' Elvgren cried, 'where the hells have you been?'

'I was having a nap, if you must know,' Dargo replied, though Elvgren could see what he would have sworn was the top of a silver spoon sticking out of the boy's pocket. 'Bloody noise out here woke me up. What's going on?'

'The major is under his control,' Barbossa called, pointing to Kana. He had grabbed a spear from somewhere and was using it to halt the vooshu's progress. 'He is using a ribbi doll. If you can destroy it, the major will be free of his influence.'

'You mean this?' Kana said, stopping and taking the doll from inside his coat. 'I have no more need of this.'

He ripped the doll in two and the major let out an animalistic scream, the scream of a leoguar's prey as the beast sinks its fangs in. Elvgren, Dargo and Holger rushed to her side.

'Her part and mine in this little piece of theatre is now over,' the vooshu said. 'The crowd has seen all the players and the curtain must fall.'

'What the fuck are you talking about?' Dargo yelled.

'You have been played, all of you, by the hands of a virtuoso performer. By tomorrow morning, the rest of the Empire shall know that the Lord Chancellor's dogs have defiled the sanctity of this place.'

'But this is all your doing,' Elvgren said. 'All these people saw you.'

'People see with their eyes, yes. But they believe what they are told. Especially when it comes from the mouth of a devout priest.'

Elvgren winced and ran a hand through his hair. 'Garand,' he said.

'Indeed,' Kana laughed. 'My role in this will be explained. The world shall know that you tried to stop me from administering justice to a murderer. I am afraid you have lost.'

'Not if I've got anything to fucking say about it,' Cirona said, rising from the ground, her face white, chest heaving.

For a second, Elvgren saw something flicker behind Kana's eyes — fear perhaps? — but it was gone too fast. 'You are tough, I shall concede that,' he said to her.

'You better fucking believe it,' she replied.

Elvgren watched, stunned, as Cirona closed the distance between her and the vooshu. From inside his long, black coat, Kana pulled out two short, curved blades. He crossed them in front of him and blocked Bouchard's strike. The major, still unsteady, staggered backwards.

'You are done,' Kana said, sword raised to deliver the finishing blow.

The hiss of steam and the whine of gears hit Elvgren's ears. Aided by his mechanical leg, Dargo flew at the vooshu, catching him round the middle and sending him tumbling to the ground.

'Run,' Elvgren bellowed at Barbossa. 'Take Midge and Crenshaw. Get to the stables, find the fittest looking horses there and get back to the *Vagabond*. We need to get out of here.'

'But—' Barbossa began.

'We'll be back before you know it,' Crenshaw said, cutting him off.

Barbossa nodded at Elvgren, scooped up Midge in his arms and set off at a sprint.

'No!' Kana cried.

He threw Dargo off his chest, sending the boy flying through the air before hitting the ground with a sickening crunch. The vooshu got to his feet and made to go after Barbossa. He was quick, but Elvgren was faster. Darting in front of the Timbokan, he made a slash at his middle. Kana blocked it with his weapons, then pressed in with a flurry of attacks. He fought with a fierce desperation, the way a drowning man battles against the tide. Elvgren managed to parry the strikes but was conceding ground.

Ducking under a wild swing, Elvgren spun on his heel and delivered a sharp blow to the vooshu's kidneys with the sword's pommel. Kana moaned and fell to his knees. Without wasting a second, Elvgren drove the point of his sword through the man's back. The vooshu let out one last cry then fell to the ground, twitching.

'Well fought,' Cirona said, coming to stand next to him. Her breathing was ragged and she looked like shit.

'Is he dead?' Holger asked, as he and Dargo joined them.

'I should bloody well hope so,' Dargo said.

Elvgren looked around him. The courtyard was in uproar. A fire had started, somehow, and the cathedral was burning. People were screaming, running any which way they could, trying to get out. The guards were trying to impose some order, but they may as well have been attempting to train goldfish. He put his fingers on his temples and rubbed as his ears began to ring. *The Palace of Radiance in uproar*, he thought, *a cathedral set to flames and a dead Timbokan holy man – could this get any worse?*

*HELP!*

He reeled back as if he had been struck. 'Did anyone else hear that?' Elvgren said.

'What?' Holger asked.

'Bellina,' Cirona said.

***

Bellina grabbed Garand's hands in a desperate attempt to stop him touching her with the vicious splinter. Arms trembling with effort, she watched the shard of wood grow in her vision, as Garand inched it closer to her face. *Gods damn it*, she thought, *if only I had full use of my powers.*

*Don't worry about that*, a voice inside her head cried. *Use what you have got.*

But what did she have? *Think, think!* Her eyes crossed as the wood crept closer, creating a blurred double of Garand and his weapon. She couldn't catch her breath, coming, as it was, in short staccato bursts. *I'm going to die*, she thought, *I'm going to die.*

'HELP!' she screamed, sending the cry out mentally as well as verbally, hating the weakness in her voice.

The purgista's eyes flashed with a sick joy. 'That's it, scream, you little whore,' he said.

He pushed down harder than ever. Bellina knew her shaking arms could hold out no longer. This was really it. Despite herself, she closed her eyes and held her breath, waiting. The sound of a dull thwack, like a cleaver striking a chopping block, followed by a startled yelp, came to her, and the pressure on her chest ceased.

'Master Ressa?' a shaking voice called.

Bellina opened her eyes and looked up into the face of Dahlia. In her hands was the *Radiana Magnifica*. On the floor to her side was a clearly unconscious Garand.

'How did you—' Bellina began to say.

'There is no time, Master,' Dahlia said, offering her hand.

Bellina took it and clambered to her feet. 'Thank you,' she said.

Dahlia's face grew pink, and she looked at the floor. 'I-It was nothing.'

'Let's get out of here,' Bellina said, making for the door. 'Oh, and keep that book safe. It's what all this madness has been in aid of.'

Dahlia nodded and clutched the book to her like a child hugging its favourite toy; if she hadn't been so tired, Bellina might have laughed.

They were almost at the door when Bellina struck her palm against her forehead. 'Our control conduits,' she said. Bellina crossed the room, kicking Garand in his side before stepping over him and retrieving their controls.

'Master, look out!' Dahlia cried.

'What?' Bellina said, turning around. She felt a sharp stinging sensation in her ankle then her whole foot from that point went numb. She looked down, her brain struggling to compute what it was seeing. From a spot, just below her ankle, she saw a splinter jutting outward.

Spreading out from it, where there should have been skin, was bark.

'Did you think it would be that easy?' Garand said, there eyes locking; all Bellina could see in them was a wild, animal hate.

She went to kick him, and Garand caught her good foot. Stumbling to the ground, Bellina just managed to give herself and Dahlia full access to their powers before the conduits once more flew from her grasp. Using her cognokinetic powers, Bellina threw Garand away from her. He hit the wall with a crunch.

Getting to her feet, the useless wooden one locking under her, Bellina saw Dahlia collecting the conduits. The girl then came to Bellina's side and lent her shoulder for support. Behind them, Garand let out a sound that was a mixture of pain and anger.

'Move,' Bellina said, pushing Dahlia away and setting off in a hobbled run.

Dahlia took the lead and headed off down a large hallway. 'We are in the purgista's wing of the palace,' she called over her shoulder. 'If we can just—'

'Murderers,' Garand shouted behind them. 'They have killed the Prima Lurista!'

In front of them, doors began to open as if the occupants had been waiting for the alarm. Bellina shoved people aside with her mind, somehow managing to keep the hallway clear ahead of them. They reached the end of it, the cries of 'murderer' now chorusing around them. Two further corridors branched to the left and right, while a doorway stood in front of them. *Which way?* Bellina thought. Then, from the branching corridors, she saw guards, purgistas and luristas rushing towards them. The door it was then. She grabbed at the handle and pushed. The door didn't move.

'Come on!' she yelled, blasting the door with her mind. The wood buckled and yielded, revealing a set of winding stairs.

'Master, let me help you,' Dahlia said.

'No! Run! I can take care of myself,' Bellina replied. Dahlia gaped at her then nodded and set off up the stairs.

Bellina followed behind, each laboured step making her heart pound, knowing that whatever slender lead they had was evaporating.

'Leave them to me,' she heard Garand say from the foot of the stairs.

Her legs froze as she heard Garand ascend the steps. He appeared behind her, blood covering his face from the broken nose, looking for all the world like a wolf who had just gorged itself on a sheep. Instinctively, she threw up a shield between them. She was glad she did, as a split second later, a shower of pebbles bounced off it.

They carried on up the stairs in this way — Garand pelting her with whatever came to hand, Bellina's legs burning with the strain of the steps and the wooden foot.

'Master?' Dahlia called.

'Just keep going!' Bellina cried.

'I … I can't.'

'What are you talking about?'

Bellina came to the top of the spiralling stairs and understood. They had climbed to the top of a bell tower. In front of them sat the giant bell, its facade defaced by pigeon shit. Around the square platform were four openings, offering what, under different circumstances, would have been a magnificent view.

'Where will you go now?' Garand said, reaching the top.

Keeping up her shield, Bellina watched as he bent down and picked up a handful of loose brick that had crumbled off one of the walls gods only knew how many years ago.

*Think!* her brain screamed. *For fuck's sake, think, woman.*

Garand advanced. 'How long can you keep that up?' he asked, pinging a piece of brick off Bellina's shield.

'As long as I want,' she replied, backing away, hoping the lie didn't make her voice waver. Her back connected with a wall.

'Nowhere left to run,' Garand said with a smile.

Bellina looked behind her, out through one of the tower's openings. Way below her she saw the glass roof of the palace's main hall.

'Not quite,' she replied, offering the purgista a mad smile of her own.

She grabbed the back of Dahlia's dress and lent back. The pair of them tumbled from the tower. They spun and twisted in the air. Dahlia was screaming, but Bellina felt awash with a strange calmness. She spread her shield around them in an invisible bubble. She saw glass and wood shatter as the bubble hit the roof. A heartbeat later and her shield connected with the floor, cushioning their fall.

Still they hit the marbled tiles with a crash that stole the breath from Bellina's lungs. Her ears hummed. Voices screamed. Blackness stole in. Fight it. Fight it. Vision blurred. Pointing. People pointing up. A shock wave rippled round the room. Garand. Why are his feet grey? No, not grey — stone. Get away. Have to get away. She crawled. Pain speared up her leg. Garand. Hands, hands grabbing, pulling. Smile. Teeth too white. A finger coming towards her head.

Black.

***

'Where the hells is she?' Cirona cried, leading the way towards the palace.

'How should I know?' Elvgren replied.

'Well, she has to be somewhere in the palace,' Holger said.

'Thank you for your input, but in case you hadn't noticed, the palace happens to be a rather large place, you dolt,' Elvgren said.

'Why don't you stick it—' Holger began.

'Stop it the pair of you!' Cirona cut in. Her body was battered and bruised, running on nothing but sheer bloody mindedness at that point; the last thing she needed was one of Holger and Elvgren's pissing contests. 'We'll make our way towards the library. Seems as good a place as any to start.'

They hurried through the main doors into the palace's reception area. The place was in uproar. Guards were running about aimlessly, luristas were shouting, asking if anyone had seen the Prima, while a few purgistas tried to instil some order, shouting instructions that no one seemed to hear.

An ashen faced lurista with bulging eyes ran past Cirona. She stretched out an arm and grabbed him by his robes. 'Have you seen Lady Bellina?' she asked.

The priest stared at her, a look of incomprehension on his face. Then a light flashed in them as something in his brain fell into place. 'You,' he said. 'It's all your fault. Garand was right. You are a bunch of thrice-damned sinners from the feckless north. You have brought doom upon us!'

Cirona belted him round the face with the back of her hand. 'Get a grip on yourself. That's a pile of hog shit and you know it,' she said. 'Now, have you seen Bellina Ressa?'

The lurista opened his mouth to answer, but all that came out was a strange gurgling sound accompanied by a trickle of blood. Cirona looked down and saw the point of an arrow sticking through the man's throat. Over the priest's shoulder, she saw a guard with a crossbow shaking in his grasp. To his side stood a purgista, a horrid mockery of a smile creasing his lips.

'Stop the Estrians! They are attacking priests, just like Garand said they would!' the purgista bellowed.

Feeling the eyes of the room turn towards their group, Cirona dropped the lurista. 'We have done no such thing,' she said. 'It was that guard there. We only want to find Lady Bellina.'

'Lies!' The purgista screamed, the veins in his neck standing out like cord. 'Get them.'

'Run,' Cirona hissed as guards and priests alike turned towards them.

Their way to the right was blocked, so Cirona took them down a corridor to the left. Feet drumming a frantic tattoo on the marble floor, they hurried on, doors and confused faces rushing past them in a blur.

'Well, that could have gone better,' Dargo said.

'What the fuck is happening?' Holger said.

'Garand,' Elvgren said. 'This is all his doing. Him and the purgistas, they've got control of the guards somehow, trying to make out we've attacked them.'

'Why?' Cirona heard herself say.

'In case you haven't noticed, Major, the man is as mad as a bull with a stick up its arse. I'm not sure if whys and rational reasoning come into it much with him.'

They reached the end of the corridor. Behind them, Cirona could hear the cries of the guards, the rattle of their armour.

'Through here,' she said, throwing open a pair of doors to their left. Once they were in, she slammed them shut again and pushed her back against them. In front of them, she saw the main hall, its massive tables laid out with a silver dinner service, ready for a feast that was never going to happen now. *Was it ever really going to?* she thought. But there was no time for that now; she could hear their pursuers closing in.

'Elvgren, help me keep these closed. Dargo, Holger, find something to hold them shut with,' she said.

'They're in the main hall,' a voice cried from the other side of the door.

Less than a second later, Cirona felt the doors bulge, the sound of splintering wood filling her ears.

'Hurry up, Dargo!' Elvgren called.

'Alright, alright, keep your bloody hair on,' Dargo said.

The doors shuddered again, the force of the blow making Cirona stagger a fraction. 'This won't hold much longer!' she said.

'Hang on, we're—'Holger started to say.

The doors flew open with a blast like cannon fire. Cirona felt herself go skidding to the ground, her back connecting with something hard and unyielding. She hauled herself to her feet, a quivering arrow striking the place where her head had been not a heartbeat before. Pulling her short sword free, she looked around her to see thirty armed guards enter.

Three men charged her. She parried their blows, chopping the sword hand from one of them, blood jetting from his wrist. The man collapsed to the floor, screaming, staring wide-eyed at where his hand should be. The remaining two lunged madly. She dodged underneath their wild swings, tucking into a forward roll, coming up behind them, slashing both behind their knees.

Springing to her feet, Cirona's gaze flicked around her. Elvgren was holding a handful of guards at bay. Dargo was sending men flying with kicks from his automaton leg, his dagger flashing in his hand. Holger was faring the worst, swinging a chair around him in a desperate attempt to hold off his attackers.

She made her way towards him, her sword flying out and dispatching any guards in her way. She saw the chair fall to pieces in Holger's hands as the last guard attacking him smashed it with a mace. Cirona grabbed a solid silver serving tray from a table and threw it at the guard. The tray spun through the air, colliding with a crunch at the base of the guard's neck.

'Thanks,' Holger said, crouching down to take the man's sword.

They didn't have time to pause for long. Four more guards came surging towards them. Cirona leapt onto a nearby table, using the higher vantage to attack. The sound of balliskets cocking reached her ears. She dived off the table, flipping it up behind her, turning it into an impromptu shield. The bullets whined through the air, smashing into the thick wood of the table with a dull thunk. *Gotta get out of here*, she thought. Rolling out from her hiding spot, Cirona grabbed the nearest guard and held a sword to his throat.

'Put down your weapons or this man dies,' she said. The sound of fighting subsided and the gaze of the remaining guards flicked between Cirona and her hostage. 'Form up!' she cried to the others. 'Get in close to me.' Holger, Dargo and Elvgren stumbled towards her, slipping and sliding on the now blood-soaked floor. The man in her grasp was trembling so violently that she had to tighten her grip on him as she began backing towards some doors at the far end of the room.

'What is going on here!' a purgista shouted, coming into the hall.

'She has Danio, brother,' a guard said.

'For the love of the Father, do we have to do everything around here?' the purgista said. Before Cirona knew what was happening, he took a ballisket and shot her captive between the eyes. 'Now, get them!'

The guards looked at each other, then at the purgista. A collective shudder ran through them, but they started to advance. Cirona dropped the corpse and held out her sword. Her and the others formed into a swirling circle as they tried to keep their enemy in view.

'We're surrounded,' Holger said.

'Why, thank you, Captain Obvious; I'm so glad you were here to point that out,' Elvgren spat.

The guards were close now, pinning them in on all sides, faces flushed with hate and fear.

'Attac—' the purgista started to shout.

He was cut off by the tinkling laughter of smashing glass. All eyes turned upwards. Two people came screaming through the shards, then seemed to hit something invisible four feet from the floor, slowing their fall and saving their lives.

'Bellina,' Cirona said, taking a step towards her.

She watched as Bellina tried to push herself up. Beside her Dahlia was also stirring. Then, rocketing through the newly created hole in the ceiling came another person who landed with a crash that sent a mini-earthquake shaking the room. Through the cloud of dust that had been thrown up, she saw the person had grey, stone-like legs. She blinked, and they were normal again. The debris drifted away, revealing a grinning Garand.

'Get away from them!' Cirona heard herself yell, her voice small and pathetic.

Time slowed. She tried to move towards Bellina as the girl struggled to get away. Garand was laughing now, his arm outstretched. Dahlia grabbed at his leg, but he kicked her aside. Cirona felt someone push past her; it was Holger. His feet tangled in a chunk of broken table and he went sprawling to his knees. *We're not going to make it*, she thought, her stomach roiling. Garand grabbed Bellina and pulled her round to face him. Still smiling, he touched a finger to her forehead and Bellina collapsed, as if all the life in her had been wrenched out by an invisible hand.

'What did you do to her?' Holger screamed.

Garand turned towards them. 'Me? Nothing. She is merely sleeping,' he said.

Heat crept through Cirona's body. *How the hells are we going to get out of this one?* she thought.

'Give her back,' Holger said, his voice now a deadly whisper.

'What's your rush?' Garand said. 'You shall all be together for your executions.'

Sweat was now pouring down Cirona in sheets. She wiped her forehead with the back of her hand. It was like she was standing next to a bonfire.

'Give. Her. Back. She's mine! We're supposed to be together. Together forever!' Holger said, taking a step forwards. Cirona noticed a haze around the young man. *It's coming from him*, she thought, *the heat is coming from him.*

'Guards,' Garand said, 'arrest them.'

Holger let out a yell, a primal scream of fury that made Cirona's head spin. Warm air rushed past her, as if she was standing too close to the edge of a locomotron platform when the contraption whizzed past. Garand's robes went up in flames. He shrieked, dropping Bellina to the floor. Cirona saw Holger stride forwards, his hands dripping fire. Guards rushed towards him, but the smashed furniture caught alight blocking their way.

'He's a mage,' Elvgren said, coming to Cirona's side. She saw a look of disgust and terror on the young lord's face.

'Whatever he is, he just gave us an opportunity,' she replied.

Cirona ran forwards, towards Bellina. Dahlia was up, cradling her fellow cognopath in her arms, shielding her. Holger was already at their side, bending down to pick up Bellina, hands still burning.

'Leave her to me,' Cirona called to him. He looked at her, then down at his hands. Realising what was about to happen, he jumped back.

'Oh, fuck. My hands. I was … they …' he said.

'Don't worry about that now,' Cirona said, plucking Bellina from Dahlia's arms, marvelling at the lightness of the girl. She placed Bellina over her shoulders and offered Dahlia her hand. The girl took it then bent to pick up a large book from the rubble.

'We're leaving,' Cirona said to the stunned guards. 'Anyone follows us, and this boy will melt your fucking faces.'

They retreated towards the doors, away from the confused and frightened guards.

'Demons!' Garand cried. 'Abominations! See, see the wickedness and sin of Estria. A mage walks amongst them. The boy's existence is an offence to the Father. Attack!'

'Run,' Cirona said.

They sped from the hall, back down the corridor towards the main entrance. Everything Holger passed was now catching alight.

'I … I can't stop it!' Holger said, as they exited into the courtyard. 'It hurts.'

'Stick your hands in the fountain,' Cirona said to him as they ran towards it.

Holger did as he was told. Steam billowed around him as he placed his hands into the water. He pulled them out, groaning. Cirona could understand why. The flesh was blackened and charred, here and there cracked, revealing a vivid slash of pink.

'Don't worry,' she said to him, 'We'll … we'll get you patched up and—'

'Where is he?' Elvgren said.

'What? Who?' Cirona replied, her head spinning.

'The vooshu. He was right here and now—'

'That's not our biggest problem,' Dargo said, pointing towards the sky. 'I think we just lost our ride.'

Cirona followed Dargo's finger. In the distance she saw the unmistakable shape of the airship flying away from them.

'Fucking hells, Barbossa,' she said, closing her eyes.

'There they are!' a voice called behind them.

Casting a glance backwards, Cirona saw Garand and a gaggle of guards coming out of the now blazing palace. She flicked her gaze towards the path leading down into the city. It was blocked by men. Shit, there had to be a way. To her right, movement caught her eye. She turned towards it and saw a lurista in the shadow of a small stone building. He waved at them then pushed himself back so as not to be seen.

'That's Drucardo,' Elvgren said. 'What the hells has he been playing at? Why wasn't he with Bellina?'

'No idea, but he's the only priest that hasn't tried to kill us in the last hour, and we need all the help we can get right about now,' Cirona replied.

She ran towards the lurista, the shouts and cries of the guards ringing in her ears. He beckoned for them to follow, leading them down some steps and to the entrance of a mausoleum. They rushed inside, Elvgren and Holger closing the door behind them.

'By the Father, what have I done?' Drucardo said, pacing the stone floor and pulling at his hair. He looked at the limp body of Bellina over Cirona's shoulder and groaned. 'My fault, all my fault.'

'What are you talking about, man?' Elvgren said.

'I didn't want to. Gods, I didn't want to. But he knows things. He … he had them and—' Drucardo babbled.

Cirona grabbed him and slapped him round the face. 'What did you do?' she said.

The priest held a hand to his cheek, his eyes focusing. 'I … gave her to Garand. But I never thought he would go this far, never, never!'

'Swine,' Elvgren said, taking a step towards the lurista and drawing his sword.

Cirona held up a hand. 'Why have you brought us here?' she said.

'There's a tunnel, a secret way out. It's beneath that coffin. Please, you have to forgive me.'

'If you get us out of here, I will,' she replied.

'Rona, you can't be serious? He—' Holger began.

'What other choice have we got,' she said. 'Show us the way.'

***

'Coast's clear,' Cirona said, pushing aside the stone sewer cover. She clambered up and out, grateful for the fresh air.

Drucardo's secret passage had taken them into the catacombs below the palace and then into Prinargo Luminaro's sewers. She had expected to hear the cries of the guards or Garand's demented shriek at every turn, but they had made it out in one piece.

Her shoulders were on fire from carrying Bellina, despite the cognopath's lightness. Drucardo had insisted that Garand was telling the truth when he said he had put her to sleep, and Cirona could feel the girl's breathing against her neck to confirm it, but she hadn't stirred once.

When everyone was topside, Cirona said, 'What now?'

Drucardo darted to the end of the alley they were in and looked about him. He waved at someone and a carriage trundled into view. A pretty woman with blonde hair sat atop the vehicle, her swollen stomach announcing that she was pregnant. She exchanged a few words with Drucardo.

'Helena says they are guarding the exits from the city, but I came prepared. Inside the carriage are clarista robes put them on and keep the hoods up,' the lurista said.

'And who in the twelve hells is Helena?' Elvgren asked.

'She is … well … I …' Drucardo murmured.

'I understand,' Cirona said, placing a hand on Drucardo's shoulder.

'Oh,' Elvgren said.

'What? What's everyone on about?' Dargo said.

'Don't worry, Dar. Just get in,' Cirona said.

Drucardo climbed up into the driver's seat and took the reins from Helena. They entered the carriage and slipped the robes over their heads. Cirona positioned Bellina as best she could then banged on the roof. She heard Drucardo gee up the horses and they were off.

From the vehicle's window, Cirona saw that the city was in uproar. The clanging of church bells reverberated on the air, mingling with the cries of the city guards. They wove their way unimpeded towards one of Prinargo Luminaro's gates. Here, they were stopped.

'What business takes you out of the city, brother?' a guard called out.

'I … well … you see …' Drucardo stammered.

*Shit*, Cirona thought, *he's the worst liar ever. How the hells did he fool Bellina?* She watched as the guard's face hardened, his hand gripping his sword tight.

'We are on urgent business,' Dahlia called out.

Cirona watched as the guard's face went slack, a misty look creeping into his eyes. 'Urgent business, of course,' he said.

'Let us through,' Dahlia said.

'Yes, yes, certainly,' the man said and waved at one of his colleagues to open the gate.

'Th-Thank you,' Drucardo said, and he moved them on through the gateway.

'Brilliant,' Dargo said.

'Yes,' Cirona added. 'Well done.'

'I-It was nothing,' Dahlia replied, her face flushing.

'What a fucking mess,' Cirona said. 'I hope that bloody book was worth it.'

# CHAPTER SIXTEEN

A smile creased Castros' lips as Whist finished addressing the crowd gathered in the tavern basement. Whist's cheeks took on a red shine, and he gave an embarrassed smile. Castros stood, applauding with the rest as his old friend got down from the fruit crate he'd used as a makeshift podium and made his way towards him.

'You've become quite the speaker,' Castros said, gesturing at the standing ovation.

'Well, these speeches always go better if the booze is flowing free,' Whist replied, pointing to the tapped beer kegs along the back wall.

Del Var laughed. 'Don't sell yourself short, man,' he said. 'You'll make an excellent politician, one day.'

'Men have fought duels over lesser insults, you know,' Whist said, taking the seat across from Castros.

'I assure you, only the minimum amount of insult was intended,' Del Var said, returning to his seat.

Castros lifted his hand and gestured towards a balding man in a stained apron. The man caught his eye and nodded. He drew two pints into tankards and weaved his way through the crowd towards them.

'Thanks, Stan,' Castros said as the drinks were set in front of him. 'For the beer *and* for letting us use your cellar.'

Stan waved a hand and said, 'It's nothing. Glad I can help.'

It wasn't nothing, and they all knew it. If one of the City Watch, or saints preserve them, the Lord Chancellor's vultures discovered Stan had let them use his premises for a rally, losing his licence would be the least of his worries.

'To the Workers' Liberal Party,' Castros said, raising his drink.

'The Party,' Whist and Stan chorused, the latter having pinched a pint from a nearby table.

Stan took a seat. 'Did … er … we have anything to do with that business in Escambria,' he said.

Castros smiled. 'Even I'm not stupid enough to burn down one of the holiest places in the Empire,' he said.

'You think what the Church is claiming is true then? That the Lord Chancellor's daughter and that did it?' Whist asked.

'Buggered if I know,' Castros said, shaking his head. 'But I intend to make full use of the distraction. Can you give us a minute, Stan?'

'Sure,' Stan said, getting to his feet and stretching. 'A purgista as head of the Church. Strange times.'

*Strange times indeed*, Castros thought as he watched Stan collect empty glasses from tables. He felt eyes upon him and turned to see Whist staring at him intently.

'Have I got something in my teeth?' Castros asked.

'How are you feeling?' Whist replied, ignoring the jest.

Letting out a heavy sigh Castros said, 'I'm fine.'

'You don't look it,' Whist said. 'You need more rest.'

'Thank you for your diagnosis, medic,' Castros said, drumming his fingers on the table. 'But I've rested long enough.'

'Do you need to do this tonight? I mean the state you ended up in after the business with the Falton heir ...'

'I'll admit I overdid it leading up to that, but I'm fine now.'

Whist raised an eyebrow.

'What do you want me to do, Whist? Turn cartwheels for you? Now are you going to give me the address or not?'

Whist chewed at his lip. 'Alright,' he said, stretching his arm across the table. In his grip was a piece of paper. Castros reached out for it. 'You better be careful.'

'Yes, Mother,' Del Var said, taking the note. He studied the information on it, nodded and added, 'See you soon.'

'Be careful, Cass ... I mean it,' Whist said, his whisper carrying to Del Var's disappearing back.

***

Standing in the night's chill, Castros grimaced. It felt like every blast of the wind was delivering an icy blade to his body. Pride had made him keep the truth of how he was feeling from Whist, but his old friend had been spot on — he did need more rest.

He didn't dare take it, though. Time was not on their side when it came to the Emperor. Each day, Castros expected to find news of the man's death staring up at him from the front of a newsprint. If that happened before he had got Aberoth into position as heir ...

*No, don't think about it*, he told himself. *We'll do this.*

With a shake of his head, Del Var returned his attention to the abandoned warehouse across from him. A single light shone out from a window on the top floor, muted and dispersed by thick curtains. If Whist's intel was right, Fredrick Winston, first in line to the throne, should be in there, out of his nut on morphium. Why the young lord would have chosen to climb out of his tree in such a squalid place was beyond him. He knew some nobles got a kick out of slumming it, but still …

*No*, he thought. *No doubts. Whist's intel has never been wrong before.*

'Let's do this,' he said aloud to himself, then began to move towards the warehouse.

Keeping to the deep pools of shadow that the other dockside buildings provided, Castros made his way to the warehouse-cum-morphium-den. As he got closer, he saw the place was unguarded. Frowning, he made his way to the large doors and gave them a nudge. He winced as one of them creaked open. *Not locked*, he thought, *strange*. Castros' eyes narrowed, and he felt his body tense. Every fibre of his being told him something wasn't right. *What to do*, he thought, running a hand through his hair.

Then a muffled cry reached him. He crouched down, skin prickling with sweat. He strained his ears. There it was again. Had someone else got to Winston or had some other poor soul got into trouble?

'Shit,' he said and slipped through the gap in the doors.

The inside of the warehouse was gloomy, but his eyes had already become accustomed to the dark. The smell of tea leaves and mouldy wood filled his nostrils. Looking about the cavernous space, he saw a staircase leading up to a landing on the first floor.

Wetting his lips, he set off towards it.

Reaching the stairs, he tested the bottom step for creaks. Satisfied, he began to climb, taking care of where he placed his feet. At the top, he saw a room in front of him. In some distant past, it had probably been the warehouse overseer's office. Now, the large windows that would have given the man a view of his workers were made blind by thick curtains.

Creeping along, Castros made it to the door. Golden light spieled under a crack at its bottom. He paused, swallowing hard.

'Arrgh!' a voice cried from the other side.

'Dammit all!' Castros said and threw the door open.

For a moment, he stood, dazed by the sudden brightness of the room. He blinked, and the room came into focus. It was empty except for a chair with an audiogram player upon it.

'What in the—'

A spike of blue pain shot out from the base of his neck. The world went black.

# CHAPTER SEVENTEEN

Cirona stared at the lifeless form of Bellina and fought back tears. A shaft of light was falling across the young woman's face as she lay in the bed, casting deep pools of shadow in the sockets of her eyes. Dahlia was squeezing a cloth over Bellina's mouth, dripping some foul concoction past her colourless lips that a medificer had made up. *She looks like a corpse*, Cirona thought, watching the scene.

The others were all gathered in the small room that had been given over to Bellina's nursing care. It was located in the Palace of Administration as the Lord Chancellor was practically living there at the moment. Cirona felt lost at sea, trapped in a vast ocean of regret and self-recrimination. If only she hadn't been drinking. If only she had been more alert to the danger. If only she had been doing her job properly.

She took a deep breath and looked at the floor. Inside, her stomach was roiling, churning its contents — what little there was, given her lack of appetite — in tumbling spasms of nausea. In her head, the images of what had happened played out in a circle; except in these, she did her duty, keeping Bellina safe.

There was a knock at the door. A clerk's head slunk round its edge. 'Major Bouchard?'

'Yes,' Cirona said, her mouth and throat feeling like they were lined with thick cotton.

'The Lord Chancellor will see you now.'

Nodding, Cirona stood. She felt the gaze of the others fall upon her but didn't have the strength to meet their eyes. Her chin dropped to her chest, and she left the room on legs that were made of lead. They walked up a corridor, the whispers of the clerks and bureaucrats reaching her ears.

'Pissed as a fart, apparently …'

'Taken hostage, I heard …'

'Should be hung, if you ask …'

Cirona scrunched up her eyes, trying to block out the noise.

At last, they reached a doorway. The clerk knocked, and the Lord Chancellor's barked command to enter came from the other side. Opening the door for her, the clerk stood aside, and Cirona entered. She heard the door close again behind her, shutting with the finality of a tombstone.

She stood there, eyes cast at the ground, silence growing pregnant around her. Cirona felt the gaze of the Lord Chancellor boring into her with the intensity of a welding torch.

*Meet his eyes, you coward*, a voice at the back of her mind cried out. *You owe him that much.*

Lifting a head that felt as though weights were hung from its jaw, Cirona met the Lord Chancellor's gaze. She had been prepared for anger, hate even, but the look of deep disappointment and hurt was a million times worse. Only vestiges of the vital, commanding man she had known hung around him now. *Gods*, she thought, stifling a gasp, *how much has all of this taken out of him.*

'So,' the Lord Chancellor said, gesturing a weary hand at a sheaf of papers. 'This does not make for happy reading.'

Cirona opened her mouth to say something, but the words died in her throat. How could she express the molten ball of regret spinning like a planet in her stomach with such a pathetic word as 'sorry'.

'You know,' the Lord Chancellor continued, 'I would have expected a balls-up like this from Lovitz, but you?'

'Lord Chancellor, I … I am ready to accept any punishment you deem appropriate.'

The Lord Chancellor gave a smile that didn't reach his eyes. 'You may regret those words,' he said. 'Follow me.'

He rose from his desk and strode out of the door. Cirona trailed behind him, her chest tightening. They stalked through the halls of the building and came to a single door. Two guards stood before it. They nodded to the Lord Chancellor and opened it. Cirona and the Lord Chancellor entered and began to descend a spiralling staircase of roughly cut stone.

Torches flared on the walls, illuminating their passage. As they went deeper, the air began to cool, the stone of the wall to her right damp to the touch. Finally, they reached the bottom. Before them was a large rectangular space, the front of which was blocked off by a wall made of iron bars. Behind the bars, she could see a thin corridor stretching away, studded here and there with thick, sturdy doors. The scent of piss, stale sweat and blood assaulted her nose, behind that, another smell, something she couldn't place her finger on … then she had it — fear.

*Gorphin's Hole*, she thought, her legs almost buckling as a wave of dizziness swept over her. There had been rumours of the gaol, the type of rumours only whispered about after a gut-load of ale, but she had never really believed the torture dungeon of Estria's most depraved Emperor really existed.

*Here you are, though*, the insidious voice at the back of her head hissed. *The deepest, darkest pit your country could throw you into. And you know what? You deserve it.*

She stood up straighter. If this was to be her fate, she would meet it with all the dignity she could muster.

From the darkness of the corridor, a small man wearing a hood came towards them. He bowed to the Lord Chancellor and opened a gate in the iron wall.

'Another for our humble home so soon, my lord?' the man said.

'No,' the Lord Chancellor replied. Cirona felt a surge of relief come over her, so powerful it threatened to send her to the floor. 'I am here to see our newest resident.'

'Right-o, m'lord. Don't think he'll be up to much talking though — we been keeping him drugged up and asleep jus' like you told us,' the gaoler said, setting off ahead of them down the corridor.

After what felt like an age, they reached a back wall with a single door in it. In front of that, stood five heavily armed guards in full armour, holding shields made from a strange black metal. Cirona looked at the shields for a moment, her brow furrowed. Where had she seen that metal before?

'Open it,' the Lord Chancellor said.

One of the guards snapped to attention and opened the door, hurrying away from the opening as if he expected a gout of flame to shoot out at him. The Lord Chancellor looked at the man. The guard coughed and turned his attention to the floor. With a shake of his head, the Lord Chancellor went through the opening. Cirona wet her lips and followed.

The door was shut behind them, and Cirona took in the cell they were now in. They stood in a thin space just in front of another wall of iron bars. *No*, she thought, *not iron ... that weird metal again; just what the hells ...?* In a flash, she knew what it was — tharg's bane. Whoever was in the cell was a person of magical capabilities.

'Do you recognise this man?' the Lord Chancellor asked, pointing towards a body covered with a threadbare blanket.

Cirona pushed her face up to the bars and gazed in, squinting to make out the man's features. She gripped the iron bars, her knuckles whitening. Blood thrashed in her ears, building louder, an army of drums beating just for her. There, in front of her, was the man who had tried to take the life of the Emperor. There, in front of her, was the man who had taken Trafford from her. There was Castros Del Var.

***

Elvgren paced up and down the room wondering just what in the hells was keeping the major. By his count, she had been in her meeting with the Lord Chancellor for over an hour now, and the wait was heightening the anxiety he always felt before a conference with the man.

As he walked, he went through what he was going to say in his mind. He had already given a written report to one of the clerks, making sure to highlight the major's drunkenness and dereliction of duty, hoping to divert the wrath of the Lord Chancellor away from himself. Despite that, the truth remained — the mission had ended in disaster.

In the two days they had been back, the newsprints had been full of the events that had transpired in Escambria. Garand had been elected Prima Lurista and had accused the Estrians of sacrilege, violating the heart of Lumanism and burning down the palace compound. *Well, I suppose we were slightly at fault for part of the fire*, he thought, looking towards Holger.

His lips curled as he stared at him, taking in the young man's bandaged hands. His natural distaste for the man had only been heightened by the revelation of his powers. A mage, a filthy mage had been by their side this whole time. A sour taste filled Elvgren's mouth, and he suddenly felt a strong desire to scrub his skin till it was raw.

*If it wasn't for him, you would never have got away*, a voice in his mind sang out. He pushed the idea back and away, squeezing it into whatever recess of his mind it had slunk out of.

'For fuck's sake, Gren, will you stand still? You're making me dizzy,' Dargo said.

'What?' Elvgren replied, his mind still a million miles away.

'Still. You. Five seconds. Don't think that rug can take much more pacing.'

Reluctantly, Elvgren forced his legs to be still.

Dargo sniffed. 'She ... er ... spends a lot of her time unconscious, don't she?' he said, nodding at Bellina.

Elvgren followed Dargo's gesture. He watched Dahlia, still nursing Bellina, before his eyes fell on his betrothed. Her face had taken on a waxy sheen, a slight yellow tinge to her flesh as if she were under gaslight. He bit his lip and looked away.

The minutes crawled by and Elvgren resumed his pacing. After what felt like aeons, the door to the room opened, and the clerk who had taken Cirona came for him. The major was nowhere in sight. *Don't read too much into it*, he thought as he followed his guide. Before long, they reached the Lord Chancellor's office and Elvgren was hurried inside.

The door clunked shut behind, making him jump just a fraction. In front of him, the Lord Chancellor sat, sipping from a teacup.

'Have a look at that,' the man said, lowering his china cup and using his little finger to point at a newsprint on his desk.

Elvgren read the headline out loud. 'Northern Heathens: Tremore supports Prima Lurista's calls to excommunicate Estria from the Church,' he said. His mouth suddenly became very dry. 'I have not seen this article anywhere, my lord.'

'That's because it is tomorrow's paper. I'm privy to such things.'

The Lord Chancellor's gaze burned into Elvgren's. The young lord looked at the floor and said, 'My lord, I … please forgive me. The whole mission was a disaster from the start and—'

The Lord Chancellor raised a hand, cutting him off. Elvgren winced, ready for the verbal tirade he was about to receive.

'I know, Lovitz. I never thought the major would take meeting her daughter so hard. I also underestimated Garand. Both things were my mistake. You did the best you could, boy,' he said.

Elvgren felt his thoughts freeze like a fox caught by a farmer on the way to a chicken coop. His mouth fell open. He had expected anger, the very wrath of the gods to explode from the man. Instead, he thought he heard … no, was damn well sure, he had heard sympathy in the Lord Chancellor's voice.

'Take a seat, lad. We have much to discuss.'

Nodding, Elvgren took the chair in front of the Lord Chancellor's desk.

'What do you make of the headline?'

Shaking his head, Elvgren tried to get his stunned mind back in gear. 'I … um … It would seem the Duke of Tremore is looking to use the … er … problems in Escambria to make a power play,' he said.

'Indeed,' the Lord Chancellor said. 'I know a pincer movement when I see one. Escambria from the east, Tremore from the west. Both have already ordered that their men be released from the Imperial Armed Forces.'

'But that would cut our manpower by more than a quarter!' Elvgren said.

'Yes,' the Lord Chancellor replied. 'It would.'

Silence descended like a winter's frost over the room.

'This whole scenario has been set up. Planned for gods only know how many years,' the Lord Chancellor finally said.

'Surely not, my lord! Such treason is … well … unimaginable,' Elvgren replied.

'When it comes to Tremore and the current duke, no treachery is beyond them,' the Lord Chancellor said with a sigh. 'Over the years I have foiled countless attempts by our dear friend, Duke Tobért Vontanza, all of the plots having one aim.'

'The Imperial Throne,' Elvgren whispered.

The Lord Chancellor nodded. 'From birth Tobért has been fed all the old myths and fantasies of his homeland. How Tremore should have been the seat of the Empire. That the Vontanzas are the true heirs of Amlith,' he said.

'Tosh,' Elvgren spat.

'Regardless of any credence the stories have, the fact remains that the duke is up to something. I need someone in his inner circle. Someone they would accept as one of their own.'

'And who would …?' Elvgren began, trailing off as he realised what the man was suggesting.

'Needless to say, it will be a dangerous assignment. My previous spies in Tremore have been rooted out, and the Tremorans will be on the alert for subterfuge. I'm sure you can imagine what fate awaits you, if you're caught.

'All further information you need is in this dossier,' the Lord Chancellor said, sliding a folder across the table. 'Leave in the morning. Tell no one. Not even Dirgo.'

'Dargo, my lord,' Elvgren corrected.

'Yes, yes, Dargo.'

Elvgren chewed at his lip, then said, 'What makes you think they will accept me so easily?'

'I will provide you with something they desire. That should help you get into their good graces. Plus'—the Lord Chancellor paused, looking him in the eye—'they will underestimate you, dismiss you as a noble fop reading the signs and leaving a sinking ship, desperate to cling to power. They will be wrong to do that … I know I was. Do you understand all I have told you?'

Fighting to keep his breath level, Elvgren said, 'I understand.'

'Good. You may leave.'

Elvgren stood, losing his balance and almost tumbling over the chair. He moved towards the door, undoing the top button of his shirt as he went.

'Oh, and one more thing,' the Lord Chancellor called after him, 'good luck.'

Just about managing a nod, Elvgren took the doorknob in his trembling hand and turned it. He took a tentative step outside and let the door close behind him.

'There you are!' a voice called at him from a little way down the hall. Elvgren turned and saw Dargo come striding towards him. 'What was all that about?'

Balling his hands into fists to stop them shaking, Elvgren said, 'Oh, you know, debriefing and all that. Nothing to worry about.'

Dargo laughed. 'The only thing I'm worried about is getting some grub; I'm fucking starving 'ere!'

Elvgren smiled, the corners of his eyes prickling. *Gods,* he thought, *how has the little rat become so important to me?*

'Well, let's do something about that then, eh? A feast is in order — all the trimmings, no expense spared.'

'What's got you so generous? You dying or something?'

Forcing a laugh, Elvgren said, 'No. I'm not dying, Dar.' He turned and walked towards the exit. No, he wasn't dying. Dying would be preferable to what would happen to him if he was caught on this next mission.

***

Castros felt his eyes creak open, though it did him little good. All he could make out was a ceiling high above him obscured by gloom. What was going on?

His mind stumbled back to consciousness, remembering. He had gone to the warehouse looking for Winston, then ... then he had been attacked. The realisation pulled his mind into sharp focus. Sweat beaded on his forehead. Where the hells was he?

He rolled onto his side, pain exploding in the base of his neck making his stomach lurch. Forcing the bile down, he sat up, eyes adjusting to the dark. Dank stone walls, iron grate, piss bucket — no doubt about it, he was in a cell. Well, whoever his captors were, they didn't know Castros Del Var. Sitting as still as he could, Castros tried to summon his powers.

Nothing happened.

Heart racing, he ran his hands over himself. His fingers came into contact with a thick curve of metal wrapped around his neck. He didn't need to see the colour of it to know what it was — an execution collar. Maybe his captors did know Castros Del Var, after all.

This wasn't good. *Now there's an understatement*, he thought. His captors knew of his abilities. They also had knowledge of his plans, had set up a trap for him at the warehouse. Whoever they were, they had excellent informants and money — tharg's bane was not cheap. There was only one person who had both of those things ...

As if summoned by his thoughts, the door to his cell opened and in strode the Lord Chancellor. 'Hello Balthazar,' he said.

'Don't you call me that! My name is Castros Del Var, and you know it.'

'That certainly isn't the name I remember giving to you,' the Lord Chancellor replied, raising an eyebrow.

Castros sat in the dark, nostrils flaring, his muscles as taut as a bowstring. 'How long have you known I was back?' he said.

'The second you set foot in Victory. Surely, you know the reach of my vultures by now,' the Lord Chancellor said, the vaguest hint of a smile tugging at the corners of his mouth.

'What do you want? Or have you just come to gloat before you chop off my head?'

'Chop off your ... no, no, no. A traitor such as you would be hung drawn and quartered. But I've not sentenced you to death, not today,' the Lord Chancellor said, fixing Castros with a stare as cold as winter frost. 'You have mastered your powers to a remarkable degree. It would be a shame to waste such an asset.'

Castros let out a harsh bark of laughter. 'You think I would ever consent to being an *asset*? I'd rather die than help you.'

The Lord Chancellor rolled his eyes. 'Why does everything have to be so dramatic with you?' He paused, examining his fingers. 'I have the book, you know?'

'The *Radiana Magnifica*?' Castros said, intrigued despite himself. Then he slapped his thigh and laughed. 'That's what all that business was about in Prinargo Luminaro! The book. Only you would take on the wrath of the Church for some dusty tome of arcane knowledge. I wonder what the humble subjects of the Empire would think if they knew *that* was your primary concern as their world falls apart.'

The Lord Chancellor took a step forwards. 'My most trusted scholar is breaking its code as we speak. Already, what we are learning confirms the prophecy—'

'Here we go! The prophecy. Superstitious nonsense dressed up as a warning.'

'Do you deny the signs? An Empire rising in the east? Civil strife? A darkness is coming, and all the players need to be on the board to counter it.'

Castros shook his head. 'You really believe it, don't you? You really think you're part of some preordained plan to fight evil. Well, you carry on. But leave me out of your madness.'

'I'm afraid that is not possible,' the Lord Chancellor said, each word spat like a bullet. 'You will travel to the Shattered Land and retrieve the White Mage.'

Castros felt his mouth fall open. 'You want me to travel to the Shattered Land. On my own. You really have lost it.'

'You would not be alone. You will be travelling with a highly decorated soldier, and a young man who you shall train as your apprentice.'

'Apprentice? What? You've found a mage and aren't going to throw him into one of the power plants?'

'At times like these, you must make use of every tool available,' the Lord Chancellor said. He looked at Castros, his lip curling. 'Otherwise, I would not be talking to you.'

'Look,' Castros said, climbing to his manacled feet, 'you could offer to send me in there with the whole Imperial Army, and I would still say no. Nothing will change my mind.'

'I wouldn't be so sure.'

The Lord Chancellor banged on the door and five guards came into Castros' cell. Four of them lined up outside, balliskets aimed at his head. The fifth opened the door to his cage. Next, the man unlocked the chains tethering Castros's legs to the wall. Coming up behind him, the guard nestled the barrel of his weapon in the base of Del Var's back.

'Move,' he said.

Sighing, Castros did as he was told. They stepped out into a long, narrow corridor, cell doors breaking up the bank of stone. Del Var knew what was going to happen. They were going to take him to one of the cells. Inside, would be a comrade. They would threaten to relieve said comrade of various body parts unless he agreed to what they wanted. It was all so predictable. All he prayed was that they didn't have Whist.

Much to his surprise, they marched past the cells. *What the hells is the old bastard playing at?* Castros thought as they climbed a spiral staircase.

'Where are we going?' Castros said.

'I'd like you to meet someone,' the Lord Chancellor replied.

Soon, they were outside a door. One of the guards opened it, and they went in. Once inside, Del Var saw a young woman next to a bed, nursing its occupant.

'How do you do?' Castros said to the girl. 'I'm Castros Del Var. Wanted terrorist and mage.'

His outburst earned him a smack between his shoulder blades with the butt of a ballisket.

'Enough,' the Lord Chancellor said, stopping the guard from any further attacks. 'I have not brought you here for her, but the one she is tending.'

Castros shot the guard a look of pure venom then turned his gaze to the bed's occupant, taking in the appearance of the second young woman. Raven-black hair surrounded a face the colour of ivory. Her eyes were closed, long lashes drawn down. Beneath an aquiline nose sat a bow-shaped mouth. Del Var felt his skin begin to tingle and a gasp escaped his mouth.

'Yes. Her resemblance to Nairne is quite striking, isn't it?' the Lord Chancellor said.

'This ... this can't be,' Castros said, his voice breaking.

'Oh, but it is,' the Lord Chancellor replied. 'Son, I would like you to meet your daughter, Bellina Ressa.'

***

Darkness ... no, that was too subtle a word. Absolute black ... that was closer but still it felt insufficient to describe what suffocated Bellina. In fact, she had no frame of reference for what surrounded her. But then that wasn't true either. She had experienced something like this before, after her fight with the kaffar.

Her consciousness spun in the black, desperately seeking something, anything, to latch onto. Fear coursed through her, but how could she be experiencing such emotions without a body?

She felt like a pinprick of light in an infinite sheet of night, a lone star illuminating nothing but her own insignificance.

Just when she thought all was lost, another speck of white flared in the black. It grew in her vision, swirling, coalescing into a shape, a person. It was Yevad, the kaffar who had rescued her from the darkness before. The wizened old man stood in front of her, his cloak of raven's feathers billowing behind him.

'Well met, Lady Bellina,' Yevad said.

Bellina went to reply, but no words came out of her mouth. Not surprising because, technically, she didn't have a mouth.

'You must focus, young one. Free yourself. I cannot save you here,' the old man said.

Twisting the entire force of what was left of her being, Bellina imagined herself. In front of her eyes, she saw her arms, legs, torso spin into existence. She looked at her hands, convinced that they would disappear at any moment.

'Where am I? What's going on?' she asked, the words not so much leaving her lips as attaining a solid reality around her.

'Easy, my lady, easy,' Yevad replied. 'You are nowhere and are also now here.'

'What does that mean?'

For a second, the form of Yevad paused, his head cocked to the side as if he heard something. He furrowed his brow before saying, 'This is the Void. the space between this life and the next. The space from which a true kaffar's power stems.'

Growing more accustomed to her new form, Bellina replied, 'The Void? But how?'

'You have been placed in this space by magic. Something powerful and ancient. The only way to escape it, to survive, is to rely on your own sense of self. Whatever else happens here, you must retain that.'

'But how? Why?' she said, a million questions buzzing inside her like a storm of angered bees.

'There is no time,' Yevad said. 'An outside force interferes with us. Stay the course. Keep yourself. Many things will make themselves known to you here — some will be truth, some will be lies. Work your way forwards and meet her. She waits for you in the deep. Perhaps, then you will understand your destiny better.'

'I—' Bellina began. But it was already too late. Yevad's form was spooling apart like a dandelion before the breeze.

'Take care, Bellina Ressa. The dangers you face here are more than real,' Yevad called as the last specks of the man were swallowed by the black.

Once more, she found herself alone.

# CHAPTER EIGHTEEN

Elvgren hefted his travel bag onto his shoulder and looked around the room. A shaft of early morning light slipped past the gap in the curtains and fell across Dargo's bed. Elvgren's gaze fell upon the boy and he smiled. He was going to miss the little bastard and no mistake.

Scrubbing a hand over his face, Elvgren crept towards the bed. On the table next to it, he lay a note and a bag of money. He reached out a hand towards Dargo's face then dropped it. He swallowed hard, forcing spit past a lump in his throat that felt like a small boulder.

Not daring to look back, he left the room.

Outside, in the crisp dawn chill, he pulled out his pocket watch — 5.30 a.m. He would have to get a move on. The information in the folder the Lord Chancellor had given him stated that he would be given a five-hour head start before the Empire would be alerted to his supposed treachery. It was all part of the ploy to get the duke to accept him. Still, it was an added tension he didn't need.

With one last look at the inn, he set off.

Already, the streets of Victory were coming to life. Shopkeepers hoisted awnings, batting the remnants of last night's rain from them with the bristle end of a broom. Delivery wagons rumbled past. From a bakery, the homely scent of fresh bread wafted. Elvgren sniffed and forced his heavy feet past it all.

Winding his way onward, Elvgren soon came to the locomotron station. The front of the building loomed before him. Bricks stained with the dirt and grime of city life formed an impressive facade. Two small towers flanked the arched entranceway. *Like hands*, Elvgren thought, the image somehow disquieting. A massive clock at the top chimed six. Cursing himself for dawdling, he went inside.

There weren't many prospective travellers at this hour. Trying to keep his wits about him, Elvgren noted the ones who were. Three elderly gentlemen were instructing a porter on how best to move their luggage, the station employee cursing under his breath as he heaved their trunks onto a trolley. A young man, dressed impeccably, looked at his watch and yawned. Calm down, Elvgren told himself, *no one's even looking for you yet.* Clutching his travel bag close, he walked to the ticket booth.

After purchasing his ticket — a non-stop service to Saprez — Elvgren made his way to the waiting locomotron, the only one in the station. He boarded the first carriage he reached and opened the door to the snug cabin. Not bothering to stash his bag, Elvgren took a seat and checked his watch — only five minutes to departure.

Stowing the timepiece, he waited. Outside his cabin, the elderly gentlemen passed by engaged in a conversation the door kept silenced from him. Elvgren chewed at a fingernail. *Just when was this bloody thing going to get moving?*

Checking his watch again, he saw that the five minutes had passed. Elvgren slid the window down and stuck his head out. A railway guard walked the length of the locomotron, a whistle dangling from his neck.

'Twelve hells, man!' Elvgren cried at him. 'Some of us have places to be.'

The man looked at him, his mouth chomping thoughtfully. He spat a jet of tobacco and said, 'Just making sure all's safe and secure ... *sir.*'

Mouth agape, Elvgren watched the man perform a sullen pantomime of checking his watch. He put his watch away, stretched, then placed the whistle in his mouth.

'For fuck's sake, blow it, you imbecile!' Elvgren roared.

The man made an obscene gesture, then finally, he gave the whistle a sharp blast.

Shaking his head, Elvgren resumed his seat. As he did, a jolt of surprise shot through him, almost forcing his heart from his chest; he was no longer alone. Across from him sat the well-dressed young man. He looked up from a book he had opened on his lap and gave Elvgren a nod before returning his eyes to the text.

Elvgren's hands fiddled with the clasp on his bag. Why in the name of the Father had the man chosen to place himself in this carriage? Elvgren found himself studying the man's face. His lips were curved in a smile, or was it a sneer? Feeling the gaze upon him, the man looked up again.

'Can I help you?' he asked.

'No ... I ... uh ... you just look familiar,' Elvgren said, offering a weak smile.

'Can't say you do, old sport,' the man replied.

'My ... um ... my mistake,' Elvgren said.

He turned his attention out the window as the man returned to his book. His nerves felt raw, like a violin string just waiting for the bow to draw across it. *For fuck's sake, get a grip*, he told himself. But it was no good. Legs shaking, he stood. The man looked up at him.

'Excuse me,' Elvgren said.

He stepped into the corridor of the locomotron's carriage, desperate to put some distance between him and the man. As he reached the door to the next car, he heard a door open behind him. He turned and saw the young man.

'Wait,' the man said.

Biting back a cry, Elvgren threw open the door with a shaking hand. Moving at just below a run he moved on.

'I say, hold up,' the man said.

Elvgren had no intention of "holding up". Instead, he barrelled forwards. *Think, think*, he told himself. Inspiration grabbed him. He sprinted to the other end of the carriage and threw open the door to the next. Doubling back on himself, Elvgren dove inside the nearest cabin and crouched just below the window. After a few seconds, he saw the young man walk past. Breathing a sigh of relief, he stood up and reached for the door handle, intending to move in the opposite direction to the man.

Behind him, he heard the sound of a ballistol being cocked.

'Don't move,' a silky voice commanded.

***

Castros stood on the prow of the small ship they were using to get to Pevontess — the closest port of call to the haunted island, which had once been the home of the mages. The morning mist was thinning, revealing the passing countryside with a dreamlike quality. Castros paid it little heed; so many thoughts spun through his head that he found it impossible to focus.

Who had sold him into the hands of the Lord Chancellor? How would Whist react to his disappearance? Was his friend the one behind it? These questions and a million others jostled for supremacy in his brain. But one kept bubbling up more than the others. How had he not known Nairne had been pregnant?

Behind his closed eyelids, the memory of the last time he had seen his love played out. They had been in a bolthole in Sylvantain, a meeting about their next operation — the hijacking of a carriage full of munitions — just ended, scribbled notes and empty bottles of cheap wine scattered around them. They were alone. A state that had been hard to come by in the weeks and months previous.

'So,' she had said, flicking her hair behind her in one graceful movement. 'You're going through with this then?'

He had bristled at the scepticism in her voice. 'If you mean to steal the weapons we need to fight our cause, then yes, yes I am.'

*Gods*, he thought, *was I really so naive? I sounded like a character in a bad play.*

'And it will be as simple as you all seem to think, will it?' Nairne had said, one eyebrow arching. 'There's going to be tons of guards—'

'We know the patterns of the guards. Their numbers. Even the route they are taking, for the Father's sake,' he had cut in, waving a hand. He met her eyes, his annoyance descending to a simmer at what he found in them. Fear. If he hadn't been looking right at her, he wouldn't have believed it, but there it was. The woman who had laughed as they robbed wealthy merchants at ballistol point, the woman who had single-handedly infiltrated a poorhouse, freeing the wretches inside, the woman who had chided him for softness, was afraid.

He had crouched beside Nairne, taking her hand. 'What's the matter?' he asked.

She had taken her hand from his and waved it around the room. 'This,' she replied. 'All of this. This isn't a life, Cass.'

'Have we ever been under the impression that it was? This is the sacrifice we make for the greater good. Yes, we're suffering now, but when we take power—'

'When we take power?' she said with a snort. 'And how long will that be? Six months? A year? What if it never happens, Cass? What if all were doing is romanticising what we really are? A bunch of people who don't fit in, taking out our frustrations on the people who have what we want.'

'You can't be serious?' he said, taking a step back.

'I am, Cass. I can't live like this any more. I want to start afresh, somewhere out of the way, living off the land like we used to talk about.'

'And we will, *once* we've achieved our aims.'

'No. It needs to be now. Not in some imagined future. We have our health. We have each other. That's all we need. And if you can't see that, I'm willing to try on my own.'

He had shaken his head and asked, 'Where is this coming from?'

With a gesture he now saw steeped in meaning, Nairne's hand moved a fraction towards her stomach. 'People change, Cass. It may be a cliché, but it's true,' she said.

'Well, I haven't. I still know what I have to do, what I *need* to do.'

Sighing, she had stood and walked to where she had a travel bag prepared with her things. 'I hope you do, Cass, I really do.'

With that, she had gone.

Pride had stopped him chasing after her. Pride had stopped him from finding her in the days that followed. Pride had made him believe that she would be back, that she couldn't possibly live without him. And then, almost a year later, he had got the news of her death, how she had been—

No. That was one wound he wouldn't dig into now.

The squawk of a bird drew him back to the present. Feeling eyes upon him, he turned. There stood Major Bouchard, a look of pure hate carved onto her face. Used to such responses, Castros smiled and waved. He knew he was adding fuel to the fire and took a small bead of delight when the woman stormed away, a vein at her temple pulsing madly.

'She'll warm to you,' a voice called from his side.

Castros looked around and saw the young man who was to be his apprentice. He had the pale hair and blue eyes of a Narvglander. An air of honest openness seemed to surround him, reminding him of Whist.

'I certainly hope so, or this trip will be exceedingly tedious,' Castros replied, forcing a smile on his face. 'It's Holger, right?'

'Yes, sir ... I mean Mr Del ... um ...'

'Call me Castros.'

'Alright ... Castros,' Holger replied.

'So, you're a flamer, eh?' Castros asked, looking at the boy's bandaged hands.

'I ... well ... I suppose I am,' Holger said. 'It's not as bad as it looks. Healing up a treat thanks to the medic's balm.'

'A fire mage can never truly damage himself with what he conjures. Still, we'll need to work through all the basics if we're going to get you to the point where your power is more help than hindrance,' Castros said.

'That would be ... good,' Holger replied, a slight frown creasing his brow.

'Don't worry, lad,' Castros said, patting him on the back. 'I'll train you in how to be one of the most reviled creatures in the Empire. Let's just hope they don't slam us in a sortilenergy plant when we return.'

*If we return, more like*, Castros thought with a shudder.

***

Elvgren felt his stomach turn into a solid lump of cold steel and plummet to his feet. Surely, he couldn't have been captured already? The Lord Chancellor's vultures worked fast, but this would be ridiculous.

'Turn around. Slowly,' the voice behind him commanded.

Licking his lips, the salt of his sweat stinging his tongue, Elvgren did as he was told. He came face-to-face with the elderly trio he had seen boarding the locomotron. Confronted with his geriatric, would-be abductors, Elvgren's first instinct was to laugh. The impulse died, stillborn, when he saw the blaze of anger in their eyes.

'Look here, chaps,' Elvgren said, forcing a smile onto his lips. 'I have no idea what slight I may have caused you, but the ballistol is a tad over the top, eh?'

'Silence, you animal,' the ballistol wielder hissed. 'Keep your serpent's tongue still. Bertram?'

'Yes, Ambrose?' one of the man's cohorts answered.

'Get the rope and gag,' Ambrose said.

'Let's talk about this,' Elvgren said. 'Whatever this is about, we can settle it like ...' The rest of his words slipped back down his throat as he saw the crystal pendants dangling from the necks of the men. 'You're part of the Order of Light.'

'Indeed, we are,' Ambrose snarled. 'You shall answer for your defilement at Prinargo Luminaro, heathen.'

Bertram finished locating the rope and stepped forwards. Elvgren's head felt light enough to float off his shoulders. This couldn't be happening? Was he really about to be captured by three old farts belonging to an obscure sect of the Lumanist faith? No. He wasn't going to let them have it that easy.

His feet inched back towards the door.

'Do not move!' Ambrose cried, the ballistol trembling in his grasp.

Another half step back.

'I will not tell you again!'

Arm reaching back, Elvgren felt for the handle. His fingers touched it. Before he could grasp it, the handle revolved.

'Tickets please!' A voice yelled behind him.

Elvgren lurched forwards as the voice's owner shoved him hard in the back. He collided with the advancing Bertram and the pair spiralled into Ambrose and the third member of the kidnapping gang.

'Argh!' Ambrose cried, falling backwards.

The ballistol went off, the sound of it amplified in the small cabin. The bullet zipped past Elvgren's right ear, singeing the flesh where it passed, and lodged itself in the roof.

Making the most of the confusion, Elvgren disentangled himself from the old men and turned towards the door. His breath caught in his throat then a smile built at the corners of his mouth.

'Dargo,' he said.

'Not too good at this covert business are you, Gren? You didn't notice my tail, and the cod-liver-oil trio caught you in, oh, let's make it an hour to be nice,' Dargo said, shaking his head.

'Yes, yes,' Elvgren replied, hurrying towards Dargo. 'Let's get out of here. Find the guard and—'

Another ballistol shot cracked the air, bullet clipping Elvgren's shoulder. He turned around, and saw the third man, weapon smoking in his hand.

'Think that might be our cue to leg it,' Dargo said.

Elvgren nodded and darted out of the room, slamming the door behind them. Dargo lifted his automaton leg and bent the handle with his heel, jamming the door.

'That should hold 'em for a bit,' he said, as the three Order of Light members started banging against the wood.

'This way,' Elvgren said, advancing down the carriage.

They made their way through the train at a sprint. At last, they saw the guard checking tickets in the dining car. The carriage's only occupant was an elderly woman, a steaming cup of black tea in front of her.

'Guard, thank the gods,' Elvgren said.

The man swung round, a crystal on a silver necklace bobbing at his throat.

Elvgren's eyes turned into saucers. 'Shit,' he said. 'Back, Dargo, back. Quickly, the other way.'

The pair spun round and headed back the way they had come, the guard's cries to stop echoing in their ears. As they entered the connecting carriage, Elvgren saw the three elderly men.

'We're trapped,' he said.

'No shit,' Dargo replied. 'Hang on a minute, though.'

Dargo pushed the outside door open. Through the gap, Elvgren saw the rocky terrain whizz past. They both cried out in exasperation; they were not going to be jumping.

'Alright,' Dargo said, 'follow me.'

He gripped the edge of the door and swivelled out of sight.

'Dargo!' Elvgren cried, rushing to the door. Looking to his left he saw the boy dangling below a carriage window, inching himself along it with his fingertips.

'Come on,' he called.

The blade of a knife buried itself into the wood above Elvgren's fingertips. Needing no further prompting, he grabbed the door frame and spun outside.

'Damn it all,' he heard a hoarse voice cry. 'Ambrose, take your men and get to the next connecting carriage. Block them off. I'll follow this way.'

'Understood,' Ambrose replied.

Edging himself along as fast as he could, Elvgren followed in Dargo's wake. A shot rang out, shattering the window above Elvgren's head.

'You're as good as dead, heathen!' the guard called, discarding his smoking ballistol and beginning to climb along after them.

'Move your bony arse, Gren,' Dargo called.

Looking towards him, Elvgren saw that the boy was almost at the next connecting carriage. The door just ahead of Dargo flew open and Ambrose appeared, a fresh ballistol in his hand.

'Up, Dar, go up!' Elvgren yelled, hoping that his voice carried above the wind whistling around them.

The weapon went off, bullet sparking against the metal of the carriage and leaving a hole where Dargo's head had been mere seconds before. Elvgren watched Dargo scuttle onto the top of the locomotron and sprint back towards him.

'Grab me hand, Gren. Quick!' Dargo said.

Elvgren took his hand and felt himself fly upwards, Dargo's strength aided by his mechanical leg.

'Oh no you don't,' the guard called and began to scale the carriage.

'Why. Won't. You. Piss. Off!' Elvgren said, stamping at the guard's fingers.

'Whoa,' Dargo hollered as a shot burst through the metal between his feet. 'Leave him, Gren; we gotta move.'

Taking one last stomp at the guard, Elvgren set off after Dargo. Shards of metal exploded around them while the elderly members from the Order of Light took potshots at them from below. They leapt from roof to roof but were fast running out of carriages. Ahead of them, the final car of the locomotron loomed. It was an old goods cart, its top made of stretched canvas instead of metal. With no other option they jumped onto it.

'End of the line,' the guard said behind them.

'I suppose you think that's bloody witty, do you?' Elvgren said.

'Yeah, talk about cliché,' Dargo said, nodding.

'Shut it,' the guard said, pulling a dagger from his coat pocket as he advanced.

He made a mad lunge at them. Elvgren and Dargo stumbled backwards, the blade whistling past Elvgren's nose and tearing a gash in the canvas roof.

'Crap!' he said as the entire thing gave way.

The air burst from his lungs when his body connected with the corner of a large wooden container. The rest of Elvgren's body crumpled to the floor, multi-coloured sparks dancing before his eyes. Struggling to gain a breath, he hauled his head up just in time to see all four of their pursuers moving towards them.

'Dar, shut that bloody door!' Elvgren called.

'Nah,' Dargo said, 'I've got a better idea.'

Staying low, Dargo made his way towards the men, fiddling with a dial on his automaton leg. Startled by his boldness, the Order of Light paused for a moment.

'See ya later,' Dargo said and promptly aimed a blistering kick at the train coupling.

With a shriek, the carriages came apart. Elvgren and Dargo's carriage fell behind as the rest of the locomotron sped away. Gaining his feet, Elvgren moved up beside Dargo and made an obscene gesture at their pursuers. Soon the men were nothing but wildly gesticulating dots in the distance.

As the car came to a standstill, Dargo hopped out. Elvgren followed.

'Never a dull moment, eh?' Dargo said with a lopsided grin.

'You can say that again,' Elvgren replied with a smile of his own.

He watched Dargo stretch, stunned as always by the boy's ability to absorb the madness around him.

'Better get going before they come back for us,' he said.

'I make you right, Dar,' Elvgren replied.

'Which way's Tremore then?'

'Oh, I don't know,' Elvgren said with a sniff and pointed into the distance, 'about five hundred miles in that direction.'

'Come on then,' Dargo said, setting off. 'And don't even think about leaving me behind again.'

Elvgren smiled and shook his head. 'I wouldn't dream of it, Dar,' he said. 'I wouldn't dream of it.'

***

Bellina fell. She fell for so long she feared it would be forever. Then her imagined body collided with something and her descent stopped. Trying to regain her breath, she lay still. Something more than air came to her as she gasped. A scent. It was the scent of wet earth, the scent of stagnant water, the scent of ... a marsh.

Gazing at her hands, Bellina saw a whole world throb into existence. Grass, trees, water ... all of it familiar. Where had she seen it before? For a moment, the knowledge danced at the edge of understanding; then she had it — it was Alcastus' marsh, part of his psychic defences.

A tightness arose in her chest, squeezing it with remorseless iron fingers. This *couldn't* be Alcastus' psychic landscape. The man was a gibbering wreck in some sanatorium or other, and she had been the one who put him there.

'Did you enjoy it?' a rasping voice echoed.

Bellina spun on the spot, her toes struggling for purchase on the wet ground, trying to find the voice's owner. A cold sweat broke across her brow as she realised it was coming from everywhere.

'Who are you?' she yelled. 'What do you want?'

'Admit it. Admit that you enjoyed it,' the voice said.

'Show yourself!' Bellina said in the most commanding tone she could muster.

'Very well.' The voice now hissed into her ear.

Feeling the icy touch of a hand upon her shoulder, Bellina turned, slipping on the sodden grass and mud. She landed hard on her arse, a jolt of pain spearing its way up her spine. The sensation soon vanished, replaced by a freezing wave of fear as she looked up into the eyes of her former cognopathic instructor.

'Alcastus,' she said, the words slipping from her lips only a breath above a whisper.

'Indeed, my *lady*,' he replied, taking a step forward.

Bellina scrabbled to reach her feet, but Alcastus placed a heel on her shoulder and forced her back to the ground. He was nothing like she remembered the last time she had seen him. Somehow, he was in fine health. No. It was more than that. He seemed more vital, more intimidating, appearing with the size and strength he had possessed in her childhood nightmares.

Straddling her middle, Alcastus hissed, 'Tell me now, tell me how it felt when you broke me.'

'I ...' Bellina said, swallowing hard.

'Yes,' Alcastus replied, leering down at her.

'I ... I loved every fucking second of it,' she said, spitting the words at him.

Alcastus howled with laughter, a base animal sound. 'Fantastic, just fantastic. It really is, my dear. And you know what?' he said, leaning forwards, his nose inches from her own. 'I enjoyed everything I did to you. Stealing into your mind when you were nothing but a girl. Exploring every nook and cranny of you. So much more intimate than sex ... at least, that's how I always felt.'

'You vile pig!' Bellina cried. 'I destroyed you once, and I'll damn well do it again.' Focusing her mind, Bellina pushed against Alcastus, pushed with every ounce of her might.

Nothing happened.

Moving his mouth to her ear, he whispered, 'You are powerless here, my sweet, sweet girl.'

'I am never powerless,' Bellina replied.

She drove her forehead into Alcastus' nose. Much to her satisfaction, she felt the cartilage smush. With a yelp of pain, the man reared back. In one motion, she pulled herself into a sitting position and, using her momentum, shoved her former tutor as hard as she could. Still clasping at his nose, he fell backwards.

Scrambling to her feet, Bellina ran. Ahead of her, she could see where the imagined landscape turned into a jungle, the freezing bog giving way to an impossible jungle. Huge leaves dripping with moisture slapped her around the face, her feet snagged on hidden vines, but on she ran.

'That's it, run!' Alcastus cackled from all around her. 'This will be fun.'

*Don't listen, don't listen, DON'T LISTEN!* A voice inside her head screamed.

This couldn't be happening; it couldn't be real. She had to remember what Yevad had told her. She had to keep hold of herself.

'You can try to, my child,' Alcastus said, seeming to read her thoughts. 'But I know you even better than you know yourself.

'I know that you sucked your thumb far beyond the point of it being cute. How you would fall asleep with it in your mouth. I know how many times you wet the bed. I know how much you feared and hated me. I know how all the other noble children would laugh and point and hit you with things when the adults weren't looking. I know—'

'Shut up, shut up, shut up,' Bellina said.

Clasping her hands over her ears, she closed her eyes, desperate to block out Alcastus' taunts. She just had to ignore them, get some space, some *time*, to think, and then she could—

'Argh!' she cried as her foot ran onto thin air.

Her eyes snapped open as she fell, body pirouetting through the air, a brittle leaf caught in a gust of wind. She landed on the edge of a sandy bank, leaving a plume of gritty particles in her wake. Skidding to a stop and coughing up a mouthful of dust, she pushed herself up. With a start, she realised that her arms were too short, her fingers pudgy and dirt rimmed. It wasn't just her arms either — it was her whole body.

Looking up, she realised she had fallen into a hole, small in circumference but deep. She watched Alcastus appear at the lip of the pit.

'What have you done to me?' Bellina yelled in the shrill squeak of a child.

'I have done nothing,' he replied, smiling. 'You have done this to yourself. You have let fear rule you. Now you will die.'

Beneath her, Bellina felt the sand begin to shift. *No*, she thought, *not shift, sink*. With the sound of her heart thundering in her ears, Bellina tried desperately to claw her way up the sloped sides of the pit. Her tiny fingers caught the surface then slipped, the now rapid suction of the sand allowing no purchase.

'I could make this stop, you know,' Alcastus said, inspecting his nails. 'But you'll have to beg for it.'

'Never,' Bellina replied.

Sighing, Alcastus said, 'You always were such a stubborn brat.'

'I don't need you. I never needed you,' she cried, still trying to climb.

A blast of ice seared through her as she realised her left foot was stuck. Turning to look, Bellina saw that it was now below the sand. Chest hitching for air, she grabbed at it and tried to pull it free. All that happened was the rest of her leg became submerged.

Faster than she ever could have imagined, her right leg disappeared. The sand was up to her stomach, then level with her chest, then her collarbone.

'Scream, plead, beg, cajole ... something,' Alcastus said with a rueful shake of the head. 'Otherwise, it will all be over disappointingly quick.'

'Screw you ... you twisted old bastard. I hope, wherever you are, you're talking nonsense and shitting yourself, knowing what happened to you, knowing what I did to you,' she said, the sand at her throat.

'Last chance,' Alcastus said. 'Not going to ask me? No? Very well. I shall savour your last moments then.'

Bellina went to reply but her mouth filled with sand. Retching she tried to clear her throat, the pressure on her body immense. Then it was above her nose.

Then she was gone.

***

Cirona sat in the ship's hold. Her eyes were fixed on the sleeping form of Castros Del Var hanging in a nearby hammock. She noted the rise and fall of his chest, the slight parting of his lips as he exhaled. She watched it all, knowing that each one he took drew him closer to his last.

In her lap sat her sword, a small whetting stone in her hand. As she ran the stone over the blade's edge, her mind turned to the Lord Chancellor. She had always known he was merciless in his punishments, but it wasn't until he tasked her with this mission that she knew how cruel he truly was.

With an unobserved eye, she had watched as the degenerate had used his charm on Holger. Hells, even some of the small, handpicked crew who had started off avoiding him like the plague were warming to him. But she saw. She knew what he was. A murderer and a traitor. You could dress it up in as many ideals as you liked, but that was the simple truth.

A black rage had settled upon her, like a murder of crows flying through her veins, spreading their wings into every corner of her being. She found it almost soothing, comforting, after all her recent second guessing. It gave her strength. The strength to endure whatever lay ahead. Not just so they could heal Bellina, but so she could claim her revenge.

Castros gave a small start in his sleep. Cirona paused to watch as the man turned over onto his side. How could he sleep so easily with all the atrocities he had been party to? She almost laughed, realising he probably never spared a second thought for the lives him and his men had taken, the families they had torn apart.

Rising to her feet, Cirona moved towards Del Var as if pulled by some dark magnet. Her hands trembled so hard at her sides she had to force them into fists. All over, her skin began to tingle, and she licked her lips.

Soon. Soon, she would kill the bastard.

# CHAPTER NINETEEN

No air. Gagging, choking. Death. Dying. I'm dying. No way out. Can't breathe, can't breathe; by the Father, I *can't* BREATHE. Movement. Upwards movement. Pain easing. Chugging, spitting. Air, glorious, blessed air. A person above her. Who? Sounds. Words. Speaking. The person was speaking.

'Master Ressa? Master Ressa you must stand.'

'D-Dahlia?' Bellina replied.

'Yes, Master. Hurry. I've managed to contain him for now, but my trap won't hold for long.'

Chest burning, Bellina managed, with Dahlia's help, to stagger to her feet. In front of her she could see Alcastus. He was trapped inside a cage of trees, the branches arching up and over him, twining together into bars.

'How in the world did you manage to ...' Bellina began.

'With a great degree of difficulty,' Dahlia replied.

Bellina looked at her fellow cognopath's face. Sweat streamed down Dahlia's brow, her face red, nostrils quivering with each ragged breath.

'Master, you must banish him,' Dahlia said.

'What? How? My powers don't work here,' Bellina replied, rubbing her temples.

'This is all coming from you,' Dahlia said, flinching as Alcastus raged at his entrapment.

'I-I don't understand.'

'Wherever this place is, you are giving form to it. It's drawing on your deepest emotions, drawing from your darkest subconscious, making this, making *him*,' Dahlia said.

Taking a step back, Bellina murmured, 'No, I can't be ... why, why can't I stop it then?'

'Fear,' Dahlia whispered, her eyes fixed on Alcastus. 'Believe me, Master, I understand why. In the compound Alcastus, he ...'

Bellina felt her breath catch. How could she have not realised? If she had felt so violated by Alcastus' training, training she had gone through in the comfort of her own home, gods only knew how he had treated Dahlia and the rest of his charges at the cognopath compound.

The sound of splintering wood resounded around them. Bellina turned to see Alcastus forcing his way through the branches.

'Master Ressa, please, I beg of you, stop him!' Dahlia said, a tear trickling from the corner of her eye and merging with the sweat.

Taking a deep breath, Bellina thrust her shoulders back and marched towards Alcastus. Strong, she needed to be strong. With each step she took, her former instructor seemed to shrink inward, shrivelling like a grape left in the sun.

'Go from here,' she heard herself say.

'No,' the shrunken creature in front of her rasped. 'I had you. You were mine!'

'You're nothing but a pathetic old man. That's all you ever were.'

Reaching out her hand, Bellina pushed against Alcastus' chest. He stumbled back, arms cartwheeling. His body hit the ground with a soft thump and burst into a million glistening particles. For a moment, the particles hung in the air, then with a puff of wind, they were gone.

Bellina tilted her face upwards, a feeling of lightness spreading through her. With a brisk nod, she turned back towards Dahlia. The girl had crumpled to her knees, chin trembling, tears beading on her lashes.

'Are you alright?' Bellina asked, holding out her hand.

'I-I will be fine, Master,' Dahlia replied, taking the offered hand.

Bellina rolled her eyes. 'For heaven's sake, call me, Bellina,' she said with a smile.

'Thank you ... Bellina,' Dahlia said, raising her eyes.

For a second, their eyes locked. Feeling heat rising to her cheeks, Bellina turned away a fraction.

'Well,' she said, 'we had best find a way out of here.'

'I'm ... I'm afraid there isn't one,' Dahlia replied.

'What do you mean?' Bellina asked.

Dahlia swallowed and said, 'You are in a coma. That purgista, Garand, he did it with some kind of magic. Do you not remember?'

The moments before she had found herself in the darkness passed before Bellina's eyes. Of course it was Garand. Bellina bit her lip, stomach rolling like a loose barrel.

'So ... I'm trapped here?' she whispered.

'Not necessarily,' Dahlia replied. 'Your father, the Lord Chancellor, he has sent the major on a mission to retrieve someone who can lift this ailment.'

'And what am I supposed to do in the meantime?' Bellina said. 'Sit here and wait?'

From the trees around them a terrible roar ripped through the air, bloodlust and destruction embedded in every note.

'I fear you will have to do a lot more than that,' Dahlia replied.

***

The locket sat in Castros' palm, cool and smooth. Hand trembling, he clicked a button on its side and watched it pop open. Inside was a lock of Nairne's hair, untouched by the years that had passed since she had gifted it to him. For so long, it had been his last physical link to her, but now there was something more.

A daughter, Bellina, a cognopath like her mother before her, a solid link between the past and the present, history locked in the atoms of her being. He wanted to know if she shared more with Nairne — a smile, a laugh, liking the same foods.

Castros rubbed at the middle of his forehead. A father, *he* was a father. The weight of the thought pressed upon him, crushing the space around his heart. Could he deal with that responsibility? Would they gel together once she was awake, slotting into his soul like a long-lost part?

Scrubbing a hand across his face, he took a deep breath. Those were questions for later. Now, he had a job to do. A job that he was one of the only people qualified to do. He would do it. He would save her; save her like he hadn't been able to save Nairne.

'L-land ho,' a tentative voice called from the deck.

Castros stood, tucked the locket back in its pocket and strode towards the entry hatch. He climbed out into a fine drizzle, the tiny droplets of rain hanging in the air like minuscule diamonds. At the prow, he saw Holger. The boy was turned away from him, observing the mass of rocky cliffs rising in front of him.

The Shattered Land.

The forbidding mountain ranges of the former island kingdom speared upwards, dark shards of glass waiting for an unsuspecting foot to tread upon them. Around him, Castros could sense the apprehension of the small crew. He certainly didn't blame them. Everything they had ever been taught as children about the place was foreboding. This was the country High Mage Excellus had set out from to conquer Estria three hundred years ago. The home of his twisted planning and grasping. From here, his army had marched, conquering all in its path. Enslaving humanity as it went. Only Victory had stood against him. A shudder passed through Castros as he thought of the ghosts that inhabited the cursed place. Shaking his head like a wet dog, Castros made his way towards Holger.

'Quite a sight, isn't it?' he said.

'You can say that again,' Holger replied.

Tension crept into Del Var's muscles. 'I know this can't be easy for you ... or the major, for that matter,' he said.

'W-what do you mean?' Holger asked, turning to meet his gaze.

'Well, this is it, isn't it? The birthplace of nightmares, a place burned into our minds as somewhere to hate. Not easy to shake those ideas.'

'Wouldn't have thought you'd find it so intimidating,' Holger said.

Castros wet his lips. 'There was a time when I didn't know I was a demi-mage. I grew up with the same stories and lessons you did. By the time I found out about my mother being a mage she was dead and my father ... well, I don't like to talk about him,' he said.

Holger frowned. 'Why are you telling me this?' he asked

'We're going to run into a lot of madness. Not just here, but in the future as well. We need to trust each other, if we're going to come out of this alive.'

Castros let the information sink in for a second. He watched as Holger's face scrunched up in thought. It had to be hard for the boy: travelling to the Shattered Land, his exposure as a mage — a whole life turned upside down.

'I-I trust you Castros. At least, I think I do,' he said. 'Plus,' he continued in little more than a whisper, 'I would do anything to save Belle.'

Del Var tilted his head to the side and let out a low whistle. 'You ... love her, don't you?' he said.

'I do. We were meant to be together. It's fate. Destiny!' Holger said, not even the smallest hint of embarrassment entering his voice, eyes burning with a passion that threatened to tumble into obsession.

A silence fell over them. The pair stood looking at the Shattered Land for a few minutes. The clouds hung heavy over it, the sea a slate grey. There were no birds above the former country.

'Sometimes, I wonder why,' Castros said, fixing the island with a glare.

'What?'

'I wonder why Excellus did it. Try to take over Estria, I mean. For thousands of years, humanity and the mages lived side by side. What did he learn that changed him?'

'I always thought he was just a nutter. That he hated humans,' Holger said.

'That's the official line,' Castros said, frowning. 'But I don't buy it. The truth is no one really knows. Never will, I suppose.' Del Var scratched his chin. 'Well, we'll be there soon. Make sure you're all set.'

He flashed Holger a smile and then walked to the steering cabin, hoping he looked more confident than he felt.

***

Cirona stared towards the smashed remnants of a lighthouse, the moss-eaten brick gaping open like a festering wound. The rest of the small harbour was in a similar state of decay, the smell of rotting wood mingling with the salty tang of the sea. She allowed herself a small shudder.

'This is as far as I'll go. You'll have to take the row boat from 'ere,' the ship's captain said.

'Fine. Thank you,' Del Var replied.

'Don't need no thanks. Orders is orders, 'specially when they come from the Lord Chancellor,' the captain replied.

Feeling angry at Castros' casual assumption of control, Cirona turned to the captain and said, 'You remember the rest?'

'Aye,' the captain replied, bristling. 'We're to return here every day at noon, waiting on your return.' The seaman gave her a look that expressed his doubt at the likelihood of this event.

'Good,' Cirona said.

With that she turned and walked forwards before clambering into the small rowboat attached to the vessel. Del Var and Holger followed her lead, and they were soon lowered onto the grey waves, hitting the water with a definitive thump. There was no turning back now.

Castros went to take one of the oars but Cirona pushed him back. She gestured to Holger to grab the other one, and they began to pull towards the shore.

A silence emanated from the Shattered Land, a blanket of quiet that stole the breath from her throat. Cirona let out a cough and felt like an interloper — a peeping Tom leering in at a world she had no right to know.

Soon, the prow of the boat crunched onto the shingle of the bay. After a short walk up hill, they came across a village. Cirona hadn't known what to expect, but this certainly wasn't it. Everything seemed so normal. The style of the ruined cottages was the same as those she had seen fishermen living in in Pevontess. Patches of grass grew a rotten brown between the cobbles and withered trees poked vindictive fingers at the sky. Not welcoming but not the magical landscape she had imagined either.

'La, la, la, la!' Castros bellowed breaking the silence. 'Come on you two, snap out of it. Don't let this place get to you, eh?'

Cirona glared at him. Del Var smiled at her. It took every ounce of self-control she possessed not to knock every tooth from his head.

'I like quiet,' she said in a voice that came out as nothing more than a hoarse whisper. She swallowed, realising how dry her mouth was; it felt like she hadn't used it for a thousand years not a few hours.

Still smiling, Castros said, 'Don't be like that! It's a long way to Primus you know, and it'll be intolerable in silence. Tell you what, ask me whatever you want; that ought to get the conversation flowing.'

*Why did you kill the only man I've ever loved?* she thought, the words spiking into her mind like the thrust of a lance. She gritted her teeth to keep them in; *that* question could wait, wait until she had her sword rammed into his gut.

For a few seconds, the silence continued, then Holger said, 'Why did you come here? The first time, I mean.'

Del Var paused for a moment and scrunched his brow in thought. 'Hmm. Well, I'd just found out I was a demi-mage. I wasn't going to get any information from my father, so I thought this would be a good place to find some answers.'

'Did you?' Holger asked.

'Yes and no. The whole place is like this. The Purge and the mage hunters had seen to that. But I did find Waltus. Well, to tell the truth, he found me.'

'How come he survived out here for so long? Why did no one find him?' Holger continued.

'He's a wily old sod. Knows the place inside out. Forages in the mountains, drinks from the streams; we'll have to do the same, all the wells have been tainted.

'As for how no one found him ... well, it's a big place, and one man is easy to miss. Plus, it took hundreds of years for the mage hunters to clear this place out. And Waltus struck a deal.'

'What kind of deal?' Holger replied.

'He healed the Emperor Isembert the First's wife. In return, he was given freedom of this place.'

'But Isembert the First died a hundred and fifty years ago!' Cirona said, despite herself.

Castros looked at her, seeming to take pleasure in her finally addressing him directly. 'Mages live long lives, usually around twice that of a human. Couple that with a White Mage's healing powers, and you've got yourself one *very* old man.'

'He not gonna mind us showing up like this?' Holger said.

'Probably kick up a stink. But he should remember me. Unless, he's gone completely mad by now!' Castros said, smiling broadly.

Cirona felt a chill run through her. Completely mad? She didn't like the idea of pinning all their hopes for reviving Bellina on a man who wasn't the whole ticket.

Seeming to exhaust his supply of questions for the moment, Holger fell silent. The quiet settled in around them again. It felt less threatening now. As much as she hated to admit it, Del Var had been right. Talking had broken the Shattered Land's spell ... if only by a fraction.

***

'We have arrived at your stop, my friend!' the cart driver hollered.

Shooing an inquisitive chicken from under his feet, Elvgren stood up. He brushed down the seat of his trousers, removing errant strands of hay and hopped down; Dargo following his lead.

'Many thanks, old boy,' Elvgren said, rifling in his purse for payment.

The driver waved his hand at him. 'That is not required. Every good deed finds reward beyond the Veil,' the man said in the soft, rich tones of a Tremoran.

'Oh. Well, please accept our thanks once more,' Elvgren replied.

The driver tipped the point of his wide-brimmed hat at them then set his horses into motion. Elvgren watched him shrink as distance and perspective swallowed him.

'Well, here we are,' he said to Dargo.

'Thank the gods for that!' Dargo replied. 'Any longer on that cart, and I never would've felt me arse again.'

'Our problems run deeper than the state of your posterior,' Elvgren said, turning to look at the city wall of Spinoza.

It had taken them three days of hiking and begging lifts, but they had made it. Before them stood their prize: the gates to the Tremoran capital ... and whatever fate awaited them therein.

'Bit fancier than the Victory ones int they?' Dargo said, pointing towards the entrance before them.

'Indeed,' Elvgren replied with an appreciative nod.

*Calling that a gate is something of an understatement*, he thought. The ancient, rough-hewn stones of the city walls were punctuated with what could only be described as a mansion. Beneath a triangular pediment supported by fluted columns was the way into Spinoza. The architecture's grandeur made you feel how it was intended: small.

'Shall we crack on then?' Elvgren said.

'No time like the present,' Dargo replied, and they strolled through the gate.

It took them a solid five minutes to get to the other side, a testament to the wall and gatehouse's thickness. Once through, the smell of frying food and freshly brewed coffee hit Elvgren's nose. On either side of the wide street, imposing buildings, pristine white in colour, rose towards the sky. The difference compared to the cramped and crowded streets of Victory was enormous, and it was one that Elvgren approved of.

'What now then?' Dargo asked.

Elvgren's forehead wrinkled. 'We make our way to the duke's palace and announce our arrival, I suppose,' he said.

'Lead on,' Dargo replied.

'How the hells should I know where it is?'

'For the love of … you could have looked at a map before you left, Gren,' Dargo said, shaking his head.

'So could you,' Elvgren replied, a slight pout to his lips.

'If you had taken the time to inform me about all o this, I woulda done.'

'This is getting us nowhere!' Elvgren exclaimed. 'Let's just wander around till we find the largest building that will … Oi! Watch yourself, you cretin!'

The man who had just barged into Elvgren responded with an obscene hand gesture and continued on his way.

'Yeah? Same to you an all!' Dargo called after him.

'Bloody great oaf,' Elvgren said with a sniff. 'Got half a mind to get the City Watch and have the rude blighter given a good—'

'Gren?'

'What, Dargo!' Elvgren replied, annoyed at having his rant cut short.

'Your bag,'

'What about it?'

'It's gone.'

'Don't be ridiculous, it's right …' Elvgren began, reaching a hand towards the strap. All he touched was the fabric of his travelling cloak. 'Bollocks.'

'Come on, maybe we'll catch him before he gets too far,' Dargo said, setting off at a sprint, Elvgren following behind.

They reached the end of the street, the tall buildings giving way to a crowded square. Many people were relaxing in a garden area at its centre. All around them, the sharp clop of hooves resounded as carriages and carts navigated their way along the straight roads.

'This is hopeless. We'll never ...'

'Over there!' Dargo cut in. The boy had scrambled halfway up an ornate iron lamp post to get a better view and was pointing away to their right. 'He's heading down that alley.'

Before Elvgren could reply, Dargo had hopped down and set off across the square, weaving his way through the traffic like a darting bird. With a sigh, Elvgren trailed after him, angry shouts from cab drivers ringing in his ears.

'Come on,' Dargo called as he drew near.

'Alright, alright!' Elvgren replied.

They followed the retreating back of the man through the city streets. After a good half hour of tailing, the thief came to a stop by a run-down building near the docks. From the shadow of a nearby street, they watched the man knock on the door and disappear inside. Nostrils flaring, Elvgren took a purposeful stride towards the building.

'Where the hells are you going?' Dargo said, catching his arm.

'To give the thieving arse a piece of my mind!' Elvgren replied.

Dargo rubbed a hand over his face and looked to the heavens. 'We can't do that! There could be a bloody army of robbers in there.'

'What do you suggest then?' Elvgren asked.

'Something a bit more subtle. Follow me.'

Dargo crouched low and made his way towards the house. Elvgren did the same. Even though the windows were obscured by thick, heavy curtains, they kept below the line of them. Soon, they reached a thin slit that separated the thieves' den from the building next to it. Forced to turn sideways, they inched along the gap and popped out into a small mess of garden.

The windows at the back of the house were covered with rotting boards. Hoping they did as good a job of keeping the garden from view as the interior, the pair stole to the back door. Elvgren crouched down and peered in through the keyhole.

'What can you see?' Dargo hissed in his ear.

'Not much,' Elvgren replied.

'Budge over and let me have a gander,' Dargo said, pushing at Elvgren's shoulder.

'No. Let me—'

'Look just get outta the—'

'Dargo, stop pushing—'

'I wouldn't have to push if you would just—'

'Hold on will you, for the Father's ... wargh!'

The door flew inward, and Elvgren and Dargo tumbled into the room beyond. Elvgren looked up. Above him, standing by the door, was the thief. Sat around a wine-stained wooden table were four more men, their heads haloed by cigarette smoke, a game of cards on the go. The man by the door raised an eyebrow.

'Er ... hello, chaps. I ... um ... think you have something that belongs to me,' Elvgren said.

'Way to give 'em a piece of yer mind, Gren,' Dargo said.

The men at the table stood, one wandering over to his companion by the door. Reaching down, the pair heaved Elvgren and Dargo to their feet.

'What shall we do with zem?' one of them said.

'Take zem to ze boss,' the bag snatcher replied.

With a shove in the back, Elvgren was forced forwards. They were marched along a short corridor. One of the men knocked on a door to their left. A series of hacking coughs emanated from behind the wood.

'Come in,' a rasping voice ordered.

The room beyond was dingy, only a thin trickle of light fought its way through the heavy curtains. Despite the hot weather, a fire crackled in the hearth, warming the feet of a wizened old man who sat, blanket covered, in a seat beside it. Upon his lap was Elvgren's bag.

'Who is zis?' the old man asked.

'We caught zem sneaking around outside, boss,' one of the men replied.

The old man coughed again, then spat a glob of phlegm into the fire. 'I take it zis is your bag, no?' he said.

'That ... er ... would be correct, Mr ...?' Elvgren replied.

'Zoland,' the old man said.

'Mr Zoland, this is all a terrible mistake—'

'What a pity! I was just about to thank you for ze lovely pouch of gold you have given me,' the elderly gang leader said.

'Yes, yes. By all means take the gold. Take it all with ... er ... my best wishes. If I could just trouble you for a few papers I left inside we'll be on our way,' Elvgren said.

'Would you be referring to zeese?' the old man replied, waving the rolled airship schematics which he grasped in his gnarled fingers.

Elvgren licked his lips. 'That's them. Just a few letters from my mother. If I could—'

'You are a terrible liar, young man,' the man said.

'I ... er ... what—' Elvgren stammered.

'Oh, for fuck's sake!' Dargo exclaimed. 'Alright grandad, enough of this crap. Give us back the papers before I kick yer false teeth down your throat.'

Zoland fixed him with an iron glare. 'You will keep quiet boy while ze adults are talking,' he said, before returning his eyes to Elvgren. 'As I was saying, you lie badly. Far from being a note from your surely delightful mother, these are plans for some kind of machine. You may not be aware, but there is a great deal of industrial espionage going on at the moment.'

'Really?' Elvgren replied, eye wide in false shock.

'Alas, it is true. Many rats sneak into our country, seeking out juicy morsels. Morsels such as zis,' Zoland said with a heavy sigh. 'And while I may be a thief, I am no traitor.' There was a knock at the front door. 'Ah, zat shall be ze City Watch.'

For a second, Elvgren felt the grip of the thief behind him lessen. Seizing his opportunity, he slammed his head back, catching his captor squarely on the jaw. Beside him, Dargo stamped on the foot of his guard and leapt for the old man, where they began a tug-of-war over the plans. Elvgren lunged towards them but was tackled to the ground.

'What is ze meaning of zis!' A new voice called out.

One of the thieves hauled Dargo off the old man and another pulled Elvgren to his feet. Elvgren's eyes met those of the uniformed man.

'These men are thieves. That bag and everything in it belong to me!' Elvgren cried.

'You have ze nerve to call my grandfather a thief?' the watchman said with a knowing smile.

Eyes bouncing between the pair, Elvgren noted the same hawk-like nose and small lips. 'Bloody hells,' he said.

'Here Jean, take zis,' Zoland said to his grandson.

The watchman took the papers. Unrolling them, his eyes widened. 'By ze Father!'

'With a catch like these that promotion should be a sure thing, no?' Zoland said.

'Without a doubt, Gran'papa,' Jean said, planting a kiss on the old man's hand.

'Enough,' Zoland said. 'You embarrass me. Get zem out of here.'

Jean nodded and blew on his whistle. The next moment three more uniformed men stormed into the room.

'Take zem to ze duke's dungeons,' Jean ordered.

Elvgren felt the cold touch of iron shiver his skin as a pair of handcuffs were snapped round his wrists. At ballistol point, he and Dargo were marched from the room. As he was pushed into the back of a barred wagon, Elvgren caught a final glimpse of the schematics tucked under Jean's arm.

'Well, we're off to a good start,' Dargo said as the wagon's doors shut behind them.

As Elvgren heard the click of the locks he stared at the floor.

*Bollocks*, he thought.

***

'This is the Vitaspiral,' Castros said, pointing a stick at the symbol he had drawn in the dirt.

Scratched into the dry earth next to their campfire was a series of concentric circles, small wavy lines extending out of them at regular intervals. Holger bent closer to examine Del Var's drawing, his face lit by the flickering flames; he didn't seem too impressed.

'Okay,' Holger said slowly. 'What does it do?'

'What does it ...?' Castros began. He ran a hand through his hair. *Patience*, he told himself, *you were as ignorant once*. 'This is the conduit we use to harness the sortilenergy; not just around us, but in us too.'

'Don't really see how that's gonna help me shoot flames out me hands,' Holger replied, scratching his chin.

Castros rubbed at his temples then closed his eyes. 'Alright,' he said eventually. 'Let's start at the beginning. Thousands of years ago the very first mages struggled to control their powers.'

'Like me back in Escambria,' Holger said.

'Exactly,' Castros replied. 'What you did is known as wrenching. It's when a mage generates magical powers forcefully and quickly. In essence, it's something you should only do as a last resort.'

'Have you ever done it? Wrenching, I mean,' Holger asked.

'Unfortunately, yes,' Castros answered, wincing at the memory of his last convalescence. 'Anyway, the first mages soon realised they wouldn't last too long if they kept wrenching sortilenergy and injuring themselves.'

'So ... they come up with a drawing?'

'No, not a drawing, a symbol, one which allowed them to tap into a vast reservoir of magical power.'

'Fantastic,' Holger said. 'How does that help me?'

'I'm getting to that!' Castros snapped, quickly realising he didn't have a knack for teaching. 'By meditating on the Vitaspiral, mages found that they could connect with something they named the Manastream.'

'Mana-what?'

'Just listen,' Castros said, holding up a hand. 'Now the Manastream is the life force of the entire world, flowing endlessly. This in itself would have been enough to draw from, but they found something else.'

Holger leaned forwards, the interest now clear on his face. 'What did they find?' he asked.

'Well, as they plunged deeper, following the eddies and tides of the Manastream, they stumbled upon five huge oceans of power. They called these oceans The Gift of The First Ones; the theory being that when the elder gods, the fathers of what became the Old Terrors, were killed by their creations their energy was locked into something. Debate raged for centuries over what form that something took: the landscape, temples, artefacts. The last of these ideas took hold, that artefacts, relics as they called them, were the storehouses for the majority of the sortilenergy in the world.'

'Did anyone try and find them?' Holger asked.

'Certainly,' Castros replied. 'Myths and legends abound about the whereabouts of the relics.'

'Where are they now then?'

'No one knows. You have to understand that so much history and knowledge was lost after the sealing of the Old Terrors. Still,' Castros said with a sniff, a picture of his father flashing in his mind's eye, 'plenty search for them.' He paused for a moment and then continued. 'Right, history lesson over; let's talk about you.'

'Me? What can you learn from that?' Holger said.

'Plenty,' Castros replied. 'When did you first notice your gift?'

'Wouldn't call it a gift, but the first time, I was around twelve. I was watching the fire dance in me mum's kitchen. Just enjoying it, you know. Then I kinda got this funny idea in me head: what if the flames just sorta flew off on their own, almost like they were dancing. I saw it so clearly. Well, you can imagine how me mum screamed when she saw it actually happening.'

'Good. Around twelve is the usual age powers will manifest in a mage. Did you try anything else?'

'Not too much. Mum flipped her wig. Me nan had been ... had been killed in one of the purges see, and well, she didn't want anything like that to happen to me. But whenever I got five minutes, I'd try it, you know. That's why I always keep these wi' me,' Holger said, reaching into his coat pocket.

He pulled out a battered box of matches. With a shy look at Castros he took one out and struck it, the smell of phosphorous filling the air.

Del Var watched as the young man's face creased in concentration. The flame twirled, then spun from the match's end.

'Excellent!' Castros cried.

'Really?'

'Really,' Castros continued. 'That shows me you have a good grasp of control and shaping, neither are easy to master.'

'Huh,' Holger said. 'I've always just thought it and it's happened.'

'Top stuff. This will halve the time I thought it would take. All we need to focus on is teaching you to tap into the Manastream, and you're away.'

'How does it happen though?' Holger asked. 'Except for back at the Palace of Radiance, I've never been able to create fire out of nothing.'

'That was an extremely rare case. Sometimes, in moments of deep emotional stress, a mage can create something from nothing. Usually though, you have to draw sortilenergy from the Manastream, convert it in your body then store it in something. That's what you have been subconsciously doing with the matches,' Del Var answered.

'Bloody hells! I didn't think there was as much as all that to it.'

'I'm afraid so. But, with a lot of practice, you'll be able to do something like this.'

Castros took out one of his waterskins and squirted a small amount of liquid into the palm of his hand. Fixing his gaze upon it, he formed the water into a ball, then into the shape of a bird. With a snap of his fingers, he turned it into ice, a tiny frozen sculpture landing in his hand.

'Woah!' Holger said.

'I know, I know; I'm magnificent,' Castros said. 'Now, let's get back to you. Ever meditated before?'

'Eh?'

'I'll take that as a no. To cut a long story short, meditation is sitting still and clearing your mind of thought. Give it a try. Close your eyes.'

Holger raised an eyebrow but did as he was told.

'Good. Now imagine the Vitaspiral. Travel along its path, let it lead you to the Manastream.'

Brow scrunched in frustration, Holger cried, 'It's no good. I can't do it!'

'It takes time. You're bloody well not going to get it on your first go. I doubt even Excellus managed that. Just keep at it,' Del Var replied.

The pair fell silent. The only sounds were the crackling of the flames and the scrape as Major Bouchard sharpened her sword. Castros looked towards her, and for a moment, their eyes met. The look of hate he saw there almost made him jump. Bouchard looked down at her weapon,

and Del Var shuddered to think that the control for the execution collar
was in her hands, that with just one click of a button, she could blow
his head off.

Clearly at some point, he had wounded her. Castros winced, a knot
forming in his stomach. He had caused a lot of pain in his youth, back
when he had thought any method was justified to achieve his goals.
Now he knew better. If only he could pinpoint what he had done. There
was something familiar about her.

A marrow chilling howl rang out. The cry carried effortlessly through
the still night air.

'What the hells was that?' Holger said, his voice a whisper.

'Malovors,' Castros replied, staring out into the night, his hand
instinctively going for one of his screamers.

'What in the world is a malovor?' Bouchard said, her eyes searching
through the dark.

'You'll find out soon enough. I'll take first watch. You two get some
sleep,' Del Var said.

Holger nodded, and the major gave a grunt.

Castros turned away from them, body tense, eyes staring. In his
hand sat one of his screamers. He prayed to every god he could think of
that he wouldn't have to use it.

# CHAPTER TWENTY

Cirona marched along behind Del Var, a vein pulsing in the side of her head. It would be so easy just to draw her sword and plunge it into the base of his neck. It would be even easier to use the execution collar. She shook her head, forcing the temptation away. *Keep calm woman*, she told herself, *the time will come.*

She wiped a hand across her brow. It came away slick with sweat. Overhead, pregnant clouds sat low in the sky, fat with a deluge they had yet to unleash. Cirona prayed they would do it soon and lessen the oppressive, life-sucking humidity.

The small party had passed through the last village thirty minutes ago. The path they were following ran straight and true, constructed from precision-cut, white stones. To either side of her, Cirona saw row upon row of stunted, withered trees, making up what had once been an orchard. For a second, she tried to imagine what it would have been like in full bloom; she found it next to impossible in this place of death and silence.

Soon the trees gave way to a barren field. She flicked her eyes to it then back to the road. *Nothing to see there*, she thought. Then she stopped and regarded it again, tilting her head to the side. There was something odd about it. Her breath caught in her throat as she realised what it was: the field had been freshly ploughed.

'What in the world?' she muttered to herself.

'Something wrong, Major?' Del Var asked.

She opened her mouth to answer.

'Can anyone else see that?' Holger cut in.

Cirona's eyes followed Holger's pointing finger. In the distance, she could make out a man-shaped form. She moved closer to the fence and squinted. She could now see the creature's elongated arms, knuckles trailing along the ground. Its skin had a greenish grey tone, like a drowned corpse. On its broad back was strapped a plough.

'Is ... is that one of those malovor things you were talking about?' Holger asked.

'Yes,' Castros said with a sigh.

'What does it think it's doing?' Cirona found herself asking.

'What it was created to do — ploughing and harvesting,' Castros replied.

Cirona turned towards Del Var, eyebrow raised. 'Created?' she said.

'That's right,' Castros said. 'By the mages. Living creatures, strong and durable. They used them for manual labour. When they were made, they were given a primary job in life. It was written into their very souls. This one must have descended from a malovor that was made to work the field.'

'Descended? What? These things can have children?' Holger said.

'Indeed; the mages found that life has a way of not following orders. But the fact they could breed turned out to be useful. It meant resources could be used elsewhere.'

'Why? Why did they need these … creatures?' Cirona said.

'The mage population was never very big. There were only fifty thousand at their height. Not enough people to do menial jobs, as they saw them. If a mage had to build a house or repair a gate, that was time wasted. The malovors freed them up to follow other … pursuits.'

'And that's all this one will do? Plough this fucking field till it dies? That's a cruel fate from a cruel people,' Cirona said, spitting into the dirt.

'I'd say the mages have paid for it. The whole being used as living power sources has been an apt punishment, don't you think?' Castros said.

'You think this is right?' she replied, not wanting to be drawn into a debate about mage liberation.

'No. No, I don't. But there's nothing I can do about it,' Castros said, a pained expression clouding his face.

'A-are they dangerous?' Holger said.

'No and yes. They'll keep at their jobs unless disturbed. They won't take orders from anyone but a mage. Problem is, in the years since the war, the survivors have bred with malovors assigned different jobs from their own. Sends them mad. Then there are the warriors—'

'Warriors? If the mages had a load of monsters to fight for them, why is it not written down?' Holger asked.

'It was. These are what we're brought up to call the Legion.'

'That can't be! The Legion are demons summoned from the Void. Not these … things!' Cirona said.

'Nope … these are the Legion. This one looks tame, but when they fight, they're as strong as bears, single-minded and relentless …'

In the distance, the malovor raised its head and turned to face them. It dropped its plough and walked slowly towards them.

'Fuck! It's coming this way. What do we do?' Holger said.

'Just stay still and let me handle it. No one speak or touch it,' Del Var replied.

The creature made its way mournfully towards them. A body with one purpose, condemned to work a field that would never yield crops again. It stood next to the wall. Small round eyes looking soullessly towards them.

'M-m-master?' The malovor said, looking at Castros.

'I am not your master. Carry on,' Del Var said.

He placed his index finger on the creature's forehead. The malovor nodded and began to slink away.

Cirona saw Holger take a step forwards and reach out after it.

'No! I know how you feel but don't. You'll only rile it up,' Del Var said.

'But it looks so miserable. Can we do nothing?' Holger said, his eyes shining.

'It's either let it get back to its job or kill it. I don't want the wretched thing's death on my conscience. Do you?'

'No,' Holger said, slowly bringing his hand down. 'Is this why they were not killed in the Purge?'

'No. Many were slaughtered. Hundreds of thousands. The ones that remain were the best hidden. The ones who live underground, their homes hard to find.'

Cirona, Castros and Holger stood for a few minutes, watching the malovor. It hitched the plough back onto its back and resumed the task it was born to do.

Cirona felt her lip curl in fresh disgust as she looked at Del Var and indeed Holger. Somewhere, in the mists of time, their ancestors had thought they had the right to produce such creatures, to meddle in things best left to the gods. If she'd had some minor reservations about the budding romance between Holger and Bellina before, they were certainly growing now.

'Come on,' Castros said. 'We've still got a long way to go.' He turned and continued along the path.

With a deep breath, Cirona got her feet moving again. In her mind, she added a new stroke to the tally of hate she kept personally for Del Var.

***

The howl rang out once more, this time joined by another, then another, the individual notes of the creature's cries mingling into a blood-freezing chord. Bellina struggled to place where she had heard the sound before.

'Wh-what is that?' Dahlia said.

Closing her eyes tight, Bellina remembered. 'Faresks,' she whispered.

'What in the world is a faresk?' Dahlia asked, her eyes wide.

Bellina felt her arms tense, her chest tightening. Finally, she said, 'A giant dog-like … thing, summoned by a kaffar.' Turning to meet Dahlia's frightened gaze, she continued. 'We need to run. Now.'

Gaze flying around the landscape, Bellina finally found what looked like the beginnings of a path.

'This way,' she said, running towards it.

The jungle swallowed her up. Her rapid movements caused colourful birds to take flight all around, and the heavy perfume of rotting fruit battered her nose. For a second, she wondered just how in the hells she was creating such a detailed environment. Her thoughts were cut short when a faresk smashed out of the undergrowth.

Feet slipping in the soft mud, she stumbled to the ground. Her head felt like it was weighed down by stone as she lifted it, her eyes meeting the bulbous gleaming ones of the creature. It padded forwards on gigantic paws, its lank, greasy fur rippling with the muscle beneath. Its lips drew back into a snarl that could have been a smile, flashing a mass of razor-sharp teeth.

'By the Father!' Dahlia exclaimed, skidding to a stop behind Bellina.

'Don't move,' Bellina hissed.

Keeping her eyes fixed on the faresk, she groped in the dirt. Her hand paused, trembling, as the creature growled softly. Inching her fingers along with as much speed as she dared, Bellina felt what she had been looking for. The digits of her left hand curled around a thick branch.

As she pulled it towards her, the beast pounced. Sounding like it came from a million miles away, she heard Dahlia scream. Bellina held the branch in front of her. The faresk's teeth sank into the wood, sending jolts of pain up her arms and splinters into the air. Her makeshift shield was not going to hold out for long.

The sound of breaking wood filled the air. Bellina closed her eyes, expecting the worst. Instead, she heard a squeal of pain. Forcing her eyelids open, she saw the faresk in front of her, a huge tree trunk pinning it to the ground. Bellina whipped her head round and saw Dahlia, panting.

'Thank you,' Bellina said.

Too tired to speak, Dahlia nodded.

As Bellina regained her feet, howls echoed around them. 'We need to get going,' she said.

Dahlia swallowed then nodded again. Bellina bit her lip; she knew her fellow cognopath had to be reaching exhaustion point, but there was nothing she could do. Not wanting to waste another second, she took off.

Sprinting as fast as she could, feet somehow missing the groping roots hidden in the undergrowth, Bellina made her way along the path through the trees. Either side of her, she could see the shadows of the chasing faresks, a blur just discernible amongst the trees. They could easily outstrip Bellina and Dahlia for pace, so why weren't they attacking?

Ahead of her, Bellina saw a massive gateway made from two colossal stones capped with a third. Where the door should have been there was only a shimmering haze. She felt the hairs rise on the back of her neck as she looked at it, filled with instinctive fear. She pushed the feeling away. The gateway was their only option.

She plunged into it at full tilt. The haze had a physical quality, gelatinous and cloying. Muscles burning, Bellina forced her way through. With an audible pop, she burst into the other side and fell to the floor. Her jaw hit the ground hard, sending little dots of light spiralling before her eyes.

'Wh-where are we?' Dahlia asked.

Shaking her head in an attempt to clear it, Bellina looked up. The breath died in her throat.

'Gods, no,' she said.

In front of her were spread the streets of Kurgobad, capital of Burkesh. Strewn here and there, like pieces of discarded paper, were corpses. Men, women and children of every age lay dead at her feet. She now understood what the faresks had been doing; they'd been herding her. They had forced her into this place.

'Is this—' Dahlia began.

'Yes,' Bellina said in a hoarse voice. 'This is what happened, what *I* did, in Kurgobad.'

Bellina forced herself to meet Dahlia's eyes. In them she saw fear mixed with disgust. Tears threatened to overwhelm Bellina.

'I-I have to go,' Dahlia said.

'Please,' Bellina said. 'Please don't leave me here alone.'

'My body it's—'

Before she could finish, Dahlia's body spiralled apart in a whirl of light.

Bellina felt the life go out of her legs and she crumpled to the floor. The tears took hold as she found herself alone in a world of destruction she had created.

***

'Oi! Oi, you bunch o bastards. Let us out! You hear me?'

'For the love of all that's holy, Dargo, will you shut up!' Elvgren said, pinching the bridge of his nose. 'You've been at it for hours, and the only thing you've achieved is giving me a poxy headache.'

Dargo shot him a pouting glance, kicked the cell door and sulked off. 'Wonder if they've worked out who you are yet?' he said, taking a seat on the floor.

'Well, it's not as if I've got any distinguishing features is it?' Elvgren said, pointing to his eyepatch and accompanying scar.

'Alright, Mr Sunshine,' Dargo said, holding up his hands. 'What's got your undies in a twist?'

Elvgren's eyebrows shot halfway up his forehead. 'In case you haven't noticed, we are locked in the Duke of Tremore's dungeons, hundreds of miles from home, with no hope of rescue, accused of being spies and at the mercy of a man who has killed every covert agent he's uncovered,' he said, checking each point off on his fingers. 'Plus, to cap it all off, we've lost our only bargaining chip.'

'What're you on about?' Dargo said with a sniff.

'The schematics, Dargo,' Elvgren replied, rubbing his eyes.

A smile spread across Dargo's face and he leapt to his feet.

'What the hells are you doing?' Elvgren asked.

'Got something to show yer,' Dargo said, his hand rummaging around inside his trousers.

'How many times have I told you — I'm not a medificer. If you've got some problem down there, you'll have to—'

'I'm not ... there's nothing ... here, just look as this,' Dargo said.

He held his hand towards Elvgren, a piece of ragged paper clutched in his fingers. Grimacing, Elvgren reached out and took it. Smoothing out the paper, he frowned. Then his eye widened.

'You ripped off a piece of the plans!' he cried, jumping to his feet. 'Dargo, you magnificent bastard! I could kiss you!'

'Alright, alright, thanks is enough,' Dargo replied, sidestepping an amorous lunge from Elvgren.

The sound of a key turning filled the cell, and a second later, a burly gaoler stood in the doorway.

'Follow me,' the man said.

Without waiting for a response, the gaoler turned and exited the cell. Elvgren shot a questioning look at Dargo who shrugged his shoulders. With a lick of his lips, Elvgren trailed after the man.

He found himself in a dank corridor, flaming torches alight along its length. The gaoler locked the cell, looked them up and down, then stormed off with a snort.

'Where are you taking us?' Elvgren asked, almost running to keep up with the man's strides.

'No talk,' the gaoler grunted back.

'But if you would just allow me—' Elvgren began.

In one swift movement, the man whipped a sword from his side, the point stopping a hair's width from Elvgren's larynx.

'No. Talk,' the gaoler said. 'Nod if you understand.'

Elvgren's head bobbed madly as he demonstrated he understood. Satisfied, the man put his sword away and carried on.

At the end of the corridor, they came across another prison guard. Without a word passing between the two colleagues, the door was opened, and the two gaolers led them up the winding staircase beyond.

By the time they reached the top, Elvgren was panting for breath, his legs ablaze. Any hope of a rest he had harboured was dashed to pieces when the two guards turned them into a long, opulently decorated hallway. Pushing himself to keep up with the gaolers, Elvgren passed beneath a collection of monumental canvases depicting women in various states of undress. At last, they came to a stop before a pair of white doors covered in patterns picked out in gold.

'You,' the gaoler who had collected them from their cell said, pointing at Dargo, 'go with him.'

Dargo looked at Elvgren, his brows furrowed. Elvgren nodded his head, and Dargo allowed the other guard to lead him away.

'You,' the first gaoler said, jabbing a meaty finger into Elvgren's chest, 'in there.'

'Through those doors, you mean?' Elvgren said. The man scowled, nostrils flaring, hand edging towards the hilt of his sword. 'Alright, alright, I'm going!'

Elvgren reached out and yanked the door open. He darted in and shut it behind him, finding himself in one of the most lavish dining halls he had ever seen.

Overhead, chandeliers dripped from the ceiling, their hundreds of lights illuminating the vast space. Everywhere was the glint of gold. A massive table — that could have seated a hundred with no cause for alarm — ran the entire length of the room. At the far end of it, Elvgren could just make out a figure tucking into a plate of food with vigour.

'Ah, Lord Lovitz, please join me,' the figure called.

Eyes narrowed, Elvgren crept forwards, half expecting more guards to descend upon him at any second. As he drew closer to the figure, Elvgren got his first look at the Duke of Tremore. The man was short with delicate, almost feminine, shoulders. Small, piercing eyes sat in the middle of a clean-shaved, youthful face.

'For heaven's sake, sit down, man; the food is getting cold,' the duke said, gesturing to an empty seat on his left.

Elvgren lowered himself into the chair. *This is it*, he told himself, *this is your chance to get him onside; don't mess it up.*

'Please, help yourself,' the duke said, pointing a loaded fork at the myriad of dishes on offer. Elvgren eyed the food. Laughing, the duke added, 'Eat man, eat! I would not be so ill-mannered as to poison you.'

Filling his plate with food, Elvgren said, 'Thank you for your hospitality, your Grace.'

'Call me Tobért, Lord Lovitz,' the duke said, 'or perhaps you prefer the title of Deputy Lord Chancellor.'

'I would prefer the title, Lord Chancellor, but Elvgren will suffice.'

The duke let out a loud belly laugh, surprising Elvgren that such volume could be produced by such a small man. 'Wouldn't we all, Elvgren. The man who holds that title may as well be Emperor for all the power he holds,' Tobért said.

'Too true,' Elvgren agreed. 'I was hoping you could help me further my ambitions.'

The duke set down his knife and fork and dabbed at the corners of his mouth with a napkin. 'Straight to the point, I see,' he said. 'Allow me a small diversion before I answer. Did you know Amlith Castria, banisher of the Old Terrors, saviour and founder of Estria, had a twin brother?'

'No,' Elvgren replied with a shake of his head.

'Not many people do,' Tobért continued. 'But the history of this twin *is* remembered by my house. A story burned into those who bear the Vontanza name before we leave the wet nurse's teat.

'Vontanza Castria fought side by side with his more renowned sibling. He won many battles and stood with Amlith when he ripped open the Void and condemned the Terrors. For this service, he was given the country of Tremore and a promise, a promise that, upon Amlith's death, Vontanza would rule Estria.'

'Well that certainly didn't happen,' Elvgren said.

'Quite,' the duke replied. 'My ancestor was tricked out of his rightful inheritance by a man named Falstaff Ressa.'

Elvgren's head snapped back as though he had been slapped. 'So Vontanza was duped by one of the Lord Chancellor's forefathers?'

'Yes. Amlith had no heirs by his wife. But Falstaff Ressa did a little digging and unearthed a bastard. And, the very day Vontanza arrived in Victory, the bastard was crowned. Do you think this was fair?'

'Of course not,' Elvgren replied with sincerity.

'So, you would not think it wrong for Vontanza's descendants to sit upon the Imperial Throne?'

'Wrong? No. Without precedence? Yes.'

Tobért clasped his hands together on the table and met Elvgren's gaze. 'I think you are a man who could help me set that precedent,' he said.

A small gasp of air entered Elvgren's lungs. It couldn't be this easy, could it?

'But first, you must prove your allegiance,' the duke said.

Tobért picked up a small bell from the table and gave it three sharp rings. Elvgren held his breath as two doors at the back of the room were opened. Two guards entered, pushing a third manacled man before them. As they drew closer, Elvgren saw who the prisoner was.

'Crenshaw!' he said.

'So, the weasel spoke true — he does know you!' the duke said. 'We caught this one and his companions in one of the Lord Chancellor's newfangled flying machines. Our scholars are stripping it down and uncovering its secrets as we speak, rendering your stolen schematics rather useless I'm afraid, Elvgren. Luckily for you, I have been much impressed with your exploits. But now I must see that you will do whatever I command.'

The duke held out a hand to one of the guards who drew his sword and placed the hilt in the duke's hands. Tobért sliced the air with two practice strokes then passed it to Elvgren.

'Kill him,' he said.

# CHAPTER TWENTY-ONE

'I … er … beg your pardon, your Grace?' Elvgren said, swallowing hard.

'I want you to kill him,' the duke replied, his eyes narrowing to slits.

Feeling his hands shaking by his sides, Elvgren forced them to be still. *Don't let them see you hesitate*, he told himself, *if killing Crenshaw is what it takes to get in the duke's good graces, well, that's what you have to do*. A sharp pain began to throb behind his eyes. Could he really take the life of a man he'd shared so much with?

*Grow some bollocks*, a voice echoed in his head. *The fate of the Empire is at stake*.

Elvgren took a deep breath, steadying himself, then took the sword Tobért was offering. The duke gave Elvgren a smile and a wink, before nodding to the guards. The men beside Crenshaw forced him to his knees, grabbed his hair and pulled his head down, exposing the man's neck.

Forcing his mind to be quiet, Elvgren stepped towards Crenshaw. Sweat was pouring down the man's face in sheets, his breathing reduced to panted gasps; to his credit, he didn't say a word, though. Elvgren hefted the sword above his head. At the very least, he would give Crenshaw a clean death. Closing his eye, Elvgren swung down.

'Stop!' A voice boomed from the back of the room.

Elvgren's arms froze. Opening his one good eye, he saw the blade resting on the back of Crenshaw's neck, an angry, bleeding scratch formed by the sword's razor-sharp edge. Legs threatening to buckle beneath him, Elvgren turned to see who had called a stop to the madness. What he saw made his heart stop.

Standing at the doors Elvgren had entered through was a kaffar. The Burkeshi was tall, his cloak of ravens' feathers draped across a set of broad shoulders. He was frowning deeply at the scene.

'Good evening, Varl Abbas. What brings you here?' the duke said.

'This man is not to be killed. His part in proceedings is not over; I have seen it in a vision,' Abbas said.

Tobért pouted. 'Very well. It's a good job your vision of Elvgren joining us has just proved true, or I would give no credence to your mumbo jumbo,' he said.

'You … you are in league with Burkesh?' Elvgren spat.

'Necessity makes strange bedfellows as you well know, Lord Elvgren,' the kaffar said with a smile. He turned to the duke and continued, 'The master wishes to speak with you, your Grace.'

'Who the hells is your master?' Elvgren blurted out. 'We … we killed—'

'No man *or* woman of normal blood could kill Arch Vizier Marmossa. And, thanks to his protection, Grand Multan Kurkeshi either,' Abbas said, the smile on his face growing wider.

A ringing began to sound in Elvgren's ears, and his head spun. Marmossa, Kurkeshi, both alive. The scene they had left in the Imperial throne room in Kurgobad flashed in his mind; brains leaking out of people's ears, blood, death, destruction. How the hells could anyone have survived that?

'Fine, fine, I'll speak with him,' the duke said, dragging Elvgren back from his thoughts. Tobért's gaze turned to Crenshaw. 'Take him back to the dungeons. And someone take Elvgren to his quarters.'

'Excuse me, Tobért, but may I have a word with the prisoner?' Elvgren asked, pointing a finger at Crenshaw.

The duke scratched his chin then looked at the kaffar. Abbas nodded. 'If you wish,' Tobért said. 'But get him to his cell first.'

'Thank you, your Grace,' Elvgren said with a bow.

'I doubt I need to remind you,' the duke said, 'that we are allies now. Do not try anything silly. I would hate to have to kill you.'

With that Tobért and Abbas stalked from the room. Elvgren turned to see that the guards were already dragging Crenshaw from the room and had to run to catch up with them. He followed them back along the hallway and down into the dungeons where he had been kept not an hour before.

Once Crenshaw was chained to the walls of his cell, Elvgren said, 'Leave us.'

The guards looked at him with something close to surprise in their eyes. Elvgren forced his most imperious, commanding look onto his face. The guards buckled under it and left the cell.

'How the hells did you end up here?' Elvgren asked as the door closed behind them.

Crenshaw's lips pulled back, his teeth bared. 'What the fuck do you care, traitor?' he spat, the veins in his neck standing out like cords.

Elvgren took a step back. He had tried to prepare himself for such fury at his supposed treachery but experiencing it in the flesh was a different story. Elvgren hardened himself. He had a role to play, and he was going to damn well play it to the best of his abilities.

'Answer my question, cretin, or I'll have you flogged within an inch of your life,' Elvgren said.

Crenshaw drew up a lump of phlegm and spat it between Elvgren's feet. Despite the hate in his eyes, he began to speak, 'Tremorans brought us down. Used arrows if you can believe it.'

'Makes sense,' Elvgren said. 'Cannon fire would've probably made the airship explode. But how did they find you?'

'Dunno. It … it was like they were waiting for us.'

Elvgren scratched his chin. If Estria had a spy — in him — placed at the heart of their enemy, then the Tremorans would certainly have done the same.

'What happened to Barbossa and Midge?' Elvgren said.

Crenshaw rubbed his eyes. 'The Vooshu took Bar. We … we tried to fight 'em off but there was too many. Where Midge is … well, your guess is as good as mine.'

In his mind, Elvgren saw Midge. He hoped that the boy was alright, but why wasn't he locked up with Crenshaw? All of a sudden, his brain began to feel like a lead weight, the madness of it all catching up with him. He would have to get to the bottom of this later.

Without another word to Crenshaw, Elvgren turned on his heel and knocked on the cell door.

'Take me to my room,' he ordered the guard who opened it.

As he forced his weary legs onwards his mind swirled with thought. Could he find a way to free Crenshaw without raising suspicion? Where the hells was Midge? How had Marmossa and Kurkeshi survived? He rubbed his temples, trying to make his mind still.

One thing was sure, though — he had to contact the Lord Chancellor.

***

Bellina walked through the corpse-strewn streets of Kurgobad in a daze. Overhead, a too large sun boiled in a sky of electric blue. Even though she knew some part of her subconscious was creating the place, it didn't lessen the heavy weight of the heat or the stench of rotting flesh.

Each time she closed her eyes, she pleaded with her brain to make it stop, to change what she was seeing, but the horror remained. Her guilt grew with every dead body she passed, an oppressive shadow that hugged close to her shoulder, whispering, telling her to look … look and see the destruction she had wrought.

Her treacherous feet led her down an alley. As she looked along it, her mouth fell open. There, in front of her, she could see the form of a small boy, his back to her. Bellina's left hand flew towards her chest; so, there *was* someone alive in amongst all this death.

She quickened her pace and sped towards the boy. Sensing her approach, the child turned. Bellina felt her stomach lurch like a storm-tossed ship at sight of the face that confronted her. One of the boy's eyes dangled from its socket, looking like it had been forced out by some tremendous pressure. A dry sliver of blood traced a path from his nose to his chin, crusted from the heat. From his ears, she could now see a grey ooze leaking.

'Why?' the boy asked, his voice hoarse, dry as the desert.

'I-I'm sorry,' Bellina said.

The boy began to advance. 'Why?' he asked again.

Bellina wanted to move, to run, but her legs weren't listening. All she managed was to shuffle backwards against the wall of a building.

'Why did you kill us?'

'I didn't mean to. Please, I'm so, so sorry,' Bellina said, taking another step, her back coming into contact with something hard behind her.

The boy let out a moan, the sound reminiscent of an animal trapped in an abattoir. He shuffled forwards, arm stretched out towards her. Bellina's vision shrank to the tiny hand groping for her. She couldn't let the boy touch her, if he did, she knew with certainty she would lose her mind.

Frantic, she tried to move further back. Her heel caught on an unseen ledge and she fell backwards, the wall behind her giving way. She landed hard on her back, the air driven from her lungs. Coughing, she climbed to her feet and saw she had fallen through an ancient wooden door and into a home. Hearing the boy's footsteps behind her, she ran.

Taking the first doorway she saw, Bellina found herself in a humble kitchen. In front of her was another person, a woman. The woman turned, a baby clasped in her arms, the same death-marks as the boy's written on their faces.

'My child,' the woman screamed as the baby began to wail. 'My child … how could you?'

Stomach writhing like a maggot-ridden cadaver, Bellina turned back towards the hallway. The boy was there, waiting for her. He reached out, fingers brushing the fabric of Bellina's dress. She stumbled past him, finding the front door. She wrenched it open and flew out into the street.

Outside, she saw that the sea of death that had been present before had gone. Now the corpses were converging on her, choking the streets, moving like birds with broken wings, jittery, unsure. She spun on the spot, looking, searching for a way out.

She saw none.

A small moan escaped her lips as black spots danced in front of her eyes. She fled in the only direction open to her, towards a well in the centre of the area she was in. Reaching her destination, she looked around her. The moving dead were closing the distance, the cries of the damned leaving their lips, mingling with the buzzing drone of the dark clouds of flies that followed in their wake.

Without another thought, Bellina climbed atop the circular wall of the well. She reached out towards the rope dangling from its middle. Her grasping fingers seized it.

'Argh!' she cried as an unseen hand tugged at the back of her clothes.

Pulling away, her feet slipped. An icy grip tightened around her heart as both Bellina and the rope shot down the well. The rope grew taut with a sudden bone-jarring jerk and Bellina tumbled to the ground.

She found herself face down in a small, shallow puddle, the remnants of the well's water supply. Gagging, she spluttered out a mouthful of the rank water. The silhouettes of her pursuers, peering after her, filled the hole above. Bellina dragged herself to the side and drew her knees up to her chin.

'Please,' she screamed up at the living corpses. 'Please … just leave me alone.'

'Never,' they hissed back, their voices mingling together.

'Die.'

'Kill yourself.'

'Murderer.'

'Witch.'

Bellina covered her ears, trying to shut out the words and curses raining down from above. Her chest felt hollow, as if an invisible hand had reached inside of her and removed everything in it. Maybe they were right, maybe she should kill herself, give up, let it all end.

'No,' a voice said beside her.

Head jerking up, Bellina saw Dahlia.

'You're back,' Bellina said. 'By the gods, you're back.'

Reaching out, Bellina pulled Dahlia into a hug. She had never been so pleased to see anyone in her entire life. She nestled her head in the crook of Dahlia's shoulder.

'I'm sorry I was so long,' Dahlia said, pulling away from Bellina and staring into her eyes.

'Y-you weren't … at least, I don't think it was very long.'

Dahlia's brows furrowed. 'Time is passing different here. In the real world, days have passed.' She shook her head. 'That doesn't matter now. We've got to do something about them,' she said, pointing up.

'I-I can't … I've tried but … but they … all of it just won't go away …'

'And they won't. Not while you keep blaming yourself,' Dahlia said.

'But it's my fault I—' Bellina began.

Dahlia slapped Bellina round the face and gripped her shoulders. 'This. Is. Not. Your. Fault,' she said. 'You never meant to harm these people.'

'I've tried to believe that, to … to put all of this out of my mind, but … but I can't go on,' Bellina said, burying her face in her hands.

Dahlia reached out and touched Bellina's chin, gently raising her face. 'You have to go on. As long as you're alive, there is always a chance. A chance to make amends, a chance to put the past behind you, a chance to be happy. Trust me. Please, Bellina.'

Bellina looked into Dahlia's eyes. She saw kindness in them, kindness and hope. A feeling of lightness stole through her body, building, filling her with strength. Above her head, the dead burst into glistening specks and danced off with the breeze.

'Good,' Dahlia said, nodding her head. 'Now we just have to find a way out of this well.'

Bellina laughed. 'We will,' she said. 'Together.'

# CHAPTER TWENTY-TWO

'Build up the fire as you normally would, Holger, but use the sticks you've stored sortilenergy in,' Castros said. The young man nodded.

Del Var wrapped his arms around himself and shivered. They had found refuge from the howling wind in an abandoned shepherd's hut, and not a moment too soon. From out of the building's small window, he could see snow-heavy clouds rolling together overhead, when only thirty minutes before, they had been bathed in bright sunshine.

'Done,' Holger called.

'Good,' Castros said, turning towards him. 'Now, concentrate, make contact with the sortilenergy you've left in the sticks.'

Holger stared at the bits of wood, brow furrowed, lips pressed into a thin line. Castros watched with only a little less intensity than his student. A smile creased his lips as the end of the sticks began to smoke then burst into flame.

'Well done, lad! You've got it,' Del Var exclaimed.

'I-I can't believe it …' Holger said, eyes wide. 'It worked.'

'Course it did! Did you ever doubt my teaching methods?' Castros said with a chuckle.

'I s'pose you were just trying to motivate me when you said I was a pig-headed imbecile then?' Holger asked, a smile on his lips.

'Exactly. Now—' Del Var began.

He was cut off by the hut's door banging open. The major stalked into the room, cheeks raw from the wind. She shot a withering look at the pair of them.

'Wind's letting up. Get moving,' she ordered.

'I don't think that's a good idea, Major. Looks like snow any moment now,' Castros replied.

'Are you defying my orders?' she asked, eyes narrowed to the thinnest of slits.

'I'm afraid I'm going to have to on this one,' Del Var said, his jaw set firm.

Bouchard stepped towards him, her massive frame filling his vision.

'What did you say?' she hissed.

'I will not go out in that,' Castros said.

'Hoped you'd say that,' the major said, a sneer curling her lips.

She reached out and pressed a button on the control conduit on her wrist. With barely a heartbeat in between, Castros felt a bolt of pain shoot from the execution collar at his neck, spreading through his body like a poisonous spider's web.

The shock could only have lasted a second, but to Del Var, it felt like hours. He crumpled to his knees, gasping for air.

'That how you rose through the ranks?' he gasped at Bouchard. 'Torturing anyone who didn't agree with you.'

'Keep going,' she said. 'Give me a reason to push it again.'

'What did I ever do to you?' Castros asked, struggling to his feet.

'What did you …? You cowardly piece of shit—'

'Woah!' Holger yelled, stopping Bouchard's rampage mid-flow.

Castros looked towards him and saw a large ball of flame had formed above the fire. He took out one of his waterskins and directed a jet at the fire, controlling the water and smothering the mini inferno.

'Got to keep your concentration up, boy,' Del Var said to Holger.

'Enough of this nonsense,' Bouchard said. 'Get your shit together; we're moving out.'

Watching her walk out of the door, Castros rubbed the restraint on his neck. For the moment, at least, he kept his opinions to himself.

***

*He was right … again*, Cirona thought, wild flurries of snow whipping against her face.

In front of her, she could just about make out Del Var's back as he struggled forwards. She pulled her cloak tight around her, but the sodden cloth made no difference. The wind screamed in her ears like howling wolves, hungry, searching for flesh to rip and tear.

'Urgh!' she cried, her voice lost in the wind.

She stumbled forwards another step then lost balance. Falling face first into the snow, Cirona swore. On numb hands she pushed herself up. Casting a look towards her feet. She caught sight of a crooked root snaking out of the ground — the perpetrator of her fall. She aimed a petulant kick towards it but soon regretted the waste of energy.

'Holger?' she called as a body became visible in the storm.

The shadow stopped and cocked its head to the side.

'Del Var? Is that you?' she barked, hoping she sounded more

confident than she felt.

The next instant, the shape crouched to the ground and sprung at her on all fours. Cirona just had time to register the grey skin and ape-like arms before the malovor crashed into her.

Together, they went cartwheeling backwards. Cirona locked her arms around the creature and used their momentum to drive the malovor into the ground. Straddling its middle, she aimed a blow at its face, but the thing was lightning fast, throwing a blow of its own that caught Cirona in the throat.

She fell to the side, gasping for air, her throat a swollen, burning lump. The malovor drove a bony knee into her side causing Cirona to collapse forwards. She barely felt the snow forced into her nose and mouth as a strange warmth came over her. Sleep, that was all she had to do; just drift off and …

'You been naughty, Miss. Master gets a-a-angry when youse is n-naughty,' the malovor snarled, grabbing the back of Cirona's hair and wrenching her head up.

*Why won't this fucker let me sleep?* she thought gazing into the thing's beady black eyes. She swung a feeble punch at it, but all she struck was air. With immense strength, the malovor smashed her head forwards into the ground again. Cirona felt searing bolts of pain bloom from her nose as it was crushed on a hidden rock. Her eyes watered, dots danced across her vision … but the pain woke her up.

The malovor began to drag Cirona by her hair along the ground, the top of her scalp screaming in protest. The fingers of her right hand groped at her side then curled round the hilt of her short sword. In one motion, she drew the blade, swinging it up, cutting away her hair and, by the sound of it, some of the malovor's fingers.

She rolled onto her side and managed to pull her body into a crouch. In front of her, she could see the creature, eyes blazing, teeth bared, as it watched its own black blood fall to the ground in steaming drops.

'You ought'a not d-done that,' the thing hissed. 'You wills have to be punished proper now.'

The malovor raced forwards. It pulled back one of its long arms and swung a club-like fist at Cirona's head. Ducking down, she dodged the punch then swung her sword at the creature's middle. At the last second, it twisted its body, turning her attack from a killing blow to a mere scratch. *Fuck! This thing's fast*, she thought.

Dropping to all fours, the thing pounced once more. Cirona swung her arm back, driving the pommel of her sword into its jaw, feeling it crack.

Wary now, the malovor retreated. Making sure her sword was ready to strike in front of her, Cirona began to inch backwards, trying to gain some distance from her attacker. Clearly sensing her trepidation, the creature, blood pouring from its pulverised jaw, crept towards her.

Cirona's eyes darted around her, searching for some form of safety, but there was nothing close to resembling *that* in the desolate snowscape. With no other option, she continued to step back. Her breath caught in her throat as her right heel came down on nothing. Stealing a glance behind her, she saw a drop of at least thirty feet. In an instant, a plan formed in her mind.

'Come on, you ugly bastard!' she yelled at the malovor.

The creature narrowed its eyes at her but still edged forwards with caution. *Damn it*, she thought, *gotta get the fucker to take the bait.*

'Your ... your master,' Cirona called. She noted the flicker of rage leap into the malovor's eyes. Good, she had hit the spot. 'Your master is a disgusting, rotten, fuckwit of an arse, who—'

She cut off her tirade when the malovor's self-control snapped and it tore towards her in a blind fury. Time seemed to slow as Cirona focused every ounce of her concentration on the creature's movements. *Wait*, she told herself, *wait till the last second, girl.*

The malovor closed the last five feet between them with a bloodthirsty lunge. Cirona's primed body spun out of its reach. Running into nothing but air, a look of bewildered fury passed across the thing's face before turning to terror as it fell, limbs flailing, into the abyss.

Cirona sank to the ground as her legs gave way. Her mouth was dry, her nose a smashed ruin, but she was alive, she had ...

Her eyes just had time to register the long, thin fingers coiling around her ankle. The next second, she was falling, falling into darkness.

***

At last, the snow began to let up. Castros came to a stop and looked down into a green valley that stretched before him. He allowed himself a smile; Primus was not far now.

'Hurry up you two we're ...' he began. 'Where's the major?'

Holger looked behind him then back at Castros his brow wrinkled in confusion.

'I-I thought she was behind me,' he said.

'No, she *was* behind *me*,' Castros replied.

'Bloody hells!' Holger cried, rubbing his forehead. 'What do we do now?'

Castros ran a hand through his hair as he weighed up the options. Any tracks the major might have left would almost certainly be covered over with fresh snow by now, and if they were caught in another snowstorm ... *Damn it to the Void*, he thought, punching his thigh.

'We'll double back, look for any traces of her,' he said.

Holger's face lit up with relief. 'Alright,' he replied.

'But if we don't find her in the next thirty minutes, we go on without her, understood?' Del Var said. Holger nodded. 'Good,' Castros continued. 'Let's go.'

They set off, but soon Castros saw that he had been right: their tracks had been covered. Despite his better judgement, he kept on looking. He and Holger had spread out but were still in hailing distance should anything appear. He cursed as a root snagged his foot and sent him stumbling forwards.

'Over here!' Holger called. 'I think I've found something.'

Castros brushed the snow off his trousers and made his way towards Holger. He soon saw what had got the boy excited. In front of him, he saw a series of large divots in the snow and ... blood. Del Var knelt down for a better look. Mingled with the usual red human variety, he saw the unmistakable raven-black blood of a malovor.

Snapping himself to attention, Castros readied a screamer in his hand and gazed around him. It looked as though Bouchard had been attacked by a lone malovor, but it paid to be wary where those abominations were concerned.

'Look,' Holger said, 'the blood leads over here and ... whoa!'

Del Var turned towards the boy. Holger was leaning back, arms pinwheeling as he tried to keep his balance. Castros gave a blast from his screamer, closing the distance between them in a heartbeat, and grabbed the back of Holger's shirt.

'Th-thanks,' the young man said.

'Don't mention it,' Castros replied, peering over the ledge Holger had almost fallen from.

'D-do you think she has fallen down there?'

'Only one way to find out,' Castros said. 'Hang on.'

He grabbed Holger round the waist and gave another burst from his screamer. The air whizzed past their ears as they plummeted over the ledge. Giving another blast of magically infused air, Castros cushioned their descent, and they came to a stop in front of the mouth to a cave.

Del Var cast his gaze around them. On the ground, he could see a trail in the snow, as if someone had been dragged along, leading up to the cave entrance. He could see blood, both human and malovor, as well. Kneeling down, he touched it. Still warm.

'She's alive … at least, she was recently,' he said, straightening up.

He stood looking into the pitch-black cave. It was undoubtedly a malovor hiding place; gods only knew how many of them would be in there. He rubbed at his temples then took a deep breath.

'Holger, give us some light. We're going in.'

***

The smell of dirt permeated Cirona's nostrils. Her eyelids pulled themselves slowly apart as she realised she wasn't cold. Above her head was a roof of mud and dirt, the roots of trees poking out like brown maggots. For a second, she had no idea where she was or what had happened. Then she saw it.

The figure of a malovor was huddled over a pot in the corner, a small fire burning beneath the pot. She wondered how the smoke was getting out of the cave then realised she didn't care. The real question was how was *she* going to get out of there? She had no hope that that piece of scum Del Var would come to help her.

As her eyes grew accustomed to the dark, she saw that the malovor by the fire was different from the one she had fought. It was bent low, the grey skin dangling like drapes from its arms; this one was older. The creature turned. In its hand was a clay mug, steaming gently.

'D-drink this p-please, mistress,' the creature said. 'It help with w-wounds idiot boy g-gave you.'

Cirona took the drink and gave it a suspicious sniff. *If it wanted to kill you, it's had plenty of opportunity*, she told herself. Lifting the mug to her lips, she took a tentative sip. A warm, hearty taste exploded in her mouth, homely, soothing.

'This … this is good,' she said, eyes wide.

'Thanking you, mistress,' the malovor said with a bow so low its nose smacked into the ground. 'Now, we must get you prepared for the ball.'

A mixture of pity and fear swept through Cirona as she watched the creature. This one had lost its mind just like the one who had attacked her; but at least this one was peaceful … for now.

She licked her lips and said, 'I think I had better go now. I … I have an appointment with … the … the master.'

'No, no, mistress, not until you've seen the others. They will be so happy to see you!'

The malovor grabbed her hand and pulled her out of the bed she was lying in. Even though the creature was old, it still possessed enough strength to drag her along, its grip like iron.

She was led down and down through winding tunnels. The walls and roof suddenly expanded, and she found herself standing in a cavernous square room. Beneath her feet, the ground went down in a series of steps cut into the dirt. At the bottom was a circle of malovors sat huddled round a large fire.

The creature holding her hand looked at her, its eyes flickering with excitement. Then she was led down towards the others.

When they came close to the circle, she saw a large malovor was sat in a chair made of roughly hewn rocks. To his side was the one who had attacked her earlier. He had obviously given his report to the large one as it looked at Cirona with withering eyes.

'Look, Vur! Look. I've found the mistress!' The malovor holding her said.

'You idiot Rez; that is not the mistress. She is long dead. These thoughts we have, they's memories of our ancestors, not ours! You know what the mages in red cloaks told us!' Vur shouted at Rez.

Cirona's mind spun. Mages in red cloaks? Surely the purgistas hadn't got here ahead of them? What if this Waltus they were searching for had already been captured. She scrubbed a hand over her face. *One problem at a time*, she thought, *one at a time.*

'Those red cloaks are liars! Filthy, crawling things. They are shit in clothes. Cock-less shrivelled jokes!' Rez screamed, eyes bulging, mouth frothing.

Vur crossed the room and belted Rez in the mouth. The creature fell to the floor and looked up with stunned eyes.

'None o that talk. The red cloaks, they have come to save us. To take us to green fields and blue skies. You remember those in your dreams? We can leave this place like our brothers have already!' Vur said. Around him, the rest of the malovors hollered their approval.

'No! They are the traitors! Deceivers! They wear the flesh of man but are less. We must—'

The rest of the group set upon Rez. Cirona rushed forwards to try and help but found herself caught by Vur. His elongated arms reaching her effortlessly, holding her in a grip of steel.

'What shall we do with them, Vur?' One of the creatures holding Rez asked.

'The red cloaks told us to gets them if others show up. But for now, we will put them in the cells,' Vur replied.

***

'This way,' Castros said to Holger, gesturing for the boy to follow him. The light from the sparkstick — an old mage term for an item imbued with sortilfira — Holger was wielding illuminated the tunnels around them. The magically made fire burned bright and strong despite the eddies of wind that whipped though gaps in the rock and earth.

Trailing Bouchard's passage through the underground lair was a lot easier than out in the snow. A thin track of blood stained the floor, a crimson thread leading them into gods only knew what kind of trouble.

'What is this?' Holger said as they turned a corner and walked into what looked like a kitchen.

'This is how the malovors live,' Castros replied. 'No doors; the tunnels just lead into each other's homes. True communal living.'

Del Var took in the home, though room was a better term for the space. The trail of blood stopped here, beside a bed with a crumpled, threadbare sheet on top of it. He wandered over to a pot, still bubbling on top of a small fire. He sniffed the contents: a basic mage healing potion. Castros frowned. Whoever had brought the major here seemed to have treated her wounds. If that was the case then the malovors here had definitely lost it, unable to tell friend from foe, confusion reigning in their small minds.

'There's another bit of blood by this tunnel, and I can hear something. Sounds like talking. Coming from that direction,' Holger said, pointing down a tunnel that led out of the room.

'Put out your sparkstick and follow me … quietly,' Castros said, tiptoeing into the passage.

As they made their way down the tunnel, following the now intermittent drops of blood, the sound of talking grew louder, accompanied by the smell of roasting meat. Castros felt his stomach squirm as he contemplated just what *type* of meat the malovors could have possibly scrounged up.

No more than a minute later, they came upon the creatures. Castros counted six of them sat round a fire, an unidentifiable lump of flesh cooking on a spit above it.

'Shit,' Del Var said, looking down at the gathering. 'We'll have to tread carefully here if we want to find out what happened to the major. Luckily, we're the only ones with mage blood around here, so they *should* listen to our commands.'

'I don't like the sound of that should,' Holger said, wetting his lips and staring down at the malovors.

'Follow my lead, and with a bit of luck, we should get out of this none the worse,' Castros said, clapping Holger on the back and hoping he sounded convincing.

He strode down the steps, the heads of the malovors turning towards him. *Keep calm*, he told himself, *have to appear dominant.* Part of him wanted to leg it, but he had Holger to think about. Stopping in their centre, he eyeballed each creature in turn. A lead weight formed in his stomach, and he had to stifle a gasp when only one of them looked away.

'How dare you treat us with such disrespect!' he said. 'Can you not sense we are mages?'

The sound of harsh laughter came from a shadowed tunnel to the right. A malovor, considerably bigger than the others, stalked towards Castros. The other creatures bowed their heads and withdrew, leaving a clear path for the newcomer. He stopped an inch away from Del Var and sniffed.

'Mage?' the malovor rasped, before letting out another bark of laughter. 'You're a half-breed, not pure blood. And as for him,' the creature said, pointing at Holger. 'Mage blood's as thin in him as week-old gruel.'

Castros felt his mouth go dry, and he had to force himself to maintain eye contact. This was not going to plan, not by a far throw.

'You have taken hostage a friend of ours. Give her back now, and you will receive no further punishment,' Del Var said.

'We do not take orders from you,' the large malovor spat. 'You will join your friends and wait for the new masters to come.'

'What do you mean new masters?' Castros said, his stomach morphing into a lead ball.

'You will see them soon enough, half-breed. Take them to the cells,' the lead malovor ordered.

'Get a sparkstick ready,' Del Var said to Holger as the rest of the creatures advanced on them.

Hunching his shoulders forwards, Castros waited. As soon as the malovors had bunched up around him, he let loose a blast from his screamer. The explosion of air struck the creatures hard and sent them spinning backwards.

'Throw your stick at the big one,' Del Var shouted at Holger. 'Once it lands, make the flame as big as you can get it.'

Holger got ready to throw, but one of the malovor's regained his feet faster than Castros had expected. It dived at Holger, knocking his aim off course and taking the boy to the ground. Del Var shot a jet of air at it, sending the creature flying backwards, smashing into the nearest wall with a bone-crunching thump. *One down, six to go*, Castros thought.

The rest of the malovors had regained their feet and were circling around Castros and Holger. The pair formed up, back to back, moving around in their own tight circle, trying to keep watch for where the next would come from.

'Got any more bright ideas, Mr Follow My Lead?' Holger hissed at Del Var.

'Keep yourself focused, smart-arse. If the big one so much as twitches, let me—'

Castros was cut off as two malovors lunged at him. He hit one with his screamer, but the second dodged and drove a fist into Del Var's stomach. He buckled over, and the next second, he felt a blow to the base of his exposed neck.

Falling face first into the ground, Castros struggled to pull himself up. He let out a gasp as a tremendous weight landed on his back, pinning him to the floor. The malovor on his back began to pound him in a manic fury. Del Var could hear Holger's cries ringing in his ears. A hot trickle of guilt poured through him. He had led the boy into this; he was sure as fuck going to get him out of it.

Aiming his screamer at the ground, Castros emptied the last of its contents. Both he and the malovor on his back sped towards the cavern's roof. The creature let out a scream of anger and fear, the sound bitten off when its skull piled into the rock above its head.

Castros fell back to the ground with a massive bang. Pain seared beneath his chest, and he knew he had busted at least two of his ribs. With no time to feel sorry for himself, Del Var hauled his body into a standing position.

'Stay where you are,' a voice called.

Turning around, Castros saw that the large malovor had taken Holger hostage, a vicious dagger pointed at the boy's throat. The remaining creatures stood behind their leader, a look of hungry expectation on their faces.

'Hands in the air,' the malovor commanded.

Del Var did as he was told. His mind spun, a tornado of thought, as he tried to formulate a plan. An idea struck him, but it would take time … time they might not have. *Got to stall him*, Castros thought.

'You have served your new masters well,' Castros said, willing a thin trickle of magically enhanced water out of its container and up his back, out of the malovor's sight.

'We is always serving our masters well,' the creature said, a look of pride in his eyes. His followers grunted their agreement.

'I'm sure that is true,' Castros said. 'Who is your new master? Perhaps

I know him?'

'The red cloaks have their own master, Garand they call him. But we be following our own. Only helps the red ones 'cos he told us to.'

*Just a few more seconds*, Castros thought, as he condensed the water into a compact ball behind his right ear. 'And who is that?' he said.

'The Heir of Excellus, the new Tharg Dessen, the new chosen one,' the malovor replied, his eyes brimming with tears.

The creature's words hit Del Var like a blow to the gut. There was only one person who might possibly fit that description, but he was dead … Castros had seen it with his own eyes. Just what the hells was going on here?

'Enough talk,' the malovor spat. 'Youse is trying to tricks me. But Vur is smart. Vur knows.'

'I will ask you once more,' Castros said, freezing the water behind his ear. 'Let my companions go, and no harm shall come to you.'

'I will never—'

Castros cut the malovor off by firing his water bullet between the creature's eyes. Vur collapsed to the ground, dead. Seeing their leader slain, the rest ran off shrieking into the tunnels.

'They'll be back before long with reinforcements,' Del Var said. 'We have to move.'

Spotting a drop of blood by a tunnel mouth to their right, they set off, Castros leading the way. After making their way through a series of winding, cramped passages, they found themselves by a wooden door. Del Var froze the crude lock on it with some sortilaqua and pushed the door open. Inside, he saw an old malovor standing over the major.

'Get away from her,' Holger said, rushing forwards and pinning the creature to the wall.

'Holger wait!' Cirona cried. 'He saved my life.'

'Who is this, mistress?' the creature asked Cirona.

'These are friends of mine, Rez. They … they have come to help us,' she said, looking at Del Var, disbelief writ large on her face.

'Major, listen to me. This is not a pet. It is a deranged creature who's got you muddled up with a memory locked into its being!' Del Var said. 'It can't be trusted.'

'I trust him more than you,' Bouchard said. 'Besides, he knows a shortcut to Primus.'

Castros watched, watched as she set her jaw firm, a steely glint in her eye. He'd seen that look a thousand times from Nairne over the years; the woman had made up her mind.

'Fine. Whatever. Let's go before any more of them show up,' Del

Var said.

The sound of shrieking echoed out of the passage they had just come down.

'Sounds like they're already here,' Holger said, his eyes wide.

'Shit! Move, all of you … now,' Del Var said.

'Lead the way, Rez,' Bouchard said.

'Of course, mistress. I will lead you from the tunnels first. We mustn't run into the ones who have been swayed by the red cloaks!' Rez said, sprinting off.

The malovor set off at an ungainly sprint, Castros and the rest trailing after him. He didn't like that they were now being led by a lunatic remnant of a broken people. But then there was a lot he didn't like at the moment, primarily that there was another mage in the Shattered Land who had the power to convince the malovors that he was the Tharg Dessen.

# CHAPTER TWENTY-THREE

'Are you sure about this?' Elvgren asked, looking out into the sea of faces.

'Yes, yes; you will be fine,' the duke replied.

'They don't look very ... er ... friendly,' Elvgren said.

'They'll love you. Just get up there and tell them how great Tremore is, that the running of the Empire from Victory is failing, etcetera, etcetera.'

'I'm really not—'

A smile made of pure ice fixed itself on the duke's face. 'My dear Lord Elvgren, one of the main reasons I decided to let you into the fold was your totemic value. If the people see that the Lord Chancellor's handpicked successor thinks his rule is cancerous, well, the little people will surely agree.'

'But—'

'No more buts! Off you go,' the duke said, pushing Elvgren towards the podium steps. 'And remember — you're being broadcast on cognovision to cities and towns across Tremore, so smile!'

Half stumbling, half falling, Elvgren lurched up the steps. The rally the duke had dragged him to was taking place at Spinoza's docks. In front of him, he saw the stern, grim faces of the cargo movers, ship hands and manual labourers, all looking distinctly unimpressed. A man at the front, chewing mechanically, aimed a large, dark squirt of tobacco juice at the base of the podium.

Elvgren took a step forwards, towards a drum-like contraption atop a metal pole that the duke said would amplify his voice.

'Er ...' Elvgren said into it, pulling back as a strange squeal pierced the air. He could already hear Dargo laughing behind him. Undoing the top button of his shirt, he tried again. 'Gentlemen, ladies, I-I would like to ... um say a few words about ... er'

'Speak up!'

'Nancy boy!'

'Noble arse-wipe!'

Anger flared in Elvgren's gut; how dare they speak to him in such a fashion!

*Easy now*, he told himself, *gotta put on a good show.*

'Ladies and gentlemen,' he began again, 'I know the pain you feel. I know how you suffer. How we all suffer under the yoke of the Lord Chancellor. How his governing has led to the loss of our foreign territories. The unsightly and unholy affair that took place in Prinargo Luminaro, which I was, to my deepest regret, some small part of. As his deputy, I have witnessed first-hand the man's tyranny and fecklessness.

'I am here today to tell you that there is another way. A prosperous way. A way that will return the Empire to its full glory. And that way will be led by Tremore and the hardworking men and women within it.'

To his amazement, the crowd erupted into cheers. Elvgren felt the warmth of the crowd wash over him. It was glorious, just like being back in the battle square.

'I thank you,' he said. 'I thank you all. Together we will make a brighter future.'

Elvgren stepped back from the voice amplifier, bowing, waving and blowing kisses to the crowd.

'That is quite enough, Lord Elvgren,' the duke said, climbing onto the stage. 'You are merely the warm-up act after all.'

'Er … yes … yes, of course,' Elvgren replied, hastening to leave the podium.

Dargo waited for him at the bottom of the steps, a huge grin on his face.

'You got there in the end,' he said.

'Managed it somehow,' Elvgren replied, still a touch stunned by the crowd's reaction.

'That microphone thingy and cognovision they've got are something else,' Dargo said, scratching his chin.

'Well the duke does pay top money to the brightest scholars from Gortrix,' Elvgren replied, looking back with longing at the stage upon which the duke was now speaking.

'Sure, your future father-in-law will be interested in all o this,' Dargo said.

'What? Oh … yes, yes, lots to put in that report for him,' Elvgren said.

'Just gotta figure out how to sneak outta the palace later.'

'That's nice, Dar.'

'Are you even listening to me?'

'Of course,' Elvgren said, tearing his eyes from the crowd. 'Escape the palace, get the report sent.'

A roar, even louder than the one Elvgren had received, met the end of the duke's speech. Smiling and waving, the ruler of Tremore left the podium and strode towards Elvgren.

'Now that's done with, shall we conclude our tour of the docks,' Tobért said.

'That would be fantastic, your Grace,' Elvgren replied with a bow.

The duke nodded then clicked his fingers. An army of valets and servants appeared as if from thin air, three men alone brushing off his clothes and fixing his hair. Elvgren nodded with appreciation; they certainly knew how to do things in Tremore. The Lord Chancellor would never allow himself, or Elvgren, to be fussed over in such a manner.

A litter was summoned and Elvgren and the duke were helped inside. Dargo climbed in as well and Tobért raised an eyebrow.

'Do you always allow your man such freedoms,' the duke said.

'He wouldn't be able to wipe his nose without me,' Dargo said, settling himself into the plush seat.

The duke stroked his chin. 'I am not sure yet, Master Dargo,' he said, 'whether I find your cheek refreshing or insolent. For the moment, I shall choose the former.'

'Where are we off to next, your Grace?' Elvgren asked, hastening to change the subject.

'Hmm? Ah, yes! We are off to see my babies,' the duke replied.

Tobért banged on the litter's roof and they began to move. Outside of the window, Elvgren saw a whirlwind of industry. Ships choked the docks, workers scurried around, and the factories belched smoke into the sky. It was a far cry from the industrial district of Victory where many of the smokestacks had fallen silent thanks to the severe dip in sortilenergy production.

'Tell me, your Grace, how is it you still have enough power for all this production?' Elvgren asked.

'An excellent question, Elvgren,' the duke said, his face lighting up. 'We are using that foul-smelling stuff the Burkeshis have — yak-something-or-other.'

'Yaksit?' Elvgren said.

'That's the one,' Tobért said, clapping his hands together. 'Can never remember the name of the rotten stuff. Works a treat though and only requires a few tweaks to a tharg engine to get it to work. Marvellous, absolutely marvellous!'

The duke settled back in his seat and produced a golden pillbox from his pocket. He flipped open the lid. Eyeing its contents with great eagerness, he took a small violet tablet from within and popped it into his mouth.

He caught Elvgren staring and said, 'Where are my manners! Would you like one? Can't get enough of the buggers. My chemisticians knocked them up for me. Give me the energy for all of this,' the duke said, waving his arm around.

'I'm fine, thank you, your Grace,' Elvgren said, swatting Dargo's hand back down as he reached towards the box.

'For the love of the Father, Elvgren, call me Tobért!'

'I … I will try, your … Tobért.'

The rest of the ride was filled with an incessant and overly enthusiastic barrage of questions and chit-chat from the duke. Elvgren offered a silent prayer of thanks when they finally came to a stop.

'Here already, eh? Time really does fly when you are having fun,' the duke said as a servant helped him from the vehicle.

*I'm sure those pills help with that*, Elvgren thought as he and Dargo exited the litter. In front of him, he saw a massive factory, doors the size of ironclad ships set in the middle of its facade. Even from outside, the buzz and whir of machinery filled the air.

'You're the first person I've shown these to, Elvgren; I hope you like them,' Tobért said, storming towards the building, his retinue of retainers practically running to keep up.

'I am most honoured,' Elvgren replied, his chest swelling. This whole "winning over the duke malarkey" was going swimmingly; the man already seemed quite taken with him.

'I'm not sure about that bloke, Gren,' Dargo said, dousing Elvgren's mood.

'Don't be such a pill, Dar,' he replied with a pout, hurrying to catch up with the duke.

'My Lords,' a man at the factory entrance said with a bow. 'It is a fine day when two such noble men attend our little workshop.'

'Richélle,' the duke said, taking the man's hand and pumping it like a crank, 'may I introduce Lord Elvgren Lovitz, the newest and grandest addition to our cause. Elvgren, this is Richélle, the factory overseer.'

Richélle turned to Elvgren and gave another deferential bow. 'Your reputation precedes you, Lord Elvgren. It is a great boon for our side to have you with us.'

'Why … thank you,' Elvgren said, shaking the man's hand, the praise crackling through his blood like a lightning storm.

'How goes the work?' Tobért asked.

'Why not come in and see for yourself, your Grace,' Richélle said.

The overseer beckoned for them to follow and opened a small door to the side of the large ones. The whole entourage piled in. It took Elvgren's eyes a few seconds to adjust from the bright sunshine outside to the gloomy interior. When they did, he felt his breath catch.

There, rising up to the dizzying heights of the ceiling were the largest automaton soldiers he had ever seen. The mechanical creations had to stand over a hundred feet tall, the tops of their domed heads brushing the rafters. The sight was so overwhelming Elvgren barely noticed that a flock of servants had begun scrubbing away the dirt and debris from his and Tobért's boots.

'Quite something, aren't they?' the duke said, slapping Elvgren on the back.

'How … how in the world … I mean, I've seen the automaton soldiers from the Mage War … but this …' Elvgren babbled.

'Pah, those rusty old relics aren't fit for scrap,' Tobért said with a sniff. 'My children, the Gomech Warriors, are the future!'

'But … there can't be enough sortilenergy in the world to fuel these … these warriors,' Elvgren said.

'Don't need any mage juice. We've got yak-i-me-bob now, and there's plenty where that came from,' the duke said, beaming up at the gomechs.

Elvgren stood in stunned silence, his head shaking gently back and forth. His report to the Lord Chancellor was going to read like a fairy tale.

***

Bellina and Dahlia fell back to the dry floor of the well with a bump. Too tired to move, Bellina lay on her back panting. So far, all their efforts to climb out had ended in failure. Swaying above them was the rope and bucket, tantalisingly out of reach. This was ridiculous; how the hells could they be defeated by something so simple?

*So much for discovering my destiny*, Bellina thought, thinking back to her conversation with Yevad.

'Come on,' she said, hauling her weary body from the floor, her jaw set firm. 'Let's give it another go.'

'Can I have a few more minutes please,' Dahlia said, panting.

Bellina looked down at the prone body of her fellow cognopath. Dahlia was covered in dust and grime, her fingers raw and bloody from their attempts to climb out. She didn't have to be here helping. A few minutes rest was small recompense for the debt Bellina felt she owed the other girl.

Sitting back down, Bellina rested her back against the cool stone of the well wall. She looked up, out through the circular window that was the watering hole's opening and saw candyfloss wisps of cloud chase each other across a violet sky. *I wonder if this is how prisoners feel*, she thought.

*Don't be so melodramatic!* a voice inside her head called out. *You're sitting next to a girl who's been locked up her whole life.*

Bellina hugged her knees and gazed across at Dahlia. 'What … What's it like?'

'Huh?' Dahlia said, raising herself into a seated position.

'The … er … compound,' Bellina replied.

Dahlia gave a small shiver, swallowed hard and, in a small voice, said, 'It's … It's not good.'

'How do they treat you there?' Bellina asked.

'Some of the guards are alright,' Dahlia replied, tilting her head to the side. 'But most are disgusted by us. They don't really talk to us, but you can see it in their eyes. Always ready to give you a shock through your power restraint too.'

'Do you get to see your family?'

Dahlia laughed, a sharp and bitter sound like a bottle of medicine shattering. 'I don't have any family. I'm a bastard. My mother was a prostitute. High-end. My father was some noble. Had her killed when she tried to use me to blackmail him.'

'By the gods!' Bellina said. 'That's awful.'

'It was alright for a while,' Dahlia continued. 'The other girls at the brothel looked after me. One of them, Allé, used to braid my hair, give me sweets. Then, when I started exhibiting signs of my powers … well, you can imagine what happened.'

Silence fell over them as Dahlia wiped at her eyes. Bellina rocked back and forth, trying to take in all that she had heard. If her recent past had taught her anything it was to appreciate the life she had led. But each time she thought she did, something else came along to put it into greater perspective. She wanted to reach out, to find the right words or gesture to comfort her companion, but nothing seemed adequate.

'Right,' Dahlia said, getting to her feet and offering Bellina her hand. 'Shall we try again?'

# CHAPTER TWENTY-FOUR

The air on top of the mountain pass was clear and bracing. A soft blue sky spread above them, a dreamy ocean studded here and there with galleons made of clouds. And beneath him, Castros Del Var could see the city of Primus.

It was a sight to take the breath away. Built to resemble a Vitaspiral, the city descended to the ground in concentric circles of terraces that throbbed with buildings. Down and down it plunged till, at its centre, a splinter of a tower rose into the sky, a white digit proclaiming its brilliance to the heavens. From where Castros stood, the bridges that crossed the span from the outer edges of circle to the tower looked like strands of thread, a spider's web waiting for flies.

'Gods that is quite a sight!' Holger said, coming to stand beside Del Var.

'I know. It was the only place the Empire couldn't destroy after the war. All the buildings have been magically bonded like the Castrian Wall in Victory,' Del Var replied.

'No wonder all those other villages were so small,' Holger said, scratching his chin.

'Yep. This is where the vast majority of the population lived. The places we've been through were built for the less magically gifted members of society. This was the capital of a king.'

'Good grief!' Bouchard said, finally catching up. 'This is a bit much.'

Castros allowed his companions a few minutes to drink in the scene. He knew himself that it took a while to get used to. His mind flashed back to seven years ago, standing in a similar place, looking down on the city. Staring down into the heart of the country whose inhabitants had tried to enslave mankind but had become slaves themselves. Del Var's thoughts were broken off by an excited squeal.

'Oh, mistress! We are almost there. Do you think His Majesty will let me serve you at his ball?' Rez said.

'I'm sure he will,' Bouchard replied to the creature.

Castros frowned, wondering how a woman so blunt could act so soft towards Rez. Despite the fact it showed an unexpected side to the major, this was a turn of events he was not happy with. An unhinged malovor was not a pet or something to be pitied, in his eyes. It was a thing, a tool. Though he had to admit that Rez had been useful in getting them here.

'Come on,' Del Var said, setting off down the mountain path towards the city.

After an hour's energy-sapping descent, the group arrived at the uppermost level of Primus. Castros had forgotten just how far down the city plunged as he took in the vertigo-inducing scene.

'Where to now?' Bouchard asked.

'Unfortunately, we have to go down to the lowest level. That's where Waltus will be, if not right now then at some point. It's also a good place to scavenge for supplies,' Del Var replied.

'That is easier said than done. I cannot see any stairs,' Holger said.

'Ha! As if mages used anything as mundane as stairs!' Castros replied.

'What are you talking about?' the major said.

'You'll see …'

Setting off around the outer edge of the top level of Primus, Castros soon found what he was looking for. In front of him, choked by weeds and grass, was a stone plinth. On its top was a Vitaspiral with a handprint in the centre. Touching the mark with his palm, Del Var waited.

A soft swooshing sound came up to them. It grew louder and louder until a round floating platform hovered before them. The blue crystal of its base shimmered and wriggled with the expelled sortilaero that kept it afloat.

'All aboard!' Castros said, hopping on. He was gingerly followed by the others.

The platform began to slowly float down through the layers of the city. White stone houses glided past as they wove their way between the spindly bridges of Primus.

'How come you know how to use this contraption? I thought you said you didn't know how to use your powers when you first came here,' Holger asked.

'I *couldn't* use this. Had to climb down!' Castros replied having to shout to be heard above the wind.

'Why are these things still working even?' Bouchard said, Rez cringing and clinging on to her trousers.

'Mages built things to last. They didn't think they would lose the war,' Castros said.

The group fell into silence as the platform continued downward.

Before long it came to rest at the bottom of Primus. What, at first, had seemed a tiny dot of a space from above stretched out around them now, the Tower of Dominion rising proudly from its centre.

As they got off the platform, Castros had to stifle a gasp. There, in front of them, was the corpse of a purgista. Del Var's brows knitted together as he went to examine the body. The throat had been crushed, squeezed into the thickness of a rolled-up newsprint; Waltus had definitely killed this man. Had more of them followed the old mage inside?

'Damn it to the Void,' he said.

'The bastards are already here then?' Bouchard asked.

'It would seem so,' Castros answered with a sigh.

Then he saw the blood. Trickles and splashes of it here and there on the pavement. All of it led towards the entrance to the tower.

'Let's go!' Castros called, praying that it wasn't too late.

They sped towards the entrance. It was unlocked. Only himself and Waltus should have been able to open the doors to the Tower of Dominion — another bad sign. Castros rushed in first, the polished marble floor squeaking beneath his boots. There was more blood on the floor and all around them were the petrified remains of malovors.

'See, see you fools! The red cloaks cannot be trusted. Filthy abominations!' Rez roared, looking into the face of one of his kind.

'Don't worry, Rez,' Bouchard said, 'your mistress will see to them!'

With that she drew her sword and sprinted ahead. Castros shook his head and followed with Holger and Rez. The trail of blood led them to another floating platform at the heart of the circular tower.

'Come on, Del Var!' Cirona called, standing in the middle of the platform expectantly.

'Listen, Major, we have to be careful. This place was designed for my kind, and it has lots of'—Castros was interrupted by an alarm blaring out—'security measures.'

Del Var knew there was no time to lose now. He ran onto the platform and placed his hand on the plinth. The device rose through the air with dizzying speed. Half-glimpsed rooms and levels flew by in stuttering snatches of vision.

Suddenly, the platform stopped with a jolt, sending all of them sprawling to the floor. From above, he could hear the sound of fighting.

'Shit!' Castros said.

'What now?' Holger asked.

'We'll have to do this the hard way,' Del Var replied. 'Come on.'

He ran off the platform and headed towards the rooms ahead of him. They would have to take the emergency stairs. The glass doors in front of him opened with a touch of his fingers.

What he saw inside made him pause. During his previous stay with Waltus, he had not been shown all the levels of the tower. Only the ones where the White Mages had carried out their research. But this room, this room was something else.

'What the fuck is going on here?' Bouchard said.

'I think this is an arsenal. Or some kind of weapons development department, at least,' Castros said.

'Arsenal? Weapons development? What the hells was this tower for anyway?' Holger said.

'The Tower of Dominion was the central hub for mage research. As well as being the home of Excellus,' Castros replied.

He did so in a distracted manner. He felt like a child in the greatest toy store ever. All around him were improvements to and superior models of his makeshift screamer and waterskin. The sun streamed through the glass windows of the tower, glinting and reflecting off hundreds of gadgets and contraptions. He wandered towards one table and picked up a thick wrist guard. On its side was a grip for a screamer and a waterskin. He placed two of the devices on his wrists and attached his sortilaero and sortilaqua containers. By flicking his wrists left and right, he realised that he could unleash the powers stored within them, controlling how much was consumed by using different amounts of pressure. He stared at it in wonder.

'What's this?' Holger said.

He was standing next to what looked like a small flat-bottomed boat. Wings of leather spread out from its side. Castros walked over and stepped into the machine. At the front of it was a control panel and a slot for his hands. Pushing them inside, he felt a click as his new weapons fitted into place. His groping fingers caught hold of two handles that could be pulled up, down, left and right.

Licking his lips, he flicked his wrist and released some sortilaero. The machine throbbed into life, and Castros realised that the bottom of the boat was made of the same blue crystal as the floating platform.

Del Var was snapped from his reverie by a huge explosion. Seconds later, there was a crash as something landed at incredible speed on the temporarily disabled platform outside. Castros watched in horror as the something stood up.

'Oh, fuck me, no!' Del Var said. 'The crazy old bastard's let 'em loose!'

'What?' Cirona said

'Not time. Get on!' Castros yelled.

The others ran onto the boat and Castros twisted the handles in his grip. The machine went shooting backwards smashing into a pillar.

'Watch it!' Holger called.

'Sorry!' Del Var said.

Pulling both the handles up, the boat rose into the air. Twisting left, they began to turn and came face-to-face with the thing Waltus had unleashed. It stood seven feet tall, made entirely of craggy rock and stone. The joints of its body were balls of molten light.

'Now will you tell us just what the fuck that thing is?' The major shouted.

'A golem. One of the tower's last line of defence,' Castros said. 'Hang on!'

'Wait! What are you—' Holger began.

Before he could finish, Del Var sent the vehicle straight at the stone monster. The pulsing blue in its eyes didn't even twitch. At the last second, Castros pulled sharply up on the handles and rose over the golem's head. The creature let out a gravelly cry and grabbed hold of the back of the boat.

Despite the added weight, the contraption continued to rise. Up and up Del Var willed the machine. They shot to the top of the tower, careering madly as the golem thrashed about. Unsure how to stop or what to do, Castros let go of the controls. The boat plummeted towards the black marble floor landing with a deafening crash. For a moment, they slid across the slick surface and then the world spun as the vehicle turned.

Castros lay panting on the floor. He felt a weight on his chest and opened his eyes to find Rez lying on top of him. For a split second, their eyes met. Then Del Var pushed him off.

'Everyone alright?' Castros asked.

'Yes,' Holger said.

'Just about!' Cirona replied.

Looking back at the boat, Castros saw that their fall had smashed the head of the golem. *Finally, a bit of luck*, Del Var thought.

'Well, well, well,' a voice said, 'if it isn't Castros Del Var. Still wandering around with a parade of freaks, I see.'

Del Var spun around on his heel as a figure strode into view. Castros saw the man's narrow face. The flame-red hair slicked back with oil, the hollow cheeks, and the eyes, those wild, staring eyes. Del Var felt the breath freeze in his throat. 'Khasal Malifa,' he whispered. 'How the hells—'

'Am I alive?' Khasal said, his pointed teeth exposed in a mockery of a smile. 'Well, it wasn't easy, especially after you fucked off.'

Castros winced at the words. 'I never … it wasn't …'

'Nuh, nuh, nuh, nuh, nuh. What's the matter? Cat got that silver tongue of yours?' Khasal said before turning to Holger and Cirona. 'I suppose he never told you that he had a companion when he first came here?'. They both frowned. 'I thought not. Dear old Castros loves to have company. They serve as good distractions while he hightails it out of danger.'

'What was I supposed to do, Khasal?' Castros said, waving his arms in anger. 'Tell me that? I thought you were dead. If I had stayed, I would've been too. I'm sorry, but whatever it is you think you're doing here, it's got to stop.'

'Stop?' Khasal said. 'Why? It's only just begun.'

With that Malifa fired a jet of flames. Castros sent a blast of air at the floor, avoiding the fire by a hair's breadth. Del Var just had time to note Khasal was wearing a wrist guard similar to the one he had just found before he had to escape another stream of fire.

For the first time, Castros could see the extent of what had been going on in the room. Bodies of malovors lay strewn about, turned to stone. At the back of the room, Del Var caught sight of the old man they had come so far to find.

Waltus was being held in place by a pair of purgistas, five more stood in front of the White Mage. All of their eyes were on Waltus. Castros didn't blame them; the old mage was a wily old sod.

'Major, help—' Castros didn't get a chance to finish his request.

Bouchard leapt at Khasal, blade swinging in a vicious arc. Holger and Rez chased after her, the young man lobbing a sparkstick at Malifa. Del Var's gaze darted between their fight and the unmoving group that had Waltus. *Gods damn it*, he thought.

Tearing towards the purgistas, Castros snapped his wrists up and sent a blast of air at them. They went flying in all directions. Del Var caught a glimpse of the old man. His white hair hung limply across his eyes. He did not look happy.

'You idiot boy! You've ruined everything!' he shouted.

For a second, Del Var was nonplussed, then he heard them. The golems came shooting from the ceiling, landing exactly where the purgistas had been a second before. They turned and smashed their giant craggy hands into the jaws of the Ruzmagi still holding Waltus.

'I … um, came to rescue you?' Castros said as the old man's reproachful glare bore into him.

'To think I would need saving by you! What's wrong with you fuckwit? Water on the brain?'

Del Var tried to find a response, but none came. Instead, he noticed their attackers climbing back to their feet.

'I think we had better go,' Castros said.

'Too right we should! I've rigged them golems to explode in two minutes,' Waltus replied.

'You've what? Shit, never mind,' Del Var said, 'I've got an idea.'

'Oh, this should be good!' Waltus said, giving a mirthless chuckle.

Still, the old man followed him as he set off back towards the flying boat. He grabbed hold of its side and pulled it upright, marvelling at how light it was.

'So, you found the aerolite, eh? Haven't seen the old girl in years,' Waltus mused, scratching his chin.

'Holger! Major! Let's go!' Del Var screamed.

Cirona, Holger and Rez broke off their fight with Khasal, the major throwing the handle of her melted blade at Malifa's face, and hurried towards the aerolite. Once they were all in, Castros brought the machine to life.

'Hold on everybody!' Del Var said.

Before any of them had a chance to comply, Castros drove the aerolite towards the massive windows of the tower. With a tinkling smash they shot into the world outside. For a moment, they plummeted as he fought to control the vehicle. The machine's intuitive handling helped him and they soon levelled out.

As they sped into the distance, monumental explosions sounded behind them. Waltus laughed and Holger cheered while the heat from the blast lapped at their retreating backs.

***

Cirona's stomach lurched as Castros guided the aerolyte through the sky. Down below, the world screamed past in a kaleidoscope of colour. It was the most terrifying thing she had ever experienced, and she hung onto the craft with manic desperation

Looking down, she saw the White Mage sitting in the centre of the flying machine. He was rolling a fag and staring intently at her arse. Cirona felt her face flush and shot the old git her death stare. The mage gave her a wink in return.

'You gonna land this anytime soon, moron? It's fucking freezing up here!' Waltus said.

'Alright, alright! Um … I'm not sure how,' Castros said.

'Stop supplying it with sortilenergy!'

'Gotcha!'

Cirona felt her stomach jump so hard she thought it might escape through her nose. The aerolyte began to plummet through the air at a startling rate.

'Power it again! And this time, stop the flow of energy slowly, you fucking imbecile!' The old mage shouted.

The flying machine levelled out and gently continued its descent. Castros turned round to look at them all, a sheepish grin on his face. Finally, they came to rest in a field of bluebells.

Holger, Cirona, Rez and Castros stepped from the aerolyte on wobbling legs; Waltus hopped out as if nothing had happened. The old man found a rock and perched himself on it. He lit his fag while the others collapsed to the ground.

'No fucking stamina! That's what's wrong with the young today. I got it to burn, just so you know, darling,' Waltus said, sending another wink at her.

'Watch it, you old goat!' Holger said before Cirona had a chance to.

Fixing the boy with a stare, Waltus touched his index fingers to his knees. As he did so Cirona noticed the same spiral that was everywhere in Primus tattooed on his fingertips. The next thing she knew, the old man was behind Holger.

'What did you say, boy?' The old man whispered in his ear.

Before the lad could respond, the White Mage touched the base of Holger's neck. For a second, the spot glowed. Then Holger fell to the ground, twitching like an electrocuted fly.

'What've you done to me?' he said through gritted teeth. 'Whenever I try to move one part of my body, something else moves instead.'

'Just scrambled your mind a wee bit,' Waltus said with a chuckle. The mage walked back to his rock, and Cirona could see the muscles bulging through his trousers. 'It'll wear off in a few seconds, wouldn't do to get a flamer riled up,'

'How did you know that?' Holger asked, regaining control and sitting up.

'Felt it when I touched yer,' Waltus said with a sly grin.

'Your … your legs!' Cirona said, pointing at them.

'Oh this? Just rejuvenated them, not the only thing I can rejuvenate either,' the old pervert said as she blushed.

'Alright, Waltus, have you had enough fun now?'

'S'pose so,' the mage replied, sitting down. 'Where you been anyway, boy? Thought you was going back to the mainland to get me pears.'

'Waltus, that was seven years ago!'

'And? What d'ya think seven years is to a true mage, half-breed? It's a fart in the face of time, that's what! Don't come round 'ere telling me about your seven fucking years!' Waltus said, puffing angrily on his smoke. 'You got 'em then?'

'Well, I did, but we lost them with the majority of our supplies on our way here.'

'So, not only did you ruin my perfect and well executed plan, you lost me fucking pears as well?'

Castros nodded meekly. Cirona was bemused by the conversation and the deferential attitude of Del Var. In all the time she had known the man, she had never seen him like this.

'We came to ask a favour,' Castros said.

'Oho! A favour, is it? Well I ain't in the favouring mood. Got Ruzmagi traipsing all over me home, that little shit Khasal stirring things up, malovors running wild and you idiots steaming into places you're not needed. All in all, favours are the last thing I'm looking to hand out,' Waltus said.

'Please! It's … well, I don't care if it sounds corny … it's the woman I love. We are meant to be together, just me and her. I can't live without her. Please help her wake up!' Holger said, looking up into the old man's eyes.

Cirona found the outburst unsettling. There was more than a hint of madness in the boy's eyes. It made her wonder if what Holger was experiencing was not love so much as obsession.

Waltus coughed up a blob of phlegm and spat it on the ground. 'Love, pah, what a load of old cobblers,' he said.

Cirona puffed out her chest and stepped forwards, poking a finger into Waltus' bony chest. 'Look, you old bastard, we need your help. Now, this girl means a great deal to me, and you're going to help, either by choice or by force,' she said, nostrils flaring.

The old mage stared at her, the fag on the end of his lip bobbing up and down frantically as he mulled over his decision. 'You're lucky I can't refuse a damsel in distress, especially a feisty one,' the White Mage said. 'Fine, I'll help yer. Got a condition, though. Come over here, and I'll whisper it to you.'

Cirona raised an eyebrow and looked at Del Var who let out an exasperated sigh before gesturing her to go over. With a great deal of reluctance, she walked over to Waltus. He crooked a finger for her to lean closer.

She pulled back, startled at the filth that came out of his mouth. 'You … you old … it's lucky for you we need you, otherwise …' she said, kicking him in the shin.

'Alright, sweetheart, don't get yer drawers in a twist. Don't ask, you don't get, eh?' the old man said, roaring with laughter.

'Now, if you're quite finished, can you tell us what the hells is going on here?' Castros said.

'Buggered if I know. Khasal and some Ruzmagi showed up a few months back, only knew about it 'cos the malovors were all riled up. Bloody gits have been feeding 'em some line about making them free back on Estria,' Waltus replied, wiping the escaped tears of his laughter away.

'What in the world are they up to?' Holger said, scratching his chin.

'I don't know, but whatever it is, it won't be good,' Castros replied. 'How long will it take you to get ready, Walt?

'Well, there's the thing, see. All my gear is back down there,' he said, pointing towards Primus. 'Gonna have to go back if I'm gonna come riding to the rescue for this juicy little peach.'

Cirona's eyes flashed and her jaw tightened at the mage's remark. It had really come to something when the fate of someone she had grown to love and respect rested in the lustful palm of an old perv.

'Hells! The tower's bound to be crawling with Ruzmagi,' Castros said.

'Not going to the tower. Gotta go somewhere worse,' Waltus said with a grin.

'You don't mean …'

'Oh yes!' The White Mage said with a smirk.

'What the fuck are you two blathering on about? Gonna let us in on this or what?' Cirona said.

'We gotta go to the Pit, lass,' Waltus replied.

***

Castros stood at the controls of the aerolyte and felt his meagre breakfast lurch inside him; he was not much taken with this version of flying. From the iron grip he saw Rez had on Cirona, the malovor didn't enjoy it either. *Not much further*, he thought, girding his stomach as the city of Primus flew past.

'What is this Pit anyway?' Cirona asked.

'Genetic research department,' Waltus replied.

'Genetic what?' Holger said.

'The study of genes, what you're made up of. Good grief, the ignorance you humans still live in! If only yer hadn't been so keen to blow everything here up, you woulda been a hundred years more advanced than you are. Learnt loads when we created the cognopaths,' he said, staring towards the sky.

'Created? What? *You* created the cognopaths?' Holger said.

'Well, I suppose created is the wrong word. More like we rejigged the human subjects' brains. This was back when we were trying to figure out why humans can't use sortilenergy. No physical difference between our races. The cognopaths were one of our triumphs,' Waltus replied. 'Had a lot of success down in the Pit. Lot of failures too …'

Castros stared at the old man. The words "rejigged the human subjects' brains" rang around his head. The old mage had uttered the phrase without a hint of remorse. This was exactly the kind of flippancy that had made mages so hated, that had led to them being used as human batteries.

Returning his eyes forwards, Castros saw they had passed the city. In the shadow of the capital, a fissure ran through the ground. Steam poured out of it in sinuous tendrils, suffocating the land it touched. A faint turquoise light shone from the crack, gleaming like light caught in a dead man's eye. The sight made him shudder in recognition.

Del Var brought the aerolyte to the ground, close to the mouth of the hole. Some fifty paces away stood a plinth like the one he had used to call the platform back in Primus. They all disembarked and set off towards it. This time, Waltus placed his hand inside the symbol.

'Right you lot, gonna have to keep yer wits about you down 'ere,' Waltus said as they waited for the platform.

'What's down there?' Holger asked.

'Hopefully, you won't find out. Try to stay together and don't follow any of the sounds,' Castros said. 'If you only listen to one thing I say, don't follow those sounds.'

'Alright, Del Var, we get it,' Cirona said.

Castros' face was a mask of anxiety as they waited for the platform to arrive. The others stepped on, but Castros found his leg hovering between firm ground and the platform. *Surely, it won't be as bad as last time*, he thought before climbing aboard.

'Nancy,' Waltus said, shaking his head at him.

With a touch of the old man's hand, the platform began to descend. The crack of the Pit swallowed them greedily. Soon the sky was nothing more than a ribbon of blue floating on the breeze. Dark pools of shadows formed around the jagged shards of rock and dirt that lined the walls of the fissure, dancing and unnerving. They ran together in places and took on shapes that were hideous and grotesque.

All the while, the mist that had been spilling out from the crack bubbled around them. It filled Del Var's nostrils with a bitter tang that made him cough. The mist also helped to obscure the floor of the Pit, stretching out and down in a thick carpet of white. The blue light still shone through it though, growing brighter and more urgent by the second.

Finally, the platform broke through the mist, and Castros could see down to the bottom. Down and down it plunged, past the point any sane person would have thought possible. The strip of turquoise grew to the width of a river as they neared the nadir of the cleft in the ground. It washed over them all, adding a shimmering veil of unreality to the countenances of his companions. Rez had curled up into a ball at Cirona's feet and was shaking. Castros felt like joining him.

At long last, they landed, and they all stepped out onto the turquoise crystal.

'What is this stuff?' Cirona asked.

'Compacted mana. It's the source mages draw their power from. The Shattered Land is the only place in the world where it occurs like this. Well, one of two ...' Castros answered.

Ahead of them, Waltus had made his way towards a giant arched door cut into the vertical face of the rock. At its centre was another spiral symbol with a place for a hand. The old mage placed his hand upon it and the doors slid apart. He turned to them and, with a jerk of his head, beckoned them over. Castros saw that Cirona practically had to carry Rez to get him to move forwards.

As they all gathered in the mouth of the door, he watched lights lining a tunnel flicker into existence.

'Stay close,' Waltus said as he set off.

The group huddled together; they would have done even without the old mage's warning. Along the tunnel, other passages dovetailed away, humming with a darkness that was absolute. The lights that had come on were giving off a feeble attempt at illumination, as if they too were struggling against the oppressiveness of the Pit.

A crushing silence fell over them as they edged their way warily along the tunnel. Even Waltus seemed to be more cautious now. A screech echoed from one of the side passages. Del Var's head jolted after it, eyes twitching and squinting into the gloom.

'What was—' Holger began.

'Keep going,' was the only reply from Waltus.

Swallowing hard, Castros willed his feet to carry on. Sensing the fear in Holger and the major, he turned and said, 'Don't worry. Worst part's almost over.'

They nodded in reply. Castros felt his mouth convulse and hoped it looked like he was smiling and not having a fit.

After what felt like hours, they came to another door. This one seemed to have some kind of warning sign on it. Waltus hovered his hand in front of it, trembling ever so slightly.

'Hope yer not afraid of heights,' he said with a dry chuckle.

The door slid apart at his touch. In front of them, a spindly twig of a path threaded its way across a chasm. Smoke billowed up from below making visibility almost non-existent. Castros could just make out the roof of the space disappearing upwards.

'Wh-what is this place?' Holger whispered.

'Used to be the maintenance passage. Used it as an emergency exit as well,' Waltus replied.

'Are you telling me this is the safest route we can take?' Cirona said.

'Yes. Yes, it is. And that alone should tell yer something 'bout the other passages,' Waltus said. 'Enough of this. Fucking nattering won't get us to the other side.'

With that he took the first step out onto the path. The others stood looking at one another. Realising that their companions couldn't offer an alternative solution, they too stepped on, Cirona having to pry Rez off her leg before setting out.

Step followed nervous step as they inched their way along the thin strand of path. Behind Castros, Rez was making a nervous whine. In front, he could just about see Holger's form, tense with concentration. As they continued, the mist grew ever denser. Soon, all he could see was the next step forwards. Heart hammering in his chest, Del Var willed his shaking feet forwards.

Suddenly, there was a faint clicking sound. It echoed around the cavern and then seemed to be answered.

'What was that?' Holger said.

'Ignore i—' Castros began to say.

The words died in his throat as he heard the clicking sound pass somewhere in front of him with a whoosh.

'Shit! Damn it all to the fucking Voi—aaaargh!' Waltus screamed.

'What's going on? Show yerself you fucking coward! I know yer out there, I can smell yoo—oohwh …' Cirona cried.

This time, Castros felt the breeze as something swooped in front of him and snatched the major. Behind him, Rez was whimpering to himself. Del Var felt the urge to comfort him, but he had to stay alert. His eyes tried to peer through the mist, straining themselves in the futility of the task. His mouth was dry, and he attempted to lick her lips, but the cracked skin passed roughly across the underside of his tongue.

The low throb of the clicking sound started again. It grew closer and closer. Castros stood frozen to the spot, his mind and body unable to deal with the situation. As the sound grew, he had a fraction of a second to turn his head towards it. Through the smoke, he saw a gigantic shadow race towards him. It burst through the mist like some kind of nightmare. Rough claws bit into his shoulder, then he was flying through the air, Rez's screams and cries echoing in his wake.

***

Castros felt himself soaring through the air. Whatever the creature was, it was holding him so he couldn't see its face. He *could* see and feel its dark bony talons penetrating the muscles of his shoulder, though.

His mind raced, and he thought about attacking the beast with his screamer. Luckily, he still had enough sense to realise what a bad idea that would be so far from the ground with no clue where he was.

The wall of the cavern came rushing towards him. His stomach lurched as he was thrown at it. A hole in the rock swallowed him, and he hit the floor hard before rolling to a halt.

Pushing himself up from the ground, he wheezed and tried to get some breath back in his lungs. Something beneath his hands felt sticky and slick, and he realised he was lying in a giant smear of white excrement. It's rancid stench attacked his nose making him retch.

Behind him, the low click that had announced the creature's arrival came to him. He turned towards it, and for the first time, he could see his kidnapper. In the mouth of the cave sat a monumental bat, its blind eyes shimmering yellow from some inner fire. The top of its head was crested with scaled horns, twisted and bent. For a few seconds, it regarded him then flew away.

Del Var scrambled to his feet, slipping and sliding in the muck. He landed flat on his face, the wind going out of him for a second time. As he lay panting on the floor he felt the wound that the creature had left in his shoulders begin to burn. It started as a low heat but slowly it built itself to a crescendo of flame. Waves of fire coursed through his body, and his mind whirled.

The walls of the cave started to melt away, in their place a room formed. An ornate lounge pulled itself into existence around him. He saw a young boy, himself, having his hair tugged into shape by the woman he had called his mother, back when he was innocent, back before he knew the truth.

Light filtered into the room glinting from the gilt-edged furniture. Paintings of the men and women he had thought were his ancestors stared down disapprovingly around him. Maids and servants buzzed around in a state of high anxiety laying out an elaborate tea service.

'There! I think that will have to do. Your hair, Balthazar, I swear one day I shall cut it all off and leave you bald the trouble it gives me,' the woman said with a smile.

'Yes, Mama,' his child self said, grimacing and scratching at his head.

'Now, go and fetch your father; our guest will be here soon, and you do not keep the Lord Chancellor waiting! Go on now, shoo,' she said, pushing him gently towards the door.

The boy set off through the marbled halls of his childhood, the mausoleum of his youth. Castros felt himself being pulled along in the boy's wake, speeding through corridors and around tutting servants. Up, up, to the second floor of the mansion. Along a corridor, rushing past closed doors, hearing a sound, coming to a halt.

Young Castros stood before a doorway. His present-self hovered behind him, stomach turning as he realised what he was about to witness. From behind the wood, he could hear grunts and slaps. A woman was crying, and the man he thought his father told her to be quiet. The grunts came faster, shorter, shallower, till, with a guttural moan, they ceased.

The door flew open and the man came out, hastily stuffing his shirt back into his waistband and doing up the zip of his trousers. The man saw the boy and looked down at him with dead eyes. From behind, a serving girl rushed past, her hair in disarray, tear stained cheeks framing glassed over eyes. The boy watched, mouth agog, as the girl ran off.

'What's the matter boy? They're just things,' the man said, gesturing at the maid before strutting off down the hall.

The world spun apart again and Del Var found himself standing in a field. He was older now, fifteen … or was it sixteen? He saw himself chatting with one of the workers, Martin, a young man his own age. His present-self stood watching as the two lads laughed and joked, staring at the clouds, finding ones which looked rude.

The scene was broken by a crashing of wheat around them. A foreman appeared in the stalks, the man who he now knew wasn't his father behind him.

'Fifth time this week I seen 'im slacking off, me lord!' The foreman said.

'Disgraceful! On your feet, boy!'

'Leave him alone, Garvin. He's with me,' Del Var's teenage-self said.

'Shut your insolent mouth you good for nothing shitstain. I've had just about enough of your love for these peasants!'

'I suppose sticking your cock in them against their will is fine though,' young Castros said.

'What did you say to me?'

'You heard me, my *lord*,' he said, walking towards the man.

'It's damned lucky for you your keep is paid for so well, otherwise—'

'Otherwise what?'

Behind them, Martin stood. He tried to make a dash past the foreman who was standing red-cheeked, eyes to the ground. The man Castros had called Father pulled out a ballistol and fired. Del Var watched as his younger self drew a sword from his side and plunged it into the gut of the man. The man's eyes bulged wide in shock, and a trickle of blood vomited from his mouth.

His teenage-self looked down at his hands, blood covering them like gloves. Wide-eyed, he turned to the foreman. For a second, their stares met before the man ran off, screaming murder. His teenage-self dropped the sword and fled as his world fell apart.

The air squirmed and wriggled itself back into form. Another room appeared, this one dark, lit by the light of a single candle. Caught in its glow, he could make out the back of his head. He was kneeling on the floor hugging someone, a woman. A gust of wind seized the flame of the candle, making it dance wildly. It fell for a second upon black hair. Nairne? Oh gods, no! Why was he seeing this again?

He watched as the image of himself knelt on the floor beside the closing door, Nairne already on the other side.

'Please Nairne, please don't leave me,' the man whispered.

His younger self smashed his fists against the floor. As he watched, he felt all those emotions coming back to him, the ones he fought so hard to keep at bay. The hurt, the betrayal, the confusion. It was the last time he had ever seen her alive.

Around him, the room flickered from his view and was replaced with the tunnels of the Warren. He was sitting with his head in his hands as Whist walked into the room.

'So, it's true then?' he said.

'Yeah,' Castros replied flatly.

'What happened?'

'She … she was flogged by some head butler. Her body just gave out on her.'

'What are we gonna do?'

'Find him, find all of them, and execute every last one who had a part in her death.'

Again, the world began to dissolve around him. This time, a hall began to form, the ghosts of dancers and revellers making their way across marbled flooring. He saw himself stepping through the partygoers, his men were in position.

Numbly, Del Var watched on, knowing what was coming next. He saw the head butler gazing on the scene with a look of smug superiority. His insides burned with rage. The butler walked out of the ballroom and Castros followed, down the stairs to the servants' quarters of the Imperial Palace where he cornered the man. There was no one else around, all the other maids and butlers attending the guests. Watching the scene before him, his present-self remembered the feel of the man's face beneath his knuckles as he smashed it to a pulp.

A shot rang out from upstairs. Pulled alongside the image of his younger self he flew back into the ballroom. The place was in chaos. Startled members of the Estrian nobility were flying everywhere. The Emperor, shrunken and trembling was being led away, surrounded by a throng of men. On the floor, in the centre of the room, a guard was lying in a pool of his own blood. Another guard, a woman, was cradling him in her arms. Not just any woman, Castros realised. It was Cirona. *Gods, that's why she hates me so much*, he thought. The scene played on. Large men appeared behind the younger Castros; they grabbed him and led him away.

Now the world was spinning, refusing to settle into one concrete vision. A prison cell, chains chafing. A man, his father, his real father, making him a deal, condemning him to exile. Boats, the sea, the Shattered Land, Khasal. More water, a land watched over by a purple sky. Digging, scrabbling, pulling up of dirt, frantic searching. Khasal lying motionless.

The world burst into flames that spun and wrapped themselves in each other like lovers. They took on the form of men. Del Var could feel the searing heat of them as they pushed in on him. He lashed out towards them, but still they pressed on. They were scorching him, the intensity of the heat burning the air from his lungs. Then everything went black.

***

The sting of the creature's talons biting into her flesh drove Cirona into a frenzy. The pain lent her strength. With no thought other than escape in her mind, she reached her arms up and grabbed the thing's legs. She squeezed hard and allowed herself a small smile as the clicking sound grew into a high-pitched whine.

The grip on Cirona's shoulder slackened, but she maintained her hold of the creature. Holding on with one hand, her body swung in the air. Using the momentum, she flung herself up and onto the beast's back.

Able to take in her attacker for the first time, she saw it was a giant bat. Cirona held on to its back and neck for dear life as the thing bucked and thrashed beneath her. For a split second, she realised quite how stupid her escape plan was as she stared down through the fog. *Ah, fuck it*, she thought, *can't change it now.*

Plunging into a dive, the bat plummeted through the swirling mist. The air was stolen from Cirona's lungs, and she tried to maintain her hold. The ground rushed up to meet them both. As it came closer, she could see that it looked like it was moving. At the last second, the creature pulled out of the dive and Cirona saw the whole floor of the cave was covered with gigantic malovors.

A roar escaped from the lips of those nearest to her. They reached up with clawing hands, gripping and tearing at her shirt. Finally, under the pulling of the malovors and the bat's wild bucking, Cirona lost her hold. She watched through the silhouettes of groping arms as the bat flew back up through the smoke.

The smell of the malovors was suffocating, filling her nose and seeming to block her other senses with its sheer force. Cirona was pulled violently left and right, her limbs stretching to the point of breaking. Her head felt like it was stuffed with cotton, the world around her blurry. *Fantastic*, she thought, *the giant bat had poisoned talons as well.*

*You're gonna die*, a voice screamed inside her. Somewhere, in the beaten dog that was her soul, Cirona was ready to accept her fate. *Coward!* the voice inside her yelled, *You don't have time to die. Get your fat arse up and fight!* Fury began to course through her body; her head was still woozy, but she could feel her body fighting off the effects of the poison. With a giant heave, she pulled her arms free.

Swinging her freed fists around her, Cirona cleared herself a small circle of space. She was hemmed in on all sides by the snarling faces of the creatures. They looked very different from the malovors she had encountered so far. They stood taller even than Cirona, broad-backed and muscled. Their faces had a low-hung bottom jaw that battled to contain a multitude of fangs. But the eyes were what got her, made her realise what she was dealing with. Glowing yellow, with slitted red pupils, the gaze of the Legion fell upon her. Mindless, merciless, the front-line attackers of the Mage War.

*Don't let them intimidate you, girl!* the voice in her head cried. *You've fought bigger and uglier bastards than these in your time.*

*A-alright, what the hells do I do?* she thought. *Think woman, think; there has to be a way out of here.* Her senses, battle-sharpened and adrenaline-fuelled, scanned around her. There! To the left, she could feel a breath of wind blowing from that direction, kissing her sweat-drenched skin, a comparatively fresh smell borne upon it.

Bursting forwards with incredible speed, Cirona raced towards the nearest malovor. She drew her short sword — the long one having been destroyed by Khasal — and drove it into the creature's stomach up to the hilt. She watched black blood gush over her arm. For a second, she felt the vibrations of the creature's death throes pulse up her sword, then with one last agonised twitch, it collapsed to the ground.

Using the creature's back for purchase, she leapt into the air. She made her way towards her perceived exit by running across the malovors shoulders. She could see it now, a mouth in the stone, coming towards her. She could also see a giant.

The malovor standing in the exit was easily ten feet tall and wide as a house. Time seemed to slow as their eyes met. The giant creature reached out his hand as Cirona flew through the air. Unable to stop in time, she felt her leg caught in an iron grip before her body was slammed into the wall.

The rocky surface kneaded her spine like a loaf of bread, stealing the air from her lungs and making her head spin. She heard something crack then fell to the floor. Cirona had no time to gather her wits. The malovor was on her in a heartbeat. Reaching down, it picked her up like she was a child and swung a massive fist into her face.

Cirona's body arced through the air and landed with a bone-jarring thud. Dots danced across her vision as she tried to pull herself up. Her left eye had been rendered useless beneath the force of the malovor's blow, eye socket cracked, cheek swollen. Still, though, she could see that the rest of the malovors had formed a circle around the pair of them, their faces full of bloodlust, creating a kaleidoscope of hate.

The creature crouched then charged at her. Cirona rolled to the left. A half second later, the malovor's foot smashed into the ground where her head had been. She jumped to her feet just in time for the giant to crash a punch into his stomach. She flew through the air and into the pack of malovors. They gave a hideous mockery of a laugh and tossed her back into the clearing.

A monumental fist sped towards Cirona's face, and she just managed to duck the blow, feeling her hair ruffle when it passed over the top of her head. Still ducked down, she drove forwards and landed a punch of her own to the creature's ribs. The giant's mid-section creased ever so slightly, and he let out a grunt of pain.

Cirona had no time to savour her minor victory. The malovor grabbed her by the throat and ran her, full tilt, into the cavern wall. Her breath coming in ragged bursts through the searing pain of cracked ribs, Cirona's vision became filled with the face of the monster.

A tongue of purple, the colour of an overripe grape, flicked across mountainous peaks of teeth. The malovor's rank breath, warm and damp, spilled into Cirona's nostrils.

Pinned to the wall by her neck, Cirona twisted uselessly in the giant's grip. Her legs dangled and scrambled to gain a foothold, to relieve the pressure, as the life began to go out of her. She dug her nails into the creature's hands, desperately trying to work them loose. Despite the sensation of hot blood covering Cirona's fingers, the malovor still maintained its hold.

Blood thundered in her temples and darkness began to creep in at the corners of her vision. Cold fury raged inside of her, but there was nothing to be done.

Then, from above, came a whooshing sound, growing louder, rushing towards them. The giant's grip slackened as it looked upwards. Seizing her opportunity, Cirona prised the hands apart and fell to the ground, gasping for breath. In front of her, she saw Waltus land on the back of a malovor, the force of his fall crushing the creature's stomach.

For a second, the eyes of the White Mage met hers, and the old git gave Cirona a wink. Then he was gone. All around, malovors started to crumple to the ground in heaps, limbs flailing madly; the giant was the last to go.

'Here, lass, let me 'elp,' Waltus said. He placed a fingertip to Cirona's shattered eye, and she felt a tingle as the wound healed. 'Reckon yer got a couple'a cracked ribs as well but time is short. D'ya think yer can move?'

Cirona gave an amazed nod when she realised she could. Waltus helped her to her feet and the pair made for the exit. Deeper and deeper, they fled into the tunnel, until finally, the old man called a stop.

'Right, girlie, yer gonna have to do a bit of lifting now,' Waltus said.

'What? Why?'

In answer, Cirona saw the body of the White Mage shrivel like a grape till all that was left was a sack of skin and bone on the floor.

***

Castros regained consciousness when a stone smacked against his spine. As his head swam, he dimly made out he was being dragged along by his ankles. Whatever was pulling him sensed his movement and stopped. Del Var lifted his groggy head and saw the featureless countenance of a ghoul.

The thing's blank slab of a face looked towards him. Castros saw the air around it shimmer as it changed shape. He shut his eyes, refusing to look, knowing what he would see if he did. He felt the ghoul's breath against his cheek. It slapped him roughly and tried to pry his eyelids apart. Still Castros refused to look.

'Look at me, Castros,' the thing commanded.

'No, no, no,' was all he could manage in reply.

'Don't you want to see me after all this time?'

'No, you're not her; you're not real!' he shouted.

'Oh, but why should that stop us? It didn't when you were here before.'

'That was a mistake, l-leave me alone!'

'Now we both know I can't do that. I'm sure your life force will be delicious. So much more fulfilling than the malovors','

He felt the ghoul's transformed body straddle his. The fleshy softness of breasts passed across his face the nipple running over his dry lips. Battling against his horror, he tried to fight down the warm swelling of his cock. The monster grabbed his member and squeezed.

With a jerk of pain his eyes shot open, and he saw Nairne's face staring back at him.

'Stop … stop it please …' he murmured.

'You know you don't want me to. Why fight it? Give yourself to me, and you need never pine for this face again,' the creature said, slowly revolving its hips over his genitals.

What was the harm? Why should he be denied pleasure? All the fighting, the loss and the pain gone in an instant. Why not …?

'No!' he said, violently flinging the ghoul off him.

The stolen, naked form of Nairne skidded across the dirt and stone of the tunnel, a thin trail of blood tracing a path from lip to chin.

'We could have done this the easy way, Castros. Well, if you don't want happiness, how about despair? How about I show you him, instead?'

'Don't you fucking dare!' Castros bellowed, pulling himself onto unsteady feet.

As the air around the ghoul started to shimmer once again, there was a tremendous rumbling sound. It filled every atom of Del Var's body, rattling his very bones. Its transformation cut off, the creature looked around with the eyes of Nairne. The floor shook, and Del Var watched in horror as a crack in the ground grew and grew. The stones beneath his feet shifted, and then he was falling.

***

Dangling precariously from the stone face of the cavern, Cirona felt the rumble pass through her. The limp, desiccated form of Waltus clung to her back, cursing.

'What the fuck was that?' Cirona said.

'I-I've activated … the self-cleansing protocol,' Waltus wheezed.

'You've what?'

'It's a … fail-safe … whole place built on top of a volcanic flow … if things get out of hand … set it off and start again,' the old man replied.

'Shit! How much time we got?'

'About fifteen–twenty minutes, tops. The bats that took us, their nests are just a bit further up, the others should be there. You think you can make it?'

'Yeah, just about,' Cirona replied and resumed his ascent with gusto.

The already perilous climb was now made worse by the gouts of flame and hot air that issued from the breaking rocks. Hand over hand, she forced herself on. The thought of Holger — the boy was no great fighter, even with his new powers — frightened and alone, driving her forwards.

Finally, she hauled herself and Waltus over the edge of an outcrop. From the mouth of the tunnel ahead of her, she heard Holger's cries. Racing forwards, she heard the cries turn into a scream. It echoed down the passage, spurring her legs to even greater speed.

In the half-light of the tunnel, Cirona could just make out Holger. He was held to the wall by two featureless things, another pair coming towards him. Catching the creatures unaware, she barrelled into one of them and smashed her fist into another. The pair holding Holger relinquished their grasp and stared at her.

'What in the name of the gods is that?' Cirona said, as Holger slumped to the floor unconscious.

'G-ghouls … they're descended from … cognopaths that went wrong … can read yer mind … work out yer fears and desires, then suck the life outta yer,' the old man said. 'You gotta stop 'em before they take shape.'

Cirona watched the air around the ghouls shimmer and twist.

Charging towards them, she grabbed the nearest pair and flung them into the stone of the tunnel wall. There was a sickening crack as their necks broke.

The other pair, the ones that had held Holger, took shape before she could get to them. Before her stood the images of her daughter and Trafford. Cirona stopped dead in her tracks.

'How could you have become so soft, Rona,' Trafford said, his mouth twisted with disgust. 'To think you're working with the man who took my life instead of killing him when you've had so many chances.'

'I-It's not what you think … I—'Cirona began.

'What a filthy disgrace you are,' her daughter cut in. 'To think I came out of you. It's … well, it's revolting. I'm glad you gave me up. I couldn't have stood the shame of you being my mother.'

'Please … please, don't say that—'

'Don't listen … you … fucking halfwit … not real!' Waltus gasped.

But Cirona was completely under their spell now.

'Forgive me, Trafford … please, I couldn't go on knowing you're angry with me,' she said.

'I'll forgive you; just let me touch your face,' Trafford said, looking towards their daughter.

'Go on, let us touch you,' the girl said.

Through the dust falling from the ceiling of the rumbling tunnel, Trafford inched towards her. Cirona watched his fingers reach out towards her face. How many nights had she longed for him to come back, to touch her? So close now, she could smell him on the air, just a little further and they'd be—

The roof of the passage gave a terrific scream and fell apart in a shower of debris. Two bodies fell through the opening, landing on the ghouls approaching her. Through the dust and the grit, Cirona saw the form of Castros stagger to his feet. With a quick glance around him, he let loose a series of water bullets each finding their target between the eyes of the ghouls.

'Th-this is why you don't follow the voices,' Del Var said with a shadow of a smile. 'What the hells happened to him?'

'Oh, Waltus used up too much of his power and … dried out is the only way I can put it,' Cirona said. 'There's no time. We gotta move; he's set off some kind of explosion.'

'What the fuck did you do that for?' Castros screamed into the old mage's face.

'Explain … later … go … emergency exits.'

'Fine,' Castros said, shaking his head. 'Cirona, you give me Waltus and take Holger,' Castros said.

With this accomplished, Del Var set off, Cirona trying her best to keep up under the dead weight of Holger. Through the strain of everything that had happened, the pair could only pick up a small amount of speed. Jets of steam burst through the rocks as they ran along, obscuring their vision and hurting like fuck.

'You know where you're going, Del Var?' Cirona shouted above the insistent hiss of the escaping water vapour.

'Y-yeah not much further!'

After a few more minutes, the group came out of the tunnel into a wide expanse of space. Lining the walls were several of the movable platforms that they had ridden previously. Letting out a sigh of relief, Cirona started to run towards them. Then she felt a great weight fall on her.

She was sent sprawling across the floor, Holger's limp body hitting the ground with a horrid thump. Cirona stared up, shaken by the attack and the shuddering ground, to see a giant malovor. The thing stalked forwards and lifted Holger by his hair. In the distance, Cirona saw Castros turn round, mouth open in horror as the giant slotted his hand effortlessly round the boy's throat.

'No!' Cirona howled, stumbling forwards, already knowing that she wouldn't make it.

Suddenly, something else fell from above them, hissing and screaming. Rez landed on the giants back and dug his fingers into its flesh.

'You will not hurt the mistress!' he shouted hysterically.

The giant lost his grip on Holger and tried to grab hold of the frantic form of Rez. The smaller malovor refused to relinquish his grip and began to gouge at the huge beast's eyes.

'Go now, mistress,' Rez yelled at her, 'you mustn't be late for the ball!'

Cirona came to her senses and plunged forwards, darting between the stomping legs of the blinded giant while he tried to shake Rez off. She grabbed Holger and ran for the platform. Castros slapped his hand into the centre of it and it sprang into life.

As they rose through the air, streams of molten lava began to pour out of cracks in the cavern wall. Cirona stared down, full of anguish, watching Rez hold onto the giant till the last.

# CHAPTER TWENTY-FIVE

Bellina wiped the sweat from her brow with a grime-stained hand. She was lying flat on her back, the perfect circle of sky above still taunting her. The frustration she had felt at their predicament was slowly being replaced by a genuine fear that she would never make it out of the well. She almost laughed at the absurdity of it. At least Dahlia could sever her psychic connection with Bellina and leave the place.

Once more, she wondered just what Yevad had meant when he said she would find her destiny here. Was being trapped down a well — and all the other things she had encountered — part of some elaborate test to prove she was worthy? There had to be a way out. If this place was responding to her thoughts, surely she should be able to do something to free them?

'Argh!' Bellina exclaimed as a drop of water fell on her head.

'What's wrong?' Dahlia asked.

'Is it … is it raining?' Bellina said.

'No, look,' Dahlia replied, pointing to a spot on the well wall.

Crouching down, Bellina spotted a tiny crack just above her. Bright, clear water was squirting out of it. Hot and parched she cupped her hands and caught the liquid, laughing and shivering as she threw it over her face and down her throat. Her laughter turned to silence as she saw another hole appear. Then another. Soon, water was flooding into the well.

'This is bad,' Dahlia said, looking down at the water, which was now up to her knees.

'Stay calm,' Bellina replied. 'If it keeps filling at this rate, we'll be able to float out of here.'

Dahlia's eyes bulged, her chest hitching as she drew in sharp panting breaths. 'I-I can't … I can't swim.'

'Break off your link to me,' Bellina said.

Nodding, Dahlia squeezed her eyes shut. 'Not working,' she croaked.

Bellina watched panic seize her fellow cognopath. Dahlia tried to climb above the chest-high water. Her wet boots slipped on the stone and she plunged back down. Heart pounding, Bellina waded over and heaved her up.

'Look at my face,' Bellina said, as Dahlia sucked in a huge gulp of air. 'You can do this. Just hang on to me.'

It felt to Bellina like her arm had been caught in a vice when Dahlia grabbed hold of it. Drawing her in close, Bellina began to tread water, just about managing to keep both their heads above the surface.

'Oh, gods, oh gods, oh gods,' Dahlia repeated, her nostrils quivering.

'It's alright,' Bellina said, battling against her companion's infectious terror. 'You're a feather. Just a feather floating on the breeze. It's fine. You. Are. Fine.'

Dahlia went to nod her head, and her face disappeared under the water. She began to thrash and flail, her grip on Bellina pulling them both under. Blood pounding through her like a galloping racehorse, Bellina tried to untangle herself from Dahlia, which only succeeded in making the girl take hold even harder.

Forcing her panic down, Bellina began to kick her legs, desperate to reach the surface of the rapidly increasing water level. Her thigh and calf muscles howled in protest, like bonfires had been started in their fibres. Her lungs were screaming for oxygen, and she watched, distraught, while the little air she did have turned into bubbles and floated away when her mouth instinctively tried to take a breath.

Clamping her jaw tight, Bellina began to kick harder than ever. Dahlia was no longer thrashing. In fact, she was no longer doing anything. Her eyes were closed, lips parted as if she was waiting to be kissed.

*She's dead already*, a sinister voice whispered in her head. *Let her go or we'll be dead as well.* Bellina shook her head, banishing the thought. There was no way she would let go.

Coloured dots danced in her vision as she strained ever atom of her being to force them up above the water. Her head was spinning, her aching limbs begging her to stop; but she had to be close to the surface now, had to be.

Bellina felt the warm kiss of the still, clammy air on her cheeks. An hour ago, she never would have thought she'd be so happy to experience it again. She filled her lungs with triumphant gasps of air.

Her happiness withered like a sun-bleached flower when her gaze fell on Dahlia.

Dragging her out, over the lip of the well, Bellina pressed an ear beneath her companion's nose. Nothing. No sudden revival. No instinctive gasp for air. Just stillness.

'Oh no! No, you don't,' Bellina said. 'You're not leaving me here alone.'

All other thoughts left Bellina's head as she tried to wake Dahlia. She slapped her. She shook her. But nothing worked. In desperation, she began to pump frantically against Dahlia's chest, she was sure she'd read somewhere that this was the thing to do. Her pale, interlocked fingers pushed and pushed.

'Come back, come back, COME BACK!' she roared.

Dahlia's body convulsed, and she coughed, spluttering out water. She made a sound like a braying donkey as she sucked in a huge gulp of air. Bellina didn't think she had heard a more beautiful sound in her entire life.

'I thought you'd left me,' Bellina said, wiping at her cheeks, surprised to find tears there.

'I think I almost did,' Dalia replied, a smile as weak as a newborn foal on her lips. 'At least we're out of the well.'

Bellina laughed. 'A gilded edge to every cloud.'

'I think I had better try and go back to my real body again,' Dahlia said, sitting up, a grimace contorting her face.

'Yes. Yes, of course,' Bellina replied, staring down at her hands.

She watched as, once more, Dahlia tried to break her link to Bellina.

'Something's wrong. I-I still can't get back,' Dahlia said, mouth quivering.

Bellina felt momentarily sick with guilt when she realised she was glad. 'I suppose we're in this together till the end then,' she said.

'It certainly looks that way,' Dahlia replied with a sigh as she rung out her sodden hair. 'What pleasure awaits us next?'

Bellina took in her surroundings. The conjured streets of Kurgobad had disappeared, leaving behind nothing but desert. Scanning the horizon, something caught her eye.

'I think there's a city in that direction,' she said, pointing into the distance.

'Well, I suppose we'd better—' Dahlia began.

She was cut off by a deep rumbling sound coming from below them. Bellina let out a gasp of surprise as the ground beneath their feet began to splinter and crack.

'What in the …? Dahlia, stay close,' Bellina cried, reaching out her hand.

Bellina watched, horror-struck as Dahlia's outstretched fingers were knocked back by a massive hedge springing out of the ground. Sand spat into the air while the landscape became filled with corridors and passages of green. Bellina's mouth hung open, the realisation striking her that she was ensnared in a perfectly manicured maze.

'Dahlia?' she yelled. 'Dahlia, can you hear me?'

The only response she got was silence.

***

'Will you stop fidgeting, Dar?' Elvgren said.

'I don't like this,' Dargo replied, shaking his head and pulling at the starched collar on his new ballroom attire.

Elvgren rolled his eyes. 'Tremoran tailoring is the best in the world,' he said. 'Besides, you'll only have to wear it for a few hours.'

'I'm not just talking about this monkey suit,' Dargo said. 'I mean this whole thing — the duke taking us in so easy, showing you his giant robots, hosting this ball in your honour; I think he's trying to turn your head.'

'So far as he knows, my head's already turned; that's the ruse, isn't it? You shouldn't be so suspicious.'

'Growing up on the streets of Tavarar will make you that way,' Dargo said.

Elvgren tapped his foot and let out a sharp sigh. 'Things are going swimmingly, Dargo,' he said. 'Now be quiet; they're about to announce us.'

Taking a deep breath, Elvgren licked his lips and waited. From behind the elaborate ballroom doors, he heard his name called. Setting his shoulders back, Elvgren puffed out his chest and stepped into the ballroom as the doors swept open for him. The applause from the assembled gathering of Tremoran nobles was deafening. Elvgren opened his arms out wide to the crowd, drinking in the adulation like an alcoholic who had found a full bottle left over from the night before. Bowing deeply, a smile stretched across his face, Elvgren glided down the sweeping steps onto the ballroom floor where the duke awaited him.

'Well met, my friend,' Tobért said, embracing Elvgren like a long-lost brother. 'Come, there are some important people I want you to meet.'

The chatter of the crowd resuming frozen conversations rose, and Elvgren was led towards two men. One was short, a gut straining at the purple military tunic trying to contain it, a walrus moustache obscuring the lower half of his face. The other was tall and thin, bald as a cue ball, wearing an expression like a kicked donkey.

'When Khasal returns, the number of boots we can put on the

ground will have tripled,' the short man was saying.

'That's all well and good, Vorian, but I still think we must strengthen the navy. The Father only knows, I could use a few more ships,' the tall man said, his mouth twisting in a pout.

The duke coughed then gestured towards the tall man. 'May I introduce Lord Tomain and Lord Vorian. Both seem to be discussing matters that have no place at an occasion such as this,' he said, eyes flashing at the pair.

Lord Vorian's moustache did a twitching dance as he bristled from the rebuke, while Tomain stared at the ground. Both bowed to Elvgren who returned the gesture.

'It is good to have you with us, Lord Elvgren,' Tomain said. 'An insight such as yours into the heart of Victory's governance is most valuable.'

'Don't care for deserters,' Vorian said with a sniff. 'Hang 'em from the yard arm when I catch any of ours. Dare say the Lord Chancellor would do a sight more, if he caught you.' Catching the dangerous glint on Tobért's eyes, he quickly added, 'But any chance of one-upping the enemy is worth taking.'

'It is a pleasure indeed to meet you both,' Elvgren said.

'How are things going on the Escambrian front?' the duke asked, taking two glasses of carbonated wine from a passing servant and handing one to Elvgren.

'All the soldiers of Escambrian descent have been dismissed from the Imperial Army and sent home,' Vorian said. 'Old Calvin doesn't want an insurrection on his hands.'

'Good,' Tobért replied. 'Have the forts along the border been reinforced?'

'Yes, your Grace, and stocked with enough rations to last a lifetime's siege to boot,' Vorian said, puffing out his chest.

'Good man,' the duke said, clapping Vorian so hard on the back he staggered forwards a step.

'My ships are out ravening as you ordered, your Grace,' Tomain said, evidently not wanting to be upstaged. 'We captured four steamers packed with spices only yesterday.'

'Excellent, excellent,' Tobért said. 'Why don't you go and find a pretty young thing to dance with, Elvgren? I have a few fiduciary matters to discuss with my men. Nothing more boring than figures and ratios, am I right?'

'I find I must agree with you on this one, Tobért,' Elvgren said with a smile.

The duke roared with laughter. 'See, gentlemen, there's that wit I was telling you about.'

'Indeed,' Tomain replied with a mirthless smile. Vorian merely grunted and checked his pocket watch.

'Come then, you pair of vagabonds, let's leave the revels to those who enjoy them fullest — the young,' Tobért said, placing a hand on each of the men and leading them away. 'I'll catch up with you in a few minutes, Elvgren. Lady Flavia is most anxious to meet you, by the way.'

Elvgren smiled and nodded his head as the trio melted into the crowd. He took a sip of his wine, the bubbles going straight to his head, making him feel light, invincible. This was how having power was supposed to be. Not dour meetings and reports to make but balls, fine company and excellent booze. The duke's court was so far removed from the Lord Chancellor's stark idea of propriety that you wouldn't be able to spot the latter with a magniscope.

'Who's Khasal?' Dargo said, yanking Elvgren back from his thoughts.

'What?' Elvgren replied with a scowl.

'Who's this Khasal, when he's at home? If old fancy pants doesn't mind us hearing 'bout his forts and what not, why don't he want us to hear about him?'

'All great men have their secrets, Dargo, the Father knows I have mine. If even half of my youthful escapades got out, there would be a national scandal.'

'But that fat bloke said when Khasal returned they'd have three times as many soldiers. Where are they gonna get that many men from?'

Pursing his lips, Elvgren said, 'I'm sure we'll find out in good time, Dargo. Now I'd best be off; Lady Flavia is giving me the eye.'

With that Elvgren sauntered towards a buxom young woman with ravishing lips. Soldiers, battleships and strategy the furthest things from his mind.

# CHAPTER TWENTY-SIX

Castros watched Waltus' body reinvigorate itself, the life-juices flowing slowly back into him like a raisin turning back into a grape. The old mage was lying in the centre of a Vitaspiral drawn on the floor of his cave hideaway, looking for all the world like a thousand-year-old mummy. Waltus' condition had been much the same for three days, all Del Var and the others could do was wait.

His mind drifting, Castros found himself thinking about what would happen once this little trip was over. What would he say to the daughter he had never known he had? Would she mind that her father was one of the most wanted men in Estria and a demi-mage to boot? Would they embrace and spend hours weeping in each other's arms? And just what the hells would he tell her about Nairne? He rubbed at his temples; the whole thing was giving him a headache.

He turned his eyes away from the ever inflating Waltus and stared at Cirona. She sat in her usual position, sword out on her lap, hands methodically sharpening its blade with a whetstone. He got it now. He knew what he had done to make her hate him with such venom. Though he hadn't held the gun that had killed her lover, he may as well have pulled the trigger. His plan had been too hasty, too full of fire. The men he had taken were raw, angry and looking to make an impact. If only he had taken the time to think. *If I had, two innocent men would be alive today*, he thought, remembering the feeling of the butler's face turning to mush under his pounding fists with a shudder. Castros fought with his guilt, fought to find the words, an action, to make things right between them. Deep down, he knew he never would.

Stomach writhing like a can of worms he looked away, his gaze falling on Holger. The boy was practising control of his flames, and Del Var had to admit he was impressed.

*Now there's a thing*, he thought; *this one has openly told me he loves Bellina; this man loves my daughter.* Castros wasn't quite sure what to make of the idea. Holger seemed like an earnest, sensible young man, though sometimes, when he spoke about her, he seemed almost possessed by the idea they were meant to be together, his eyes blazing with a manic fire. Was a man like that good enough for his daughter? Did she feel the same way about Holger? Argh! Questions, questions and more damn questions. He felt his shoulders droop then, as his gaze lingered on the boy, a deep sadness coursing through him, he realised Holger knew more about Bellina than he did.

'What … um … what's she like?' he asked him.

'What's that?' Holger replied, the flame he'd been playing with snuffing out of existence.

'Bellina, I mean,' Del Var said, inspecting his nails.

Holger tilted his head to the side and bit his lip. 'She's strong,' he said. 'Probably the strongest person I know. Speaks her mind. Elegant but not snobby.'

'She … she sounds quite the young woman,' Del Var said, swallowing around a melon-sized lump that had appeared in his throat.

'She certainly is,' Holger replied. 'Why do you ask?'

'Just thought I should know a little bit about the person we've come so far to save,' Del Var said. 'Think I'll pop outside for some air.'

'Don't bother, lad,' a croaking wheeze of a voice said. Everyone's gaze turned to Waltus.

Castros used the distraction to wipe his eyes.

'Finally up, you old goat?' Del Var said.

'Like to see you take on a legion of malovors at my age and only need three days to recover,' Waltus said, a hacking cough shaking his body. He spat out a great clump of phlegm. 'Where's me tobacco? Never mind, yer useless bastards, I've found it.'

'Please tell me you found what you were looking for in that gods forsaken place,' the major said.

'Don't worry, sweetheart, Uncle Waltus has got the goods … in more ways than one! Sure I can't tempt yer?' he said, licking at his lips. Cirona's face contorted into a mask of anger — a look Castros had got much used to. 'Alright, darling, keep your drawers on! Now, are you gonna tell me what that git Khasal is up to?'

'I don't have a clue,' Castros replied. *I wish I did though*, he thought.

'Who is he anyway?' Holger said. 'I mean, why is he not in a sortilenergy plant? He seemed pretty powerful …'

'He is. The only full mage at large today. As for why he's not in a plant … I … well … I helped him escape,' Castros said.

'How the hells did you manage that?' Cirona asked.

'It's a long story,' Castros said with a shudder. 'Anyway, we need to get moving. You up to it, old man?'

'Yeah, yeah; just give me a few minutes.'

***

Half an hour later, they left the cave. Castros hopped onto the aerolyte, the others following suit, and fired it up. Quicker than a bird, they took flight, skittering over the rugged terrain of the Shattered Land. Soon, Castros could see the sea, the small boat just where they had left it on the beachhead, the steamer ship waiting for them, a glistening toy in the distance.

'Shit, we've got company,' Cirona yelled.

Castros turned his head. Behind him, he saw Khasal piloting an aerolyte of his own, red hair flapping in the breeze like a crown of fire, a gaggle of purgistas huddled behind him.

'Damn it to the Void!' Castros bellowed. 'Alright, everyone, hold on.'

Gripping the aerolyte's controls harder, Castros increased the flow of sortilenergy he was pumping into it. The flying machine responded with vigour, bursting forwards with a high-pitched whine. A clunk sounded beside him. Shooting a glance towards the noise, Castros saw a small, flat pebble, the area around it fossilised.

'Yer missed, you fucking traitors!' Waltus screamed back at their pursuers. 'Bollocks. Incoming, moron, can't you fly this thing with a bit more cunning?'

'I'd like to see you do it!' Castros roared back, throwing the aerolyte into a sharp dive.

Del Var saw three more stones whistle past and heard the dull thwack of one hitting the side of the vehicle. More and more stones pelted the craft; the purgistas' aim wasn't good enough to pick out Castros or the others individually, but the cumulative effect of the aerolyte's gradual fossilisation was slowing them down.

'You're not leaving me behind this time, Cass!' Khasal screamed, wild eyes bulging, his aerolyte catching up with theirs.

'Khasal, you madman, you'll kill us both!' Del Var shouted back.

'We'll see if that's true, won't we?' Khasal replied, ramming his ship into Castros'.

The aerolyte shook like an electrified snake, sending painful vibrations up through Del Var's arms. He gritted his teeth and willed the craft to go faster; they were so close to the beach now, the sandbanks rising to greet him.

'Duck!' Cirona cried as another shower of stones rained down on them.

Castros crouched as low as he could without relinquishing the controls. One pebble bounced an inch from his nose. A manic cry sounded behind him, and he turned to see one of the purgistas making a death-defying leap from Khasal's ship to theirs. The man landed with a thud, making the aerolyte drop alarmingly.

'Get him off!' Castros called.

'We're trying,' Cirona grunted back.

There was a series of dampened thuds.

'What the hells was that?' Castros said.

'They've … they turned their own man to stone,' Holger replied, horror in his voice. 'Why would they …?'

The added weight caused the aerolyte to plummet from the sky like a pigeon having a sudden heart attack. *There's your answer, boy*, Castros thought.

'Pull her up you imbecile, we're going to—' Waltus began to say.

He was cut off when the bottom of the aerolyte clipped the top of a sandbank. Castros felt his stomach cartwheel as the vehicle flipped over and crashed to the ground. Sand forced its way into his nose and mouth when he was thrown from the flying machine and onto the beach, his shoulder almost popping out of its socket as it took the full force of his fall.

Ears ringing, dots flashing in his eyes, Castros pushed himself up in time to see Khasal leap from his ship and aim a blast of sortilaero at him. Del Var felt his body lifted up into the air before he took another bone-shuddering crash to the ground.

'Leave Del Var to me,' he heard Khasal shout. 'You get the others.'

*Oh no you don't*, Castros thought, adrenaline alone pulling him to his feet. He aimed his own blast of magically infused air at the purgistas and sent them spinning in all directions before they could get to the others.

'Lightweights,' Khasal spat at them. 'Still, you won't be able to keep them away for long, Cass, not with me to deal with.'

Khasal flicked his wrist and a gout of flame roared at Castros. He was just quick enough to send a gust of air towards it, the two magically charged elements twining together in a mammoth blaze that shot towards the heavens.

'What are you waiting for?' Castros screamed at his dumbfounded companions. 'Run!'

***

'You heard the man — move!' Cirona said, grabbing Holger by the shirt and throwing him forwards. She took one last look at Castros, blood pouring from a cut on his cheek, then set off at a sprint towards the small boat they had left behind.

'Can't you do something about them?' Cirona cried, a handful of pebbles falling around them.

'Sorry, love,' Waltus panted. 'Ain't stored up enough sortilenergy yet.'

'Fan-fucking-tastic,' Cirona spat.

Stealing a glance behind her, she saw the remaining three purgistas giving chase. *Damn it fucking all*, she thought, *there's no way we'll get the boat in the water on time.*

'Holger, Waltus, keep going and get that boat off the beach. I'll hold them back,' Cirona said.

'But, Rona—' Holger began.

'Ain't time for buts, boy. Leave the fighting to the professional,' Waltus said, racing ahead.

With a spray of sand, Cirona came to a sudden stop. The chasing purgistas came to a stumbling stop of their own, surprised by the major's sign of aggression. Years of battle gave her the upper hand. War-sharpened reflexes sprang into action as she found her footing and drove her sword through the neck of a shocked purgista.

One of the purgistas threw a stone at her, and she swatted it away with her sword, it's razor-sharp edge turning into a useless pointy rock. *Maybe not completely useless*, she thought, swinging the heavy weight into the attacking purgista's head. It connected with his temple, a sickening crunch accompanying it, and the man crumpled to the ground like wet tissue.

The last purgista eyed her warily from a distance. She may have evened the odds, but she had learnt the Ruzmagi were enemies not to be taken lightly. They circled each other, the stony sword hanging low, her arms aching from its weight. The purgista clasped a nasty shard of wood in his hands.

'Run out of stones, have you? Why don't you fight like a man? Oh yeah, I remember now, you can't can you, you fucking freak!' Cirona spat at him, but the man was not to be goaded into rashness.

The purgista darted forwards, and she swung her sword. *Slow, too slow*, she thought as the man danced back out of reach. There was no way she would be able to move fast enough to keep up while she was holding the petrified sword, so she dropped it to the ground. Inching forwards, she dug the toe of her left boot under the sand. The purgista kept his eyes on hers. *Now that's a mistake*, she thought, kicking sand up into his face.

As the purgista staggered backwards, Cirona pounced. Tackling the man around the waist, she pinned the hand in which he clasped the splinter of wood to the ground. She let out a triumphant yell as she pummelled a fist into his nose, the cartilage flattening under the force of the blow.

'Quickly, Rona, the boat is ready!' she heard Holger yell.

She turned her gaze towards the cry, catching a half glimpse of Holger and Waltus knee-deep in the surf. The purgista pounced. *Stupid girl*, she thought as she was forced onto her back, the positions of her and the purgista reversing. The man snarled, his teeth bared in a battle-fuelled sneer, while he writhed on top of her, trying to jam the shard of wood into her eye.

Muscles quivering, Cirona grabbed hold of the man's hands and tried to force them back, away from her face. The purgista grunted, blood from his destroyed nose dripping onto Cirona's face, and let his whole weight fall onto her. With a twist of her shoulders, Cirona just managed to deflect the blow. The wood tore into a spot just below her collarbone. A hot sliver of pain seared up from the wound then stopped when the left side of her chest and her left shoulder became petrified.

'You dirty fucker!' Cirona roared, smashing her forehead into the man's already battered nose.

Rearing back in agony, the man howled his pain. Cirona shoved him off her, lifted her good fist into the air and drove a club-like blow into his face, knocking the purgista senseless.

'Don't worry, girl, I'll get yer fixed up,' Waltus said as she staggered towards him and Holger.

'Boat … in … now,' she said, panting.

'But what about Castros?' Holger said.

'The boy will have to look after himself, look,' Waltus said, pointing a gnarled finger back up the beach.

Cirona's gaze followed the outstretched digit and saw a host of purgistas landing aerolytes on the beach. 'Come on,' she said.

'But—' Holger began.

'Move your fucking arse. Now!' Cirona screamed in his face before shoving him forwards.

She collapsed into the boat, still panting, struggling to catch her breath. As Waltus and Holger began to row the boat towards the waiting steamer, she caught a glimpse of Castros battling on the beach.

She was surprised to find a faint flutter of guilt twirling in her gut.

***

Castros saw the major push Holger forwards and get them all moving. The purgistas gave chase, but all he could do was place his faith in

Bouchard. Khasal had been right when he had said Del Var would have his hands full with him; taking on a true mage without any tharg's bane tools was a task to be reckoned with.

Across from him, Khasal twitched his fingers. Castros had no way of knowing how much sortilenergy the mage had stored in the containers strapped to his wrist guard, but he had a feeling it was a lot more than his own.

'Something the matter, Cass?' Khasal called across to him, his teeth bared in a twisted smile. 'Well, if you're not going to make a move, I suppose I'll have to.'

With a twitch of his wrist, Khasal let out a burst of sortilaero and shot into the air. Castros followed his movements, waiting. With a snap of his hands, he sent out a sliver of water, freezing it into a lance, in the perfect position to skewer the falling Khasal.

'You'll have to do better than that,' the mage said, melting the ice with a gout of flame.

'I'll try,' Del Var replied with a smile as he blasted Khasal with his screamer.

Shooting back through the air, Khasal landed with a crash in the sand. Castros was already steaming forwards, aqua bullets at the ready. He let them fly with a wave of his hand, the compacted balls of water sizzling towards their target. Khasal deflected the projectiles with a blast of air. Castros kept them under his control. Khasal was powerful, but Del Var had always had the upper hand when it came to manipulation of his abilities. He was a dagger next to his foe's hammer, but a dagger wielded with skill was just as lethal. Swinging the liquid bullets back round, Castros felt a surge of triumph when they zeroed in on Khasal's face, a face that was now filled with fear. His head snapped back, and the mage tumbled backwards.

Castros ran towards his former friend, bending down to check he was dead. With a yelp of pain, he pulled his hand away from Khasal's neck. The mage's entire body was red-hot, a shimmering haze coming off him.

'Gotcha,' Khasal said, opening his eyes.

*The bastard must've heated the air around him*, Castros thought, *turned the aqua bullets into steam*. Half a heartbeat later, Del Var was blasted back by a gust of magically infused air.

'Let's have a little fun, shall we?' Khasal said.

As Castros looked on, reeling from yet another hard smash against the ground, Khasal emptied what must have been an entire water skein, heating the liquid into a swirling mass of steam. Spinning on his heel,

Castros felt his heart pound in his chest, his visibility going to zero in the stinging fog. He saw angry red patches begin to spread up his arms where the hot air attacked his exposed skin. He had nowhere near enough sortilaero to disperse the cloud; there was nothing for it, he'd have to wrench.

Del Var took in a great gulp of the scalding air, felt it burn his throat and lungs raw, but it was his only choice. Quickly fusing it with his own life force, he let loose a howl of spinning air, blasting the steam from around him, sending it skywards in great rippling albino tentacles.

'Behind you,' a sing-song voice called.

Castros spun around. He just had time to see the thin blade of fire, temperature brought up to a white heat by Khasal's powers, before it plunged into his gut. For a second, Del Var felt nothing at all. Then his abdomen became a vast reservoir of agony, deep and seemingly endless. With a howl he fell to his knees, clutching his hands to his stomach, lifeblood coursing out of him. Khasal stamped on both his wrists, breaking his magical containers, the precious sortilaqua coating his hands, the sortilaero returning to the aether.

The world twisted when Del Var felt a kick crash against his temple, then he was choking, mouth and nose clogging with sand as Khasal trod on the back of his head and ground his face into the beach. Castros wriggled free and pushed himself up, shivering at the sight of the blood pooling beneath him. A pair of boots came into view.

'How the tables have turned, eh Cass?' Khasal said. 'I would tell you to try begging for your life, but we both know me well enough to see the futility in that. I'd like to tell you this will be painless, old friend, but quite frankly, it won't be.'

With a desperate lunge, Castros lurched forwards and grabbed Khasal's trousers, trying to hoist himself up.

'For the love of … will you just stay down!' Khasal sighed. 'You're making a scene.'

'No,' Castros hissed.

With the last ounce of his strength, Castros morphed the sortilaqua covering his hand in to a sharp blade, crimson red where it mingled with his blood. A bright flare of triumph pulsed through him as he punctured Khasal's side, the mage squealing like a pig in an abattoir. Khasal collapsed to the floor, and Del Var crawled, inch by inch, up the stricken mage's body, till his face was no more than a fraction away from his foe's.

'Goodbye, Khasal,' Castros said. 'I hope you find peace on the other side of the Veil.'

'Cass, wait! Listen to me!' Khasal babbled. 'I-I've been to the Scorched Earth, stood beneath the purple sky, met one of the fate weavers, a Fargazer. She told me, Cass, told me my destiny, told me where to find the Heir of Excellus, told me of the Twelve Terrors' return, how we would live like kings in the new world they shall bring!'

'You really are mad,' Castros said, swinging his makeshift dagger at Khasal's face.

'I saw your mother!' Khasal screamed.

Del Var stopped the blade just a hair's breadth from Khasal's manically bobbing throat. 'What?' he said.

'I saw her, Cass. Your mother, your real mother that is.'

'No ... no ... she's dead,' Castros whispered.

'No. She's not.'

'Tell me,' Castros spat, his crimson dagger biting into the flesh of Khasal's throat. 'Tell me where she—'

Castros was cut short as he felt something pierce his shoulder. Eyes wide he looked down to see a splinter of wood jutting from the bone. He could hear his heartbeat pummel in his eardrums as the area around the splinter petrified and terror seized him. He could hear Khasal laughing.

'I'd love to keep chatting, but it looks like the cavalry has arrived,' he said. 'Oh, we're going to have such fun, me and you. Just like old times.'

Del Var went to reply but found he couldn't. He reached up and felt another splinter lodged in his larynx. His body jerked in a wild dance as more and more shards of wood bayoneted his flesh. The last thing he saw was Khasal's smiling face. Then the world went black.

# CHAPTER TWENTY-SEVEN

Bellina stopped at the latest intersection of the maze and bit her lip. Which way now? Thin gravel paths branched off around her, but she recognised none of them. She felt like tugging at her hair and screaming to the heavens. This was *her* maze, part of *her* psychic defences, so why couldn't she find the right path?

*Just choose one!* a voice cried in her head.

'Fine,' she muttered to herself, rolling her eyes skyward. 'Left. I choose left.'

Overhead, the sky had grown bloated, an exhumed corpse ready to expel a swollen, rotted fury upon her. The air was still and close, vampiric, sucking moisture from her body in steady streams of sweat.

'What in the ...?' she said, coming to a stop.

Leaning her head to the side, she listened.

Nothing.

But she could have sworn—

Her head snapped to the right. She had definitely heard it that time. A strange sound, a sound that made the hair on her arms stand on end, made her skin tingle. A child laughing. The spit in her mouth had gone as sour as off cream. She swallowed, but it felt as if someone had jammed a large rock in her throat.

*It's just your imagination*, her inner voice said. *Stop being ridiculous and get moving. You're the only person around here. Well, you and Dahlia, but the Father only knows where she is. Gods, I could use her now.*

Bellina balled her hands into fists, banging them into her legs to get going. Once she had whacked some life into them, she set off, a lot slower than before. Step followed creeping step, her head jerking left and right, a metronome trying to keep time with the frantic beating of her heart.

'Huh?' she said as she felt her dress snag on something.

She turned her head, everything slowing, breath catching in her throat. Her eyes grew wide, wide as cartwheels, a pathetic yelp trembled from her lips. There, holding the back of her dress, was a hand, a child's hand, smooth and blemish-free poking out of the hedge. She took a step backwards, trying to free herself, but the hand, though small, had a grip like iron. Eyes appeared in the hedge, large and full of giggling malice, then a mouth full of tiny spikes of white teeth beamed at her in a wicked smile.

'Play with us,' a voice called.

Her breath now came in ragged bursts, unblinking eyes stinging. She pulled at her dress, yanked and grasped, until finally, the fabric tore, the small hand still gripping the white cloth like a lover waving goodbye at a locomotron station. More hands shot out of the hedge, hundreds and hundreds of them, tiny fingers wiggling, beckoning.

'Play with us …'

'Yes. Play …'

'It's fun here …'

'Why won't you be our friend?'

A moan escaped Bellina's lips and she began to run. She ran blindly, not knowing where she was running to, the hands making the hedge ripple like a wheat field caught by a gust of wind. She felt the touch of tiny fingers brush against her skin, and it was all she could do to stop herself from screaming. *This isn't real*, she thought. *It's not, it can't be; I must have gone mad.*

Pushing her hands against her ears, Bellina tried to block out the beckoning, pleading calls from the hedge. She screwed her eyes tight shut.

'Not real,' she babbled. 'Not real, not real, not real, not real … ow!'

Colliding with something solid, she fell to the ground. She lay there, eyes still shut, not wanting, not daring to see any more.

'Open your eyes, lass,' a familiar voice said.

She did. Her jaw dropped at what she saw. It was Torkwill.

'How are ye darlin'?' Torkwill asked, gazing down at her.

'You're not real!' she screamed. 'None of this is real. I can't take it any more. Go away. Leave me.'

'Can't do that, Bellina. You needed help an' I've come,' Torkwill said with a sniff. 'Now gimme yer hand, and we'll get you on your feet.'

'You promise you're real, that this isn't some new bloody trick?'

'Oh, aye. I'm real alright,' Torkwill replied, reaching out to her.

Bellina flinched back then stretched her hand out to meet Torkwill's in a series of short jerks. Her took her hand in his, comfort rushing through her at the touch, and pulled her from the ground.

'There we go,' Torkwill said, offering her one of his crooked smiles. 'Nothing to it, eh? Now come on, let's get ye outta here.'

'How … how are you here?' Bellina asked, the shock of seeing Torkwill again wearing off.

'A cognocast stone, at least that's what I think they're called anyway. Some sort'a device the Tremorans have cooked up to amplify cognopathic powers. Makes folks like us able to transmit our thoughts over massive distances. Got it off a fella in Chenta who had stolen it from a fella in Kurgobad. Lotta Tremorans hanging about there these days. Once I had that, it was just a case of following your ribbon and here I am,' he said.

'That's … that's amazing,' she said.

'You're telling me. Scared me shitless when I wound up in this place. What the fuck is wrong with yer brain, girl? I thought I was messed up, but this shit is mental.'

'I don't know,' she said, rubbing at her temples. 'I know I'm making this stuff appear, but I've got no control over it.'

'Well isn't that fantastic,' Torkwill replied. 'Lucky for you, Uncle Torkwill reckons he's got this place sussed.'

'Really?' Bellina said, raising an eyebrow.

'Yep. I think we're travelling deeper into yer subconscious. I may be wrong, doubt it though.'

'But the hands,' Bellina said with a shiver. 'What about those hands?'

'Maybe it's a part of you trapped in that hedge. Some desire left over from when you were a wee nipper. I can't say for certain. Let's just be thankful for now that they're gone.'

For a while they pushed on in silence. Bellina wrung her hands then said, 'I'm … I'm glad that you're alive, Torkwill. After we left you, I thought you were dead.'

'Me? Dead?' Torkwill replied. He let out a gruff laugh. 'Gonna take a lot more than a rabid mob to kill me, poppet. They've been trying though. The Tremorans are after me. But I'm giving 'em a merry chase, that's for sure. But hang on now … I think we're out.'

Peering past him, Bellina saw Torkwill was right. The hedge-lined path they were walking along had come to a sudden stop. At the very point the hedgerow ended, a massive wall rose up, a large gate gaping at the bottom of it.

'That's … that's the Castrian Wall,' she said. 'This is Victory.'

'Aye, I think yer mebbe right, lass,' Torkwill replied, scratching his chin. 'Well, anything's better than that bloody maze, eh? Come on.'

With that he stalked through the gate. Bellina followed, her head swivelling as she tried to work out where exactly they were in the Estrian capital. Her thoughts were cut short when a massive bolt of lightning fell from the sky, accompanied by a bone-shaking crash of thunder and a downpour of rain.

'Tell yer brain thanks from me,' Torkwill said, pulling at his already drenched clothes.

'I told you — I can't control this!' Bellina shot back.

'Can't or won't?' Torkwill said.

'Just what the hells are you implying?'

'You need to get—'

Torkwill was cut off by the sound of hooves pounding against the cobbles. A heartbeat later, a covered wagon came tearing into view, sweat steaming from the horses in the freezing rain. Bellina could see the driver casting frantic looks over his shoulder, terror written large on his face.

'What's going on here?' she said, looking at Torkwill.

'Gods,' he whispered. 'We've gotta get outta here, lass. You don't want to see this.'

'What are you talking about?' Bellina said.

Opening his mouth to answer, Torkwill was cut short by the blast of a ballisket. The driver's head whipped to the side, his hands letting go of the reins as his corpse toppled from the vehicle. Bellina stepped forwards, her guts swirling, wide eyes staring down at the dead man.

'Bellina, get back here!' Torkwill roared. 'This was what I wanted to tell yer about but … but not like this.'

But Bellina was transfixed by the scene unfolding before her. Out of the shadows stepped a man with a ballisket hanging from his shoulder. He strode over to the man he had just killed and gave the body a shove with the toe of his boot. Satisfied, he gave a nod then walked to the back of the carriage. Following him, Bellina watched when he paused by the wagon's back doors. From inside came the sound of a baby crying and a soft voice trying to hush it. The man's jaw set firm and he pulled the doors open.

Bellina stared in, craning her neck to see past the man's large frame. Inside, she saw a woman huddled in a bundle of blankets, the light from the street lamps illuminating half of her face, catching on a shock of matted, midnight-black hair. On her lap was a mewling baby.

'Get away from her!' the woman screamed. 'You can't have us!'

'I only need the child,' the man said, his eyes glass-like as he lifted his weapon.

'You're an animal!' the woman spat. 'Nothing more than a glorified lapdog. I hope you rot in the Eighth Hell for this. Who sent you?'

The man smiled, over-large teeth flashing. 'The Lord Chancellor,' he said.

'You're … no … it can't be. He would never harm us. He would never want his granddaughter to be motherless.'

Bellina felt her stomach plummet. This couldn't be … there was no way …

'For what it's worth, the girl will be well cared for. She'll never know the horrors of the compound.'

'She has a name, you know,' the woman gasped, looking down at the child, her tears splashing on its pink, pudgy cheeks. 'It's Bellina.'

'A fine name,' the man replied. 'I'll let you say your goodbye.'

The woman moved the baby so it was cradled in front of her. 'I know you're going to be fine, my little angel,' she said. 'You're going to be strong and beautiful, and you won't take any shit from people, just like me and your dad. Live well, my precious girl. I will always love you.'

The sound of the ballisket firing tore through the night air as tears streaked down Bellina's cheeks. She felt sick, the back of her throat burning like she had inhaled a poisonous vapour. Everything around her began to bulge and sway. She clutched a hand to her chest, trying to force air into a pair of lungs that were not working.

'Calm down, lass,' Torkwill said, stepping towards her. 'You've had a massive shock. You never should've had to find out about yer mam this way.'

'Calm … calm d-d-down!' Bellina managed to gasp. 'I've just seen my m-mother murdered on the f-fucking orders of the man I thought was my father, and you're telling me to calm down?'

'It's going to be alright,' Torkwill said, edging closer. 'Just … what in the name of all that's holy …?'

Torkwill's eyes stared past Bellina's shoulder, wide and full of fear.

'What is it?' Bellina said. 'What's behind me?'

She felt the pressure of a palm being placed on her shoulder. Then she was gone.

***

Castros awoke to the sound of the sea, the gentle splash of its waves, the harsh caw of a seagull's call. For a moment, he was in another time and place, sitting by the seashore, the sun baking his skin a lobster red, a beautiful woman by his side and a world of possibilities ahead of him. Then he was jolted to the side, white hot lances of pain shooting through his body, and he remembered everything. That was probably the worst part of all.

Pulling his gummy lids apart, Castros waited for his eyes to grow accustomed to the world around them. In front of him, he saw a ghostly reflection staring back from a pane of glass. He saw a bruised and battered man, covered in makeshift bandages, arms and legs in chains that stretched off to the side of him. *Not again*, he thought, trying to move his manacled arm. *Being captured is starting to become a bad habit of mine.* Past the glass he could see pistons, gears, gauges and levers; it looked like a ship's engine room.

It was then that he realised there wasn't just one pane of glass in front of him. No, he was completely trapped inside a large sphere of the stuff. Cables and tubes, coiled like over-large snakes, slithered away from the sphere, connecting with the room's other equipment.

'Oh gods, no,' he whispered as, with dawning horror, he realised the fate Khasal had planned for him.

'Glad to see you're awake, Cass; I was beginning to worry about you,' the man himself said, coming through a door at the back of the room. 'I do hope your quarters are to your liking; I went to a lot of trouble to arrange them for you.'

'I know you hate me, Khasal, and maybe you have a right to that hate, but *this*, this is wrong.'

'Is it really?' Khasal replied, his face a picture of innocence. 'I thought it would do you a world of good to experience what every other mage has undergone for the last one and a half centuries; your rather blessed birth gave you an exception to the unpleasantness of a vorosphere.'

'Just kill me,' Castros replied. 'If you have any shred of decency left in you, kill me. This is a far worse fate.'

'Oh, I'm well aware of that, Cass,' Khasal replied, walking up to the glass so the tip of his nose was touching it. 'But this is two birds with one stone, you see. I get to inflict a whole universe of pain, and you get to be useful and fuel the ship back to Spinoza. You still … maybe … no, I can sense you're not happy, but you have to understand — this is a win–win for me.'

'I know you've suffered—' Castros began.

'Do you?' Khasal hissed, his eyes flashing. 'Do you really? How did you spend your twelfth birthday, Cass? Hmm? Some cake? A party? Do you want to know about mine? It was a great day! The first time I was chained inside a vorosphere, the first time I was choked with ether, the first time my life force was ripped from my body to fuel some noble cunt's lights, the first time I heard the screams of my mother while she went through the same thing in the sphere next to mine. No, Cass, you'll never know how I've suffered.'

With that Khasal moved to one of the control panels and pulled a lever. Castros heard a soft hiss coming from behind him. He turned around, heart hammering, to see a violet plume of ether spooling out from a hole into the sphere.

'Stop this,' he yelled, banging on the glass. 'Stop it, right now, Khasal; it's not too late.'

'Sorry, can't hear you,' Khasal said, cupping a hand to his ear.

'You … you fucking bastard,' Castros said, wheezing as the gas stole into his lungs. 'I'll fucking kill you for this … you wait Khasal … I … will … kill you … aaargh!'

Castros felt his body tense, his back arching almost to the point of breaking. Every atom of his being howled in agony as the sortilenergy was forcibly pulled from his body. For what seemed like an eternity, the pain coursed through him, then just as he thought he would lose consciousness, it subsided. His chin dropped onto his chest, drool dribbling from his slack mouth.

'Don't get too comfy, Cass; things are just getting started,' Khasal said.

'F-fuck y-you,' Castros spat.

Khasal just smiled and pulled the lever for a second time.

# CHAPTER TWENTY-EIGHT

'Are you happy now, Dar?' Elvgren said, putting down his pen and picking up a fork laden with scrambled eggs. 'I've finished encoding the report for the Lord Chancellor.'

'What do you want?' Dargo replied, his frosty glare boring into Elvgren across the breakfast things. 'A medal?'

'I should bloody well think at least *one* is in order for my derring-do in the heart of the enemy's territory,' Elvgren replied, jabbing his fork towards Dargo.

'Oh yeah, it's been such a trial for you. All those parties and galas must really be taking it outta yer.'

'I'm not sure I like your tone,' Elvgren said. 'You've been getting far too cocky lately. Tobért said I should keep you on a shorter leash.'

Dargo's nostrils flared. 'Oh, did he now? Just a fucking dog, am I? Just a noble's lackey? Well, you can tell your precious *Tobért* to stick it up his arse,' he said, rising to his feet.

'Oh, sit down you *utter* ham,' Elvgren said. 'Can't we go five minutes without your histrionics? We've done a fine job getting our intel back to the Lord Chancellor, even though he's a po-faced git who wouldn't know a bit of fun if it sashayed in front of him in nothing but a pair of stockings. Our troops have been put in exactly the place they need to be, extra help has been sent to guard the ports. Hells, I even gave them the name of the next town Lord Tomain's ships are going to ravage. All in all, I think we're playing the duke like a well-tuned fiddle.'

'Then why do I feel like he's playing us?' Dargo replied.

'Give me some credit, Dargo,' Elvgren said, rolling his eyes. 'I think I'd know if he was leading us down the garden path.'

'Then why don't he tell you everything, hmm? Why don't he tell us what happened to Midge? Why don't he tell us who this Khasal is?'

'We still have plenty of time to work out those things.' Elvgren sighed, waving his hand dismissively.

'Just like we had plenty of time to work out how to free Crenshaw?' Dargo said.

'What can I do, Dar? The man was a wanted criminal long before we met him. I'd love to be able to do something for him! In fact, I was talking with Tobért just last night about reducing Crenshaw's sentence to fifteen years hard labour.'

Dargo rested his hands on the table and shook his head. 'What's happened to you?' he said. 'What's happened to the bloke I travelled halfway around the world with? What's happened to the man who chopped my leg off to save my life? What's happened to the bloke who planned the infiltration of the Imperial Palace in Kurgobad?'

'I'm still that person,' Elvgren said.

'No,' Dargo said, turning away and walking to the door. 'No, you're not.'

'And where in the twelve hells do you think you're going?'

'To get things done,' Dargo said, slamming the door.

Elvgren raced over and pulled it back open. 'Don't you embarrass me, Dargo! If you do something stupid, you're bloody well on your own!'

The last thing Elvgren saw was Dargo giving him a mocking salute, before he disappeared down the stairs at the end of the corridor.

'Ungrateful little shitter,' Elvgren said, closing the door and returning to his breakfast.

***

Elvgren spent the rest of the day touring the city of Spinoza, a thing he never tired of. The duke had left Elvgren in the hands of his top assistant while he went to inspect a ship that had just returned from some mission or another. Elvgren was constantly wined and dined by the cream of Tremoran nobility, each showering him with praise and adulation.

Feeling rather pleased with himself, Elvgren had dismissed the assistant, sending him back to the palace while he met the man who was helping him get messages back to Victory. The chap was a stoic sort who ran a small tavern. He'd lost a leg in some battle or another and had no love for the duke, thus his — rather well paid, Elvgren thought — position in the Lord Chancellor's intelligence service.

Elvgren entered the spy's bar and was led to a hidden room that contained a scribograph with a direct link to the Lord Chancellor — totally untraceable, or so he'd been told. An hour later, with the Lord Chancellor's rather curt reply to "carry on" in his hands, Elvgren left the tavern after a few drinks and stepped into the night air.

And what a night it was. The sun was a trembling arch of orange hovering on the horizon, catching the tops of the waves and setting them alight. A cool breeze as refreshing as a glass of ice water was lifting the heat and stink of the day into the sky. Whistling a tune, Elvgren made his way along the waterfront before hailing a cab.

Thirty minutes later, the vehicle came to a stop by the palace's gates. The driver rushed to open his door and Elvgren flicked a gold coin to him. The man tipped his hat and sped away. Elvgren frowned at the cab's quick exit then strutted into the palace grounds. As he walked up the driveway, he began to feel as if something was off, something, something, something … but he couldn't quite put his finger on it.

Then it came to him: there was no one else in sight.

The palace and its grounds, so usually full of life, were as silent as a mausoleum. No bustle of servants. No stomp of a guards' boots. Nothing. His brow wrinkled as he squinted up at the building. With considerably less spring in his step, he pushed open the doors and went inside. The magnificent entry hall was in almost total gloom, a single galvanic lamp casting a pale yellow orb of light.

'Dastôn? Marcellené?' he called, but no servants came scurrying to help him with his coat.

He heard the soft thump of something falling above him. *This is ridiculous*, he thought, *where can everyone be?* Then it dawned on him. It was so obvious he should have seen it sooner. He smacked his left palm against his head, stunned at his own stupidity. The duke must've planned a surprise party for him.

He gave a small laugh and began to climb the sweeping stairs to the second floor. It all made sense now. This was why Dargo had had a fight with him in the morning, so he had an excuse to go off by himself and get things ready. This was why Tobért had made up that cock and bull story about inspecting a ship and sent Elvgren out for the day.

'Hello?' Elvgren called, a smile stretched across his face. 'I wonder where everyone could possibly be?'

At the top of the stairs, he saw a light shining from beneath the door to the duke's study. So, they were all in there waiting to jump out and yell surprise. Well, two could play at that game. Creeping along on the balls of his feet, he inched closer to the door. Suppressing a chuckle, he took the handle in his hands.

'Found y—' he began.

The words died in his throat when nothing except a rather ordinary-looking study met his gaze. Elvgren had never been in this room before and was surprised by how small it was. Still, he decided to go behind the desk and make sure no one was there. As he moved closer, an open dossier, paper spilling out from it in all directions, caught his eye. He cast his eye over the papers, phrases jumping out at him.

*All goes well on our end. The idiot suspects nothing …*

*… report has been received in Victory, pleased to state LC has taken the bait …*

*… only a matter of time before she trusts me completely …*

*… it's almost like a bad play, the servant being smarter than the master and all that! Still, an accident might have to be arranged for that street rat of his …*

'You weren't supposed to see those,' a voice called from the doorway.

Elvgren looked up and saw the duke stood there, arms behind his back. 'What in the—' Elvgren began.

'Father save us!' Tobért said. 'Just how thick are you? You've been played, you idiot.'

'Played? What do you mean played?'

'I knew from the start who had sent you, you imbecile. I must say, Calvin's schemes are usually a lot better crafted than this one, but I suppose he's got a lot on his mind, what with the Empire falling apart and all.'

Elvgren felt his stomach clench, his head growing dizzy. 'You … you knew all along … but … the parties … the rallies?'

'The vain man is the easiest to deceive. Who said that? Doesn't matter, I suppose. It's a shame, you know — you've been most entertaining. Useful too, don't think anyone else could have got the Lord Chancellor to leave Victory defenceless.'

'So that's what you needed all the extra men for, the men this Khasal is bringing.'

'Well, I wouldn't call them men. But in a nutshell, you're right. Though I am hoping the taking of Victory will be bloodless. In fact, I think the citizens of that fair city might just welcome me with open arms after what we have planned,' Tobért said with a smile.

'That's why you've packed everything up? You're moving your court to Victory.'

'The Imperial Palace, no less. Moving on to bigger and better things. Won't need this poky little place any more. That's what the dynamite is for, but I'm getting ahead of myself.'

He clicked his fingers and two guards appeared at the door.

'Did you find the boy?' the duke asked.

'Not yet, your Grace, but it's only a matter of time,' one of them replied.

The duke frowned. 'Very well. Keep looking. In the meantime, take this one to the dungeons.'

The men moved forwards and grabbed Elvgren by the arms. His legs began to shake and he had to fight down a scream. Dungeons? Dynamite? It certainly didn't sound like a good combination.

'Tobért! Tobért, wait!' Elvgren called as the men dragged him from the room. 'Please, I can help you!'

'I'm afraid your usefulness has run its course, old chap. This place is scheduled to blow in … oh, thirty minutes — can't leave any loose ends.'

'That's … that's mad!' Elvgren yelled. 'How will you explain your palace exploding?'

'I shall play it as yours and Calvin's last desperate ploy to be rid of me, keep the general public nice and riled up,' the duke said.

Now Elvgren did scream, long and loud, the sound echoing along the now deserted halls.

Castros let out a shuddering breath and opened his eyes. He looked down at his smoking body, saw the last wisps of the sortilenergy that had been ripped from it curl away, and prayed, prayed for the pain to end, prayed that the boat would strike a rock and sink, prayed for release. But the Father's attention was elsewhere, and the only response his prayers received was the clicking of Khasal's boot heels as he entered the room.

'Well, my old friend, I must say you have proved more powerful than I would have credited, especially for a half-breed,' Khasal said. 'We have arrived in record time, all thanks to you. Doesn't that make you feel all tingly inside?'

Del Var pulled apart his cracked lips, tried to say something back, but all that came out was a pathetic puff of air.

'What was that, Cass? I'm afraid you'll have to speak up,' Khasal said, stepping forwards and cupping a hand around his ear.

For a second, Castros thought about trying to speak again. Deciding it wasn't worth the effort, his chin slumped to his chest. *Ignore him*, he thought, *ignore him and sleep, just sleep.*

'Uh-uh, my dear old thing, you're not getting away from me like that; I'm just—'

Khasal was cut off by a frantic hammering on the engine room's door. The mage's face contorted into a furious snarl.

'Enter!' he spat over his shoulder.

'Mr Malifa, sir,' a man's voice called. Castros lifted his head and saw a squat man, belly as wide as he was tall, standing in the doorway.

'I have told you to address me properly,' Khasal replied. 'Must you be taught another lesson?'

'I-I am sorry!' the man squeaked. 'Please forgive me, Karn Malifa.'

Khasal snorted. 'What is it then?' he snapped.

'I-it's the … um … creatures, sir … the … er … malovors.'

'For the love of the gods, spit it out man!'

The man licked his lips and said, 'They've … well, some of 'em 'ave got loose sir, on the other ship like. Won't calm down. Keep saying they want to see the master and only you have keys to the boy's—'

'Enough!' Khasal said. 'I'll be there in a moment. At least this hadn't happened during the duke's visit.' He turned towards Castros once more. 'Well, Cass, it seems you've got yourself a moment's reprieve. Use it to muster that stout heart of yours. You're going to need it.'

Khasal spun on his heel and stalked out of the room. Before the door closed, Del Var caught the sound of shouts and cries ringing on the air. Then silence again. He shut his eyes, mind inching towards unconsciousness.

'Oi! Oi!' a voice whispered. 'You're in a right bloody state, ain't ya?'

'L-leave … m-me … be …' Castros managed to rasp. He didn't have the energy to deal with another deckhand come to gawp at him.

'Fair enough. I'll take these keys to your chains with me as well, shall I?'

'What?' Del Var said, his eyes snapping open.

In front of him stood a short youth in his early teens. A pair of mischievous eyes stared back at him, a crooked smile beneath them. As Castros scanned the boy, he wondered what the kid had been through to require an automaton leg being grafted onto him at such a young age.

'Wh-who are you?' Castros said.

'Name's Dargo,' the boy replied, looking him up and down. 'So, you're Del Var then? Thought you would a been a bit more … I dunno … imposing.'

'I'm sorry … having the life sucked out of you tends to leave you in a bit of a state,' Castros rasped.

Dargo let out a short cackle. 'Well, I reckon we better get you down, mate. Bought us a bit of time, letting them monsters loose, but they'll round 'em up eventually.'

'How did you—' Castros began as the boy opened the vorosphere and undid his chains.

'Get here? It's a long story, but the short version is I followed that oily bastard, the duke. Wanted to find out who this Khasal was. Snuck on board and blended in — I'm good at that sort o' thing — pretended

I was a cabin boy. Saw them monster things and damn near shit meself. I stayed close, listened in on 'em. Heard them talking about you and thought I'd have a look-see, wanted to know what you was like; you *are* pretty notorious, mate! I'd already nabbed the keys off that ginger git for letting out the monsters, so I made me way down here. When I saw yer looking like this, well … it wouldn't be human to leave yer. Plus, I reckon you're not gonna be the biggest fan of the duke, and we're gonna need all the help we can get stopping him and this motley crew.'

'Why do you care? About stopping the duke, I mean?'

Dargo sniffed. 'Well we was s'posed to be trying to bring down the tosser, scupper his plans like; Lord Chancellor himself gave us the mission … but me mate kinda got suckered in by the duke.'

'Y-you know the Lord Chancellor?'

'Course! Me mate is engaged to his daughter,' Dargo replied.

'What!' Castros cried.

'Hey! Keep it down will yer? Look, the time for questions is later. Let's get off this bloody tub first, eh?'

Castros shook his head, battling his thoughts, trying to get them in some semblance of order. He failed.

'Lead on,' he finally said.

''Ere wrap this around yer,' Dargo said, tossing him a coarse piece of fabric that had been covering some machinery. 'Can't 'ave yer walking around starkers, now can we?'

Wrapping the material around his emaciated body, Castros felt old and withered, a smoke-shadow of the man he had been just days before. His entire body throbbed in agony, each step a minor miracle. He bit down on his lip, tasted the salty tang of blood in his mouth. No. He wasn't beaten yet. He would make it. He had to make it.

Dargo had scuttled ahead and poked his head out of the deck hatch. He turned around and beckoned Del Var over to him. 'Coast's clear,' he said. 'They're all preoccupied with them … things. Am I a genius or what?'

'You've done well, lad,' Castros said with a smile. Gods! Even that hurt.

Following behind the boy, Castros climbed out into the cool night air. The salt from the sea stung his sore skin, but he didn't care; he was free again. Yes, he was free … and now Khasal would pay.

'Which way are the cabins?' Castros said.

'Fancy a little lie down, do yer?' Dargo replied with a shake of his head. 'Need I remind you we are trying to escape?'

'I-I just need my things. Khasal would have kept them.' *Kept them as trophies*, Castros thought.

Dargo rolled his eyes. 'Fine. This way,' he said, pointing across the deserted deck. 'But you better be quick.'

'I promise,' Castros said, putting a hand to his heart.

Gesturing for him to stay low, Dargo led the way. They arrived at an ornate-looking door — well, ornate for a ship anyway — and the boy fumbled through the keys, searching for the right one.

'Hurry up,' Castros whispered.

'Alright, alright!' Dargo hissed back. 'There are a bloody million of … hang on, there we go.'

The door swung open and revealed the cabin beyond, a large window at the back offering a view of the ocean. The room had obviously once belonged to the ship's captain and been reappropriated by Khasal. A scrimshaw paddle made from the tusk of a garwhale had been flung onto the floor where it lay next to a Vitaspiral, a harpoon with a handle made of silver was propped against a traditional mage's cloak of black. All in all, it was a bizarre mix of styles and personality. Castros entered the room and began rummaging through the drawers of a desk.

'Come on,' Dargo called.

'I know, I know, I'm coming … where in the bloody hells would he have put them? … Aha! Gotcha! Alright, Dargo let's …'

But the words died on Castros' lips as he turned around. There was Khasal, a ballistol pointed at Dargo's temple.

'Oh dear, oh dear, oh dear,' Khasal said. 'You *have* been getting into some mischief, haven't you?'

'Let the boy go, Khasal,' Castros said, his eyes meeting Dargo's. The boy winked at him and gestured, ever so slightly, at his automaton leg.

'I don't think you're in any position to … arrghh!' Khasal screamed as Dargo's leg hammered down on his foot, the bone breaking with a rippling crack.

Wasting no time, Dargo dashed forwards, grabbed hold of Del Var and leapt out of the large cabin window. They plunged into the still, warm water, accompanied by Khasal's curses and screams of fury. Castros felt his wasted limbs try in desperation to propel him forwards, to reach the surface, but they wouldn't respond. Icy fingers of fear caressed his insides.

Then he was grabbed round the neck and pulled to the surface. He took in a great lungful of air and heard Dargo do the same.

'Th-thanks,' Del Var spluttered.

'Don't mention it,' Dargo replied. 'I can pull you along but you've gotta kick your legs — my automaton one got too wet and I've had to ditch it.'

'I-I'll try,' Castros said.

Feeling some life returning to his body, Castros was able to help move them towards the shore. The effort was immense, but fifteen painful minutes later, they were clambering up the stone steps of the wharf.

Castros lay on his back, panting. 'Where now?' he said.

'Gotta go and get that mate I was telling you about,' Dargo said. 'Gods only know what trouble he's got himself into by now.'

'And where will we find him?' Castros asked.

At that moment, a dull boom sounded, a deep bass note that made Del Var's bones shake. He sat up and looked to the horizon, saw a great plume of smoke and flames licking the roof of the sky.

'Reckon that's where we'll find him,' Dargo said with a sigh.

***

Elvgren sat with his head in his hands on the cold stone floor of the cell, rocking backwards and forwards. *Idiot*, he thought, *vain, selfish, arrogant idiot; how could you have been so blind?* The duke had played him like a hand of cards, and now, all that awaited him was a fiery death. *If only I'd listened to Dargo*, he thought as his stomach tied itself in an elaborate knot. *If only I'd taken it more seriously, maybe then, all of this…*

Fear gripped him then, hard and relentless, pounding him again and again like a blacksmith's hammer. The walls seemed to shrink in on him, their quivering shadows reaching out, an early caress from death's cold, raven fingers. *No, no, no*, he thought, *not like this, nonononono…* A high-pitched whine escaped his lips as he clawed at the walls, the bars. How much time did he have? Was it already too late? Was the bomb igniting this very second? He collapsed to the floor, hugging his knees, his muscles twitching and spasming.

Then, by his head, he heard a scratching, scraping sound. He turned his eye towards it and saw one of the bricks down the bottom begin to move, the centuries-old mortar disappearing in small, white puffs, till the stone was shoved all the way out. Elvgren peered through the newly formed hole and saw a pair of wide, staring eyes looking back at him.

'So, it *is* you in there,' a disappointed yet familiar voice said.

'Crenshaw? Is that you? It is, isn't it! Oh, you magnificent bastard, you've found a way out, haven't you?' Elvgren cried.

'No,' Crenshaw replied. 'Well, not one that you'll be taking anyway. See you later. Or not, I suppose.'

'Crenshaw? Crenshaw! Don't you dare leave me here!'

'And why shouldn't I? Come on, tell me that,' Crenshaw hissed, his eyes reappearing in the hole.

'You're not still angry about the whole almost-killing-you thing, are you?' Elvgren said.

'Believe it or not, it is still a sore point for me,' Crenshaw said.

'It was all a ruse!' Elvgren cried. 'I was supposed to be gathering intelligence for the Lord Chancellor. I had to get myself in the duke's good graces. I … er … never would have gone through with it. Anyway, we don't have time for this. The duke's rigged the palace to explode.'

'Pity you ain't got a way out then,' Crenshaw said.

'I just told you—'

'You just spouted a load of jibber-jabber. You still ain't given me a reason to help you. Come on, tell me why?'

'Because … because … because you're a better man than I'll ever be … because you could never leave someone to die like this,' Elvgren said.

He heard Crenshaw make a disgruntled growl. 'It's a good job for you Dargo would miss yer,' he said. 'Come on then, let's see if we can pull some more of these bricks free.'

Letting out a huge sigh, Elvgren rolled his eye to the heavens and muttered a prayer of thanks. He grabbed at the edges of a brick and pulled with all his might. With Crenshaw's help, the ancient brickwork gave way and soon there was enough room for him to crawl into the other cell.

'Well,' Elvgren said dusting himself down, 'that was—'

He was cut short when Crenshaw's fist connected with his cheekbone. Elvgren staggered backwards, clutching at his face.

'I won't say we're even,' Crenshaw said, 'not by a long way. But I feel a lot better. Come on'—he offered Elvgren his hand—'let's get out of here.'

Head still swimming from the blow, Elvgren followed Crenshaw to a dark corner of this other cell. He crouched down for a closer look and saw that a hole had been made, just big enough for a man to belly crawl through.

'How did you manage this?' he asked.

'With this,' Crenshaw replied, holding up a long rusty nail. 'Been using it to gouge out the mortar, loosen up the bricks. Worked on it in the nights. Been going at it like a hyperactive blacksmith ever since I saw the guards leave earlier.'

'I think I can hear running water,' Elvgren said, still peering down the hole. 'Where the hells does it lead?'

'Dunno,' Crenshaw said. 'Let me know once you're down there.'

'Whaaargh?' Elvgren screamed when Crenshaw's boot pushed against his arse and sent him sprawling through the hole.

Elvgren felt the world spin and lurch as he fell through the darkness. The air sang while it whipped past his face. Then, with a terrific splash, he was submerged. He fought his way to the surface of the foul-smelling water, emerging coughing and spluttering, and tried to stop himself being thrown along with the current, but it was no use.

He was dimly aware of a sound like cannon fire as he tried to keep his head above the waterline. Huge chunks of stone and brick began raining around him, hitting the water with deep, booming thuds. Elvgren gave a small prayer of thanks that the current was taking him away from the murderous masonry.

His body was tossed and turned, spun and flung, along the length of the underground river. His world shrank to a handful of sensations — cold, wet, fear, pain. The last of which became the prevalent feeling after his back smashed into something solid. Spinning around, Elvgren saw moonlight reflected off the ocean through the bars of a grate. He tugged at them with his numb wet fingers, rust coating his hands. They were old and rotten. If only he had a bit more force to attack them with ...

At that moment, he heard a garbled scream. He flicked his head round and saw Crenshaw and what looked like a mountain of stone, rushing towards him.

'Oh no,' Elvgren said.

Crenshaw hit him first, crashing into him, slamming Elvgren's back once more against the bars. He only had a brief heartbeat to register the pain before a chunk of fallen brickwork hit his shoulder. He let out an agonised yell.

'L-look o-out!' Crenshaw babbled.

'W-what?' Elvgren replied.

Then he saw it. A massive hunk of stone racing towards him in the churning water. His eye grew wide; there was no way he would get out of the way in time, not when his body had frozen like it had. Elvgren felt like a lifetime passed while the stone grew bigger and bigger in his vision. He closed his eye, waiting for the end, to feel the rock pound the life out of him. Instead, he felt icy fingers grip him round the neck and pull him to the side.

There was a sound like a hundred rusted gates swinging in a gale, then he was rushing forwards once more, out, out into the ocean. For a while, he drifted, until eventually, he could tread water.

'Crenshaw?' he called. 'Crenshaw! Where the devil are you man?'

In the moonlight, he saw a body floating to his left. He swam towards it. *Gods*, he thought, looking at Crenshaw. Something had caught him just below the eye, caving in his cheek, shadows pooling in the newly created crater. Elvgren held the back of his palm under Crenshaw's nose. He was still breathing.

Fighting against the slowly rising tide, Elvgren managed to drag the pair of them back to shore. For a while, he lay on his back, struggling to get his breath under control. When he did, he could smell fire. He turned his head and saw, on a promontory above him, the smoking remains of the duke's palace. *Good riddance*, he thought.

'Fucking hells! Is that you, Gren?' a voice called out.

'Dargo?' Elvgren replied, turning towards the voice as he pulled himself into a sitting position. 'What are you doing here?'

'We was trying to find you,' Dargo said, nodding his head towards a tall, gaunt man who stood beside him.

Elvgren met the man's gaze. There was something very familiar about the haughty stare that met his; he just couldn't quite place it …

'Oh, this is Castros Del Var,' Dargo said, noticing the stare-out.

'What?' Elvgren spluttered. 'Castros Del Var, the terrorist?'

'Yeah, but he seems alright though. Plus, he was on a mission from your father-in-law, just like we were. Went to get someone to heal Bellina.'

'I know,' Elvgren replied. 'The duke and Marmossa are counting on it.'

'What are you talking about?' Del Var said.

'There's no time,' Elvgren replied, hauling himself to his feet. 'We have to get back and warn the Lord Chancellor before the Emperor's birthday. That's when their plan will be set in motion.'

'But the Emperor's birthday is tomorrow. How could the duke get there in time?' Del Var said.

'They … they could, if they took the *Vagabond*,' Crenshaw said. 'That's what they kept me alive for — to show them how to pilot it.'

'Gods damn it!' Elvgren spat. 'We'll never catch up with them now.'

'I might just have a way,' Del Var said, looking over his shoulder at a row of ships.

# CHAPTER TWENTY-NINE

White. The whole world had turned into a pulsing, throbbing whiteness. Bellina spun, trying to find anything to latch onto, to anchor her in the space, but she found nothing.

'Greetings, Variable Seven Point Eight. Please, do not be alarmed,' a disjointed but distinctly female voice said.

Bellina turned around. Behind her, somehow brighter than anything else was the form of a woman. She was clothed in a swirling white gown, a stark contrast to the midnight-black of her skin. A pair of glowing eyes set in a face as dark as ravens' feathers and, atop her head, a writhing, curling mass of hair, a crown of albino flame.

'Who the hells are you?' Bellina said.

'Vital signs of Variable Seven Point Eight oscillating wildly. Syntax change required. Initiating colloquial mode. Change implemented. Hello, Bellina. I am Nexus Hub Four, a part of the Infinity Machine Network. In your mythology, I am referred to as a Fargazer,' the woman said. 'You need to calm down, or your body will shut off and our connection will be lost.'

'Calm down?' Bellina spat. 'Calm down! I've been attacked by faresks, chased through a city I helped destroy, stuck down a well, lost in a maze, made to watch my mother's final moments, and then, to top it all off, I've been kidnapped by a badly made-up ghost who's claiming to be a mythical figure *and* talking bollocks. I'm sorry, but calm is the furthest thing from my mind.'

'I am sorry for the distress you have suffered, but it was necessary to bring you to me. Many have sought me through the years. Some have travelled like you, overcoming the obstacles in their mind. Others have made the more perilous physical journey. All who have made it are worthy of my words,' the Fargazer said.

'Where are we, anyway?' Bellina said, her curiosity getting the better of her.

'We are in my Somnus Cortex, my dream space, if you will. If you prefer, I can change our surroundings to something you are more familiar with,' the Fargazer replied.

'Hmm, something familiar or this eerie blank infinity? What a choice!'

'Would you like some more time to think?'

'In the name of … no! Change this … please.'

The Fargazer waved her hand and a cosy study morphed into being. In front of her, Bellina saw a pair of leather chairs, the seats scuffed and worn by the passage of time and a desk complete with a steaming tea service sat upon it. In almost every detail, it was the same as her grandfather's study. A million conflicting emotions erupted inside of her as she contemplated the fact that, despite everything that had happened, she still found this place a comfort. She forced herself to remain calm and flopped into one of the chairs.

'So,' she said, watching the rather improbable scene of the Fargazer taking a chair, 'what is this Grand Destiny of mine?'

'It is not as simple as that,' the Fargazer said, cocking her head to the side. 'It is your destiny, but it is also the destiny of this world.'

'Oh, how dramatic!' Bellina replied, raising an eyebrow. 'Do you have to speak in riddles?'

'I speak in riddles for riddles are what I see,' the Fargazer said. 'It was never the intention of my creator that I see the exact future. They knew such a thing was an impossibility. They created me, my brothers and sisters, to perceive the possibilities lying dormant in this world, to piece them together and dream the permutations, all so that another Cataclysm could be averted, though our interpretations of the data can be different.'

'Cataclysms? Permutations? Just what in the world are you talking about?'

'The Infinity Machine, the hubs like me that make it up, we were created as a fail-safe, a guard against the Old Terrors ever returning. Unfortunately, our data pool only included the variables for the Twelve Terrors,' the Fargazer said.

'Well, that's how many Terrors there were,' Bellina said with a shrug.

'No. A mistake was made. A thirteenth Terror, weaker than the others, existed, unknown to my creator, unheeded, waiting, waiting a thousand years to be unleashed. He cloaked himself in the flesh of man and preyed on their weaknesses, seducing them with his demon's tongue. Each day, he grows more powerful. He is already in possession of the first of the relics as well as the Heir to Excellus. These, combined with possibly only one more of the relics, will give him the strength to open the portal and rend the fabric of all worlds, releasing the other

Terrors from their prisons.'

Bellina's mouth had gone dry, and she had a fight to swallow a sour mouthful of spit. 'Who … who is this thirteenth Terror?' she asked, already fearing she knew the answer.

'He has chosen the name of Marmossa,' the Fargazer replied.

'But … he … I …'

'He lives. As does the human, Kurkeshi, who unwittingly set him free. To kill a Terror is no mean feat. They have powers beyond the scope of humans. In fact, it was the illicit liaisons between the Terrors and humans that brought the first mages into the world, a chance happening that would lead to their downfall. But I digress and our time is running short. Soon, the healer will arrive to free you.'

'Healer? What—'

'Listen well, Bellina Ressa, Variable Seven Point Eight, you are the axis, the convergence point for those who will fight him. The boy whose powers are newly awakened, the one with the blood of Amlith flowing in his veins, the thief, the healer, the scholar, the warrior, the lover, the father and the fallen king; you must bring them all, bind them all. Your love will be blessing and curse, elevating and damning all at once. You will lead them to the Scorched Earth, you will take them into the final battle. What happens next, I cannot see.'

Bellina's head was spinning, a cyclone of confusion and fear twirling together in her mind. 'I don't—' she began.

The Fargazer held up her hand for silence, cutting Bellina off. 'Someone is trying to follow you in here. This must not be allowed,' she said. 'Initiating Flamepost Protocol.'

'Flame what?' Bellina cried. 'What the hells are you doing now?'

'I am putting you back into stasis. Until the healer arrives, the rest of your sleep shall be dreamless.'

'You can't just tell me all that and then leave me!' Bellina said. 'Wait … wait … wa—'

'Sleep now.'

'W—'

***

Cirona stood at the front of the barge, the Castrian Wall growing in her vision. Night had fallen some time ago, the sky choked with clouds, starlight stabbing through them at irregular intervals. She had watched the water around the boat turn from clearest blue to a sludgy, turgid brown as they closed on their destination. Cirona couldn't think of a time she had seen Victory look so miserable.

They had switched from their boat to the barge in Pevontess, not daring the roads. All along their journey, Cirona had seen signs of the battle that was brewing — great columns of men marching towards the Escambrian border, carts laden with supplies, the general caravan of smiths, whores and ale-sellers; a part of her itched to be with them. But she knew her duty and understood her debt. She would get Waltus to Bellina if it cost her life. So, she had sat, like a strange prow-beast at the front of the barge, scowling into the distance while the ship crept towards the capital.

And now they were there.

She looked up in wonder as the massive portcullis that allowed entry by boat passed overhead, the giant pointed ends, so much like dragon's teeth, suspended above her, just waiting to bite down on the water. No doubt, they would soon, but for the moment, the iron teeth waited. On they travelled, up the Tollfaith river, through the Merchant's Arch, the wind whistling a mournful tune through the deserted streets and squares. *It's like a corpse*, Cirona thought, *like the whole city is just a giant grey corpse.* She shivered and pulled her travel cloak tight.

'It's horrible, isn't it?' she heard Holger say.

She turned to see the boy standing beside her.

'Aye,' she said.

'It's … it's like the whole city has taken a breath and is just … waiting.'

'Aye,' Cirona replied, not knowing what else to say.

The barge whispered towards the docks and came to a stop. The tiny crew busied itself securing the ship in its berth. A gangway was lowered, linking them to the wharf.

'Where's Waltus?' Cirona asked.

'Below deck. Said he was getting changed.'

Sighing, Cirona stalked along the deck and banged on the door that led below. 'Waltus? Waltus! We're here; get a bloody move on!'

'Alright, alright!' Waltus yelled as the door swung open.

Cirona felt her jaw drop at what she saw. There, in front of her, stood Waltus, dressed head-to-toe in a white robe with an accompanying pointy hat. If not for the tears and stains on it, he would have looked like an illustration from a book on the Mage Wars.

'You can't wear that!' she cried.

'Yes, I fucking can. This is my ceremonial garb, been handed down my family for generations.'

'At least leave the hat?' she said.

'No chance,' Waltus said, pushing past her.

Shaking her head, Cirona followed him off the barge. She climbed up a set of steps slick with scum from the river and found Holger and a carriage waiting. A valet opened the door for them, climbed in, and banged the roof to get the drivers moving. As they wound through the streets, Cirona stared out at the city. Every other streetlight was out and hardly any lamps shone in the homes they passed.

'Sortilenergy is being rationed, Major,' the valet said, noticing her frown.

Giving a grunt of reply, Cirona returned her attention to the empty streets of Victory. Outside a shop, she saw an advert for the *Chronicler* bearing the heading, "Lord Chancellor refuses to step down!". *Things have really gone to shit*, she thought, pinching the bridge of her nose. Outside, she noticed a large box, a flat, blank screen taking up its centre, dials, tubes and rods sticking out of it at odd angles.

'What the hells is that?' she asked the valet.

'Oh, those,' the valet replied with a sniff. 'The Duke of Tremore sent them as a gift to the people of Victory. Says he's got some way of showing the Emperor's birthday celebrations on them. More pot-stirring from the little git. It's him who's got everyone riled up against the Lord Chancellor.'

The rest of the journey passed in near silence, the only sound the clop of the horses' hooves and the trundle of the wheels as they wound their way towards the Palace of Administration.

Finally, they arrived. The valet opened the door and led them towards a waiting servant holding an old-fashioned gas lamp. The servant merely nodded at them then began to lead them towards the palace. Cirona looked up at the building. Without the usual lights glaring from its windows, the palace's facade was a jagged mess of lopsided shadows.

Following the bobbing light from the servant, they entered the building. Cirona felt like the shadow of a ghost stalking the still corridors, even the echo of their footsteps was muted and sombre. At last, they came to a stop by the room that had been given over to Bellina's care. The servant reached out a hand and knocked. The Lord Chancellor himself answered.

Cirona felt her stomach grow heavy with a numb, cold weight, like she had swallowed a stone. *By the gods*, she thought, *what's happened to him?* The Lord Chancellor stood before them, his broad shoulders sagging, confused eyes staring out of two sunken pools of darkness, a phantom of the man who had ordered her to retrieve Waltus.

'Is … is this him?' he croaked, pointing a gnarled finger at Waltus.

'Yes, my lord,' Cirona replied.

'And where is my … where is Del Var?'

Taking a deep breath, she said, 'He didn't make it, my lord.'

'I … I see,' The Lord Chancellor wiped a hand across his face. 'I suppose you'd better come in then,' he said.

Entering the room, Cirona saw the servant with the lamp bow as he closed the door, leaving them. She turned her face, not really wanting to see. Bellina lay in the bed, thinner, her skin the colour of curdled milk; if it wasn't for the steady rise and fall of her chest, Cirona would have thought her dead. In a chair next to her sat Dahlia. At first Cirona thought the girl was napping, then she saw that her flesh had also lost its colour.

'What happened to her?' Holger asked, pointing at Dahlia.

'She … uh … she followed Bellina into the space she was sent to … to help her … but she … she has not returned for some days now,' the Lord Chancellor replied.

There was a pregnant pause. 'Bloody hells!' Waltus cried. 'It's like a fucking funeral in 'ere. They're not dead yet. And you've got the greatest White Mage that ever lived to fix 'em. So … cheer up, eh?'

'You … you can do this … you can fix her? I was beginning to lose hope,' the Lord Chancellor said.

'Only one way to find out,' Waltus said, pushing past him.

The White Mage crossed the short distance to Bellina's side. From his pocket, he retrieved the red crystal they had battled through the Pit for. *The red crystal that had most probably cost Del Var his life*, she thought with a grimace. Waltus placed the gem on Bellina's forehead then tapped it with one of his tattooed fingertips. Cirona had to stifle a gasp when the veins of Bellina's body began to glow with a pale orange light.

Waltus frowned. 'She's in deep. Just about knocking on death's door, I reckon,' he said.

'Bring her back … please … bring her back …' the choked voice of the Lord Chancellor replied.

'What d'ya think I'm trying to do, you great idiot?' Waltus said. His brow knitted in concentration as he hissed, 'Come on, girl!'

Bellina's body began to convulse, her back and neck arching to bone-snapping contortions.

Still, her eyes remained closed.

'Come on,' Waltus said again, sweat beginning to gush from his head in torrents.

Cirona felt pain in the palms of her hand. She looked down at them and saw blood trickling out from where her nails were digging in. She tried to unclench them, but they wouldn't respond, tried to drag in a deep breath but couldn't. *Please let her come back, wherever she is, let her come back.*

For a second, her mind was whipped back, back to a tent in the deserts of Burkesh where Yevad the kaffar battled to bring Bellina back to the world of the living, to rid her of the poison she had ingested. *Never again*, Cirona thought. *I'll never let you get hurt like this again, just come back, and I'll protect you. Come back, and I'll keep you safe. Never again.*

The gas lights in the room flickered and danced, pulled to and fro by an invisible wind. The window began to rattle in its pane, harder and harder, a thin crack blossoming from one of its corners. Waltus' lips were moving ceaselessly, mouthing unheard words, commands, summoning Bellina back. The girl's veins stood out, stark on her limbs, thick as cords, turned from orange to a midnight-black. Her body was now hovering above the bed. She opened her mouth, a sound filled the air, sucking, gurgling, like the last gasp of time itself. She collapsed back to the bed then …

Silence.

Cirona leaned forwards. Her eyes were stinging from lack of blinking; still, she kept her gaze fixed on Bellina. 'Come on,' she said, her voice hissing through gritted teeth. 'Come on!'

***

Bellina pulled her eyes open, each lid feeling like a ten-ton weight was attached to it. The effort it took was monumental, and the only reward she got was a blurry ceiling looking back at her. Around her, she heard voices, muted, hushed voices, and tried to work out who was speaking. Then a face swam into view. Her eyes trailed across to it, focused on it. It was her grandfather. Tears poured down his face as he reached out a quivering hand. She tried to flinch back, but her wasted body refused to respond. The feel of his calloused fingers against her skin was almost more than she could bear. Her mind flicked to the image of her mother dying, and she let out a hoarse sob.

'Shush,' her grandfather whispered. 'Shush now, my love. It's alright. You're home.'

Each word he spoke made Bellina's flesh writhe. Her chest hitched as the braying sobs were wrenched from her body.

'I think that's enough for now,' a new voice said.

Bellina turned her head towards it and saw on old man dressed like a mage. *Mad*, she thought. *I've lost my mind back there.*

'But—' the Lord Chancellor began.

'No buts. Out! All of you. Now,' the mage said. 'I'll have her and the other one right as rain by morning.'

*The other one?* Bellina thought. *Who's the … Dahlia!* With a supreme effort, Bellina turned her head a fraction more. Her eyes met Dahlia's and the girl smiled. Bellina returned a weak one of her own and reached out her hand, fingers interlocking, her fellow cognopath's, strength flooding into her.

'Out, go on. That means you too, lover boy, and you, Major. You can all visit in the morning,' the mage was saying.

'We're back,' Dahlia said, her voice nothing more than whisper. 'Thank the gods.'

'Yes,' Bellina replied, her eyes locked on the back of her retreating grandfather, her stomach churning. 'Thank the gods.'

***

Cirona stood looking down at Victory. She had climbed to the higher levels of the Palace of Administration and found a balcony. Before, in what now felt like another life, she would do the same at the Imperial Palace. The view there had been better, but she doubted even *that* building's magnificent vantage point would make the tomb-like city beautiful now.

'It's a sorry thing, isn't it?' a gruff voice croaked behind her. Cirona spun round and saw the Lord Chancellor behind her.

'It … it is,' she replied, unable to bring herself to lie. She turned back towards the city.

The Lord Chancellor moved forwards, stood next to her. 'I am grateful for the service you have performed,' he said.

'Merely doing my duty, my lord,' she said.

'No. No, it was more than that, and we both know it. She has a way of getting under your skin, doesn't she?' he said.

A brief smile appeared on Cirona's lips. 'That she does.'

'I am glad she has earned your love, Major. It gives me comfort for what's to follow.'

'What is to follow, my Lord?'

The Lord Chancellor merely took a deep breath and shook his head. 'I always knew she was special,' he said, ignoring Cirona's question. 'It was prophesied.'

'Didn't know you were a man who believed in such things?' Cirona said.

'There is a lot about me you don't know, Major. A lot nobody knows.'

The pair fell into silence. Cirona's gaze scanned Victory once more. The clouds overhead moved like a crippled giant, filled with a slow, brooding menace. Everything else was still, a nail waiting for the hammer to descend, foreboding squeezing every street, every home in its gnarled grip.

'How did it come to this?' she said.

'How all great things are brought low — treachery,' the Lord Chancellor replied. 'Do you know how Amlith Castria took Gar, capital of the Old Terrors?'

Cirona frowned, this was a story every child knew. 'He led a charge against the Horde, took the walls by the bravery of himself and his men,' she said.

'That's the official story, not the true one,' the Lord Chancellor replied. 'Amlith himself was the child of Hapthor, Third of the Terrors. Amlith knew the secret ways into the city. Knew the men to bribe, the ones to threaten, the ones to disappear. He brought down the city of his own family.'

'Regardless of his methods, he overthrew the Terrors and cast them into the Void. If it wasn't for him, none of this would exist,' Cirona said. 'How is that treachery?'

'One man's hero is always another man's traitor,' the Lord Chancellor said with a sigh, his whole body sagging with the expelled breath. 'But I never thought Tobért would sink so low.'

'Tobért?' Cirona asked.

'The Duke of Tremore. He knows enough to understand what he has sold us for and to whom. Understands there will be no coming back from this,' the Lord Chancellor said. He slammed his hand against the balcony, some of the old fire returning to his voice. 'If only I had more time, hadn't been so distracted. I was so close, so close …'

The Lord Chancellor's voice died, his tone tumbling from cold fury to a whimper, the whimper of a beaten man used to be being beaten, expecting to be beaten. Cirona stood by his side, eyes glued to the ground as she tried to find the words to lift him, to raise back up the man who had been Estria's rock for so long.

Nothing came.

Instead, her eyes caught sight of a cigar-shaped shadow hovering in the distance, the first tentative rays of dawn's light stroking its underbelly. 'What's that?' she said, unable to stop the words spilling out, despite the fact she already knew the answer.

'There lies our Amlith,' the Lord Chancellor sighed. 'Enjoy the sunrise, Major. I pray to the Father we'll all live to see another.'

***

The wind ripped through Castros' hair, snapping stray strands out behind him. In the distance, he could just make out a long cylindrical object cutting through the clouds. Despite the distance, Castros smiled; they were gaining on them. He leaned forwards, his battered body coiled with anticipation, and forced himself to inject more sortilenergy into the aerolyte.

Del Var had known that Khasal wouldn't have been able to leave the flying machines in the Shattered Land, so back they had crept towards the ships, caught a small group of men unloading one and reappropriated it for themselves. It wasn't a fight to be proud of, not one to be turned into song, but it had served its purpose. By the time the dockers cries of distress had been answered, Castros and the others were long gone, speeding through the night sky, safe in the knowledge Khasal couldn't give chase while he had the malovors to control.

'Fucking hells, this is incredible!' Dargo cried.

'For the Father's sake, Dar, stop jumping up and down; you're making this … *thing* wobble,' Elvgren replied.

Castros cast a look at the young man, still handsome, despite the eyepatch and ugly scar that flowed from it. This was his daughter's intended? This queasy-looking youth, clutching on to the rails for dear life? Del Var shook his head. So far, he had met Bellina's fiancé and a man who had admitted his love for her without hesitation. It was a stabbing pain that he knew more of *them* than of her.

*All that's going to change*, he thought gripping the controls tight. *We're going to catch them, we are going to stop them, save Bellina.* His chest ached at the thought of the duke's plan. It would leave many dead, Bellina included, if he pulled it off. The audaciousness of it stunned him like a slap to the face. It almost brought a smile to his lips. Here he was, racing after a group of people who, in a few small months, had affected more change in the Estrian Empire than he had managed in a lifetime of struggles. It almost brought a smile … but not quite.

A dark grey fuzz stole into the corners of Castros' vision. His stomach lurched as the aerolyte dived down, clipping the dark roof tiles of a house beneath them. Castros gritted his teeth, jaw aching, and forced the vehicle back up. There was no doubt about it, he would need another dose.

'Are you alright, Mr Del Var?' the man called Crenshaw asked. 'You … er … look a bit peaky.'

'I'm fine,' Castros lied. 'Just tell me this thing is faster than theirs.'

'It is, aye,' Crenshaw said. 'But they've got a good lead on us.'

'We'll soon remedy that,' Castros replied. 'Dargo? Be a dear and pass me a vial of blue liquid from my bag.'

The sound of rustling and clinking came to Castros' ears then Dargo said, 'Here yer go! Is this it?'

'Perfect,' Del Var said, flashing the boy a smile. 'Mr Crenshaw, can you take out the stopper and place three drops on my tongue?'

'Well I'm no medificer, but I can do that,' Crenshaw replied. 'What is this stuff anyway?'

'Condensed ether,' Del Var said.

Crenshaw let out a low whistle. 'Sure you should be taking this? Don't it … er … send your … kind … loopy?'

'It can, if it's used unregulated. We first came up with it as a stimulant, something to bolster your life force when you're flagging. If you know what you're doing, it's a powerful tool,' Castros said.

'And you know what you're doing with it, do yer?' Crenshaw said.

'I do,' Castros replied, telling the man a second lie.

'Alright then,' Crenshaw said, unscrewing the bottle.

Castros stuck out his tongue, felt the liquid hit it, ice-cold, felt the stolen power flood his battered body. *Gods! There will be hell to pay for this*, he thought. He forced the idea down. No time for that. No time for doubt. He squeezed the controls, a surge of power flowing out of him. The aerolyte jumped forwards.

His gaze fixed on the airship in the distance, his whole focus centring on it. They would catch them. He would save his daughter. He wouldn't lose anyone else.

'Am I seeing things,' Elvgren said, the dawn light catching the back of his head, 'or is that Victory?'

'You ain't seeing things, boy,' Castros said. 'We're almost there.'

# CHAPTER THIRTY

Bellina placed her feet on the floor, took a deep breath, then stood. Her legs didn't buckle, didn't shake, and she strode across the room laughing. Dahlia let out a laugh of her own and Bellina pulled her in for a hug, before doing the same with the old mage, Waltus.

'Thank you,' she said to him. 'I can't believe it. How can I ever repay you?'

'A kiss from a beautiful young lady is payment enough for me,' Waltus replied.

'Then you shall have it,' Bellina said and planted a peck on the old man's wrinkled forehead.

'Lovely,' the mage said. 'But I was … er … thinking you could apply that somewhere a bit further south?' and he grabbed at his crotch.

Dahlia let out a hiss of surprise, but Bellina merely suppressed a laugh, raised an eyebrow and said, 'Not in this lifetime, old man.'

'Then I'll wait till the next,' Waltus said with a sigh. 'Anyway, girls, it's been a long night, and I need to get a bit of kip.' With that the White Mage left the room.

'The dirty old bugger,' Dahlia said, eyeing the closed door, her cheeks red, affront shining from her eyes.

'He was only joking,' Bellina said. 'Plus, he did manage to heal us in a night like he said he would.'

'I suppose,' Dahlia replied with a frown. 'But still …'

'Oh, stop being such a prude,' Bellina said, flopping back onto the bed. 'There's more to worry about in this life than a randy old man.'

Tucking her hands behind her head, Bellina lay back, staring up at the ceiling, eyes following the path of a crack that divided it in two. Yes indeed, there really was more to worry about than Waltus. Her baffling conversation with the Fargazer split through her brain; she desperately tried to make sense of it, to glean some insight from what she had been told, but the memory faded, dreamlike, to the back of her mind, replaced by something much worse.

The image of her mother being murdered flashed before her eyes, pain spreading out into her body like venom. Then came the image of her grandfather, face streaked with tears as she opened her eyes.

Was what she had seen the truth? Yevad had warned her that not everything she saw in that place would be. And what had happened to Torkwill? Was he trapped there now, or had he managed to escape? Was he ever really there at all? She rubbed the middle of her forehead, trying to fight back the headache that was building behind it.

'Are you alright, Bellina?' Dahlia asked.

'No,' Bellina replied. 'I … when I got separated from you, I met an old friend.'

'Really?' Dahlia said, surprise writ large upon her face. 'How?'

'He was … is another cognopath, a Master. His name is Torkwill.'

Dahlia let out a gasp. 'I remember Master Torkwill. He was a good man. Always arguing with Master Alcastus … till he was sent away, that is. I am glad he's alive.'

Bellina nodded. 'I met him travelling into Burkesh. He taught me so much. He told me that he knew my mother, that he would tell me about her one day,' Bellina took a deep breath and closed her eyes. 'Somehow … when we left the maze … I … I saw what happened to my mother … I heard her say … say her last words to me before … before she was killed.'

'By the Father!' Dahlia hissed, sitting down beside Bellina and taking her hand.

Letting out a humourless laugh, Bellina said, 'That's not even the worst part. The man … the man who took her life, he … he said that the Lord Chancellor … that the Lord Chancellor had given him the order.'

The tears came then, hot and furious. Bellina felt her body shake and heave. She tried to stop, but she couldn't, the tears had her and were not going to let go until they had run their course. Dahlia wrapped her arms around Bellina, rubbing her back, making soothing noises. Bellina buried her face in the crook of Dahlia's neck and let the sobs have their way. After what felt like aeons they subsided.

'What will you do?' Dahlia asked.

'I don't know,' Bellina replied, throwing up her hands. 'I don't even know if it was the truth.'

'You'll have to ask him,' Dahlia said. 'The Lord Chancellor, I mean.'

Bellina let out a sharp bark of laughter. 'As if he'd tell the truth. He's lied to me my entire life.'

A silence settled over the pair. Finally, Dahlia said, 'There is a way you could get the truth.'

'What do you mean?' Bellina replied. 'How?'

Dahlia bit her lips then said, 'By going into his mind.'

'It's no good,' Bellina said, shaking her head. 'He has all kinds of psychic defences, I'd never break through on my own.'

Dahlia leaned forwards, took Bellina's hands in her own, looked her dead in the eyes and said, 'No. Not on your own. Together.'

***

Cirona stared over the heads of the chattering crowd gathered in Dunsen's Square, at the man she had been sent to capture: Jean-Paul Vontanza, Tremoran delegate and the duke's son. Apparently, the little shitstain had been holding rallies like this all over Estria, denouncing the Lord Chancellor's rule. Now he had brought his sideshow to the capital, timed no doubt for his father's arrival.

So far, he had managed to evade capture. *Luck's run out today, sonny boy*, Cirona thought, looking around at the five vultures — the Lord Chancellor's most loyal and ruthless men. The idea was to use him as a bargaining chip, to stop whatever madness the duke had planned before things went too far. Cirona watched Vontanza step onto the stage, heard the crowd's chatter turn into a massive round of applause and wondered if maybe this was all too little too late.

'Let's move,' Cirona said to the men at her side and began to worm her way to the front of the crowd.

'Ladies and gentlemen!' she heard Vontanza say. 'It brings me much joy to see you here on such an auspicious day, a day when we come together to celebrate the birth of our Emperor and, in so doing, the Empire itself.'

''Scuse me … look out …' Cirona muttered as she wriggled through the crowd.

'Watch it!' a man shouted when she trod on his foot.

'But this year I know, as we all know, that the Empire has little to celebrate. Our eastern territories have been lost. Blasphemy has brought down the wrath of the Father, we are at war with enemies both foreign and domestic. All thanks to one man. I think you all know his name.'

'The Lord Chancellor!' a man next to Cirona roared along with the rest, his eyes bulging, spit flecking his lips.

*This is bad*, Cirona thought, sensing the bloodlust, the urge to destroy, emanating like a poisonous fog from the people gathered.

'Yes, my friends,' Vontanza continued, his voice quieting the crowd. 'The Lord Chancellor. A man who would have us make war with

Burkesh, a man who has sent your sons, your daughters to fight and die for his own selfish interests. A man who does not understand the word, peace.

'While he has been making war, while he and his cronies in government have been stoking the fires of hate oblivious to the blockade and the deprivation it has brought to so many of us, my family have been in search of peace. A peace Burkesh also desires, despite the fact the Lord Chancellor sent his freak daughter into their capital where she used her dark powers to kill thousands. No. Despite all this, the Burkeshis still desire peace, just as we all do. A peace that will bring an end to the hardship we are enduring.'

*Peace?* Cirona thought. *Peace with the Burkeshis? You haven't seen their Kaffars, their Naffirs; you haven't seen them raise the dead and send hounds from the Void to hunt you down. Peace, but at what price?*

'Yes, my friends, we can … oh, what's this? Look friends, the Lord Chancellor has sent his lapdogs to stop me, to stop the truth!'

Feeling the eyes of the crowd swivel, pinning her to the spot with their intensity, Cirona stopped. She looked up into the smiling face of Jean-Paul, her skin prickling.

'S-stop this at once,' she yelled. 'By order of His Majesty the Emperor, you must stop!'

'The order of His Majesty?' Vontanza said, tilting his head to one side. 'Speak the truth, woman. Say his name, the name of the man who really sent you!'

Cirona opened her mouth to answer, but the breath died in her throat. She swallowed a mouthful of sour spit, tried again; but still, no words would come.

'Answer him then?' a woman next to her shouted, shoving at Cirona's shoulder.

'Yeah!' a man screamed in her face. 'Go on!'

'Get back, all of you,' Cirona said. 'This … this is your only warning.'

'Oh, yeah,' another man said, pushing her in the back. 'What yer gonna do?'

The sound of a shot rang out. Cirona spun round to see one of the vultures, a ballistol smoking in his hand. *Gods, no! What have you done?*

'See!' Vontanza screamed. 'See! Now he sends his men to kill the very people he has sworn to protect. Do not let these murderers leave!'

'Murderer!' a woman shrieked, darting forwards and grabbing Cirona's hair.

'Bitch!' someone screamed as a glob of spit splattered against her cheek.

Punches, shoves, kicks began to rain in on her. The world shrunk to a swirling mass of snarling, angry faces. Curses, threats, broken shards of vocal hate assaulted her ears. Cirona fell, curled herself into a ball, protecting her head. She was dimly aware of more shots ringing out, of screaming, of rushing trampling feet.

She felt something catch the back of her head, felt blood, hot and sticky, course down her neck, felt the fear grip her stomach, cold and hard. *I'm going to die*, she thought. *I'm going to die, I'm going to die, I'm-going-to-die-die-die-die…*

A sound escaped her lips, a low, guttural, animal sound. With a monumental effort, she hauled her body off the ground, drew her sword, swung it about her in a great arc, driving her attackers back. As her eyes focused, she realised there was no need. The crowd was running now, scattering like leaves caught on a breeze, the City Watch advancing on the square, balliskets lowered, bayonets fixed.

'Stop,' she yelled at the men, 'for fuck's sake, stop!'

But her voice was lost amongst the chaos. Cirona spun round, saw the now empty stage where Vontanza had stood.

'Shit,' she swore. 'Now *this* is a fucking mess.'

***

'Where are all the guards?' Bellina asked, stepping into the hallway outside her room.

'Gone,' Dahlia answered. 'Pretty much every able-bodied man has been sent to the Escambrian front or is on Watch duty.'

Bellina shivered as a slight chill travelled up the length of her spine. She had never seen the Palace of Administration look so empty, so hollow, so devoid of life. She remembered the first time she had visited the palace when she was a child, the man she thought her father proudly taking her on a tour of the place, showing her the people whose decisions shaped the Empire and the rooms those decisions were made in.

Shaking her head to clear it, Bellina pushed the memories away; now was not the time for reminiscing, not with what she had to do. She reached out and took Dahlia's hand.

'Come on,' she said.

Swallowing hard, Bellina led the way down the corridor, passing beneath the portraits of former Lord Chancellors, their stern, somehow knowing, glances bearing down on them. Their eyes seemed to follow Bellina, adding to her sense that she was being watched. Time seemed to slow as she approached the door to her father's office. She reached out a hand, a hand that did not seem like her own, and gripped the handle of the door. With a jerky twitch, she opened it.

And there he was, hunched over a desk stacked high with papers, his hand furiously scribbling in the scribograph. It was a position she had seen him in so many times; but had she ever seen him look so fraught, so frail? He didn't so much as look up at them, just kept on penning his missive.

She opened her mouth to say something, to make him stop, but no words came. Everything she could think of saying seemed small and pathetic. She almost fled then, almost dropped the whole thing, but the image of her dying mother was seared across her mind.

'Stop that,' she said. The Lord Chancellor gave a startled jump.

'Bellina!' he said, a broad smile breaking across his face. 'You look fit as a fiddle.'

He disentangled his hand from the scribograph, pulled himself heavily from the chair, and came towards her, arms outstretched. Bellina flinched away, her hand held high to ward him off.

'No,' she said. 'I don't want you to touch me; I don't think I could bear it.'

A frown wrinkled her grandfather's forehead. 'What? I … I don't understand.'

'No more words. All that comes out of your mouth are lies,' Bellina whispered, a tear escaping from the corner of her eye. 'Now it's time to see if you are a monster as well as a liar.'

With a trembling finger, Bellina pressed the buttons on her and Dahlia's power controls, giving them full access to their cognopathic abilities. The Lord Chancellor's eyes grew wide, flicking between Bellina and Dahlia.

'No,' he hissed. 'No! Bellina, don't do this. We've been fooled; you have to listen to me!'

She felt Dahlia give her hand a reassuring squeeze. 'I've listened to you for long enough,' she said, closing her eyes and reaching out with her mind.

When she opened her eyes next, Bellina found herself on a moor. Low clouds pressed down on rolling hills. A fine mist hung in the air, coiling itself around her feet, wrapping itself amongst the scrubby bushes. The smell of wet earth and stagnant water assaulted her nose.

From the ground, at irregular intervals, there rose small mounds. Then she saw some of the mounds had entryways made of rough-hewn rock.

'Barrows,' she murmured.

'What?' Dahlia asked.

'Those are barrows … graves … but what are they—'

She was cut short as a skeletal hand, scraps of flesh still clinging to the knuckles, appeared out of the barrow nearest to them. A skull followed closely behind, worms writhing in gaping sockets, a thin band of gold on top of its brow.

'Go back,' the dead thing rasped.

Its command was echoed by dozens more creeping from their burial places. Some hefted rusty swords and axes, one was even sat atop a fleshless horse.

'By the Father!' Dahlia exclaimed.

'Keep calm,' Bellina hissed, fighting back her own rising sense of panic. 'His defences were always going to be strong. We just have to find his psychic centre. I reckon the right way will be through one of these barrows.'

'But which one?' Dahlia cried. 'There are hundreds of the bloody things!'

*Think*, Bellina told herself, *think; there has to be a clue somewhere.* Her concentration was broken when one of the skeletal warriors made a shambling lunge at them. Dahlia let loose a cry. Bellina pushed the thing back with her mind, her eyes still scanning the barrows. Then, on one of the rock entryways, she saw a symbol, a crudely carved sword covered in flames. She recognised it; it was the symbol used to represent the Sword of Amlith.

'That one,' Bellina said, pointing towards the grave.

'Are you sure?' Dahlia asked.

'I'm sure,' Bellina replied, grabbing Dahlia's hand and setting off at a sprint.

Bellina heard the bones of the skeletons grating as they turned to follow. She sent the closest one spinning away, saw it hit a rock and explode into tiny fragments, only for it to begin reassembling itself like a revolting jigsaw puzzle. Bellina kept running, pulling Dahlia along with her. They were close now, the entry to the barrow yawning before them.

Thin fingers clasped Bellina's ankle in an ice-cold grip, tripping her, sending her sprawling to the ground. She hit the ground hard, biting her bottom lip as her jaw was jarred shut. Bellina tried to scrabble forwards, slipped again, twisting on the rain-soaked ground, turning to see the hollow face of her attacker, sword raised, ready to strike.

'No!' Dahlia cried.

The skeleton froze, weapon still poised, skinless arms trembling as it fought to attack. Bellina felt Dahlia grab her under the arm and heave her to her feet. Together, they half ran, half stumbled into the barrow's doorway. Once inside, Dahlia raised her hand and summoned a vast clod of earth to bar the undead army's way, leaving them in total darkness.

'D-do you think that will hold them?' Dahlia asked.

'I don't intend to stay long enough to find out,' Bellina replied. 'Now, let's have some light.'

She stretched out her hand and concentrated on the spot where she knew her palm to be. Within a few seconds, Bellina had willed a small ball of flame into existence, its flickering light illuminating a long, thin passage that descended sharply. Muscles tense, blood throbbing in her veins, Bellina took a tentative step forwards. She shook her head and pulled herself up to her full height. *Stop being ridiculous*, she thought. *You bested Alcastus; you can beat this place. Besides, this time you have help.*

Bellina turned towards Dahlia and gave her a small smile. 'Come one,' she said.

Together, they set off down the passageway, the small flame making the rock walls glisten. In front of her, Bellina saw an arched doorway grow in her vision, a curious smell of mildew emanating from beyond it. She stepped through, her breath catching in her throat.

'What is this place?' Dahlia said.

'I think it's a cavern or grotto,' Bellina said.

She gazed up at the vast expanse of rock above their heads, saw stalactites, outcroppings of moss-covered stone and, beneath it all, a floor made of some black, reflective material. Bellina took a step forwards onto the dark floor and gasped when ripples spread around her feet. *Not a floor*, she thought, *a lake, a massive, underground lake.* The water was ice-cold. She stepped back, shivering.

'I can see another doorway,' Dahlia said. 'On the other side of the water, but ... how in the twelve hells are we supposed to get over there?'

Bellina took a deep breath, focusing her mind. *Weightless*, she told herself, *I am weightless.* She felt her body rise a few inches from the ground and then fall back to earth. So, she couldn't control *everything* in her grandfather's psychic realm. Frowning, she cast a glance around her. There, to her far left, hidden in a corner was a small, bobbing rowing boat.

'We'll have to use that,' Bellina said, pointing towards it.

Dahlia frowned and bit her lip. 'It ... er ... looks a bit rickety,' she said.

'Well, it's that or swim,' Bellina replied and set off.

Feet snagging and slipping on the wet stone beneath her feet, Bellina eventually made it to the boat. She placed a hand on the side of it, felt the waterlogged wood squish beneath her fingers and climbed in, the craft rocking like a child's crib.

'See,' she said, turning to the hesitant Dahlia, 'It's … it's perfectly fine.'

Dahlia still looked reluctant but nodded her head and got in next to Bellina. Taking an oar each, they set themselves skimming across the still water of the lake.

'There you go,' Bellina said through gritted teeth when they were halfway across the lake. 'We'll be across in no—'

'What was that?' Dahlia said, letting go of her oar, head swivelling like an owl.

'What was what?' Bellina replied.

'That!' Dahlia said.

'I can't …' Bellina began.

Then she felt it. A swelling of the water, as if some huge thing was pushing itself up from beneath them. There was a massive splash, then a roar, and she realised a huge thing had pushed itself up from beneath them.

In front of them loomed a monumental serpent, jaws wide, fangs dripping, water running of its sleek scales in small waterfalls. Bellina felt the blood freeze in her veins. She flinched, pulling the oar in front of her to form a feeble shield. The creature let out a rippling hiss then dived back below the water. The small boat was rocked and tossed by the wave the serpent created, only just staying afloat.

'Row!' Bellina yelled.

Arms pumping in wild desperation, Bellina and Dahlia rowed for their lives. The far side of the lake was getting closer. Just a few more seconds and—

With a deafening screech, the serpent reappeared, blocking their way. Bellina dropped her oar and stood at the prow of the boat. She pushed against the beast with her mind, but it was like trying to move a mountain by blowing at it.

'Help me!' she cried to Dahlia.

Her fellow cognopath scrambled up beside her, lending her power. A look of confusion came over the serpent's face as it was forced back a foot. *No good*, Bellina thought, sweat trickling down her brow, *we'll get nowhere like this*. She looked about her, hunting for a solution. Something caught her eye above the creature's head. A gigantic stalactite dangled above it.

'Focus on that,' Bellina said, pointing at the rock.

The serpent reared back, hissing and spitting. Bellina focused all her mind on the stalactite. *Come on*, she thought, *move, damn it!* There was a grating sound. A shower of loose stone fell onto the serpent's head, leaving it blinking and unsure. It looked up only to see the stalactite break loose and spear down at its flat nose.

The rock connected with the beast's head, and it let out a forlorn scream that was soon cut short. Fragments of stone crashed around the tiny boat, casting it to and fro on the water. Taking up the oars once more, the pair rowed. Five feet from the shore, a chunk of rock smashed into the vessel, shattering the already weak wood.

Bellina and Dahlia bailed from the craft. The water here was shallow and they gained their footing, but still, the rocks continued to fall. Every sinew straining, Bellina forced her way through the water. She staggered up the incline towards the passageway, dragging Dahlia with her. With a mad dive, they lunged for the door, crossing its threshold just as a boulder blocked it off.

'It's a good job we don't have to go back that way,' Dahlia said.

Bellina looked over into her companion's sweat-streaked face, saw eyes wide with fear and relief. A mad giggle escaped Bellina's lips. Dahlia joined her and soon they were laughing hysterically.

'Wh-why a-are we laughing?' Dahlia said.

'I-I think sometimes it's laugh or go mad,' Bellina replied, wiping tears from her eyes.

'Shall we?' Dahlia asked, extending her hand to Bellina and giving a fake bow.

'Yes,' Bellina said, 'let's.'

Arm in arm, like two lovers promenading, they walked down the passage. Their way was lit by faltering torches held in sconces attached to the stone. Soon, they came to a door made of large, shimmering, brass cogs. In its centre sat a small square of numbered buttons, above that, a slot showing six blank spaces.

'What is that?' Bellina said, leaning in to inspect the numbers.

'Perhaps, you have to put in a code?' Dahlia replied.

Bellina cocked her head to the side then typed in 123456. The passageway reverberated with the sound of a gong followed by something akin to a sword being drawn.

'Er …' Dahlia said, inching close to Bellina, 'I don't think we're going to get too many tries at this.'

Following her companion's trembling finger, Bellina saw a host of sharp spikes poking out of the walls and floor.

'Right,' Bellina replied.

She turned back to the panel. *Numbers*, she thought, *numbers important to the Lord Chancellor*. Licking her lips, she typed in the date of his marriage. There was a teeth-rattling grinding sound, and the spikes shot another foot outward.

'Careful!' Dahlia cried.

'I'm not getting it wrong on purpose,' Bellina hissed.

'I … I know just … really think before you put this one in, eh?'

Bellina gave a snort and shook her head. She placed her twitching fingers back on the keys. *What the hells could it be?* she thought. A number flashed through her mind then. But no … it couldn't be. Taking a deep breath, she punched in the numbers. Her finger hovered above the last one; she closed her eyes as she pushed it.

There was a faint click followed by the whirring of gears beginning to move. Bellina watched in amazement as cogs pulled themselves apart leaving a perfect doorway in their wake.

'By the Father!' Dahlia cried. 'What was it?'

Bellina looked at the ground. 'It … it was my birthday,' she whispered.

'Oh …' Dahlia said.

With that they passed through the door.

Bellina found herself in a space she had visited once before — the Lord Chancellor's psychic centre. The walls of the vast space were covered in clicking, spinning, whirring machinery, but her eyes weren't drawn to that. Her gaze settled on a chair in front of a control panel, more specifically on the man sat upon it.

'So, you've made it,' the Lord Chancellor said, standing up. 'I don't know what kind of lies this witch has been feeding you, but there is still time my love. Stop this now, before it's too—'

'Silence,' Bellina said.

She pushed out with her mind and sent him tumbling back into his seat. With a twitch of her thoughts she conjured rope and a piece of fabric which twined itself round her grandfather, binding him, gagging him.

'What now?' Dahlia asked.

'Now we find his psychic core. It could be something small … or large … it—'

'Could be anything,' Dahlia finished for her.

Bellina bit her cheeks and cocked her head to the side. She began to pace up and down alongside the machinery. She noticed that one bank of machines was producing copper punch cards, the kind used to programme automatons. One finished being made and was whisked away to another part of the room on a small conveyor belt. She followed it and watched in wonder as the small card was filed away with a vast number of other ones. Picking one up, she saw that they had titles. The one in her hand read: Meeting with Scholar Fontaine RE latest find, and it had a date from two days ago upon it.

'It's these!' Bellina exclaimed. 'These are his memories. All recorded and filed away.'

'Really?' Dahlia said, a strange, hungry look in her eyes. 'Let me see.'

'If we can find the one with my birthday on, we should be able to ...'

Bellina's voice trailed off, realising Dahlia wasn't listening. Her fellow cognopath was flicking through the memory cards, her eyes darting over the dates and titles so fast she looked like a cat following a piece of string. Bellina began to peruse the cards as well. She noticed that, the further left she went, the further back in time the cards descended.

'This should be the right date. How about we try this one first,' Dahlia said. 'You know, just to make sure you're right about what these contain.'

'I don't see how ...' Bellina began, but Dahlia had already crossed the room and slotted the card into another machine.

The room around them disintegrated and Bellina found herself upon a windswept hill, surrounded by a semicircle of standing stones. In front of her, she watched the figure of a man digging beneath one of the obelisks. He paused, panting, threw his shovel to one side and stood up straight, the hood of his cloak falling back. Bellina let out a gasp when she saw the face of her grandfather; a face many years younger but unmistakably his. He reached inside the folds of his coat and pulled out a large sword made from bone. He placed this in the ground then began to move the excavated earth back on top of it.

'So that's where he put it!' Dahlia exclaimed.

'What?' Bellina said, spinning round to face her.

Dahlia ignored her and closed her eyes. 'Father? Yes, it's me. I've found it. I know where it is! Tell Lord Marmossa that he was right; she did prove useful. Shall I carry on as planned? ... Very well ... see you soon.'

'Dahlia who were you talking to? Just what the hells is going on?'

'We can leave now,' Dahlia said, her face lit up with a twisted smile Bellina had never seen before.

'What do you mean leave? I need to find out what happened to my mother! This isn't the right memory!'

'It is for me,' Dahlia replied, eyes flashing.

'Dahlia? What are you …? We need to keep going. I need to know if he really had my mother killed.'

'Of course he didn't!' Dahlia chuckled. '*My* father did. The Duke of Tremore.'

'What are you talking about?' Bellina replied, her head reeling.

'Gods, you're dense! My father sent that man to kill your mother, to steal you away to be reared by him. Unfortunately, your grandfather got in the way and stole you back.

'But I saw—'

'But I …' Dahlia replied, imitating Bellina. 'Bah! I was controlling what you were seeing almost the whole time you were in that other place. It was so easy! Thanks to that meddling bastard Yevad, your subconscious was already creating psychic landscapes.

'I may not be as powerful a cognopath as you, but I use my powers better; a dagger compared to your war hammer. All it took were a few tweaks here and there and … poof … you were mine. I lost you for a while at the end, gods only know where you went, but I had already won you over, already knew you would do whatever I told you.'

'This can't be … you … you're an orphan … raised in the …' Bellina said, struggling for breath.

'Oh, my little back story was true enough. But my father only pretended to disown me. He knew and appreciated what my powers could do. He and Alcastus groomed me for this day, and now I have won.'

'You … you lying bitch! I'll kill you!' Bellina screamed.

'Uh-uh,' Dahlia said. 'Don't want to bring the whole shebang down on granddaddy's head now, do we? So, do exactly as I say, and maybe my father will let the pair of you live. We'll need a few fools to liven up the Imperial Palace when we move in. Now break off your psychic link.'

Bellina's hands clenched into fists, her pulse a tribal drumming in her ears. She wanted to tear, to cut and claw and maim. But she didn't dare, not then. She would wait.

Disengaging her psychic link, Bellina opened her eyes and found herself back in her grandfather's office in the Palace of Administration. She saw Dahlia standing by the Lord Chancellor, chucking him under the chin like you would a baby.

'So many people have feared you for so long, old man,' she hissed at him. 'Now you're under my control. But I must thank your precious Bellina. Without her, I never could have broken you.'

'Get away from him, you fucking bitch!' Bellina spat.

'Oh dear,' Dahlia said, shaking her head. 'That's quite the temper.

Perhaps a little demonstration will bring you in line? Pick up the letter opener.'

Bellina watched dumbfounded as her grandfather did as he was told.

'Now,' Dahlia said with a smirk, 'press it against your throat.'

Watching in horror, Bellina saw her grandfather's muscles twitch as he tried to fight the command. Then, with a snap, the blade was at his throat, a thin bead of blood blossoming where its tip met his skin.

'I do hope this has been a convincing performance,' Dahlia said with a bow. 'He is very suggestible after being broken by us, and it would only take one wrong word to—'

'Alright!' Bellina bellowed. 'Alright. What do you want?'

'First, give me your power controls. That's it … don't want you getting any silly ideas now, do we?' Dahlia said. 'Now, we're going on a little trip. I think it's time we all offered our birthday wishes to the Emperor.'

***

'I … um … think we might need to get a bit higher,' Elvgren said as the Castrian Wall grew alarmingly in his vision.

'I know,' Castros hissed at him.

The wall was now the only thing Elvgren could see out of his one good eye. 'Pull up! For the love of the gods, man, pull up!' he screamed.

He heard Castros let out a strangled roar and the aerolyte reared up in a near vertical line. Elvgren felt his feet slip and he fell onto his stomach with a bang. He began to slide down the vehicle's deck, hands scrabbling, fingers trying in vain to gain some kind of purchase.

Still sliding, he saw Dargo clinging to the rail on his left. The boy reached out his hand to him. Elvgren flapped his own hand in the boy's direction but missed Dargo's grasp by a long way. *This is it*, he thought, as his feet shot out into thin air, then his knees, his torso. His hands were clamped round the rim of the flying machine, the rest of his body dangling in nothingness. One by one, his sweat-slick fingers began to lose their grip.

'Help!' he cried, knowing it was pointless, knowing he was doomed.

Then, with a lurch, the aerolyte returned to a horizontal position. Elvgren's body swung forwards, his ribs connecting with the edge of the ship in a breath-stealing collision. He let out a strange whooping noise then lost his grip. A second later, he felt a hand wrap his wrist in a grip of iron. He looked up into Crenshaw's straining face.

'No, you don't,' Crenshaw said. 'Dargo, quick!'

With the help of Dargo and Crenshaw, Elvgren was dragged back onto the vehicle's deck. For a moment, Elvgren lay there, drinking in air, forcing it down in great gulps. His ribs burned with a deep ache, his wrist felt as though it had been pulverised where Crenshaw had grabbed it, but he was alive.

'Hope you got deep pockets, boy,' Crenshaw said. ''Cos you owe me more than a drink.'

'Thanks,' Elvgren wheezed as he hauled himself to his feet.

He shuffled back towards the front of the aerolyte and looked out. Down below, the Merchant's Quarter and the docks flew by in a blur. In front of them, the *Flying Vagabond* was a massive dark oval.

'What are they doing?' Elvgren managed to say, pointing a finger at the airship.

'Whatever … it is … they aren't stopping,' Castros said, panting, a sheen of sweat covering his brow.

'Looks like they're headed straight for the Imperial Palace,' Crenshaw said, scratching his chin.

'We have to get there first!' Elvgren bellowed. 'If Dahlia has already convinced Bellina to break the Lord Chancellor's psychic defences—'

'More,' Castros cut in. 'Give me … more … ether.'

'I don't know if that's a—' Crenshaw began.

'Just do it!' Del Var yelled back.

Elvgren watched as Castros held out his tongue and Dargo dripped three more drops of ether onto it. The reaction was instantaneous, the aerolyte lurching forwards. The shadow of the airship fell over them as they raced past. They were level with the top of the Olphant Hill now, the Imperial Palace within their grasp.

'We're only gonna fucking do it!' Dargo yelled.

'Excellent work, Mr Del Var,' Elvgren said. 'You can slow down now. Mr Del Var, you can—'

'Shit, he's passed out!' Crenshaw said.

'Get his hands outta there,' Dargo cried.

'How! It's like he's welded onto something in those holes—'

'All of us pull him, on three!' Elvgren said. 'One … two …'

'It's too late, Gren,' Dargo said. 'We're gonna cra—'

***

There was something in the air. Cirona could sense it, almost taste it at the back of her throat. She knew it well, had felt it before while standing in line waiting for the call to charge, but there was no word for it, none that she knew anyway. There were things close to it: chaos, anticipation, bloodlust and, most terrifying of all, change.

'No sign of him, sir,' one of the Lord Chancellor's vultures informed her.

'Thank you for stating the bloody obvious,' Cirona spat back, her nerves stretched too taut for pleasantries. 'Try Skelm's Den and get eyes on the Olphant Hill. I'm going on to check Tailor's Row.'

'Yes, sir,' the vulture replied.

Cirona turned from the man and set off. She had been following the general path the fleeing crowd had taken, sword and ballistol drawn in case any more of Victory's citizens tried to exact vigilante justice upon her. Part of her knew it was madness, that with the manpower available they would never find the duke's son, let alone capture him. But there was still a chance, a bloody faint one, admittedly, but a chance, nonetheless, that they could still defuse the situation.

She turned a corner and found a small crowd gathered around one of the mammoth-sized, glass-fronted boxes the duke had had set up. Her eyes darted over the assembly, but there was no sign of her prey. Cirona turned away but was drawn back when a strange hum filled the air. The crowd let out a collective gasp and the major felt herself do the same.

The glass front of the box had lit up, a black and white image upon it. The box crackled and hissed, the picture going in and out of focus. Cirona squinted her eyes, trying to make out what it was she was seeing. It looked like the Imperial Palace, but there was a bloody great hole in one of the walls. Next thing she knew the Duke of Tremore's face was on the screen.

'Friends,' the duke intoned. 'A great crime has been foiled by my men. These … traitors!' he spat as the view changed to show four people, hands bound.

Cirona felt her stomach contract into a solid lump of cold steel when she realised who they were.

'Some of these traitors are known to you. Deputy Lord Chancellor Elvgren Lovitz here, for instance. But this … thing is someone you've only heard of when his name is cursed. He is the terrorist, Castros Del Var.

'I ask you, friends, what would the Deputy Lord Chancellor be doing with one of the most wanted men in the Empire? I'm sure you have reached the same conclusion as myself, that Lord Lovitz, under order from his master, the Lord Chancellor, is aiding Del Var in assassinating the Emperor and finishing what he attempted years ago!'

The assembled crowd let out a collective gasp.

'Why, you may now ask? Why would anyone do such a thing? I shall tell you, friends. To keep power. That's right. All to keep power in the twisted talons of the Lord Chancellor!'

At this, the crowd erupted, hissing, booing, some even throwing things at the screen. This wasn't good. In fact, it was just about as far from good as Cirona could imagine. Damn the duke's son, she had to get up to the palace; but how could she get there with the streets packed?

'Excuse me,' a voice called behind her.

Cirona spun round, pointing her ballistol at the face of a man she found stood there. 'What?' she spat.

'Are you Major Bouchard, Major Cirona Bouchard?'

'Aye,' Cirona replied. 'What do you want?'

'The Lord Chancellor sent me a scribograph, telling me to find you. Weren't easy, let me tell you that, right now!'

'Who the hells are you?' Cirona said.

'My friends call me Whist.'

***

Bellina stared past her grandfather at Dahlia. She watched the back of Dahlia's uniform ripple as her fellow cognopath set a brisk pace through the courtyard of the Imperial Palace; the bitch was even whistling a little tune. Bellina's jaw ached from clenching it so hard, her skin was a bristling, living thing, itching with the desire to hurt. *If only I could get my controls back*, she thought, then she'd see. But how? A moment would come, it had to, and when it did, Bellina would be ready.

The scene at the palace was one that would, ordinarily, have left Bellina stunned. Overhead, the *Flying Vagabond* hung in the air, a great smoking hole smouldered in the left wing of the building, what looked like a flat-bottomed boat sticking out of it, and a pair of smirking purgistas standing guard at the great doors. They bowed to Dahlia as she approached and stood to the side to let her, Bellina and the Lord Chancellor in.

They strode through the palace and into the Grand Hall, the mural of Estria's illustrious history on the ceiling above them. A further two purgistas stood in front of the doors to the throne room. They opened the way and Bellina followed Dahlia into the space beyond.

This time, Bellina did feel stunned at what she saw.

Before her stood Elvgren, Dargo, Crenshaw, and a man she did not know; though he looked familiar, like she was staring at a portrait of a long-lost ancestor. They were covered in cuts, their clothes ripped and torn, dark smudges up their arms and legs, as though they had been cleaning chimneys. A guard stood behind each of them, ballisket pointed at the base of their skulls. More guards lined the back of the room. She took a step back when a man in a cognopath uniform leered in at her while adjusting a dial on a pair of bizarre brass goggles.

'Papa!' Dahlia squealed, running towards the Duke of Tremore.

'My darling girl!' the duke replied, pulling her into a tight embrace. 'You have done well.' Then he turned to the cognopath in the goggles. 'And now, my friends, the conspiracy is complete. All the players in this treachery are revealed!'

'Liar!' Bellina spat at him, unable to stop herself.

Dahlia crossed the floor in a few quick strides and belted Bellina round the face with the back of her hand. 'You had best keep that pretty mouth shut,' Dahlia whispered in her ear, 'or you and your little group of freaks will be nothing but a pile of corpses.'

Bellina's eyes blazed. She wanted to spit the blood from her bust lip at Dahlia, wanted to stick her thumbs in the corner of the other girl's eyes and pop them out as if she were shucking peas … but she forced all that down. *Keep waiting*, she told herself.

'Your Majesty,' the duke said, bowing low before the Emperor. 'I'm afraid my gift hasn't arrived yet. But may I wish you the happiest of birthdays.'

'This,' the Emperor replied, waving a shaking, claw-like hand at Bellina and the rest. 'This … treachery … your discovery of it … is gift … enough for me! Kill them!'

'Your Magnificence, please!' the duke said. 'I know they should pay with their lives for such treason, but I beg clemency. As yet, they have not done—'

At that moment, the Lord Chancellor let out a scream of fury. Bellina watched, mouth gaping, as her grandfather lunged forwards, the letter opener still in his hand. *Yes*, Bellina thought, *this is it*. Her body grew tense in anticipation. But instead of setting upon their captors, she saw the Lord Chancellor plunge the small blade into the Emperor's heart.

Everything seemed to slow for Bellina then. The shouts and screams that echoed around her were merely murmured messages. The guards at the back of the room raced forwards. They seemed like bad actors to her, their faces twisted in caricatures of rage. *Perhaps that's all it is*, she thought, *just some farce that will end with the drawing of a curtain*. But then they had her grandfather, had forced him to his knees before the duke.

'There can be no forgiveness now,' the duke said, looking down at the Lord Chancellor.

'Wait,' one of the guards said. 'The Emperor is saying his last words.' The man leaned in close and Bellina watched the old man's withered lips mumble something into the guard's ear. 'He … he says he has chosen an heir. He says … all hail, Emperor Vontanza the First!'

'All hail!' the guards and purgistas yelled in what seemed like scripted unison.

A tear rolled down the duke's cheek. He took the dying Emperor's hand in his and said, 'Thank you, your Majesty. I will try to bear this burden as gracefully as you did.'

The Emperor smiled, patted the duke's hand, then was still.

'My first act as Emperor,' Vontanza said, raising himself up, 'is to condemn you all to death!'

'Wait!' Bellina yelled as the guards readied their weapons. 'You said—'

'I lied,' Dahlia hissed, cocking the hammer of a ballistol and pointing it at Bellina's temple. 'This is for Alcastus.'

*No*, Bellina thought, *this isn't right!* The moment … where was the moment she had been waiting for? She looked round, into the eyes of Elvgren, Dargo and Crenshaw, saw the same look of disbelief on them all. Then she met her grandfather's gaze.

'I'm sorry,' he mouthed at her.

'On my order,' the new Emperor said. 'Fi—'

He was cut off as the throne room doors flew open and a living flame shrieked across the room. Bellina just had time to register that it was a man wreathed in fire, before he jumped out of the window. She turned towards the door, saw Holger and Waltus standing there and her heart leapt.

'Kill them! Kill them all!' the duke screamed.

The guards pointed their guns at Waltus and Holger. The old mage touched his legs and disappeared. Around the room, the guards buckled over as if hit by some invisible hand. Then Waltus was behind Elvgren and the others, untying their bonds. Not wasting another second, Bellina drove the point of her elbow into Dahlia's gut. The girl made a satisfying groan of pain when she buckled over, and Bellina sent a smart blow to her forehead. She pounced on top of Dahlia, wrenched the power controls free and hissed in her ear, 'You'll burn for this.'

'Will I?' Dahlia sneered.

Bellina felt herself pushed back, the controls spinning from her hand. She groped after them, but the boot of a battling guard kicked them out of her reach. She scrabbled across the floor on her hands and knees, slipped, stretched out her hand, felt a finger brush the controls, then she was sent spinning away as though she had been kicked by an unseen foot. Bellina lay on her back, staring at the ceiling, panting.

'I will make you suffer,' Dahlia said, looming over her.

'Belle!' she heard Holger cry.

'Silence!' Dahlia screamed, throwing a hand out towards Holger. There was thump and then Bellina could hear him groaning. 'I am going to make your brains dribble from your ears, just like you did to all those poor little kiddies in Kurgobad.'

'Fuck you!' Bellina yelled back.

She felt pressure at the sides of her head. It was like her skull was being crushed by two colliding mountains. There was no way she could last much longer …

'Belle,' Dargo called, as if from another world. 'I've turned your power on. Now get her!'

Reaching out with her mind, Bellina pushed at Dahlia. Her fellow cognopath went soaring across the room, smashing into the wall. Bellina stalked across the floor, past the individual battles, pushing, pushing harder and harder with her mind, enjoying the way Dahlia was squirming against the wall, just a little more and—

'Leave her,' a voice said behind her, as a hand grasped her arm.

Bellina looked round into the face of her grandfather. 'But they—' she began.

'We need to go. Now,' the Lord Chancellor said. 'Reinforcements are arriving and we must regroup.'

Bellina took one last look at Dahlia then let her tumble to the floor where she landed like a puppet with cut strings.

'To me!' she heard her grandfather cry, looking like the man he used to be.

Running for the door with the rest, Bellina followed the Lord Chancellor through the Grand Hall. He made a series of turns, leading them through reception rooms, dining halls and studies.

'Where are we going?' Bellina asked.

'To the library,' the Lord Chancellor replied. 'There's a secret tunnel there. With any luck my man and the major should be waiting for us as well. We just have to—'

The sound of a ballisket shot thundered down the hall. Bellina watched, her brows furrowed as something blasted through her grandfather's chest, a plume of blood trailing after it. He staggered forwards, Bellina rushed to help him. The man she didn't know darted towards them to help too.

'They're down here!' a gruff voice shouted behind them.

Turning around, Bellina saw a solitary guard, ballisket still smoking in his hand. Rage, pure and undiluted pulsed through her body. She reached out with her mind, grabbing the man in invisible hands, slamming his head into the ceiling, again and again and again.

'Stop,' the Lord Chancellor murmured. 'The library is there. Get me inside.' Bellina and the others got him into the room. 'Now, barricade the doors ... for the love of ... what good will a vase do, Lovitz? Use your head, boy! You two, put me down. There's something I need to tell you.'

'Father I ... I don't know what to ...' the unknown man said.

'Wait! Did you just call him Father?' Bellina said. 'Then that would make you ...'

'Yes, my love. He is my son, your father, Balthazar Ressa; though he goes by Castros Del Var.'

'Er ... hello?' Del Var said to Bellina. Bellina simply stared at him, her mind reeling.

'You will have time for that later,' the Lord Chancellor said. 'Now, listen. The prophecy is true, son, every last word of it. The Terrors will return to this world stronger than ever. You ... you must get ... get to the ... the summer house in ... Sylvantain ... you will find answers there ... locate Scholar Fontaine and give him this; he will know what to do with it.' He pushed a piece of paper into Del Var's hand.

There was a grating sound from the back of the room. Bellina turned and saw the fireplace swing round. Cirona and a man stepped from behind it.

'Whist!' Castros cried. 'What in the ... you work for my father? I never knew—'

'There's a lot you don't know about him, Cass, me as well; but the time for questions is later. The duke's men are flooding the place,' the man replied.

'We can't just leave you,' Bellina said to her grandfather.

'Don't be soft, girl; of course, you can. My race is run.'

'But you could still—'

'I can't, and I won't. You, boy,' the Lord Chancellor called, waving towards Holger. 'Make sure you burn this place after you leave. That should give you a bit of a head start.'

'No,' Bellina said. 'I won't leave you, I won't.'

'Come on, Bellina,' Cirona said, resting a hand on her shoulder.

'You have been,' the Lord Chancellor said, his voice breaking, 'the singular most wonderful thing that has ever happened to me, Bellina.

You brought light and laughter into my life when I thought such things were long since passed for me. I love you more than words can express, so please — go. Don't let me die thinking you didn't get away.'

Wiping away her tears, Bellina leaned forwards and kissed him on his forehead. 'Don't … don't you go getting all soppy on me, old man,' she said with a sniff.

'I wouldn't dream of it,' the Lord Chancellor replied.

'I love you,' Bellina said to him. Then she turned on her heel and strode towards the fireplace. 'Let's go.'

The others rushed in beside her. Holger tossed a wooden stick into the room and she watched it erupt into flames, attacking the room beyond with abnormal speed. She turned her gaze towards her grandfather. He was completely still. *At least he won't burn to death*, she thought, almost laughing at the dark horror of it all. Then the fireplace slid back into position and the scene disappeared.

# CHAPTER THIRTY-ONE

Bellina gazed back at the city she had lived in her whole life, watching smoke rise from the top of the Imperial Palace. The secret tunnels the man called Whist had led them through had taken them into a patch of woodland miles from Victory. Despite the distance, the mighty Castrian Wall still loomed before her gaze, a brooding, grey dragon coiled around its treasure. A lump formed in her throat as she watched the Estrian flag lowered across its length and the Tremoran one raised.

'Well, we've certainly got a talent for burning palaces,' Dargo said, coming to stand behind her.

'I suppose we have, Dar,' she managed to reply.

'I'm sorry for your loss, Belle,' Holger said, walking towards her.

'We all are,' Cirona added.

'What do we do now?' Elvgren asked.

Bellina turned to them all, met each of their gazes. She heard the words of the Fargazer whisper in her head, "You will lead them …" She felt her fists clench, felt her insides harden like cooling metal.

'Now,' she said. 'Now we get revenge.'

# EPILOGUE

'… that is how he died, my lord, though, you will be pleased to know that, with the girl's unwitting help, we know where the relic is located. They managed to get away but—'

'It matters not,' Arch Vizier Marmossa said, staring into the projected face of the Duke of Tremore. 'She played her part as I knew she would and that is enough. Her role in this story is over. Do you have anything else to tell me?'

'No, my lord. Now we await your arrival.'

'Very good. You have done well. Your reward will be great in the world that is to come.'

'Thank you, my lord,' The duke replied.

Marmossa waved a hand and the screen went blank.

'Truly it is a magnificent thing,' Grand Multan Kurkeshi said, gazing at the cognovision box.

'Bah!' Marmossa spat. 'A bauble. It is nothing compared to the technology of the first ones. Nothing compared to the world my brothers and sisters made.'

'A world we shall make again,' Kurkeshi said, his eyes gleaming.

'Indeed,' Marmossa replied. 'A world we shall make again.'

www.ingramcontent.com/pod-product-compliance
Lightning Source LLC
Chambersburg PA
CBHW050817190726
48286CB00007B/1898